TWO RIP-ROARING ADULT WESTERNS IN ONE VOLUME!

RAWHIDER'S WOMAN

Spur takes on the infamous Jamison gang, a band of ruthless rawhiders, and a pretty young captive who won't let him out of her sight.

SALOON GIRL

Spur investigates the suspected murder of a land agent in La Grande and comes face-to-face with notorious outlaw John Ringo—and body-to-body with a sultry saloon singer named Colette.

Other Spur Double Editions:

GOLD TOWN GAL/RED ROCK REDHEAD
SAVAGE SISTERS/HANG SPUR McCOY!
INDIAN MAID/MONTANA MINX

Spur Double:

RAWHIDER'S WOMAN

SALOON GIRL

Dirk Fletcher

LEISURE BOOKS NEW YORK CITY

A LEISURE BOOK®

January 2007

Published by

Dorchester Publishing Co., Inc.
200 Madison Avenue
New York, NY 10016

Rawhider's Woman copyright © 1986 by Dirk Fletcher
Saloon Girl copyright © 1986 by Chet Cunningham

ISBN 0-8439-2954-5

The name "Leisure Books" and the stylized "L" with design are trademarks of Dorchester Publishing Co., Inc.

Printed in the United States of America.

Visit us on the web at www.dorchesterpub.com.

RAWHIDER'S WOMAN

ONE

In the year 1875 a good man could work ten hours a day for twenty dollars and "found" on a cattle ranch or as a hired hand on a farm. A clerk in a store might draw down twenty-five or even thirty dollars a month. That's a yearly income of $240 to $360. President U.S. Grant was in his second term in the White House, and the first nine inning no-hit baseball game was played in Philadelphia, Pa.

The twenty-cent piece was authorized this year as a silver coin, and the first typewritten book manuscript was completed by a relative unknown, Samuel L. Clemens. He called it, "Adventures of Tom Sawyer." The transcontinental railroad had been completed for six years and Isaac Charles Parker took over the position of judge of the Federal Court of Western Arkansas. Judge Parker at Fort Smith became known as the "hanging judge."

Will Jamison hitched up his pants, settled the .44 New Model Remington army revolver on his hip and glanced at his two sons beside him. Will was a tall man, six-one, lean and stringy with a brown drooping moustache and now a four day's growth of beard he hadn't taken the time to shave off. His clear green eyes checked the street again, then he nodded and stepped into the Willow Creek Fiduciary Bank.

The boys, Dale and Phil, were slightly smaller versions of their father. Behind them Matthew Rorick pulled up a red and white bandana from around his throat and covered his face right up to his eyes. The three ahead had done the same thing.

Will charged up to the waist high metal cage, pushed aside a woman customer and waved his pistol at the surprised male teller.

"This is a stickup!" Will bellowed. "Everybody raise your hands and shut up!"

Dale and Phil leaped across the barrier and ran to the two teller cages. Quickly they took out all of the paper bills there, then grabbed the man sitting behind the president's desk.

"Open the safe!" Dale bellowed in much the same angry tone of voice that his father had used. Dale was softer, twenty-eight, smaller and lighter. He also had a sandy drooping moustache. He jabbed his six-gun in the man's face.

"Move! Get the vault open or you're dead right now!"

The bank president, Aloysius Nestor, groaned as he rose from the chair. Dale slammed the heavy revolver across his forehead and jerked him forward with his left hand.

"The vault, dead man, now!"

Nestor cringed, then walked stolidly forward to the vault. He stepped inside first, grabbed a loaded pistol from the rack near the door and turned trying to aim it at the vicious gunman in back of him. It was too far to turn. Nestor was too slow and clumsy. He tried to pull the trigger.

Dale shot him through the throat. Nestor went

down with a gurgling scream. The shot in the small vault echoed as the sound slammed around and around, deafening Dale. He ignored the drumming in his ears. It had happened several times before. He watched Nestor drop his weapon and crash to the floor. A growing pool of blood puddled the vault. Then Nestor whispered something and died.

The blood pool stopped growing. Blood never flows from a body after the heart stops pumping it.

Dale Jamison stepped over Nestor and began pulling out drawers in the vault. The third one was stacked with paper money. He fished out stacks of banded bills and pushed them into a brown cloth sack he carried. He rushed as he cleaned out the first drawer, found three more that contained paper money. He emptied those also, passed over stacks and sacks of gold coins.

Early on the Jamison gang had learned that gold was valuable but ten pounds of it was worth only $3,300. Ten pounds of twenty-dollar bills could be worth three times that much. They never took gold unless there was no paper currency.

"Hurry it up in there!" Will Jamison barked from outside the vault. He held two pistols now, staring down a dozen workers and customers. "Everybody sit down!" he barked again, this time at the customers and clerks. "Down on the floor! Do it right now!"

The customers sat slowly. Rorick pushed down two older men who were having trouble getting on the floor.

Phil Jamison walked around making sure everyone was sitting down. He had his weapon out, an old Colt. He was good with it, but his dad said he always wanted to shoot too much. Privately Will called Phil a bloodthirsty sonofabitch, but he never told him that to his face.

Phil snarled something at a pretty girl. She

blushed and turned away. He reached down and cupped one of her breasts where it bulged against her dress. She edged away. Phil laughed.

Roger White had sat down with the others. Now he was sweating. In his pocket he carried a Derringer, a two-shot loaded with .45 rounds.

What was happening here was wrong. He knew that. He should be doing something about it. Damnit! He had to do something! He eased one hand around and pulled the weapon out when the robbers looked away. Now he held the small weapon between his legs where he had crossed them. The younger robber looked at him, scowled and then looked away. He carried only one gun. But the older robber was closer.

White had sworn to Mr. Nestor that he would help protect the people's money. If the robbers got away with this, half the people in town would be broke, bankrupt!

Roger watched the younger robber touching Lucy. He had been sweet on her for a year now. They kind of had an understanding that when she was a year older they would be married. He hated it when the kid touched her breasts. He had never even touched them! It drove him wild.

He had to do something! There was no one else. That's why Mr. Nestor had bought the Derringer for him. He had to use it now!

Phil caught the girl's face in his hand. "You be good to me, big tits, and I'll be nice to you." He reached down and squeezed one of her breasts.

Roger felt a cold sweat break out on his forehead.

"Nooooooo!" he screamed, lifted the Derringer and fired at the molester who touched Lucy.

His shot missed from eight feet away and smashed into the wall.

Will spun, the big six-guns both coming up. He fired one round from each weapon. The first caught

Roger in the chest, punctured one lung and slammed out his back. The second round hit almost at the same time as the first and drove through Roger White's black suit coat, through his shirt and shattered a rib before it cut a deadly path through his heart and lodged against his rear ribcage.

Two women screamed.

Roger jolted backward by the impact of the two .44 rounds. His head hit the floor with a crack, but he was already dead. His eyes blinked open and stared unseeing at the ceiling.

"Don't nobody trying nothing else foolish!" Will bellowed. "That fool died for trying it. Anybody else does the same thing gets lead poisoning. You understand?"

Heads nodded in shock and grief. Unbelieving eyes looked at the dead body of what only a minute ago had been the most popular teller in town and the best church soloist the little Baptist congregation had ever had.

Dale came out of the vault. He had two brown sacks crammed with banknotes.

"Done!" he said.

The four robbers backed toward the front door. Phil was out first. He turned casually as he had done so many times and slid his weapon against his thigh as he watched the street. Nobody had noticed the robbery. Good. He nodded to Gabe Hinckley who had been on guard outside. Gabe's rifle stood innocently beside his leg where he leaned easily against the brickwork of the best bank in town.

Inside, a six-gun roared again and a man passing the bank looked up, then began to run. Gabe Hinckley grabbed the rifle, a Henry repeater, and swung it by the barrel. The heavy stock hit the running man in the right shin, breaking the bone in two places and dumping him on the boardwalk. He screamed. Gabe kicked him in the head, saw that the others were out of the bank and ran for his horse.

Across the street the hardware store owner Fred Jones heard the scream and saw his friend hit with the rifle. He grabbed his Winchester 1866 model from behind the counter, ran to the door and slammed a round through the open door at the man with the rifle by the bank who kicked his friend on the sidewalk.

Jones took more time with his second round and sailed it through the tough's right leg, trying to bring him down, not kill him.

Gabe went down with a scream of pain. He had no idea where the round came from. Before he could move, another round from up the street dug into his chest and he fell flat on his back.

To Gabe it seemed everything had slowed down. He saw the other four members of the robbery gang leave the bank, leap on their horses and ride toward him on their planned route out of town.

"Will!" Gabe screamed. "Will, help me!"

Will and the other three had started firing behind them, driving two gunmen back inside storefronts. Will rode toward Gabe, saw his bloody chest and shook his head.

"Got no time to nurse you, Gabe," Will said. His .44 came down and he blasted a round through Gabe's right eye, then spurred his horse as he fired three more times behind him and the four horsemen pounded down the street, turned up an alley and were soon out of sight.

Behind them, the dazed little town came back to life. People looked cautiously from doors and windows. Then a few men came out. Sheriff Victor Adams used up ten precious minutes gathering a posse. He used three of his deputies and four volunteers. Finally they were riding, each man with rifle and pistol.

But it had taken ten minutes to get moving. The

robbers were two miles down the trail by the time the posse kicked up dust out of town.

Back in the bank two women had fainted. Three bodies lay on the floor. The woman who had pulled away from Phil Jamison's touch was the third victim.

"She pulled away from that filthy man and shouted at him," one of the men customers in the bank said. "Then the bastard ripped open her blouse and laughed as he shot her twice in the chest." The man looked at her body and tears crept into his eyes. He never noticed that he had blood splatters on his new blue suit.

In the vault, Aloysuis Nestor lay on his back, his blood soaking his jacket and a packet of one dollar bills. Dale Jamison had dropped them, evidently deciding they were not important enough to pick up.

The cashier of the bank, the number two man under Mr. Nestor, shook his head at the tragedy. Tears stained his cheeks and he wiped his eyes and blew his nose. His voice was barely a whisper.

"They won't catch them, not unless Will Jamison wants them to. That had to be the Jamison gang. I've been reading about them in the St. Louis newspapers. They had it all planned out. They must have had one man outside." He shook his head.

"Sheriff Adams certainly will not catch the Jamisons, that's a fact." He stared at the bodies a moment, then wiped his eyes again. "Will somebody go fetch Harley the undertaker? We're going to have four funerals tomorrow."

The trail that stretched south of Willow Creek was not as defined as some others. This track led to the Indian Territories, a huge area north of Texas and west of Arkansas where the Federal Government had brought in six or eight Indian tribes from the east and southeast and dumped them. The land was supposed to be theirs.

Will Jamison always scoffed at that idea.

"Damn Indians don't deserve nothing!" he roared. "Push all the fucking heathens into Mexico. Hell, I kill every one I see!"

Now he turned and checked his riders. His two sons were jolting along just behind him, Rorick was close. Not bad for a haul, he decided. He had lost only one man, and he wasn't family so it didn't matter so much. Gabe should have been more careful.

From what Dale said there must be thirty thousand at least in his brown bags. One of them rode tied to Will's saddle horn.

Christ he was glad they didn't try to carry that much gold away! They would be burned down by the posse by now.

Rorick had hung back and spotted the posse coming. He left the last little rise behind them and gave Will the word.

"Looks like six or seven of them. Riding hard, Will. But they got to be a mile behind us."

"Far enough," Will said grinning. "About time we taught these shitcake posses a lesson!" Will roared. "Teach them a damn good lesson."

He rode on scanning the trail, and came to what he wanted a mile down the path. It was a rocky ledge where a small stream cut through. The ledge lifted twenty feet on each side of the creek. The trail elbowed through the cut next to the creek. Any buggy or wagon going through would have one set of wheels in the water.

Will put Dale and Phil on one side and he and Rorick went on the other side of the cut. They hid their horses and then slithered up so they could peer over the top of the grassy, rocky ridge.

It made Will remember the war. Christ but that

had been exciting! He'd never lived so high or had so much fun in his life. Too quick the fighting was over. The killing was over. Will shook his head in wonder. He never would understand it, but in the heat of battle he went wild. He counted more Bluebellies dead than anyone in his unit. Every time.

His bayonet was always bloody at the end of a battle. He loved it! War was the greatest game man had ever invented. The only trouble was that a man had trouble finding others to play. Now he had a pale substitute.

The look of stark terror in the banker's eyes! The way the customers jumped to obey his commands! It was power, raw, life and death power and he reveled in it.

He saw a puff of dust on the downtrail. Will squinted his eyes and watched closer. They were coming. A good mile and a half away, and trotting, he figured. They would be making six, maybe seven miles an hour. Fifteen minutes they would be at the cut. Fifteen minutes and half that posse would be dead.

The idea of it surged through him and he checked his rifle. He lay on his stomach and as he watched the riders come, he fondled his Henry repeater, aware of his growing hardon. Christ, he was at it again! Yeah, this would be a good one, they always where when he got his cock up. He licked his lips and sighted in on the moving figures.

The gun motion gave him a surge of sexual feeling and he knew the jism was rising, getting ready to surge forward.

"Won't be long now," he told Rorick. "Remember, you have the second man into the cut."

Rorick nodded and laughed softly. "Gonna get me a lawman today!" he said and laughed again.

The boys on the other side of the cut knew their targets. This way they would not all shoot at the same man.

Dale rose up on the far ledge about fifty feet away and waved. He saw them coming too.

The posse stopped a hundred yards out from the cut, all grouped around and talked excitedly. Then one man yelled at them and rode hard for the gap in the ridge and they all followed. They were spread out by the time the first man hit the cut. Will waited until he was almost through to put the others in range. Nobody would fire until he did. He had taught his unit that much.

Will sighted in, led the lead rider two clicks and fired. The Henry spoke loudly and the lead man pitched forward as the round took him in the side and drove him off the thundering sorrel.

Will worked the lever and cranked a new .44 caliber slug into the chamber.

He heard rifles crack from both sides of the cut. The first four men through the gap were hit, two of them on the ground, a third one fighting to stay in the saddle, and a fourth slumped over and gunning out the other side.

The rifles spoke again and again. Three of the posse turned and fled back the way they had come, sending ineffective pistol rounds toward the concealed men on the little cliff.

The "battle" was over in twenty seconds. Will sent one more round thundering after the retreating riders, missed and moaned in delight as his hips slammed four times against the hard ground where he lay. He panted for a minute as the climax powered through him quickly and he turned to Rorick.

"Good day's work. Get your horse and run down that last sonofabitch who got through. Give him another dose of lead poisoning!"

Rorick yelped with pleasure and raced down the slope for his mount. Will and his sons checked the

carnage below. Dale raced ahead, picked up a
Spencer repeating rifle and two six-guns. Phil found
two good rifles, a Winchester and a Lee, and they
checked the men. All three were dead and their
horses had run off. They would go back to town.

"Hell, don't worry about the horses. We got
better mounts than they ever thought of getting.
Check them for cash and watches, then let's move
out. No rush now. No damn posse gonna come near
us before we hit the Territories."

Dale scowled and looked at each dead man again.

"None of them has a badge on," Dale shouted. "I
thought we was gonna get us a lawman today!"

"Hell, Dale, they all lawmen," Phil said. "They
got to be deputized 'fore they can ride on a posse.
Them guys is all deputy sheriffs of whatever damn
county we're in."

Dale snorted. "Hell, I wanted me a badge. None of
these fuckers got a badge!"

Will cut it off with a round from his Henry into
the air.

"Enough of this caterwauling! We done it good.
Now let's get the hell out of here and into the Territories before somebody else comes along."

Rorick rode back a few minutes later, met them at
the horses and held in his hand a shiny silver star.

"I got myself a fornicating sheriff today!" he
yelled.

"Lucky bastard!" Dale screeched.

Will stared them both down, turned his horse
down the trail. It was no more than half a day into
the Territories. He grinned.

Once they crossed into the Indian Territories
there was no sheriff or town marshal who had jurisdiction. It was a beautiful haven for all sorts of hard-
assed characters. But no lawmen. Once in a while a
U.S. Marshal came around, or one from Judge
Parker. But more of them were buried in the Terri-

tories than Parker would ever know about.

Will kicked his mount and moved out faster. He was anxious now to get to their hideout and see if anybody had found it and was trying to claim it.

He fingered the Henry, half hoping some claim jumper had tried to stake out his concealed cabin.

TWO

Spur McCoy rode into Willow Creek, Mo. about noon the day after the bank had been robbed.

He had guessed right. For two weeks Spur had been following the track of the Jamisons. His assignment had caught up with him at a small railroad line in Missouri where they had a telegraph office.

General Wilton D. Halleck, his boss at the Secret Service in Washington, D.C., was a man of little humor. When the secretary of the treasury upbraided him about the rash of Western bank robberies, the retired army man fired off orders to every agent he had East and West.

Spur still had his telegram in his pocket. It read:

SPUR McCOY ROCKFORD MO

DROP ALL PRESENT ASSIGNMENT STOP CONCENTRATE ON WILL JAMISON AND HIS GANG OF BANK ROBBERS STOP LAST KNOWN TO BE IN EASTERN MISSOURI STOP IF CONTACT MADE WIRE AT ONCE

THIS OFFICE SO MORE MEN MAY
BE SENT STOP THIS IS YOUR PROB-
LEM, McCOY SO SOLVE IT STOP

Spur threw his reins around the hitching rack in
front of a hotel and pulled his saddle bags, blanket
roll and small carpet bag off the saddle and carried
them into the hotel.

At least he figured it had to be a hotel. It was the
only one in town, two stories, unpainted, but with a
sign out front that said: *"Rooms 25 cents a night.
Bath extra."*

There was no one behind the small desk in the
lobby that was less than ten feet wide and half that
deep. He rang the bell but no one came. Spur found
the register, signed his name and left a one dollar
greenback beside his name. He wrote the room
number 16 on the edge of the bill, took key 16 from
the rack behind the desk and went down the hallway
to his room.

It was grim, but better than sleeping on lumpy,
hard ground as he had for the past three nights.

There was a bed with blankets and sheets that
would remain on the bed for the length of his stay, a
small wash stand with the usual porcelain bowl and
big rose-decorated porcelain pitcher filled with tepid
water. There was no dresser or chiffonier. The walls
were covered with the worst looking wallpaper he
had ever seen.

He dumped his gear on the floor, pushed it under
the bed but let the Spencer seven-shot repeating
rifle lie on the hand made comforter.

The Spencer was his favorite all around rifle. It
weighed ten pounds and was forty-seven inches
long, but it was hard to beat in a close in, wide-open
firefight. It had saved his skin more than once. It
held seven rounds in tubular magazines, and one

more round could be kept chambered for a total of eight.

That was eight shots compared to the Henry's thirteen rounds. But over thirteen rounds it was no contest. Spur would have two or three of the long thin tubes loaded with rounds ready to slip into the Spencer that would keep firing. The Henry had to be loaded one round at a time by hand.

He stretched, took off his dusty brown shirt and tossed it on the bed, then scrubbed his face, arms and torso with the tepid water and dried himself on a big soft towel. Spur put on his "dress up" shirt from his carpetbag but didn't bother changing his pants.

He had a midday dinner in the hotel dining room, then talked to the undertaker. The man had put four bodies in the ground that morning and was exhausted, but richer. He had four more funerals slated for the next day.

The coroner, Harley, told Spur what happened, and that the services for the sheriff and the three members of the posse would be tomorrow.

Spur did not reveal his official status, nor did he bother checking in with the acting sheriff, the lone deputy who had not ridden with the posse.

Spur next talked to an officer in charge at the bank. He explained that the bank had been declared insolvent. He said that all available monies would be paid out to depositors on a percentage of the dollars owed, as soon as the total assets were gathered.

His name was Norton Dunlap and he was the only living officer of the bank. He sat at his desk, one down from the larger one the president had used. The front door was closed and bolted. Spur had come in the back door after persistent knocking.

"You said it was the Jamison gang," Spur questioned. "How are you sure?"

"The bunch was moving across the state. I read about it in the St. Louis papers. We should have been warned. Why weren't we warned?"

"Your town has no telegraph, Mr. Dunlap. There was no way to warn you, or to know which way the gang might turn. I rode in here by chance today hoping to get a reading on their next move."

"Now you know, and now the residents of Willow Creek are the losers of forty-three thousand, two hundred and twenty-eight dollars. That's more money than this whole town is worth. I work for thirty-five dollars a month, do you realize that, Mr. McCoy?"

"You said they took no gold?"

"That's right. There were drawers in the vault opened that contained over ten thousand dollars in gold coin. None of it was gone. They wanted only paper money, it's light, easy to transport, especially when a posse is chasing you. When are we going to get some protection from gangs like this?

"The Jamison gang has robbed twenty-six banks as of two weeks ago. The St. Louis paper said they had killed over thirty people in those robberies. Now you can add three more bodies to their bloody record."

"One of the gang was killed during the robbery, is that right?" Spur asked.

"True. Our sheriff wounded him, and then Will Jamison himself shot his own gang member because he didn't want to nurse him on the trail. Also I figure he didn't want to leave any witnesses who might talk."

"Mr. Dunlap, I would like to guarantee you that yours will be the last bank the gang will rob, but I can't do that. I am on their trail, and it's my job to capture, or kill them, but I can't say just when that will be."

"Good, I hope you kill them all," Dunlap said. He

lifted his brow and wiped moisture from his forehead. "Yes, I know, that kind of talk is not very charitable, not Christian at all. But I don't feel charitable after seeing Roger White and Lucy shot down in cold blood. It was the most brutal, terrible thing I've ever had to watch."

Spur turned his hat around in his hands. "Mr. Dunlap, I can only say I'm sorry. I'll do what I can. Thanks for your help." Spur went to the back door where the banker let him out quickly.

Spur McCoy walked down the alley to the street. He was a big man for the day at two inches over six feet and weighing two hundred pounds. The weight was toned, supple muscles that let him walk with the lithe prowling quality of a big cougar. He was in superb physical condition and used to the hard life of the saddle and camping out.

Reddish brown hair showed under his low crowned gray Stetson, and full sideburns grew well below his ears. Green eyes peered curiously at the Wild West where he had sworn to protect and uphold all laws, federal, state, and territorial.

His hands were hard, but did not show the rope burns, callouses and scars they would have if he was a working cowhand. But he was good on a horse, with a rope, and had spent time rounding up and driving cattle.

Right now he was on the trail of some ammunition. He turned in at the general store and went to the back where he saw a gun rack. On the shelves lay boxes of cartridges. He picked out two containers of .45 rounds and two boxes of the longer .52 caliber loads for his Spencer rifle.

When he looked around for a clerk, he saw only a woman behind the counter. She was tall, probably five feet eight. Her long black hair fell over her shoulders and down her back.

"Finding what you need?" she asked, a smile

coming naturally, unaffected.

"Yes. Have it right here. Do you work in the store?"

She laughed and he liked the way her eyes twinkled and the way she appraised him.

"You could say that. I also own the mercantile." She checked the ammunition boxes, added up his bill and he paid it. She put the shells in a small paper sack and handed it to him.

"You're new in town, talking to people about the bank robbery. Which makes you either another bank robber learning his trade, or a federal lawman. I'd guess the latter."

Spur pushed his hat back on his head and looked at her. She had an attractive face with a slightly sharp nose, penetrating brown eyes and a rounded, full figure.

"Do I pass inspection? Or do I have a hook and eye unfastened somewhere?" She was laughing at him with her eyes.

"No, nothing unhooked and everything is in place. You are an attractive woman. In fact you're the prettiest lady store owner I've ever seen."

"Because I'm the first. I know that old story. How would you like to have a nice home cooked meal for a change instead of that old hotel food?"

"Are you suggesting that I go to a boarding house?"

"Not really. It's closing time, and I live in back. If you'll snap the night lock on the front door I'll close up and see what we can find for supper."

"Isn't that taking quite a chance?"

She frowned for a moment, put her hand to her chin, then in a darting move drew a Derringer from the top of her dress and aimed it at him.

"I don't believe in taking chances." She smiled and lowered the small, deadly .45 two-barreled weapon. "Besides, I'm a good judge of men. I hardly ever make a mistake that way." She watched him and smiled. "Hungry?"

"I'm getting hungrier by the second." Spur turned, went to the front door and engaged the lock, then came back to the counter. She had lit one lamp which she carried as she waved for him to follow her.

The rear door of the storeroom for the mercantile opened into an attached five room house that fronted on the alley. It was comfortable, clean, well furnished and pleasant. It definitely had a woman's touch.

"This is home," she said. Then she held out her hand. "I'm Ester Cooper. My husband ran the store here for ten years, then caught the shakes one day and died two days later. Our doctor had no idea what was his trouble. I've been running the store myself for the past three years. If you're counting, I'm thirty-one years old and not ashamed of it. No children."

Spur took her hand and was surprised by her firm grip.

"My name is Spur McCoy. I am a federal lawman but I would appreciate your not telling anyone. I am delighted that you offered me a home cooked meal. I'll even help do the dishes."

She smiled and went to the kitchen. "I think I'm going to like you, Spur McCoy. Ever peeled potatoes?"

Two hours later the meal was over, the dishes done and everything put away. Spur held a drink of whiskey and branch water and watched the pretty woman who sat on the couch beside him.

"I'd weigh three hundred pounds in a month if I ate all my meals here," Spur said.

Ester smiled. "Thank you. I think a man should eat. I love to cook and like even more seeing someone enjoying the food." She looked away, then stared at him. "I'd guess you're not going to be in town long."

"Have to leave at sunup. I'm after the Jamison gang."

"Oh damn!"

He looked at her quickly. He was not used to hearing women swear. She grinned and lifted her brows.

"I know, nice ladies are not supposed to use bad words, but sometimes I do. Our relationship had been moving along so well. I do like you . . . now you're leaving before we even get to know each other."

She looked away, then back at Spur. "I'm not the kind of person to sit around and wait for things to happen. And I am not bashful about going after something I want."

She slid closer to him, leaned in and kissed him on the cheek. "If you'll turn around I'll show you exactly what I mean."

Spur turned and she put her arms around his neck and drew his face toward hers, then kissed him hard on the mouth. She broke it off, leaned back and looked at him, then kissed him again, this time with her mouth open, her tongue washing his lips. They came apart moments later.

"Mr. McCoy, we don't have much time. I would be ever so thankful if you would make love to me, right now."

She caught his hand and pressed it against her breasts. She watched him, then kissed his lips again and this time his mouth was open as well and she moaned softly, pushing closer toward him, trapping his hand between them.

Spur could feel the heat of her body through her clothes. Her tongue battled with his for a moment, then withdrew and let him penetrate her mouth.

She leaned away from him, pulling him with her as she lay to the side on the narrow couch. He was half on top of her, the kiss continuing.

His hand moved on her soft flesh and she moaned again, then one of her hands unsnapped the top of her dress and she pushed his hand down inside.

Her mouth left his and she whispered to him, her voice heavy with wanting him.

"Spur, you don't know how long it's been! I always have liked making love but now it's been almost three years! I knew when I first saw you that you were the one. I'm so much in need that I can hardly sit still. You do understand, don't you? I wouldn't do this for just anyone. You are something special, and big, and wonderful!"

Spur let his hand wander through the fabric until his fingers found her warm flesh. Her breast was more than warm and when his hand closed around it she kissed him quickly.

"Yes, wonderful Spur! Yes! That feels so wonderful. Oh, yes! I love that. It feels like it did the first time a boy ever touched my breasts. At first I was shocked and upset and then on top of that came the most wonderful, warm, marvelous feeling, and I didn't ever want him to stop touching my titties. Then my father came out on the porch and the boy pulled away and a minute later he left and I had to go inside."

She pushed him away gently.

"Let's go into the bedroom," Ester said.

The bedroom was small, decorated in soft pink with a four poster bed and pink canopy, pink bedspread and three pink satin pillows on top.

She sat on the bed unfastening the buttons on the top of her dress. She paused.

"Spur, how much do you know about women?"

He sat beside her, kissed her gently on the mouth, then shook his head.

"Woman is the most complicated animal God ever invented. I'm usually at a dead loss."

"As you seduce them, you're wondering how and why. Not too likely." She kissed him back, shrugged the dress off her shoulders leaving her chemise in place.

"Most women like to be loved, but they want the cuddling, the petting, the soft, lying words, the hugging and all the tenderness they can coax out of a man. A woman exchanges sex for love. Did you ever think about that? A woman gives in to sex after she has been cuddled and petted and told how wonderful she is.

"Men put up with a little petting and loving and holding in order to get to the sex. True. So this is going to be a long, slow process." She tenderly patted the bulge behind his fly. "Big man, you just take it easy down there, and wait your turn."

She shifted her skirt and pulled the dress off over her head, then lay on the bed in her chemise and long, silk, loose drawers that came to her knees. She patted the place beside her.

"Come and lay beside me and hold me and pet me and tell me how wonderful I really am." She grinned. "Of course you're going to have to lie a lot, but I bet when your thing down there is hard and ready and a girl is half undressed, you're one of the best liars around."

Spur lay beside her, kissed her eyes, then her mouth and bored his tongue deep inside her. Then he put his arm around her and drew her to him.

"Frankly, Ester, you are a marvel. You are tall and sexy and have big breasts and you're honest about sex. That's rare in a woman these days." His hand covered her breast through the chemise, then crept under it and found her bare flesh warm and inviting. When he touched her nipple it was already stiff and pulsating with hot blood.

"Oh, yes!" Spur said. "This is going to be a wonderful night. I have right here in hand a generous, sexy woman who has a great body and fine, full breasts."

She scowled, reached up and kissed him.

"Darling Spur, talk dirty to me, use all the bad words ladies aren't supposed to hear, like cock and cunt and fuck. I like that!"

Spur did. For fifteen minutes he teased her and coaxed her and petted her breasts and got her chemise off and talked her into sitting up. Her full, heavily nippled breasts thrust out beautifully. He kissed them and chewed on them until she could stand it no longer.

"Get your clothes off, Spur McCoy! I want it right now! Push your big cock into me as hard as you can!"

She undressed him, tearing at buttons and pulling off his boots, then his pants and underwear until he was naked. She had kicked out of the long legged silk panties and lay beside him, eyes half closed, her hands fondling his genitals. She wailed and pulled him on top of her.

Slowly she spread her legs, and lifted her knees offering herself to him. Her vagina lips were pink and swollen, the wetness showing that she was more than just ready.

Spur went between her legs and eased forward, penetrating her and driving in deeply. She gasped and then smiled and lifted her legs around his neck. A soft purring sound came from her as she thrust her hips upward as far as they would go, crunching their pelvic bones together.

"Oh, God yes!" she said. "Now that is good fucking!"

Spur thrust three times and she climaxed. Her whole body vibrated and series after series of spasms pounded through her big frame. She tensed and rattled and her voice raised in a soaring wail with each new series of shakes.

Spur waited for her for a moment, then the pressure caught up with him and he slammed hard into her, driving her hips deep into the feather bed on the springs until at last he could hold it no longer and he erupted in a jolting series of thrusts that spewed his seed deep inside her.

On the last few thrusts she lifted to meet him and they both grunted in surprise at the force of the meeting. After the last mighty thrust he dropped half on top of her, half on the bed and panted to feed his oxygen starved system.

"Glory, glory, glory!" she said softly. "It has never been that good before!"

"Three years," Spur said.

"Well, not exactly three since I've had a lover. Still it has never been so dramatic, so beautiful. Never with anyone else, not even the first time."

They rested for a few minutes then sat up.

"You're staying the rest of the night," she said. It was not a question, not an order, just a fact.

"Yes," he said and kissed her.

They lay back down and he put his arm around her shoulders and she cuddled against his warm body. They talked, as strangers often do when getting acquainted. She told him where she was born and raised, and how she had come from Ohio in a covered wagon with her family, out on the frontier! He had settled for southwestern Missouri. It was already a state, and there was land to be homesteaded.

The day Ester was sixteen she got married to John Cooper who had just opened a new mercantile in the small town of Willow Creek, ten miles from her father's farm.

"I was young, and inexperienced. John taught me everything, first about sex and making love and how to be a good wife. I wanted to learn, but I was disappointed in sex the first year or so. John had no idea that a woman was supposed to climax too. He thought only of himself."

Spur told her about his early life growing up in New York City where his father was a prosperous merchant and importer. He told her wild stories about his days at Harvard University in Boston and his graduation. Then about his working in his father's firms for two years and going into the Civil War as a second lieutenant in the infantry.

"Before the war was over, I was a captain, and my friend, U.S. Senator Arthur B. Walton of New York, asked me to come to Washington, D.C. to be his military aide. The Army said of course.

"Then in 1865 the U.S. Secret Service law was passed and I applied to be one of the first agents. With the senator's help I was accepted, and here I am."

They got up and had a snack, but before the food was gone they were touching and holding each other. They never got out of the kitchen that time, making wild, shouting love on the rough boards of the kitchen floor.

Twice more that night they became one, and before dawn they lay holding each other.

"I'll never let you go," Ester said. "I may just get my Derringer and shoot us both so we can be together forever in heaven."

"But what if there is no heaven, only a long sleep without dreams?" Spur asked.

"Then I won't shoot us, and I'll hope you'll stay another day or come back and see me every week or so."

"Whenever I can." He kissed her and reached for his clothes.

"At least I can seduce you with breakfast. Hate to see a grown man go to work without a hearty breakfast."

It was hearty. Flapjacks with fried eggs on top, biscuits and gravy, hash brown potatoes, coffee, jam and toast and a firm hug and squeeze before he headed for the hotel and his gear.

At the door she put his hand down the front of her robe so he could touch her breasts.

"Spur McCoy. You promise me on your Secret Service badge that you will come back."

"I promise," Spur said. He squeezed her breast and kissed her deeply, then he walked out the door. It was time he got on the trail of the robbers. They would not be expecting anyone to be trailing them two days after the robbery and massacre. That would be his advantage.

THREE

Spur rode due west on the track that led toward the Indian Territories. Scarcely two miles out of town he came on the site of the ambush. A dead horse lay to one side of the small creek where a million flies buzzed around it. Hawks and crows had been at it, opening huge bloody landing zones for the insects. Everyone fed on the surprise meal.

There were cartridge cases in the roadway where the ambushed posse had been attacked. He found dark pools which had once been blood that soaked into the dirt. Farther along the trail he found another shootout and more of the dark red-black stains on the ground.

· It was a military operation. Will Jamison must have been in the big war. He was putting his training on how to kill to a practical if highly illegal use.

Spur watched the tracks, and soon saw all of them fade except four that moved straight ahead toward the west. These would be the four Jamison gang members. They were making no effort to hide or conceal their direction or route.

They knew no other posse would come after them. They would soon be across the line . . . into the Territories. No Missouri lawman could touch them in the Territories.

But Spur McCoy could, and he would. It also was prime killing ground for the bounty hunters, those strange individuals who enjoyed tracking down and capturing a wanted man like some game animal. Most of the posters on wanted men read "Dead or Alive," and every one was a sure death warrant for the fugitive, whether he was guilty of not. A body slung over a pack mule or a horse was much easier to handle than a live prisoner.

Spur pushed all thoughts out of his mind and moved forward. He had supplied himself from Ester's store and now had a sack of provisions and minimum cookware tied over the carpetbag in back of his saddle. He had no idea how long he might be in the wilderness that was Indian Territories.

He had been in it once or twice before. It was off limits to settlers, but some white men had set up houses, scratch farms, and a few cattle here and there. All such uses of Indian lands were illegal, but usually little was done about violators. The place was a new refuge for all kinds of outlaws, since state officials and lawmen could not chase them inside the Territories.

There would be no hotels, no friendly farmers, no support if he ran into trouble.

Spur kicked his horse into a faster walk and stared ahead. He could see little difference in the lands: broad central plains, with a few gentle hills and rolling lands. There would be no marked change when he went across the state line from Missouri into the Territories.

He had never agreed with what the federal government had done with the Indians, especially those on the east coast that were marched out of their homelands and walked hundreds of miles and tossed into the Territories with little support, supervision or help. Congress called it "removal."

The removal of the Indians dated back to 1838 when the first of more than 60,000 Indians began the trek to the Indian Territories. The Cherokee, Chickasaw, Choctaw, Creek and Seminoles were all rounded up at gunpoint and marched across the plains from their wooded homelands to the mostly treeless prairie beyond Arkansas and above Texas.

Spur had heard stories that one of every four Indians who began the long march died on route from dysentery, measles, whooping cough or some other "white man" minor ailment.

Spur watched the rolling land and knew that sooner or later the emigrants would want to take even this away from the first Americans and use it for farms and ranches.

It was not his fight, not at the moment anyway. He saw a crude sign ahead and rode up to it. It had been hand lettered with a paint brush on a long board a foot wide and nailed to a sturdy cedar fence post. It said:

"Howdy! Your arse is safe here, this is Indian Territories! No lawmen allowed. Bounty on U.S. Marshals . . . $50. On Judge Parker deputies . . . $100. Welcome!"

Spur checked the tracks, leaning out of the saddle, looking over the now faint imprints on the ground. The same four horses he had been following went through the border into the Territories. The gang was safe, now the men would relax and move to their hideout, or set up a new one.

The tracks continued west along a little used trail for a mile, then turned sharply south, cutting across a broad rolling plain that extended as far as Spur could see. It was grasslands, with a few small rises, and a brush bordered creek snaking here and there in every direction as the water sought a route down the slight tilt of the land.

Near one small stream he saw a dozen Indian tipis. He circled around them, cut the trail again and saw that it bore almost due south. They were heading for a given point, and all the time they were coming closer to Fort Smith, Arkansas. That was Judge Parker's jurisdiction. He was the new Federal judge who had as his special responsibility crimes committed in the Indian Territories. Quickly he had become known as the hanging judge.

Spur rode all morning, paused in a small copse of trees for a quick drink from a stream and ate the sandwiches Ester had made for him. She was a delightfully interesting person. He just wished he had more time to get to know her better.

Spur had one more drink from the pure little stream, then leaned back just as a rifle bullet slammed through the space where he had been and splashed into the water. He dove to the side and rolled toward a fallen tree. Three more shots came in rapid succession all from the left where a small rise gave the gunners the advantage.

His rifle was still in the boot on his saddle where the horse stood a dozen paces away. Two more rifle slugs slammed over him, pinning him behind the log. All they had to do was run around to his flanks and nail his carcass to the log. He fired twice over the log, but the gunners were out of range of his Colt .45 pistol.

He knew he had to move, and made a desperate dash for his mount, but six rifle slugs drove him back to the log.

For a moment there was silence, then a different sounding weapon boomed from fifty yards above the first ones, on up the small rise.

Spur could not see any of the shooters. The newer weapon that sounded like a Sharps barked four more times, and there were only two return shots from the lighter sounding rifles below. None of the rounds were aimed at Spur.

A man surged around a rock and raced down hill twenty yards, then slid behind a scraggly tree and waited. One shot came at him, and he put three more slugs into the area where the ambushers had been. He stood and fired once more, then watched for a moment.

Spur could hear the sound of horses as someone moved away at a gallop.

The man on the slope above tried one more shot, then cradled his weapon across his chest and led his horse down the hill toward where Spur still lay behind the log.

When Spur looked over the log again, the man had stopped thirty yards up the hill.

"Hello down there. Don't shoot. I'm one of the good guys. I'm coming into your camp." He slung the rifle over his shoulder with the barrel pointing down and walked the animal down the hill.

Spur checked him out as he moved. He was tall and thin, wore clothes that had been on the trail for at least two weeks. Black hat, a Sharps rifle, and a six-gun on his hip. His boots had spurs that jangled as the horse moved.

When the rider got close enough, Spur saw that he was just a kid, no more than seventeen, maybe eighteen. Blond hair fell down the back of his neck. He wore thin leather gloves and pulled his bay up ten yards from Spur.

"Friend," he said lifting both hands when Spur rolled over and came up with his Colt .45 pointing at him.

"Is it all right if I get down?"

"Whenever a man saves my life, I let him alight and introduce himself," Spur said, standing. "My name is Spur McCoy."

The kid slid off the horse and held out his hand.

"They call me Longjohn Ferrier. I know about you. You're hunting down the Jamison Gang. I figure you could use some help, since your odds are four to one. With me on your side it would be two to one, much better odds."

"True." Spur shook the hand and tried to evaluate the young man. "Thanks for getting me out of a jam. They had me pretty well in a hole there."

"Yeah, they did. But old Matilda and me knew what to do." He patted his Sharps-Borchardt rifle. "This old girl scared off two of them and wounded the other one. Bunch of rawhiders from the look of them. You got to be more careful traveling alone in this country."

Spur nodded. He had heard about the new Sharps-Borchardt, a single shot rifle that fired a .45 center fire round. But the thing was a half inch longer than four feet and weighed nine pounds.

"I've been here before," Spur said. "The fact is I work alone, not looking for a partner."

Longjohn grinned. "You lawmen never are. How did I know you was packing a badge? The way you look, the way you ride. You're too damn clean to be living out here. There's still even a woman's perfume smell on you. I wasn't trying to be your partner, teacher would be more like it."

Spur scowled and started to reply.

"Let me have my say. Out here you look like a lawman, every killer and petty thief in the Territories is gonna be gunning for you. Nothing personal, nobody out here likes the law, and especially federal lawmen. Get dirty or get dead."

Spur nodded, realizing the young man had a good point. "You got any other free advice?"

"Lots of it. First off, don't ever stop or camp in an open place like this, makes you a sitting duck. A man out here will kill you for your horse, saddle and your guns. He don't need no other reason. You gonna be here a while, suggest you toughen up a little."

"Thanks, that *is* good advice."

"Also, watch your backtrail better."

"What?"

"I saw you in Willow Creek, been following you ever since. Good thing I was friendly."

"And you're interested in the Jamisons?"

"A mite bit, yes. Four of them got wanted posters out. There's two thousand dollars a head on them four."

"Dead or alive?"

"That's the ticket! Neater, cleaner, that way," Longjohn said.

"And you aim to collect?"

"Hell, a lawman like you can't collect no reward. Might as well be me as anybody."

Spur nodded. "Might as well, but don't look for any help from me."

"Real neighborly. After I saved your ass just now."

"I didn't need all that much help."

"You took it."

"Not much I could do about that. How old are you?"

"Old enough. I've collected three bounties already, five hundred each. All alive when I turned them in, in case you're wondering."

Spur put his gear together and mounted up.

"Free country, Ferrier. Man can ride any trail he wants to around here. I can't stop you."

Longjohn pushed his light brown hat back on his forehead and rubbed his chin with his hand covered with the skin-thin leather glove.

"You shore don't sound none too friendly. Maybe you just don't like bounty hunters."

Spur nodded. "You could be right."

"We serve a purpose. No way enough lawmen to bring in all the riff-raff that is running around, especially here in the Territories. I've heard some bounty men hunt guys down like animals, kill them on sight. I never had to do that."

"How old are you, Ferrier?"

"Old enough. Eighteen."

Spur laughed. "More like sixteen."

"Yeah, well I'm over seventeen by two months. If a man is big enough, he's old enough. I can pull a trigger and shoot straight. That makes me just as big and as old as the next guy."

Spur turned his mount and rode south. He cut across the trail again after a ten minute search.

Longjohn Ferrier rode behind him.

"You ain't much on friendly," the young man said.

"I am with friends," Spur said.

A mile on south Longjohn was still there.

"You know anything about the Jamisons?" Spur asked him.

"Bank robbers, killers. Robbed over thirty banks by now and probably killed more than thirty people. Usually they kill one or two at each bank. Favorite targets are lawmen."

"You been shot at before?"

"Lots of times, like today."

"Which way did those guys you rousted head out?"

"North," Longjohn said.

"Good, I don't need no extra trouble. I didn't come down here to fight every outlaw in the Territories."

"With two we could stand guard at night," Longjohn said.

Spur lifted his brows, threw up one hand in defeat.

"You know how to fast track?"

"Of course," Longjohn said.

They galloped their horses down the long, shallow valley for half a mile, then each made a hundred hard arc round the center of the valley, trying to find the tracks of the four horses.

Longjohn found it first and whooped. Spur rode up, checked the tracks. They were at the far side of the valley, and soon they angled up and over the low rolling ridge. They followed slowly, but when the tracks headed down the next valley south, Spur and Longjohn nudged their mounts into a gallop again for a quarter of a mile, then they checked the ground the same way.

An hour before sunset they had moved what Spur guessed was fifteen miles. The trail led over another small rise and to the left they could see a fair-sized Indian village.

"Everything peaceful with the injuns," Longjohn said. He lowered a pair of old army binoculars. "Seems strange. Most guys would have raided the place for a young girl if nothing else. These guys all hate the Indians."

"Which means they were in a hurry, and maybe they were close to their hideout."

Before they could move from the cover of the trees, gunshots echoed up the valley. They saw two white men on horses charging the Indian settlement. To their surprise, the small Indian village went to ground, the women and children vanished into tipis or into brush, and six braves dropped behind log barricades and began shooting at the charging raiders.

One of the attackers took a round in the chest and slammed off his horse, hit the dirt and rolled half a dozen times before he stopped. His horse veered off from the shooting and soon vanished down the valley. The second white turned back toward his partner, stared at him on the ground for a minute, then seemed to shrug, dropped down and took the pistol from his holster. He mounted and rode off into the brush at the end of the short valley.

"Maybe that was why the Jamisons didn't hit the village," Spur said. "Some of these red men are learning how to protect themselves from raiders."

They rode on. Spur not pleased that the bounty hunter was with him, but for the moment he could not think of a good reason to send him packing. He had a point, two men were three times as effective in this lawless land than one man alone. It might work out. He would try it for a day or two and see. Spur McCoy had no thoughts of helping Longjohn to get any reward. He didn't even want to think about it. If it happened, it happened.

By dusk they turned into a thicket, found a small clearing and built a fire. Longjohn had a full sack of supplies. They ate canned beans, had a mess of potatoes, and bacon along with their boiling hot coffee.

When the food was gone and gear cleaned, Spur left the fire going, built it up a little and then took his horse and his rig a hundred yards into the thicket.

Longjohn began to follow him. Spur stopped and looked at him.

"I thought you were an experienced man out here in danger territory," Spur said.

"I been here before."

"Good. Then you know not to sleep near your campfire. That smoke is a beacon for five miles for anybody smelling it. You go on the opposite side of the fire. If anyone comes, one of us should hear them."

"Yeah, yeah. I was just about to ask you if I should do that." Longjohn scowled as he turned, walked his mount past the fire to the brush on the far side and kept going.

Spur could have ridden away from him right

there, but he decided to wait another day. An extra gun might come in handy, even if it was in the hands of a relatively raw seventeen year old who was playing it much older.

Spur tied up his mount, left the saddle on and hunkered down on the soft mulch of leafmold under the trees. He leaned against a tree for a time, then stretched out, put his hands under his head and pulled his Stetson down over his eyes blocking out the stars that winked at him through the leaves overhead.

It would be a quick night. He figured they had covered about twenty miles into Indian Territories that day. If the trail kept moving south, he guessed it would end soon. The Jamisons would not want to get much closer to Fort Smith, which sat only a hundred yards from Indian Territories just across the Arkansas river.

A night hawk called but Spur did not hear an answer. Everything seemed natural enough. He would sleep, but the slightest noise out of place within fifty yards would awaken him.

Spur McCoy closed his big right hand around the butt of his Colt .45 and drifted off to sleep.

FOUR

Three men rode up a small valley, then turned into the headwaters of a creek. Each man trailed four horses behind him. Some of the mounts had saddles, others only bridles. All seemed to be riding horses and were broken, trailing quietly. The men agreed on the spot and hid their horses in the brushy woods.

Back at the creek and the shade near a little open spot, they kicked off their boots and splashed in the cool water, then brought out their grub sack.

One man gathered wood for a fire and the others looked over the supplies.

The older one was nearing fifty, with a sun and windburned face, stringy, long hair showing from under a weathered and dirty low-crowned hat. He wore a shirt that was once blue but now was so stained and dirty that color became a mottled blue black. Over the shirt he had a grease spattered leather vest that was never buttoned.

The next man at the food sacks was thirty, with a full beard and bleary eyes. His nose ran and made a mess of his moustache, but he didn't seem to care.

He wiped his sleeve over his nose now and then, watching the older man.

The bearded man wore overalls, with only red long johns showing on top. He had a gunbelt strapped around his waist, and was never far from his rifle, an old Lee.

The younger man came back with wood. He put it down, hollowed out a small spot and began to make a tipi of dry grass. Over the grass he put a second tipi of small dead twigs, then slightly larger ones, until he could cross inch-thick branches over the fragile structure.

He put rocks around the outside of the small fire ring, then struck a stinker sulphur match and pushed it between the larger sticks to the center where he lit the tinder dry grass and small twigs.

The grass flamed up, touched the small twigs that resisted a moment, then burst into flame. From then on it was a gradual warming process as one small stick burned and lit a larger one over it. Soon he had a blazing fire going. He carefully built a square of larger wood around the tipi, then stood back when the older man strode up.

"Finally got a fire going, huh?" the older man said. He pushed the younger one aside. "Damn, you ain't good for nothing, is you, Wort?"

Wort frowned, puzzled, then lifted his brows as he tried to think through the question.

"Not good . . . ?" He grinned. "No sir, Mr. Walton. No sir, I guess not. If you say so."

"Damnit Wort! Keep out of my fucking way! Now stand over there and be quiet."

Wort scowled. "Don't like you swearing at me, Mr. Walton," Wort said, his voice low, nearly an apology.

Walton turned, snorted. "Damn, Wort, don't think I can put up with a crazy like you any longer." He lifted an old Colt .44 from leather and fired once from the hip. The round jolted through Wort's chest, puncturing his right lung, broke a rib and brought a froth of blood to his lips.

Wort stumbled backwarks and sat down, fear and anger on his face.

"Shot me!" he screeched through a mist of blood.

"Damned if I didn't," Walton said.

The third man came running up, his pistol out. He looked at Mort, then back at Walton.

"Hell, Bill, I just couldn't stand the idiot any longer. We just took him on to help with the horses."

"Doctor!" Wort said, his voice losing volume. "Take me to a doctor!" He screeched the last but it ended in a gurgle of blood seeping from his lips.

"Hell, you don't need a doctor, Wort," Bill said. Both the men turned toward him. They glanced at each other, then both lifted their pistols and fired three times each. The rounds ripped the last shreds of life from the mentally retarded man's body, and sprawled him on his back on the rich black soil of the Territories.

"Hell yes, Wort. We'll take your horses to the doctor. You just gave up your third in the string we got!"

Walton chuckled. "Bill, you are bad! Remind me not to get you mad at me."

Bill laughed and motioned toward the food. "Not as long as you feed me good. What the hell we having for chow?"

On a rise thirty yards away through a fringe of trees, a rawhider with a four day's growth of beard stared through a small bush down the slope at the three thieves. He jumped when the shots slammed into the quiet noon time.

He was between fifty and sixty years old. A greasy railroader's bill cap perched on his head hiding dull, dirty gray hair. His face was spotted with sores and he coughed quietly as he watched the killing below.

He had seen the three riders come up the valley, watched them hide the horses and grinned in anticipation. His clothes were so dirty they would stand up by themselves. His name was Spivey and he held the stolen Winchester rifle in his hands like a lover.

Spivey had counted the horses, fifteen! Christ, there was a fortune in horses down there! He could get plenty for them in Fort Smith, no questions asked. The brands might have to be dealt with, but that would be little problem out here.

He reached below him and whacked the girl lying in the grass.

"What the hell you want, old man?" she asked. She rolled over and sat up.

Spivey grinned. She was maybe fourteen, she never had told him. The man's shirt she wore had so many holes in it her breasts both showed through the front. She had a lot to show. Christ, she was built like a brick shithouse! Spivey reached down and grabbed one breast and pulled her up the hill so she could see over the top.

"Right down there is our ticket to Fort Smith. Fifteen horses we can sell. Should mean five, six hundred dollars, we work it right. And I might even buy you some pretties and maybe a new dress."

"Fuck, you better, all the loving sweet pussy I give you even if you is an old bastard." She laughed softly.

Spivey pushed his hand down the front of the shirt and grabbed her breasts and played with them. He rubbed his growing hardon, then scowled.

"First we blast these cruds, then we have a party."

"You promised to save the next young one for me," she said, her dirt caked young face pouting.

"Hell!" He spat into the dirt. "If'n it works out,

girl I'll save you one young prick down there. If'n it works out."

"Good!" she said and tried to snatch his balls. He pushed her hand away.

He let go of her breast and lifted the rifle. One of the targets worked over the fire. Spivey waited until the man was on the side of the fire, then lifted the Winchester and sighted in. When it was just right, he squeezed the trigger. The rifle fired and the heavy round bored through the back of Walton's head and exploded out his right eye, taking half his face with it.

Walton slammed forward, fell full length across the fire and the flames soon licked at his pants legs.

Below in the small camp, the rifle shot was a warning to Bill who dove to the ground, then rolled toward the water where the stream had gouged a two foot deep gully.

"Damn't!" Spivey said. "Only got one."

"Save the other one for me!" the girl whispered, as one hand stroked her breasts.

"Hey! You up there with the rifle." The words came from below in the creek bed.

"Talk up, stranger," Spivey called.

"You got us good. Old Walton, he's cooking on his own fire, dead as a toad. Me, I'd like to live a while. I got me fifteen good horses down here. Split them with you. You get ten, I keep five. Been working two months rounding up these nags. Fair is fair. What do you say?"

"How can we do that?" Spivey called. "I got the rifle, you can't go nowhere." He kept watching but the man did not show himself. Spivey's rifle sight worked over the edge of the cut where the man had vanished. Spivey could kill a fly at a hundred yards with the rifle.

"Hell," Bill called getting some confidence back. "You hold up your rifle by the barrel so I can see it, and I'll go into the woods and take five of the horses and you get the rest. Give me an hour's start and then they are yours.''

"Sounds reasonable," Spivey said. "You got a bill of sale for them all, I'd reckon.''

Bill laughed. "Hell yes, and I'm the Bishop of New Orleans, too."

Both men laughed at that. Bill lifted up to scan the hill above him, but dropped quickly.

"Well, what do you say?" Bill asked. "Those ten horses should bring you forty dollars a head in Fort Smith.''

"You got a deal," Spivey said. He held up the rifle by the barrel.

Below Bill couldn't believe his good luck. He had talked his way right out of getting killed! He eased up a moment, stood, then dropped down out of sight. The rifle stayed high in the air held by the barrel.

"Got to be sure," Bill called. He bent to step up the two feet to the slope and out of the stream bed. As he did he looked down at the ground.

When he looked up again he saw a gaze of blue smoke just as the Winchester fired and felt the slug slam into his shoulder and pitch him backward into the six inches of water in the small creek.

By the time he got to his knees, the Winchester was six feet from him, and the man behind it not the kind to take ten horses when he could have all fifteen. Bill swore and lifted his hands.

"Up here on dry land," Spivey said.

Behind him the girl stood watching. Her skirt had been cut off halfway to her knees, showing delicious curving calves.

Spivey turned to her and motioned.

"Hurry up, we ain't got all day. Fuck him quick and let's get back to the wagon."

She watched Bill. He went to his knees and she saw his shoulder was still bleeding.

"Got to stop the blood draining out of him first," she said. She tore part of his shirt off and made a pad, then pushed it against the wound and told him to hold it there. Then she unbuttoned her shirt and spread back the sides.

Bill stared at her breasts and wailed.

"Them tits of yours are real that are hanging out there?" he asked.

She stepped closer and pushed one breast into his mouth and he moaned as he chewed on it. He remembered what the old man had said.

"Look, girl, I can fuck you good, that what you want. I can stick you where it feels good, any hole you want filled. I got the prick that can do the job five or six times, without stopping. You can ask any of the fancy women in Fort Smith."

"Get on with it!" Spivey shouted. He was collecting the weapons of the three men. So far he had found four six-guns and three rifles.

They all looked up as they heard a wagon coming. It drove up the little valley as far as it could go. An old woman eased down and stared at the pair, then walked up twenty yards to the death scene.

She was a match for the old man, maybe fifty years old, shrunken and thin, with a pinched face as dirty as the others. Her hair was hidden under a sunbonnet. Her breasts had sagged years ago and now hung down almost to her waist, small flopping globs of useless flesh.

She wore a dress that had at one time been a fancy ball dress, but after she had worn it for six months without washing it, the beautiful fabric and its colors had turned into dirt brown and tattered. The skirt drug the ground and was grimy black on the bottom.

She swore at Spivey, then walked over to the man
on his knees where he was chewing on the girl's
breast. She backhanded the girl across the face, and
pushed her away.

"You know it's my turn first around here! This is
a young one. Help me undress him."

The girl cringed back for a moment, then with the
resiliency of youth smiled and jumped forward
tearing at the buttons on his shirt. They stripped his
boots off, then pulled down his pants and jerked
them off so he was naked.

"Go slow, women! I got enough here for both of
you." Bill sat on the grass now, his member stiff and
ready. "Lordy, let me see some of them young tits!"
he yelped.

The girl opened her shirt and flipped back the
sides, then covered herself.

The old woman bent over him, playing with his
stiff penis for a minute, then straddled him, lifted
her skirts and held him upright as she lowered her
crotch squarely on his shaft. She grunted once, then
a smile covered her dirt streaked face as she began
to bounce up and down on him.

"What the hell you doing old woman? That's no
civilized way to fuck! You're an animal. Now big tits
over here, yeah. I bet the girl knows how to fuck
proper on her back." He wailed.

"Christ, woman, you do know how to get a guy's
cock going!" He roared and tried to thrust up as he
climaxed, but the woman kept on lifting and
dropping.

At last she screeched a bellowing claim of satisfaction and stood up.

She snorted. "Hell's bells, he warn't half good.
Look at how fast he shriveled up. Not a stayer. He's
all yours, girl. See if you can get him hard again. Bet
you can't."

The old woman walked away with a little swagger and went inside the covered wagon.

The girl sat on the grass a dozen feet away from Bill. She had her hands inside her shirt slowly stroking her breasts as she had done as she watched the two coupling. Now she slowly took off the shirt.

She made a little ritual of it, a strip tease, letting him see her pink tipped breasts one moment, covering them, then showing both and covering. Gradually she let one breast show fully, then both and turned to face him.

"Now them is tits!" Bill screeched. He got on his hands and knees and crawled toward her.

"Stay there!" she said. She went down on her hands and knees letting her big breasts hang and sway as she did. She crawled six feet toward him, then rolled on her back and back to her hands and knees making her breasts jiggle.

"God almighty!" Bill breathed. "Them is damned pretty boobs and I want to eat them off you!"

She moved closer but stayed out of reach.

"Sit down," she said. He did and she saw his penis was still not hard.

Slowly she began to stand, then went into a little dance that made her breasts shake and bounce. She worked on the buttons of the long skirt and when it was undone, she began to tease it off her body. It dropped from her waist, lower and lower until pubic hair showed.

Bill moaned and crawled toward her. She scurried away and pulled up the skirt, then bunched it high on her white thighs inching it up and up. Bill screeched in delight and tried to catch her.

By now his penis was stiff and tall and she twirled the skirt away and showed him her back, then she turned slowly until she was facing him and he gasped in wonder and passion.

She walked to him, letting him grab her thighs, then she bent, rubbing her breasts over his face until he caught one and sucked it into his mouth. He was not concerned with the weeks of build-up of dirt and grime on her breast. He sucked and licked and washed it.

When she tired of that she stood, forced him down and stepped over him with her crotch inches from his face.

"Eat it!" she said, her voice husky.

"What?"

"Lick my pussy, stick your tongue up inside me!"

"Goddamn!" He pushed forward and up until his face was buried in the muff of her crotch hair and his tongue worked wonders in a act he had never done before. He tried to move away but her hands caught the back of his head and forced him against her harder and harder until she climaxed and he fell away shaking and laughing.

He grabbed his penis and began pumping it with his hand.

She kicked him in the side.

"No!" she said sharply. She pushed him down with her foot and then fell on top of him and pulled herself up his hard, lean body until they matched and she forced him into her tight vagina.

She screamed as he penetrated and then shrieked in total pleasure as she rode on top of him like a young stallion.

"Christ, woman. Can't you get enough?" Bill exploded after she had climaxed four times. She had stopped him every time he started to drive toward his own satisfaction.

"Twice more," she said and looked over at the old man. She nodded and he lifted his brows in reply. He would do it again! Christ but that made her feel even sexier!

She made it last a long time, working up slowly

54

and then on the second time she raced fast and hard toward her own climax. She rocked and rolled and surged up and down until he thought she would break him in half.

She surged higher and higher and saw the old man move up beside her. Her passion mounted again and again, then as her face distorted with the surging release of the tremendous pressure she nodded at the rawhider.

Just as she screamed and shivered into a tremendous spasm of fulfillment, the old man lowered a Colt .44 and blasted a round through Bill's forehead.

The girl sensed Bill dying inside her and it pushed her climax to a higher level. She screamed and her whole body went stiff with a sudden paralysis.

Then it was over and she came off him quickly and without looking at his face she began gathering up her clothes. She went over and sat down naked in the small stream and began to wash herself.

"Ain't had a bath in three months," she told the old man. She stood and humped her crotch at him. "I'll get it clean and sweet smelling so you can eat it, too." She laughed and sat down in the water again.

He hardly heard her. He was busy checking the bodies for anything else of value. He had the guns, horses, saddles, and all the paper money and gold coins they owned. There was nothing else.

The old rawhider stood, looking down at the dead, naked man a minute. "Damn fool!" he said. The naked, dead man should have known better than to trust a fucking woman. He should have been thinking how to get away.

The rawhider sat down and watched the young girl in the stream. Look at them tits! Damn it was nice having her along on the trip. They had found her in a wagon after they attacked it just over the line in Arkansas. Her parents had got themselves killed in the fracas. That didn't seem to bother her a lot. She said she didn't like them.

She had been a year younger then, but already she had big tits. The old woman had objected, then realized her man wanted the young body for fucking. That was fine with her. And the young girl could do the cooking and cleaning up, too. It had worked out well.

The first three or four times had been a struggle for both the old man and the old woman to get the girl's clothes off and her legs apart. But after half a dozen times, she realized that she loved to fuck more than anything. After that she had come to him every two days. At his age every two days was about right so he didn't get worn out.

The old rawhider shook his head. Today he couldn't get it up, not even watching her wash herself and teasing him. But tomorrow he would have her again.

Damn, tomorrow would be a day. They would move this string of saddle horses into Fort Smith, and then sell them one at a time over the next two weeks. By the end of that time he would be a rich man!

Christ but she was a pretty woman. He didn't care if she was just fourteen. He rubbed his crotch but nothing happened.

The old rawhider went to look at his new string of horses. What a day tomorrow was going to be!

FIVE

Spur and the bounty hunter Ferrier met back at the dead fire a little after sunup. Spur had the feeling the young man had been waiting for him for some time.

"Figured you for an early riser," Ferrier said.

Spur checked around the fire area. There had been no horses nearby and he found no strange boot-prints.

"Coffee," Spur said.

Ferrier got a fire going while Spur dug into the supplies on his horse and came up with the coffee pot and a jar filled with fresh ground coffee.

By the time the brew was boiling, Ferrier had drawn a rough map on the ground of the Indian Territories, and outlined several spots where he figured the Jamison gang could be holed up.

"All depends if they are new here or if they come back here after every five or six robberies," Ferrier said. "Heard about one gang that had a regular cabin they used. Even hired somebody to stay in it while they was gone so nobody would ruin it or take it over."

Spur sipped the hot black coffee and looked at the map. "We follow the tracks as long as we can. There's a chance we could lose them, but by then we should have some indication which general direction they're headed."

Ferrier nodded. "Fine by me. Not sure I could have read their tracks this far."

Ten minutes later the sky was bright enough to see the hoofprints and they were on the trail. It wasn't poor tracking, rather too many animals that proved their downfall.

Spur quickly found that one additional horse had used the trail since the Jamisons. Two miles farther south two more horses joined the set of prints that showed plainly in the damp places on the trail.

They came to a spot where the faint trail forked. One trail led on down south within spitting distance of the Arkansas border.

Ferrier sat on his horse as Spur got off and tried to read the hoofprints on the packed ground. Now there were eight or ten more sets of marks for him to figure out.

Longjohn Ferrier shook his head. "Don't look like there is much of a chance that the Jamisons would head toward the east. Arkansas is not more than five miles over there, and down another ten or twelve is Fort Smith, state lawmen and the home base for the hanging judge, Mr. Parker. Nosiree. I had my druthers I'd be moving away from Judge Parker."

"That cave you talked about is over that way to the west?" Spur asked.

"That's a fact. Somewhere eight or ten miles. It's possible we could find out something over there." Longjohn stopped. "Damnit no, you look too clean. You'll have to dirty up your clothes and stop shaving for a few days. You got to fit in with the rest of us out here."

Spur kicked at the dust in the road, swung up on his horse and looked at the young bounty hunter.

"Let's try the cave. There are so many tracks right here that I can't even tell if they got this far." Spur rubbed his chin. "How can you travel around out here, being a bounty hunter? Outlaws hate you guys ten times as much as lawmen."

"That's a fact. But they don't know what I do. Had a poster printed up on me. Shows me wanted in Texas, but the reward is only fifty dollars for me as a sneak thief. I use it when I get cornered or need some help. It's a good way to throw them off the track. Just be sure you don't shave any more. Nobody out here shaves."

They rode along the new trail heading east for a mile, then Ferrier pointed off the way to a small stream.

"Let's go down there and we'll get you dirtied up some. Won't be foolproof, but it could get you by."

"Is this absolutely necessary?"

"Only if you want to live a few more days so you can smile as a pretty lady takes off her chemise for you with promises."

"You win."

At the creek Spur took off his shirt and hat and let Ferrier trample them in a muddy shoreline. He wrung out the shirt and the mud smeared it again. The hat he stomped into the mud and water and mashed mud into the brim and crown until it looked unfit to wear.

"Now your face. Get it wet and smear it with dust. Keep at it until it won't wash off. Get some in your hair too, you look too damn much like a federal lawman."

An hour later Ferrier decided Spur McCoy looked as though he had been living in the Territories at least for a few months. He still wasn't dirty enough. What he needed was the kind of grime and greasy dirt that had to be earned, not smeared on.

They got back on the trail and Spur felt gritty and grimy. If he had lived in the same clothes for a month he would have been used to the slow accumulation of dirt. Not this way. He sighed. If it would keep him alive and help him finish his assignment, he could put up with it.

"Tell me about this damn cave," Spur said.

"Only been there once. Guy I was chasing went in and out of there like a shot one night, and I was a day behind him.

"It's a natural cave, a cavern place that some guys say is more than a mile long deep underground. It's got a small stream flowing through it, so water is close at hand, and it's pure too, none of that mineral stuff."

"Men live in there?"

"Damn right. Nobody gets in unless he's vouched for or can outshoot the guard. I gave the guard a twenty dollar gold piece and proved to him I could outdraw him if he got greedy. The man on duty keeps whatever he charges."

"Fires, food, how do the men live?"

"Bring in their food. If somebody gets lucky and kills a deer, they share it. Firewood is carried in, you'll see."

"We can get in?"

"How else can we tell if the Jamisons came this way? When a bunch like them comes past or stays a night, every man Jack of the people inside know it."

"Any women in there?"

"Damn few. I heard there were two whores way up in back by the air shaft, but I never got back there. Guess they could charge whatever they wanted to."

Spur spotted two horsemen riding toward them half a mile ahead. He motioned Longjohn off the trail and they sat on their horses behind some brush as the pair went by. Both were Territories dirty, both looked mean and carried three weapons each.

Spur put his Colt back in leather as the horsemen moved out of sight down the trail.

"Friendly looking pair," he said.

"Friendly ain't important out here," Longjohn said. "Staying alive is the first order of business."

They approached the cave just past midday. The sun was out brightly burning away the morning chill. They had moved into a river valley with a real canyon feel to it. Cliffs sixty feet high rose on both sides of the small shallow stream that seemed to come out of the face of the sheer cliff.

It did.

"This is the underground river I told you about," Longjohn said. "We get to the cave entrance by riding right up the creek. Be sure to duck at the cliff. The opening is just a little higher than a horse's head."

They turned into the water and walked their mounts toward the cliff.

"Let me do most of the talking. Be ready to use that Colt, but don't draw first. We don't want a real shootout."

"I got the idea. Why haven't we seen anyone?"

"This place is like a fort, everyone inside. Duck."

Spur went flat against his mount's neck as the animal walked through the opening in the cliff wall. For a moment it was as black as the inside of a gambler's heart, then his eyes adjusted.

He followed Longjohn who swung to the right to dry ground and eased off his horse.

The cavern sloped up sharply from the small doorway. Sun streamed in lighting the front part. Spur guessed it must be forty feet high ten feet back from the entrance. Beyond that he could see only a few fires burning, and a torch or two.

Somewhere a rough, raucous voice sang a bawdy

song.

"Who the hell are you guys?" a sharp unpleasant voice boomed at them.

"Who the fuck you think?" Longjohn spat back. Then he laughed. "Louie, that you? You still got the door concession? Damn, you must be rich by now."

"Kid, you back so soon?" The voice laughed. "Bet your mommie is chasing you, huh kid?"

"Right, her and a sheriff, Missouri type. We had a misunderstanding about who owned the cash in a general store safe." Both men roared with laughter.

"Longjohn, the bounty on you any higher yet?"

"Nope, still fifty bucks. I keep changing my name so I don't get too valuable. You thinking of turning bounty hunter?"

Spur could see the man now. He sat in a rocking chair beside a formal dining room table. Both were on a wooden floor someone had built. There were two other chairs, and the table was well stocked with whiskey, water and tins of canned meats and at least a few cans of sliced peaches, the cowboy's favorite dessert.

"Who's your ugly friend?"

"Louis, this is Sam Spur, a phony name if I ever heard of one. But a hell of a good gun to have on your side. He threw in with me back about ten miles when a damn rawhider decided he liked my horse."

Louis laughed. "Yeah. Rawhiders is for shit, but we got a few. Bad for the neighborhood!" He laughed again. Louis was fat and filthy. Spur guessed he was a short man. Since he was sitting down, rolls of fat flowed around his belt.

"Hey Sam, can you talk?"

"Fer damn sure," Spur said using a slight Texas drawl.

"Oh, shit, another Texan. Hell, five bucks a head to get in. Any argument we shoot out a candle. You win, you get in free. I win, it costs you fifty bucks."

Spur dug out a ten dollar gold piece, an eagle coin, and walked over to Louis. He held it in the palm of his hand, then tossed it in the air. Louis caught it, bit it, then nodded.

"Welcome home. But don't you expect no damn sheets on the beds." Louis laughed. "Hell, don't expect no beds!" His laugh soared into the reaches of the cavern, as Longjohn and Spur walked their horses into the cave.

They passed the first campfire Spur had noticed on the left. Behind it two men lounged on straw mattresses and blankets. They were eating the remainder of a pair of roasted rabbits. The men touched their weapons as Spur and Longjohn walked past.

Around an abrupt turn in the cavern they came to a lighter area, where a thin shaft of light penetrated through a natural chimney opening above.

In the center of the big "room" was a campfire. Horses were picketed around the rim of the oval area that was a hundred feet across. Spur and Longjohn ground tied their mounts against the wall, then moved toward the blaze.

"This is the campfire, the meeting place," Longjohn said. "We should be able to hear anything about Jamisons if they passed or came in."

The fifteen or twenty men around the campfire were all sitting on the rocky floor, resting, talking or just watching the fire. It was a haven for them. If they wanted to talk they talked. Two men played poker in the light of the fire, using gold coins instead of chips. Loaded pistols lay close by each man's hand. It was a warning that to cheat was to die.

Longjohn looked for a familiar face around the circle, at last saw one and moved next to him on the outer ring and sat down.

The man next to them stared at Spur for a moment, then looked at Longjohn and grinned.

"Hi, kid! You make the big time, or you just playing at being an outlaw? Sure as hell hope your hide is worth more than fifty bucks by now."

Longjohn laughed. "Hell no! I ain't gonna tempt any damn part time bounty hunter inside here. Just had a small argument with a sheriff, that's why I came by."

"You two didn't see eye to eye about somebody else's money, I bet," the man said.

"True, true. It was only three hundred, and the damn mercantile had plenty. I only borrowed it for a few years. Damn sheriff was going to put me in the calabose."

"But you shot him?"

"I refused to dicker about such a small amount. I left town."

"And the sheriff came after you."

Spur could see the other man plainly now. He was about thirty, had a full beard and gleaming white teeth. His clothes were not as dirty as some of the others, and he spoke well, as if he was an educated man.

"Johnson, wasn't that the monicker?"

"Not my current one but it will do for now," Johnson said with a laugh.

Longjohn waved at Spur. "My traveling companion, Mr. Sam Spur. Leastwise that's what he said his name was. Handy man in a pistol conversation with a sheriff, though. I can guarantee that."

Spur nodded at Johnson. The other man stared at him for a minute, then bobbed his head once.

"Spur, unusual name," Johnson said.

"It was White last week," Spur said and they all laughed.

Longjohn plunged on. "Least wise I found out why that Missouri sheriff was so nasty. Will Jamison and his boys had relieved the bank of all its paper currency the day before. My timing ain't too good in these matters."

"Jamison again," Johnson said. "Wish he would retire and let the rest of us have a chance. He keeps things all riled up and makes it damn hard for a man on his own."

"I just hoped he hadn't pulled in here and taken over the place," Longjohn said.

"Hell, no chance of that. He's got his own place somewhere, fixed up like a damn fort I hear."

"Heard the same thing," Spur said. He looked at Longjohn. "You said we'd fix some chow in here? We need our own fire?"

"True," Longjohn said. "After we buy some wood." He paused. "Johnson, you got a fire we could rent?"

The man shook his head.

"Hell, come sit by ours then. We'll dig up some grub, too. Don't pay to sit around here by yourself too damn long."

Johnson sat up straighter. "I thank you, young feller. I was starting to feel a mite like bait in somebody's trap. Should be some vacant spots down this drift a ways."

A half hour later they had bought five dollars worth of wood from a man who had a stack, built a fire in a side tunnel and settled down to coffee and slabs of bread and cheese that was just a day from spoiling.

"Glad that damn Jamison ain't coming our way," Longjohn said between sips of the scalding black coffee. "He always brings a new batch of bounty hunters and federal men chasing him."

"He ain't this deep into the Territories," Johnson said. "Hear his place is over near the Arkansas line. That way he gets to his hideout quick and can strike back across the line again."

"No shit?" Longjohn said.

Johnson ate another sandwich and refilled his coffee cup. "One guy who was through here said he stumbled on their place once and it wasn't more than fifteen miles from Fort Smith. Ain't that a belt! And with old Judge Parker just ranting and raving about law and order!"

"Funniest thing I ever heard!" Spur said, faking a laugh that sounded faked even to him.

"Yeah, I figured on him being a hundred miles west of here," Longjohn said.

The voices from farther into the main cave came plainly. Two men were shouting at each other.

A few men began moving past Spur's spot, walking toward the fight. There was no alarm given, no announcement made, but the audience was assembling. Spur, Johnson and Longjohn walked that way. Twenty feet up the cave two fires lit the scene. Two men were facing each other across one of the blazes. Each was bare to the waist. Each held a knife with a six-inch blade. The sharp edges glinted in the firelight.

"You stole it, you sonofabitch!" one man snarled.

"Like hell! It was mine all the time. Come take it away from me you want it so bad."

Those were the last words spoken. The larger of the two men jumped the fire, his knife slashing at the other man who pivoted away and sliced a three inch gash on the attacker's shoulder.

A howl of pain and anger echoed through the cavern.

The smaller man feinted one way, drove in from another angle and sliced the tall man's knife hand.

Now the strategy changed. The big man knew he was outgunned as far as knife fighting skill. He took a big breath, surged one way and then the other to force his target against the wall with no escape, then he drove straight at him, lifted his left arm to take the knife slash he knew was coming from the smaller man.

The blade bit through his arm to the bone.

The wounded man screeched in pain, but rammed against the smaller one with his chest, pinned him against the rocky wall, then drove his knife into the man's side, tugged at it, ripping and slicing forward until the blade came out the smaller man's stomach.

The victor stepped back, watching the man die. He was ripped and sliced to pieces inside, but no vital organs had been touched.

The big man roared in anger, stabbed his bloody knife into the fallen man's groin and slashed at his genitals. Then he bent over the victim who was barely conscious and stabbed his knife into the dying man's eyes one at a time. Screams so agonizingly painful that Spur could scarcely believe they were human bounced off the walls.

With a bellow the big man slashed his knife across the dying man's throat severing both carotid arteries.

He turned, stared at the watchers. Three cuts on his arm and shoulder dripped blood. His knife was blood bathed. He roared and shrieked and charged at the men at the edges of the firelight, then pulled back.

"Leave me alone you sonsofbitches!" he screamed once more and the crowd of watchers began to fade away.

Spur caught Longjohn's elbow.

"Time to go," he said.

Longjohn shivered and nodded.

Back at their fire, they gave it to Johnson, found their horses at the wall of the big room, and led them back toward the front of the cavern.

At the entrance, Louis demanded a complete report on the fight. Spur gave him a brief version of it.

"Just stopped by looking for a friend, but he ain't here," Longjohn said at the door. "So best we be on our way."

"Still to do that candle shooting out?" Spur asked Louis.

"Not a chance, no stakes now."

Spur pulled his horse around, mounted and watched the small fat man. The Secret Agent pulled his .45 and shot the top off a bottle of whiskey sitting on the table beside Louis.

"Just in case you want to know, I'd have beaten your tail off," Spur said. He pushed a new round into the spot just fired and holstered his piece.

Spur touched his hat, moved into the stream and walked his mount to the entrance, leaving his back open to the fat guard if he wanted to try it.

Louis chose the better part of valor and decided to live to fight another day.

Outside, Longjohn stared at Spur in disbelief.

"Christ, you almost ruined the whole thing! Why you have to do that fancy shooting thing? Now he'll remember you and me too. He'll want to know which Fancy Dan outlaw you really are. I won't be able to go back there for a year at least."

Spur grinned. "I had a bad day. There I was rubbing shoulders with a hundred outlaws, and I couldn't even arrest one of them. It was the most frustrating few hours of my life. What did you expect me to do, play poker with those cutthroats?"

Longjohn lifted his brows. "Hey, I never thought of it that way. I guess it was tough for you. Where we heading?"

"Back the other way, east again, back toward the Arkansas line. I want to see where the other fork in that road goes."

"I'm with you. Maybe now that we have it narrowed down a little we should split up so we can cover more ground quickly."

Spur thought about it as they rode. It was a good idea. By the time they got to the fork in the trail it was late in the afternoon. They could camp together one more night, then lay out the territory to cover and arrange a meeting place for each day at sundown. Spur nodded and they looked for a good place to conceal themselves for the night.

SIX

Will Jamison and his band approached their hide-away cabin the way they always did when all of them had been away. They came at it on foot from four different directions. They moved slowly, stalking it, rushing quietly from one bit of protection to the next as they came up on the small building.

Unless one knew exactly what to look for, the cabin itself was extremely hard to see.

Will moved twenty feet and stopped, every nerve in his body alert to danger. Someone could have found the place and taken it over while they were gone.

He moved again and could see the shape of the door through the branches and vines that covered the structure. His breath came quickly now as he watched the place.

Will saw no movement, no sign that anyone had been there since they left. No smoke came from the stone chimney. They never came to the cabin in the same way so no trail could be established.

A mockingbird chattered a shrill cry and Will

made the same sound back at it. The call meant Phil had seen nothing unusual.

He heard one more call on the far side, then Dale broke from behind a tree and raced to the cabin door and jolted it open, a pistol in each hand.

He vanished inside and a moment later was back, hogslegs leathered and he waved.

"All clear, come on in," he said and went back inside.

Will came from behind the tree and moved forward. They had looked a long time before they found this place. It had been built maybe forty years ago, and the brush and small trees of the Brushy Mountains had grown over and aroud the place until it blended in perfectly with its surroundings. They did a little work to make it even harder to spot.

They put in new windows, hung a solid strong door and dug an escape tunnel out the far side that exited ten feet the other side of the wall. It had been home to the Jamison gang now for almost two years.

As far as Will knew, nobody had ever found the place, at least not while they had been there.

The Brushy Mountains were an ideal spot for them to hide. The growth reminded Will of the Big Thicket country in Texas. The brush and vines were so thick that no man in his right mind would try to plow through it without some kind of a trail.

A native to the area could get lost in five minutes, and would need half the morning to find his way out. Only two trails crossed the area anywhere near their cabin.

They had built a small pole corral in a little canyon half a mile away, and kept their horses and spares there. They had worked out several general routes to get to the cabin from the corral. None was exactly a trail, and in spots they crawled under the thick brush rather than through it. The difficulty of the entrance was what gave them such good protection.

Will walked into the cabin and saw that Phil had a lamp lit and was laying a fire in the stove. They made it a habit never to light a fire in the stove or the stone fireplace until after dark. It made tracking the smoke damned near impossible through the thicket at night.

Will tossed his saddlebags on the table and the sack of currency.

"Counting time, boys," he said. His sons and Mat Rorick grinned and gathered around the two sacks.

As usual, Will did the counting and dividing. He was the boss. He laid out the wrapped bundles of bills according to denomination. He stacked the loose bills the same way for counting later. There was one bundle of fifty dollar bills and one of hundreds.

None of the men had ever seen a hundred dollar bill before. Will put them aside and concentrated on the rest. When he had it all laid out, he began dividing it into four piles.

The expressions on the men's faces grew as the stack he had claimed as "his" grew and grew.

"Must be forty thousand here!" Will said. "Damn, one of the biggest hauls we've ever made. One more like this and I can go back to New York City and live like a king for the rest of my days."

Dale grinned. "I think I'll keep Milly in Fort Smith instead of her going back and forth to Missouri at the time. Hell, we could buy that house we been using! But I ain't ready to quit yet. Nosiree bob. Got me a lot more banks to do!"

Will preened his drooping moustache and stared at his oldest. "Don't push it too far, boy. We been damn lucky up to here. We kept things under control. But it can't last. One of these days the surprises will all be against us, and some of us could get killed."

"Like Gabe," Rorick said.

"Yeah, like Gabe. He was hurt bad and we couldn't help him none riding on a horse."

"Pa, would you have finished me off that way if it had been me gut shot back there?" Phil asked.

Will Jamison looked at his youngest son and shook his head. "Don't rightly know, Phil. Hell no! I'd have brought you back, nursed you myself. Gabe, he never fit in with the family all that well. Not like Rorick here does."

By the time the money was divided they each had a little over ten thousand dollars.

"Christ, a cowboy would work for thirty years to make this much money!" Dale said. "We made it in a day and a half!" He jumped up and danced a little jig on the hard packed earth floor.

Will laced his fingers together in back of his head and leaned back on the box he sat on by the table.

"Yeah, right. So maybe we should just hang up the iron and enjoy our money. Sure is sounding better to me all the time."

"But you're old, Pa. You got to be over forty now!"

"Ain't exactly in the grave yet, boy!"

"Didn't mean it that way. Hell, I'm only twenty-two. I figure I'm just getting started."

"You found a good woman yet, Phil?"

"Hell no. When I got time to meet a nice woman? I just barely got time to fuck a whore now and then."

Phil left the table and went to the corner where his bunk stood against the log wall. He moved the bunk out and scraped an inch of dirt away from the floor until he uncovered the top of a sturdy metal box. He wiped away all the dust and dirt from the top, then swung it up.

The rest of them ignored him as if he wasn't there. He looked down at the stacks of bank notes.

"God damn!" he said softly. On a scrap of paper he had written a figure. It said $38,325. He laid the new money in the hole, put the loose bills that amounted to $187 in his pocket and then made a note on the total. He added the two figures and grinned. He had a total of $48,854!

Phil put the top down softly, spread the dirt over the spot and pounded it down hard with a board, then stepped on the board to make sure. He swung his bunk back in place and dusted off his hands.

Will pointed at the fire and Dale lit a match to the paper and kindling. Dale was their chief cook.

Will had spread out a game of solitaire on the rough wood table top. He glanced up at Phil.

"You still don't trust banks, do you, Phil?"

"Hell no. I seen too many of them go busted." He chuckled. "Hell, I made about thirty of them go bust!"

"How much do you have salted away down there now in that box?"

"Why you wanta know?"

"It's a mighty big temptation."

"How? Nobody but us know it's there!"

"How much, Phil?"

Phil wrote a figure on a piece of paper and handed it to his father. Will read it and pushed it in the small cast iron stove.

"Too damn much, Phil. I got my cash in a bank. I dress up and shave and wash and everything when I go in there as Marshal Jones. In that town I am Marshal Jones. I could ride in there tomorrow and buy a house, go to church and start breeding me some race horses."

"If the bank don't go bust."

"Yeah, that's right."

They didn't talk about the fortune under Phil's bunk again.

"Hell, me, I'm gonna buy myself a big saloon," Dale said. "Have about thirty gambling tables, and a long bar and big goddamn mirrors, and maybe about six fancy women upstairs!" He nodded. "Shit! I got enough money now to buy the best saloon in almost any town I want. Maybe one of the bigger cow towns where there's lots of money floating around. Or maybe one of them fancy-schmantzy places in Houston!"

"Quit dreaming and cook our supper," Rorick said, grinning. "You want any help? I'm starved half to death."

"Sure, peel the potatoes," Dale said. Rorick was almost like family, had been with them since their second bank job. "Rorick, what the hell you gonna do with all your money?" Dale asked.

"Me? Told you. Gonna head out for Wyoming and buy myself a spread and get the best beef breeding stock I can buy, and go into the cattle business. Intend to have me five thousand beef on the hoof by the end of three years."

Phil laughed. "Damn, you must flat out like to work. You ever been a cowboy? You get rained on and step in cow shit and sleep on the damn hard ground and have beans and salt pork to eat a dozen days in a row. I never worked so hard in my life as I did on that damn cattle drive to Kansas."

"I'll be the boss," Rorick said. "I got me enough money to sit back and drink good whiskey and pay somebody to do the dirty work."

Will went outside and checked the exterior of the cabin. It was just as it had been. Vines and young trees had grown up around it giving it a natural camouflage. The roof had long since picked up enough leafmold to sprout grass, and now a heavy grass thatch covered the old roof, helping make it warmer and more waterproof.

The cabin had been built backed up against a twenty foot sheer rock wall. Nobody could get behind it. The front and sides could be defended, and shooting holes had been built in to give complete protection all three ways. The windows were small and high up so a man would have a struggle coming through them. The door had a pair of oak two by fours that dropped in half-inch thick iron straps to bar the outward opening door.

Safe as a babe in his crib.

Will went back inside. He could smell the fried potatoes and onions now. They had brought fresh provisions with them, picking them up at the general store just before they hit the bank up in Willow Creek. He was hungry enough to eat half of Texas.

Will looked toward the trail that ran a half mile from them through brush. He heard nothing. Will Jamison grinned. Just goes to prove what a man can do when he plans ahead. But a man has to plan everything. Even the end of the game. He was thinking about that more and more.

He had meant what he said about being lucky. Their luck could not hold. They had lost only two men, killed in thirty-seven bank robberies. It simply couldn't last.

Will shrugged and went in when Dale called that it was suppertime.

The next morning Phil and Mat Rorick lounged in a shady spot outside the cabin. Rorick heard it first. He sat up and stared into the brush. Phil caught the sound and reached for his rifle.

Rorick caught up his from beside the door and without a word they faded toward the sound. They had no idea who or what the sound might be, but it was too close to the cabin to be ignored.

They glided through the dense brush and woods without a sound. Both had learned to be expert woodsmen, and now they put that to good use. They looked at each other, made signs and split twenty yards apart. They paused, listened, caught the sound again and moved angling to the right.

Phil watched the brush and woods ahead. In a small open space he saw nothing and moved without a sound to a large shortleaf pine. He edged around it staring ahead.

Out of the corner of his eye he saw Rorick move up and pause. They both waited. The sounds came again this time to the left. They moved that way keeping their twenty yards separation.

Phil wormed his way through a tangle of sycamore, gum and hickory trees, then paused beside a huge oak.

Rorick was slightly ahead of him.

He caught movement in front. Phil concentrated on the scene then picked out the movement near a gum tree. An Indian crouched there, bow and arrow in his right hand, three more arrows in his left. He seemed to be naked, but Phil guessed he had on a loincloth.

It was the first Indian Phil had seen this close to the cabin. Phil would make short work of him. He lifted his rifle, then looked at Rorick. The other man held up his hand in a wait signal and pointed to his right.

Before Phil could sight in on the Indian, a four point buck deer wandered from behind a screen of brush and grazed directly in front of Rorick, no more than thirty feet away.

They looked at each other, both nodded and each aimed at the closest prey.

Phil and Rorick fired almost at the same time. Phil saw the Indian move just as he shot. The native stood, and started to draw his arrow. The round slammed into his right leg. The Indian bellowed in pain, then limped around the tree out of sight.

Phil looked at the deer. It was hit, but it bounded away to the right.

"Let's get them both!" Phil shouted. He chased his Indian and Rorick went after the wounded deer.

Phil knew the Indian was still armed. An arrow through the chest could be as deadly as a .45 slug. He ran from cover to cover, then darted across an open spot. An arrow whispered as it cut the air just to his right. He dove to the ground, rolled and came up behind a tree.

Ahead he saw only a big oak tree which the Indian probably stood behind when he shot. The redskin was gone. Phil jumped up and ran for the tree, made it and checked around the base in the grass and leaves. He found splotches of blood.

"Bleeding like a stuck hog!" Phil said softly, then moved ahead, watching both ways, pausing and listening.

Soft sounds came from directly ahead. Indian walk! He moved silently for ten feet. The brushy area opened and Phil ran forward as fast as he could, the rifle at port arms but ready to fire.

He saw the Indian through the light timber, brought up his Springfield .45 army rifle and fired. He saw the slug hit the Indian in the shoulder and slam him down.

Phil ran forward, but used the protection of the foot-thick shortleaf pine when he stopped to watch. He could see one leg of the Indian sticking beyond a big tree.

Phil paused, then jolted ahead again. He was in an open space twenty feet from the redskin when the brave sat up and fired an arrow at Phil. The shaft caught him in the side, sliced through his shirt and nipped a half inch of skin then tangled in his shirt and hung there.

Phil stopped, looked down at his side, then roared in anger. His long rifle came up just before the Indian could loose another arrow. Phil's shot caught the Brave just under the chin and drove down through his neck and ruptured four discs in his spinal column and snuffed his life out in an instant.

Phil left the arrow where it hung in his shirt and eased up to the savage. He wore a loincloth and a headband. Phil kicked him but saw that he was dead, so he bent over and pulled the bow from the death grip and picked up the two arrows he had dropped. The bow was short but effective. He took them with him.

It took Phil ten minutes to find Rorick after he heard a second and then third rifle shot to the right.

If the buck had been lung shot it could run a half mile before it died. Rorick must have stopped it sooner than that.

Phil found Rorick in high spirits. He had just cut the deer's throat and hung it on a stub branch low on a pine tree to let the animal bleed out.

"Got the sucker!" Rorick shouted. "Damn are we going to eat tonight! Liver and brains! Tongue sandwich and then all the venison steaks we can hold. If we can find enough sun I want to slice some of that venison thin and try to dry it, you know, like the Indians do."

He looked up. "You got an arrow sticking in your side!"

Phil laughed. "Near miss. That's one fucking redskin who ain't gonna bother us no more. Let's clean that critter there and cut him in half and I'll help you carry it back to the cabin."

When they struggled to the hideout with the venison, they were met with aimed rifles.

"Heard the shooting and didn't know what the hell was going on," Will said. "Next time you go hunting, you goddamned well better tell me about it. I might have blasted both of you!"

"Sorry, Pa. Happened all sudden. Caught a damn injun stalking this buck, so we stalked them both!"

"Yeah, all right. For venison steaks for dinner I'll forgive you."

Dale was already examining the carcass. He took out the liver and then hung the halves at the side of the cabin. He cut off steaks and took it all into the cabin to start a smokeless fire. Will had just given him permission for a noontime fire, unusual, but he wasn't going to argue.

Rorick stuffed his hands in his pockets and walked up to the other man.

"Will, I been wondering if I could take off for town. I'm getting hornier than an old he-goat."

"Want to spend some money, right? Hell, I don't know. Let's eat first, then we'll decide. I'm still mad as hell about all that shooting so close to the cabin. That venison helps, though!"

The fried liver and onions and venison steaks put them all in a good mood. Phil counted his money again, Rorick decided to have a long nap in the shade, and Will contemplated his future. Rorick figured he'd get a good night's sleep and build up his strength for another day.

Besides, Rorick wanted to stay and eat as much of the venison as he could hold. He got up from his nap, carved out some big steaks from the buck and began slicing them into thin strips half an inch wide and a foot long. He'd heard the thinner the better.

When he had twenty of them done he hung them on a rack he had made with sharpened pointed sticks. He set the rack in the sun and used a pine branch to scare the flies away. After a half hour he got tired and took another nap.

The flies returned, the sun started drying out the venison which might someday become jerky.

Will leaned back in the chair he had taken outside and thought about where he wanted to settle down. His wife had died in an epidemic of smallpox ten years ago. Now with money he could go anywhere he wanted to.

Before he decided he fell asleep.

SEVEN

McCoy and the bounty hunter, Longjohn Ferrier, split up at dawn that morning. Ferrier went farther south to check out some hideouts he knew of where the Jamison gang might be. The Secret Agent worked back toward the fork in the road where he first lost the Jamison gang's tracks. He wanted to try the other fork in the hope that he could pick up the quartet's prints again.

The spot he sought was farther than he remembered. He met no one on the trail and when he came to the fork he moved down it a quarter of a mile before he got down and checked the ground.

Here and there he could still find evidence of the four horses. Most of the prints were leading the other way, toward the interior.

Spur checked for sure, then began walking the ground, checking out the prints every ten yards. They continued. Three miles later they were still showing.

Around a bend in the trail, Spur stopped quickly. In a small side valley he saw a wagon being driven by an old woman. A young girl on horseback led a string of ten or twelve mounts. The little caravan came out of the valley onto the trail heading toward Spur.

He jolted into the woods until he was out of sight and listened for the group to go by. The girl's voice came suddenly through the woods as she shrilled at the old woman. Then she laughed as the older woman screamed in rage and swore at her for as long as Spur could hear them. Sounded like a friendly country family. When he was sure they were out of sight, Spur went back to the trail and worked south. A half mile on he found a change. Spur studied the tracks for ten minutes before he figured it out. There were only three set of prints. Why?

He moved down a quarter of a mile and studied the narrow trail once more. Now there were only two sets of hoofprints in the ground. They showed plainly in the soft spot where a spring wet the trail for fifteen yards.

The riders were leaving the trail one at a time. It could be that they were near their hideout so they didn't want to wear a trail to it. They went through the woods, a different way each time to prevent pounding a trail. Which side had they ridden away on? Spur backtracked until he found three sets of prints he was sure belonged to the same horses.

Then he moved forward until he spotted the spot the third horse left the main trail. It moved to the left. Spur studied the country. The main north-south trail wound along the edge of the low rim of hills. They were called the Brushy Mountains he'd noticed on his map. The hills were covered with shortleaf pine and a million hardwood trees. Around, through and between the trees lay a mass of low growing, hedge-thick brush.

He'd seen spots like that before that you couldn't cut through with a team and a mowing machine.

All he had to do was follow the tracks to the

hideout. Spur frowned. It should not be that simple. He guessed he was in for some surprises.

Tracking the lone horse through the dense woods was easier than Spur had figured. A hundred years of leafmold on the forest floor meant the horse left deep gouges in the six inches of dead leaves, pine needles, molding leaves and newly formed soil.

The trail led through sparse pine, around a dense thicket Spur could not even see through, back near the main trail, then turned dead into the mountains and went up a small ravine, over the top, around more thickets and into a heavily timbered section of hardwoods: oaks, hickory, elms and sycamore.

Spur battled his way through low hanging branches as he followed the trail. Anyone who went to this much trouble to hide his camp had to be an outlaw. The gang members had to do this each time they left or entered the hideout.

Ten minutes later he had followed the tracks to a small open place. He figured it to be a quarter of a mile across. He could see the tracks starting through the center of the meadow. He paused in the heavy brush. Should he show himself and follow the tracks? Or should he stay under cover of the brush and ride around the edge of the opening, and find the tracks on the other side?

It would take longer to go around.

Spur shrugged. There was no choice. He had to go around and stay hidden. He worked as quickly around the meadow as he could, but found heavy brush again and had to detour. He figured it took him almost an hour to move a mile.

When Spur came to the middle of the valley on the far end, he picked up the tracks easily as they left the meadow. The woods were more open here and for a moment he thought he smelled wood smoke. After being in the open for a few days, he could pick up the scent of wood smoke five miles downwind from a small campfire.

But this time he was not sure. It could have come from a fire a dozen miles away and carried here, settling in a spot with little wind.

He moved on.

Spur came out on the edge of a small cleared space no more than thirty yards across. It looked as if it had been a small lake at one time. Now it held only swaying green grass. His horse reached down for a mouthful. As Spur pulled up her head he saw a horseman ride into the opening directly across from him, and then another man behind him.

Both men looked up, startled.

Spur jerked his mount to the side, driving her back into the deeper woods.

Two pistols cracked almost at once as the men fired. They were out of range for anything but a lucky lofted shot. Spur got deeper into the woods and listened. The others were pounding across the dry lake bed directly toward him.

Now he was the hunted, not the hunter!

In the second and a half it had taken Spur to see the two riders and react, he noticed that both wore full beards and rode dark horses. That was all he remembered.

He paused now, checking his escape routes. The two men could be in the Jamison gang, maybe heading out to town or another camp site. He had blundered into them. Now he had to stay alive.

He charged through the most open spot of woods he could find, cut around a thicket and moved generally east. He would touch the main trail south sooner or later.

A rifle slug whined over his head and he jerked the horse to the left behind another heavy growth of thicket. He could try for an ambush, but these two would follow his prints and sniff it out. Maybe,

maybe not. It was worth a try when the right spot showed itself.

Spur charged ahead like a man running for his life. He smashed through light brush he usually would go around, he slithered down a ravine and bulled up the other side. Then just over the small ridgeline he brought the blowing horse to a stop, slid off and jerked the Spencer from the boot.

He bellied up to the top of the little ridge just as the first rider showed on the far side. Spur sighted in on the lead man and was about to fire when he jerked the horse downhill and rode hard. Spur didn't have a chance at the second man who cut through some timber and angled toward his leader. Spur decided he would hold off on his ambush until he could nail one of them and not just warn them.

He rode hard again, passed a small Indian camp, but saw it was a temporary affair. There was nothing there to offer protection or ambush potential.

He continued downhill working toward the trail. Spur had no idea how far from it he might be. Then he remembered that the survivors in Willow Creek said the Jamison gang had the best and fastest horses they had ever seen.

What he had to do was turn this surprise into an advantage. They had no idea who he was. So why shoot? They probably shot at anyone who got close to their cabin. So he must have been close to their hideout.

Spur turned back away from the trail, found a small rise with an open area in front of it and tied his horse to a tree, then slithered up to the top of the rise.

They charged into the opening, cut back to the trees, but not before Spur put two rifle rounds after them. He had no chance to aim, and at two hundred yards it was a chancy shot. At least he had tried. It would slow down their tracking.

He got back on his mount and circled back the way he had come, hoping he was moving toward their hideout again. That might make them furious, and force them into a mistake.

He rode for ten minutes then stopped in some heavy brush and waited and listened. He heard nothing for five minutes, then far behind he heard a horse snort and blow before a hand quickly gripped the muzzle.

They were coming. Spur scowled. He needed something special, unusual that they wouldn't expect. He looked around the woodsy area. Lots of brush, spots of thicket and a few big pine trees.

Pine trees!

Yes! He spurred his horse forward until he found a good one, then rode the animal fifty yards to the side out of sight. He took the Spencer rifle and hurried back to the tree. Spur slung the Spencer over his back by the sling, then using the convenient hand holds the lower dead branches made, he climbed.

When he was thirty feet up the looked for a good perch. Ten feet higher he found it, three four inch thick limbs that came out of the trunk within a few inches of each other. They made a good platform for him to sit on.

There was enough new growth of needles to completely hide him from below. He moved several small branches until he could see his back trail, then he settled down to wait.

Within a few minutes he heard them coming, then saw the first one round a big pine and pause. They were two hundred yards away. Spur waited. They came closer and the next time he had an open shot, he aimed, sighted in carefully and fired.

The round went over the man's head. Spur berated

himself. How often had he told troops that when you're high and shooting down on someone, the round often carries high?

At the crack of the rifle, both the men on horses jerked the animals into the heavy brush and big trees concealing and protecting them. He sent two more rounds through the brush but there was no chance to hit the men.

Spur waited five minutes, then realized the pair had known their position and retreated prudently. The big trees masked their withdrawal and he had no shot.

McCoy climbed down the tree, ran for his horse and kept moving. He was sure they would circle his position to pick up his tracks.

He had no mind to keep running. It was not his style. He would rather stand and fight any day, but it would be on his own terms. If he picked time and place he would have the advantage. He watched his back trail now more frequently.

Backtracking! Yes, he should have thought of it before. He was in a fairly open woods now and sent the mare at a gallop for a quarter of a mile. Then he hid her in some brush, took the Spencer and hurried back along his own trail. He would move up on them, knowing they would be coming along his tracks like a steam engine.

What he needed was a good firing position. A spot where he could do a proper ambush, be safe and at the same time have a marked advantage.

He found it fifty feet ahead. A pine tree had grown tall, but it split when it was small into two trunks. Now the tree was four feet wide at the base, and eye high off the ground the trunks went their separate ways, leaving a perfect "V" slot for firing.

Spur rested the Spencer in the slot. He could sight down the barrel when standing flat-footed behind the tree. He had perfect cover and concealment except for six inches of his head. That would be a tough target. All he wanted was one good, clean shot.

As he waited he saw that the sun had passed its zenith. It could be a little after one in the afternoon. The sun would set around five o'clock. He had four and a half hours of daylight left.

Ten minutes later he heard them coming. Both men were mounted, reading the trail, picking up the pace where the brush thinned. The man in front held up his hand and stopped. He listened for a moment, shook his head and they moved foward. They vanished into a small dip, then came up and directly toward him only sixty yards away.

Spur sighed on the man's chest as the target rode forward. Spur knew the man had a beard from the time he had seen him up close before. He remembered the people in Willow Creek said two of the robbers had full beards and two were clean shaven except for drooping moustaches.

Spur refined his sight, tracked the target past a patch of brush, then had a clean shot. He squeezed the trigger.

On the lead horse, Matthew Rorick seemed to sense the shot. He looked straight ahead at the split tree, started to raise one hand, then the heavy .52 caliber round smashed into his chest, tore through his heart and exploded out his back splattering Phil Jamison with his friend's blood.

Rorick slammed off his horse and onto the ground. His arms flew wide, he hit on his head and shoulders, then tumbled over on his back, his eyes staring straight upward.

Phil Jamison seemed frozen in place for a fraction of a second, then he screamed, jerked his mount to the side and charged through the brush and out of sight.

Spur put three more rounds into the brush where

the man had vanished, then he lifted up and watched the whole area. He saw movement through the brush and fired again, but heard no cry.

Now the hunted became the hunter again.

Spur waited ten minutes, than ran and got his horse and rode up to the spot where the body lay. He checked the surrounding area, found only the trail of one horse moving away quickly. He went back to the body and checked it for identification. Spur found one letter addressed to Matthew Rorick. The name clicked.

Rorick was listed as one of the non-family members of the Jamsion gang. The body held no other personal items.

Rorick's horse munched grass a dozen yards away. Someone would find her eventually.

Spur took the nearly new Henry repeating rifle from the boot and a .45 caliber pistol from the dead man, mounted up and began tracking the survivor.

In the back of his mind, Spur was hoping that the other member of the Jamison gang would ride straight back to the hideout. After a half hour of tracking, Spur realized the man ahead of him was too smart to run right home. He was a tracker, too, and knew that such a move would endanger the rest of the clan.

The man would try to even the score, to put Rorick's killer down. Spur began to watch for an ambush. He changed directions suddenly every two or three minutes, moving ahead but hoping to confuse a sniper.

The prints in the soft footing showed that the rider was making fast time whenever possible. Spur discarded his elusive tactics and pressed foward faster. It was plain now that the rider was heading due west, away from the border, and perhaps away from his hideout. That was a natural move.

Twenty minutes later, Spur came to the north-south trail and figured that the man he was chasing had turned his mount south. The lawman had guessed the rider would go the other way. Now the chances for an ambush were greater. There was room for an open shot from the brush at almost any point along the wide open trail.

Spur had no choice. He had to ride the trail, he had to move slowly and track.

Again he tried fast tracking. He rode a hundred yards at a jump, checked for the prints, when he found them he rode fast another hundred and searched.

The sun was just touching the tops of the Brushy Mountains on his left with the last rays of the day, when Spur came to a large meadow with patches of hardwoods sprinkled through it. The beaten trail cut through the left of the open place.

Spur saw with surprise that the tracks of his man veered to the right and angled for a patch of oaks and hickory trees two hundred yards away. Spur rode quickly back into the woods for protection, then he studied the meadow.

A small stream issued from the woodlands, and cut across the meadow. In times of flash floods, the small stream must be a roaring torrent, because it had dug a channel eight feet deep through the meadow. The wandering stream came to within fifty feet of the first batch of woods out in the flat space where the rider had headed.

Spur figured the stream would be shallow. He rode into the hock deep water and hunkered down to be out of sight of the oak woods, then turned downstream and walked his horse quietly until he could see the target batch of trees.

He came out of the stream on a sloping bank and galloped flat out for the treeline. A rifle spoke once, then again, but Spur had dodged his mount and the lead missed. By then he was in the cover.

The shots had come from his left.

Spur rode forward slowly, watching every direction, listening for the smallest sound that was out of place. He heard nothing. He saw no one. Remembering his tree climb, he checked the oak trees as he moved, but found no sniper.

Now he had a time deadline. If he could not find the other man before darkness, the game would be over. The enemy could slip away in the night, then lay a confusing, impossible to follow trail and vanish.

The man had to be a Jamison. There were only the three of them left in the gang now. If this Jamison got away, it would be ten times as hard to sneak up on their hideout and take them.

No matter how slowly Spur rode, the horsehooves made noise in the dry leaves and twigs. Spur was at the point of leaving the mount and walking when he smelled a foreign element. A moment later he knew what it was.

Smoke!

He looked behind him and saw the smoke trails. A fresh fire billowed to his right and then he saw torches thrown directly in front of him and to the side. They had set on fire the dry grass and ten years of dry leaves and gushed up into a fierce fire before he had time to ride forward.

The horse reared. He pressed toward the right side where there was no fire. Before he got there, the wind whipped a sheet of flames over the escape route and he was surrounded!

Spur sat on the horse holding the frightened animal in check. The fire directly ahead blew at him on a strong wind and came at a surprising speed. There was no chance to ride through the fire on either side.

He began backing away from the flames, then he turned the mare and walked back with the wind toward where the fire burned behind him.

Spur knew he had only one chance of getting out of the firestorm circle alive. He had helped fight a fire in Colorado one summer. They used to do what they called backfiring. For this they would go in front of a roaring fire and do a controlled burn in the path of the flames.

They would backfire it, so when the raging, out of control, firestorm came to the burned area, it would have nothing else to burn and would go out.

Spur stared at the flames behind him. The wind whipped them away from him toward the edge of the grove. On the upwind side was a growing black and smoking ribbon of fire free land! It expanded slowly as the sudden flames burned the ground cover and some small brush, but they were not hot enough to set the larger trees on fire.

Spur checked behind him again, fighting the smoke that swept in on him. The fire was twenty yards away and moving quickly. He urged the mare forward. She refused to step onto the charred ground. Spur jumped off, grabbed the reins, then tied his kerchief over the horse's eyes and led her gently into the blackened, still smoking remains of the backfire. Smoke still drifted up, but it was better than the flaming alternative just behind him.

The horse moved obediently, then shied to one side as her foot hit a hot spot. She walked forward again and Spur came close to the flaming brush on the up wind side of the fire as it burned closer to the edge of the woods.

When he stopped he was fifty feet from the raging flames behind him blowing on the wind. It would burn itself out in another ten feet. He nodded slowly, lifted into the saddle and moved toward the edge of the woodland which had burned through to the grass as the flames died out. Only a few tendrils of smoke remained.

He took the blindfold off the mare, kicked her in the flanks and galloped the last dozen yards, broke through a smoldering section of dry grass into the open meadow where the green grass resisted the flames.

Spur lifted the Spencer from the boot and made sure the safety was off, then began circling the fire blackened island of trees. He found no one. It took him a second circle moving slowly to discover the tracks.

They were fresh and showed that one horse had galloped north toward the trail.

One Jamison had escaped. He would soon be back with the rest of the family in the gang's hideout. Spur didn't have a prayer of catching him now, or tracking him in the darkness. He would report Rorick's death and warn them that someone was hot on their trail.

As Spur rode back to the track he turned off just before the sun went down and found a thicket where he could sleep in comparative peace and safety.

Tomorrow he would return to the trail and move toward the Jamison's hideout. Now he was certain that it was somewhere south of where he had been surprised by the pair of gang members. He would have little trouble finding that spot again, he was sure of that.

But from there on it would be much harder to get to the hideout, especially with the Jamison's expecting him to be coming and waiting for him with all rifles loaded and ready and held by itchy trigger fingers.

EIGHT

Coffee boiled in the small pot sitting on the side of the coals of the dawn fire Spur had built. It was a small fire so it would not attract any attention. He had moved from the thicket to a fairly well protected brushy spot near a chattering creek. Coffee would take care of his breakfast.

Spur thought ahead, remembering where he had been when the two gang members had stumbled on him. He would be able to find that little meadow again, he was sure.

He lifted the tin coffee cup, drained it and was about to stand when the serene morning quiet was shattered with a rifle shot and his coffee pot slammed off the fire as a heavy slug tore into it and knocked it a dozen feet into the brush.

Spur's right hand darted to his holster but a voice stopped him.

"Sonny, you touch that iron and the next slug goes through your chest. You aimin' to die young?"

Spur turned his head slowly, his hand frozen against the butt of his Colt .45.

Twenty feet away three rifles aimed at him over

the top of a fallen log. Spur let out a long held breath and slowly lifted his hands over his head.

"Damn smart!" an old woman's voice croaked.

"This one is all mine," a younger woman said, her voice surging into a wailing high laugh.

They stood one at a time, the old man first. He was in his fifties, rawhider dirty, unshaven, matted hair, an ugly high-crowned hat and below the rim, beady eyes that took in Spur's rig, horse, fire and sack of grub.

The younger woman stood. Spur had no idea how old she was, under wenty, dirty blonde hair in strings around her face and shoulders. The man's shirt she wore had been cut off at her waist and had holes and tears in it. Through one of the holes a tanned breast peaked showing all of the softly pink areola. She didn't notice or didn't care.

"Cover him!" she said and moved forward like a wild creature, ready to jump away at any time. She went to the side, careful not to get between the rifle and Spur, came up behind him and slid the six-gun from his holster.

"Check for a hideout," the old man said.

She did, from the back, her hands feeling his chest, his arms, and torso, then she came up each leg, took a knife from the boot sheat, then patted around his crotch more than was needed.

"Can't find nothing else," the girl said.

The old woman stood, cackling. Her face was drawn, wrinkled, worn out. She laughed again. "If'n you can't find nothing else at his crotch, you don't know where to look!" She roared again, slapping her thigh. Her fancy dress had seen better nights. Now it was filthy and showed how her shrunken breasts sagged almost to her waist.

The girl stepped back, looking at Spur.

"He's a pretty one, ain't he?"

"Mine," the old woman said.

"You got the last one first!" the girl screamed. "My turn. Fair is fair!"

"Ain't no such thing as fair, girl," the old man said. He walked up to Spur and stared up at him. Spur was nearly a foot taller than the slender rawhider.

Suddenly the man's right fist jolted out and crashed into Spur's jaw. The move was so quick and such a surprise that Spur staggered backward.

The old man punched Spur twice in the belly and another shot at his jaw before Spur caught his hands and held them.

"Let go!" the old man screamed. "Let go or I'll shoot your goddamn knee into pieces so you'll never walk again!"

Spur let his hands go and stepped back.

"He's a fancy one, Pa. You said he was mine."

"Got to teach the bastard a lesson first. Take off his gunbelt, and be careful."

The girl slid up beside Spur while the old man covered him with his six-gun. She unbuckled the gun belt and pulled it off to one side, then she rubbed his crotch and his fly.

The old man swatted her to one side and slammed the side of the pistol into Spur's belly. This time Spur saw it coming and deflected it, swung once at the smaller man, but missed and took a sharp blow on the jaw with the side of the six-gun. He dropped to his knees, his head groggy.

The girl prowled around the area and came back.

"Just the one horse, Pa, but he's got two repeating rifles. A Spencer and a Henry! I get me the Henry, you promised me I could have a new gun."

"Yeah, yeah. Now you want this one, you hurry. We got to move on."

The girl moved up close to Spur where he sagged on all fours. She knelt in front of him and unbuttoned the last two fasteners of her shirt and let it swing open. Spur was eye to nipple with her breasts. They were the cleanest part of her.

"You like them?" she asked softly.

Spur blinked, trying to make the four breasts collect into two. At last they steadied. He nodded.

"You want them, first you got to play my game. You slap me. I like to get pushed around a little sometimes. Go ahead, slap me."

Spur slapped her gently. She slugged him in the side with her fist. It was a kidney punch and he almost gagged, but breathed deeply and sat back on his haunches.

"Slap me hard!"

He swung at her and his open handed slap spun her around and dumped her into the dirt.

She came up with tears in her eyes nodding. "Oh, yes! Do it again!"

"No."

A six-gun roared and the slug drove into the ground an inch from Spur's thigh and buried itself.

"Hit the crazy bitch!" the old man bellowed.

Tears in her eyes glistened as she nodded.

Spur hit her, jolting her into the dust again. There would be a bruise on her cheek. She got up quickly and crawled to him, rose to her knees and pushed her breasts into his face.

"Chew on me! Bite my tits. Make them hurt!"

Spur looked at the old man who had one hand filled with a .44, the other rubbing his crotch.

Spur did as she demanded, all the while trying to figure out this trio. The girl called him Pa, but that meant little. He doubted that she was this couple's child. She looked more like a new toy they bought or stole.

Spur realized he was chewing on good sized breasts yet he was not excited; he was as soft as a marshmallow.

"Yes, yes that feels good. Take my shirt off."

Spur left her breasts and took off her shirt. Her breasts were smaller than he had first thought, but still a handful. She pulled his leather vest off one arm and told him to drop it. Then she unbuttoned his shirt fasteners and snaked it off him.

She played with the black hair on his chest and smiled.

"We're going to have a party! Do you know that? A fine party, and we're going to get undressed and go over there in the grass where it's soft and we're going to just have a fine time!"

She rubbed his crotch, but found no erection.

"What's the matter, don't you like me?" She pulled open his belt, then unbuttoned his pants and reached inside.

The old woman snickered. "Got a big one but he must like little boys better than pussy, I bet!" She cackled and slapped her leg.

"Shut up, you old dried up crone!" the girl screamed. Then she smiled as she looked back at Spur.

"You just need a little help, some pussy help!" The young girl slipped out of her skirt that had been cut off around her calves, short for that time. She twirled it in front of her a minute and he saw that she had nothing else under it.

Her hips and belly were starkly white against the soft suntan brown of her back and chest. Even her breasts were tanned.

She knelt in front of him, took his hand and rubbed it between her spread legs.

"Now, you do like it, don't you, pretty man?"

Her blonde hair crotch was soft and damp and as she pushed his fingers against her outer lips, Spur could not help but feel his own hot blood surging.

"I don't believe this," Spur said softly.

"Believe, honeybear. You can have all of it you

want for as long as you want it!"

Her hand went inside his pants and came out with his long hard erection.

"Yes! That is more like it!" She stroked it once, then tugged at his boots. He had to help her with them. Then she stripped down his pants. When they both were naked the old woman hooted and shot twice near Spur just to see him jump.

"You crazy old loon!" the girl screeched. "You're just jealous you don't have tits anymore!"

The girl took Spur's hand and led him near the creek under some trees to long, soft grass and pushed him down. Then she lifted him.

"I want you to do it standing up!" she said. "Nobody has ever been able to fuck me standing up. Try it."

She spread her legs and Spur bent down and tried to enter her, but it didn't quite work. Then he bent over and grabbed her around the waist.

"Put your arms round my neck and hold on," he said. Spur lifted her off the ground. Her legs went around his waist and she used one hand to guide his turgid tool as he positioned her, then slid her forward, impaling her with his lance.

The girl laughed and screamed.

"You did it! You did it! First time ever standing up!"

The old woman shot twice into the tree. "Hurry it up, fucking young whore. Let a real woman get to him."

But the girl did not answer. The way they fit together put her clit under pressure with every stroke and soon she was reeling and wailing and jolting through a climax.

She went from one satisfaction to another and for five minutes she kept up the series of climaxes until she hung on him, spent and wasted.

Spur couldn't remember if he had shot his wad or not. She sagged off him and he let her slump to the ground. She panted, then went and sat in the creek where it was only a few inches deep. The cold water revived her.

The old man walked near her, his six-gun out. "What's the matter, you didn't call me. Weren't you ready yet on this one?"

She shook her head and smiled. "No, I want to keep him for a while, a few days at least."

Grunting with unhappiness, the old man went to Spur and tied his hands in front of him with wet rawhide. Spur knew at once that when the rawhide dried it would shrink up and cut off all circulation to his hands. He could lose his fingers in a big hurry!

He also knew there was no sense in trying to talk the rawhider out of it. He would as soon shoot Spur as tie his hands. Spur had to be patient and wait. There had to be a time to make a break for it.

Any of them would kill him for the horse, saddle and the two repeating rifles. They had nothing to lose.

The three rawhiders had a late breakfast then, and Spur could smell venison steaks frying over a small fire. They did not offer him any food or coffee. He knew better than to ask. When the food was gone, the old woman snarled at the girl to get things cleaned up.

The girl had put on her skirt but was still topless. She spat something back at the old woman who threw a tin plate at her. The girl held the fry pan with the venison drippings, and she swung it and threw it at the old woman. The hot grease splattered on her bare arm bringing a wail of fury and hatred.

"That was the worst mistake you ever made, slut!" the old woman screamed. She grabbed a foot long butcher knife from the cooking box and moved toward the girl.

"Don't start it!" the girl yelled. She reached behind her, found a six inch blade the old man had used for skinning the deer. It was sharp as a razor. She caught it in her right hand and waited for the older woman.

After two swipes with the knives failed to find flesh, the pair moved away from the fire and the wagon to a circle of grass.

"Put up with your mouth and your big tits long as I can stand!" the old woman bellowed. She slashed in with the knife, missed and stumbled away. The girl darted after her and before the old woman turned, the girl sliced her left arm near the shoulder bringing a crimson flow down the dirty shirt sleeve.

The old woman did not make a sound. She turned and glared at the girl, touched her wounded shoulder, then advanced.

The old man had seen the fight start. He moved over beside Spur, sat in the grass and chewed on a stem of grass.

"Seen it comin'. Bound to happen. Old woman just shriveled all up. Picked up the girl most a year ago now. She growed up nice. Taught her how to sex myself." He laughed. "That made the old woman mad as hell."

The women circled each other, each looking for an advantage. Spur sensed that the older one would die. The girl had all the advantages of mobility and strength. There was no way he could stop it.

The old woman charged the girl, darted in one way, then the other and continued the first way and sliced an inch long gash across the girl's left breast.

She screamed and jumped back. Holding the bleeding breast, her anger rising.

"Picked up the girl when her parents fell on hard times. Actual their whole farm and house fell on hard times, and hot times!" He laughed remembering. "Leastwise we took the girl and raised her a year. Built them girl bodies damn good back there. Now she's a real looker.''

The girl moved with a purpose now. She went on the attack. Her first charge produced a new cut on her opponent's right arm, then one on her leg.

The girl kicked off her skirt to give her more mobility. She fought naked like a frenzy, slashing, darting in and out. She took one small cut on her leg, but paid it back with a six inch slice through the old woman's shirt and blood pulsed down her stomach staining her dress.

"Enough?" the girl demanded.

The old woman shook her head. She looked at the old man for a moment, then charged at the younger woman, trying for a fatal blow a thrust into the heart or lungs.

The strategy backfired. The girl accepted a small cut on her left arm as she caught the knife and powered it upward. Then her strong right arm drove the skinning knife deep into the old woman's chest. She pulled it out and stabbed her again.

Both stood still for a moment. Then blood seeped from the old woman's mouth, her eyes went wild searching for life.

The girl screamed a message of victory and slashed the razor-like skinning knife across the old woman's throat. She tried to gasp, but no sound came from her mouth. She fell, the knife dropping from her hand. She hit the ground and a rattling of her last breath gushed out.

The girl screamed again, dropped to her knees beside the dead woman and stabbed her chest a dozen times. When she finished and sat back, her hands and torso were bloody. Her breast still bled. She had blood on her legs.

She stood on wobbly legs and walked to the old man. There she lay down beside him, spread her legs and held out her arms to him. "Do me! Do me right now the way you taught me!"

The old man had been rubbing his crotch during the fight. Now he dropped his pants and drove into her. The girl climaxed again and again and when the old man came away from her she was so exhausted and drained that she slept at once.

He stood, picked up the rifles and two pistols, threw Spur's food sack and equipment sack on the horse and kicked Spur in the leg.

"Let's go," he said. Spur rose and looked at his clothes. The old man shrugged, cut Spur's tie and let him dress. Then he tied Spur's wrists again with dry rawhide.

The moment the horse moved, the girl sat up, then came to her feet and grabbed her skirt and ran to catch up with the other two.

None of them looked at the old woman where she lay in death. She no longer existed, her body was not their problem.

A quarter of a mile down the trail a small valley opened to the left and the wagon sat in it, concealed behind some brush. A small camp had been built with a cooking fire ring, forked sticks and two make-shift benches.

At the camp, Spur's horse was tied with the rest of the string on the lead line. Then the old man tied Spur's ankles together.

"Don't want you running off 'till we decide what to do with you. Thought we had decided that, but 'parently not." He winked at Spur. "Ain't she a cracker! Tits like I ain't seen in years and that snatch of hers just grabs you and won't let you go till you do her good and proper."

Spur only shrugged at his captor. He wasn't expected to reply.

Just after a cold noon meal, the girl came to where Spur lay under a tree. She offered him a biscuit with homemade jam on it, and fed it to him a bite at a time even though he could have held it in his tied hands.

"You was good this morning," she said, big open blue eyes measuring him. "Pa said I shouldn't feed you. No sense wasting good food, he said. But I been figuring me some. Pa is gonna have nigh on to four, five hundred dollars once he sells the string. I could get most of it." She looked up at him and shrugged.

"You know what I'm talking about, pretty man?"

"Not entirely."

"Trying to figure me out which one of you to go with. Pa—he's got the rig and horses, and I know him." She rubbed her hands over his bare chest and down to his crotch.

"But, Lordy, you got something a lot better to fill me up and make me scream in the night. Course you're younger, but, Lordy how you can love!" She watched him. "I never use naughty language. My folks were honest, hardworking people."

She sat closer to him. She wore only the skirt which now she hiked up around her waist.

"Feel my titties, pretty man," she said. She lifted his hands to her breasts. He rubbed them and petted them until she sighed.

"I could do lots better if you untied my hands. I could pet you both spots."

"Pa would whip me."

"He'd never see, you move over a little bit."

Her eyes widened, and she licked her lips. He tweaked her upright nipples and brought a gasp of pleasure from her. Slowly she took a small pen knife from her skirt pocket, opened it and without looking at the old man, sliced through the rawhide thong.

Spur rubbed his hands and wrists. She did the same for him, then when the feeling was back, he touched her breasts and with one hand touched her leg under the skirt and worked up.

The old man lay down in the shade and a few minutes later Spur heard him snoring.

The girl was beathing heavily then, scratching at his crotch.

"Do me!" she said. "Pa won't care. When he sleeps like that takes a thunderclap to wake him."

"Want me to tie you up and pretend I'm raping you?" Spur asked.

"Lordy! Yes! Ain't never had that done. Tie my hands first."

Spur did with the rawhide. Then he took off his shirt and tore off a strip off the tail.

"Have to gag you so you can't scream and yell," he said. She looked puzzled.

"If I'm raping you I don't want your folks to hear us, so I gag you so you won't scream and tell them."

He kissed her, then probed with his finger between her legs and she nodded.

He put the gag around her head and over her mouth so it wouldn't choke her. Then he bent and cut the thongs off his ankles. He tied them around her ankles, then kissed both her breasts and laid her on the grass.

Spur looked at the old man. He still snored. He touched the girl's cheek.

"Don't struggle too much. The old man will let you go when he wakes up." Spur stood, slid the Spencer out of the wagon and found his Colt .45 and gunbelt. Then he stuffed his shirt tail in his pants. He walked to the end of the trail line and untied his horse. A moment later he swung up and walked the mare out to the road and turned south. There were still three hours to sundown. With any luck at all he should be in Fort Smith before it got too dark to find his way.

He needed to touch base, and to get some new

supplies. Getting away from the rawhiders with his horse and guns was enough for one day. He wasn't going to push his luck!

NINE

When Spur rode into Fort Smith, it was nearing ten A.M. the following morning. In the darkness the night before he had lost his way in the thickets, missed a turnoff for Fort Smith and become hopelessly lost. He decided to spend the night along a small friendly stream deep in the brush. He had survived the night.

Now the Secret Agent rode into a dust filled conglomeration of dirt streets and one and two story wooden buildings, most of them unpainted, that went by the name of Fort Smith, Arkansas. He heard there were about 2,500 people in the town which had both a railroad and docks for river traffic along the Arkansas river.

More than twenty saloons catered to the trailmen and river rats, as well as a flood of cowboys halfway back home after driving cattle up the various trails to Kansas for shipment to the eastern markets. A good number of settlers also picked Fort Smith as a spot to jump off for points West.

Fort Smith began as a real army fort built on the site in 1817 and long since abandoned by the military. Now the fort buildings themselves remained a hollow shell, a large squat structure enclosed by sturdy stone walls with cannon emplacements on top. Adventurous children often played there, at night down and outers sometimes slept there and robbery victims often ended up breathing their last gulps of precious air before their deaths.

Spur realized he looked little better than the raw-hiders from whom he had just escaped. He had not shaved in four days, he had not been able to take time to wash himself or clean his clothes.

Respectable women crossed the street when they saw him coming. A drunk swore at him, and Spur got no response from a man in a black suit when he asked where he could find the telegraph office.

At last he saw the railroad tracks and followed them to the station and the telegraph facility. Spur pushed into the small room and found no one there but the operator.

The man with wire rimmed glasses perched on his nose and a green eye shade, pushed back the garters that held his sleeves in place and glowered.

"Get your bones out of here before I call the sheriff!" the small man roared.

"I would appreciate that, sir," Spur said with his most polite tone of voice and his cultured, Eastern diction.

The telegrapher squinted and cocked his head.

"Would you say that again?" he asked.

"I would appreciate it if you would ask the sheriff to come here, since that is my second point of business today, to look up that lawman and hold a conference with him."

"Ummm. What's your first business?"

"I'd like to send a telegram." Spur lifted his Colt .45 from the holster by the barrel, pushed all five rounds from it and lay it on the counter top near the telegraph operator.

"I wish to send a telegram and have no funds. You may hold the weapon until I get money to reclaim it."

"We deal on a cash only basis."

"Sir, I am a federal lawman working in disguise. I wish to contact my office in Washington, D.C. for identification and an introduction to Judge Parker where I will draw funds. I hope we have no problem over this small matter."

The telegrapher looked Spur steady in the eye. Spur stared back at him openly with no threat.

"I think we can arrange that," the small man said. "Write out your message. 'Course as a goodwill gesture, I will retain your piece until you bring the money. No offense meant."

Spur smiled. "No offense taken. A prudent man is a good man." He wrote the message on a piece of paper with a stub of a pencil from the counter.

"Gen. Wilton D. Halleck, Capitol Investigations, One Pennsylvania Avenue, Washington, D.C.

I am without funds in Fort Smith, Arkansas. Please wire Judge Isaac Parker here my credentials and authorization to draw funds. Have contacted subject. Group number reduced to three. Urgent need here. Reply soonest. Signed C. Spur McCoy."

He handed the message to the telegrapher who read it, nodded and told him the cost. Spur motioned to the weapon. The man in his fifties grinned and turned to the key.

Spur heard the key stop chattering and go clear for a moment. The Fort Smith operator jumped on while he could and clicked out the message. Then he signed off. Spur had watched him, saw the man look up and nod.

"It's on the wire. Depends how fast the people in

Washington get it delivered. Sometimes they move quickly to government offices."

Spur thanked him and looked at the two wooden chairs. He avoided them and sat on the floor leaning against the wall.

"I'll wait. I have nothing else to do until that message comes in. Then I'll be glad to deliver it to the judge."

"Don't usually work that way," the telegrapher said.

"But you can do it this time, right?"

"Reckon so. Looks like you need a nap. Want some coffee? Got some warming in back."

"Please, then I might take that nap."

The telegrapher brought Spur a hot cup of coffee. "You been in the Territories I'd guess."

"Yes, kidnapped, shot at, trapped in a circle of grass fire, tracked, trailed and within an inch of being blown straight into hell. When I go back in, things are going to be different."

The telegrapher nodded. "Sure as hell hope so. And I got to feel a mite sorry for the bunch you're looking for."

"The bunch has killed more than forty people already. Don't feel sorry for them."

Spur had sampled the coffee. It was twice as good as any he had made. He sipped it slowly, then leaned his head back.

The next thing Spur knew someone shook his shoulder. He came awake slowly, reached for his pistol but found only the empty holster.

"Mr. McCoy?"

"Huh? . . . Oh, yes. I'm awake."

"Your wire came through. I sealed it in an envelope for you and put the judge's name on the outside. Like I say, usually I take them over or hire a boy. Guess it will be all right this time."

Spur stood and stretched. Then he took the envelope, got directions to the judge's chambers and left the station. He found the courthouse, and the offices of the judge who had become well known in only four months of work here.

A deputy marshal stood in front of the judge's chambers. He drew his six-gun as Spur approached.

"Hold it right there!" the deputy marshal barked.

Spur stopped.

"What the hell you want in here?"

"I have a telegram for Judge Parker, then I hope to talk to him," Spur said with his best diction and his slightly affected Eastern accent.

The marshal blinked. "Sound a hell of a lot better than you look."

"Thank you. Will you see that the judge gets the telegram and tell him that Spur McCoy would like to see him?"

"Judge is busy."

"This is important."

The marshal laughed. "Everybody says that these days. I get dozens of people trying to see the judge."

Spur walked closer. "I'm a federal lawman. I've been working in disguise in the Territories. You've been in there, you know how rough it can be. This wire concerns me. It is of significant importance."

"Got any papers that prove you're a lawman?"

"Lost them back in the Territories."

"Possible." The marshal stared at Spur. "Damn if I won't give it a try. Can't promise. Sit down over there in that chair and don't move your ass a foot. I'll be back."

It was an hour before Spur McCoy walked into the private chambers of Federal Judge Isaac Charles Parker.

Judge Parker stood ramrod straight beside his desk. He was big for that day, six feet tall and two hundred pounds. He was clean shaven except for a trimmed moustache and a neat but thick goatee. His straight black hair was parted on the right side and he stared with a hint of concern at McCoy.

"Judge Parker, I'm Spur McCoy. I hope the wire identified me and confirmed what I need."

"Mr. McCoy, I have my own deputy marshals who work in my jurisdiction."

"And I've heard they do a good job, Judge Parker. I'm on special assignment to end the rampage of the Jamison gang of bank robbers. They seem to be holed up in the Territories and I am authorized to go in and get them. I have no wish to usurp your command or your contol here."

"Secret Service," Judge Parker said softly. "Heard of it. Thought that was set up to handle counterfeiting."

"It was, sir. But then other problems came up and since we're the only real inter-state federal law agency, we have been overburdened with a hundred other types of crimes."

"Including bank robbers. Yes. I see by the St. Louis newspaper the Jamisons have killed forty-two people now in their rampage."

"Yes sir, but their gang is down from five to three. One was killed in Willow Creek, Missouri in a robbery, and I shot a second one in the Territories."

"You found their hideout?"

"No sir, but I know the general location."

"On the far side of the Territories?" the judge asked.

"No sir. I'd say it's not more than fifteen miles from your courtroom."

"That's outrageous!"

"I hope to do something about it, sir. But I need new supplies and a short rest."

"Yes. I concur. You look like you could also use a bath and some new clothes. Although your present ones would be a good costume for the Territories from what my deputies say."

"Did you know there's a sign that posts a bounty on your deputy marshals? A hundred dollars I think it was."

"The criminal mind is hard to decipher," Judge Parker said. "When I arrived four months ago I had ninety-one cases waiting on my calendar. I've hardly made a dent. I work twelve hours a day, but there is progress."

He reached in his desk drawer and took out a stack of twenty dollar bills. He counted out ten of them and handed them to Spur.

"Your General Halleck has instructed me to advance you two hundred dollars, no questions asked. He said he would reimburse the cost to me by post. Is there anything else I can do for you?"

"You might suggest a hotel with a good dining room. I haven't been eating too well lately."

The judge allowed himself a small smile.

"I can recommend the Arkansas River House. Fair beds, and an excellent cook." He nodded and his smile grew slightly. "I'd say you had a slightly Boston accent."

"Yes, sir. I put in four years up there until I graduated from Harvard so I picked up some of the twang. I grew up in New York."

They talked for a while longer, then the judge seemed to be thinking about something else. Spur thanked him, and went out the door with the two hundred dollars deep in his pocket.

Spur wasted the rest of the morning buying new clothes. He concentrated on rugged trail outfits, a checkered wool shirt, jacket, a dozen pair of good socks and a small carpetbag. He bought two boxes of new rounds for his pistol and rifle as well. Then he checked in at the hotel, ordered a tub of hot water and soaked for an hour. He had a relaxing early dinner and sat outside the hotel in his new denim pants, checkered cotton shirt and leather vest and a new low crowned brown hat pulled down over his eyes, as he surveyed the little town.

The Federal Court seemed to be a big part of the town's activity. Witnesses as well as lawbreakers were being brought back from Indian Territory. The forays were made by teams of deputy marshals, five or six to a group who traveled together for protection, and took with them a wagon that worked as a jail and chuck wagon for the trip.

When six or eight teams came back with an average of twenty lawbreakers each, and maybe twice that many witnesses, it taxed the small town's facilities. Witnesses flooded the place and some slept in the jail because they could not afford a hotel.

Spur watched the flow of people on the boardwalk and moving up and down the dusty streets.

Then he edged his hat lower and watched a couple walk past him. He had not even bothered to put on his six-gun after getting it back from the telegrapher. It lay in his room on the dresser.

Now he stared in frustration at the couple walking past. The man was the same one he had chased in the brush with Rorick. He was one of the Jamisons!

The bank robber carried two pistols low on his hips. He walked with a fancy lady who flaunted her new self importance as if she were loving it.

Spur was torn between following them and trying to get a gun. He saw several men moving past with pistols, but to ask to borrow another man's side-arm was simply not done in a town like this.

McCoy moved behind the couple trying to figure out what to do. If only he had worn his gun! He was almost never without it. Now he was paying the price. The couple kept moving past shops and headed toward the edge of the business district.

The girl waved at a painted woman who stood in the door of a saloon urging men to come in.

They went down a street and then into the residential section. Spur could only figure that the woman was from a dance hall saloon. She would be a working girl, and the Jamison would be buying her services. But why the flaunting?

He followed well back as the couple turned one more corner and went up the steps to a small white house and walked in without knocking.

Spur was flooded with questions. Did the girl live there? Was she a proper girl? Why did she know the whore at the saloon? Had the Jamison rented the house, or bought it? How could he attack a house not knowing who else might be inside?

Spur ran back to the Arkansas River House Hotel and took his pistol and the Spencer and went down the back steps to the alley. Again he trotted the six blocks to where he had seen the Jamison enter the house.

For a moment he thought of going to get the sheriff, or to call on a half dozen of the Judge Parker marshals, but he decided not to. This was his job, and he would do it.

It had been late in the afternoon when Spur first saw Jamison, now he checked the sun and saw that it was fading fast. It would soon be dark. He was not sure how good a look Jamison had of him in the Territories. At last he decided he could not go to the door and bluff his way inside. Too risky. He would wait until darkness and hope that Jamison came out.

Now, could he pick the man off with the rifle? Spur needed a positive identification first. While he was trying for a sure I.D. on the man, Jamison could be shooting Spur down. He snorted at the advantages the criminal always had. He knew it had to be that way to protect the innocent. This man could be a look-alike for Jamison, but Spur had a feeling he was not.

Darkness came as Spur crouched in an alley awaiting some movement from the house. Jamison was probably in bed with the floozy and would probably stay there the rest of the night.

Spur wondered if he should break down the front door and crash in on them. Or should he slip in the unlocked rear door and catch Jamison in bed with his guns hanging on the bedpost?

Spur discarded both ideas. He had to wait.

An hour after dark, he saw the front door open and someone come out. The figure walked his way and he saw it was the girl. He slid out of the shadows and stepped in front of her.

"Miss, I won't hurt you, I just have some questions to ask you, I'm a law officer. Will you cooperate with me?"

She stared at him, the fright fading. He saw that she was young, no more than nineteen or twenty.

Slowly her head bobbed. "Yes, I've done nothing wrong. Want do you want?"

"The house, is it yours, a friend's, or rented?"

"It is rented . . . I . . . we rented it this morning."

"Is it furnished?"

"Yes."

"Who is the man with you?"

"Phil Johnson."

"You know him from before today?"

"Of course! He comes to town now and then. I've been with him six or eight times. He's thoughtful and tender. A gentleman."

"What kind of work does he do?"

"He's a cattle buyer. Goes up to Kansas a lot."

"Where are you going now?"

"To get some more whiskey. We drank up what we had."

"Do you usually work in a saloon?"

"That's not a way to talk . . ." She sighed. "Yes, The Silver Horseshoe."

"Is there anyone else in the house?"

"No."

"Does Phil have a gun with him?"

"Yes, he says it can be dangerous on the trail. He has two pistols and a rifle."

Spur reached in his pocket, took out his wallet and handed the girl a ten dollar greenback.

"What's this?"

"I want you to forget about Phil . . . Johnson and go back to the saloon. Was he paying you more?"

"Fact is he was, twenty dollars."

"Had he paid you yet?"

"Of course, business before pleasure."

"So you must made thirty dollars for the night you didn't even have to work. Did you know Phil's last name isn't Johnson?"

"It is too."

"Afraid not. His real name is Phil Jamison, he's one of the Jamison bank robber gang."

"I don't believe you!"

"It's true."

"Impossible."

"What's your name?"

"Hettie."

"Well, Hettie, you wait and see if it's impossible. I'm going to have a talk with Phil. If he doesn't start shooting, you win and I go back to my hotel and you can climb back in bed with him. If he starts shooting you get back to the saloon. Fair enough?"

She bit her lip, then nodded. In the darkness he could see only her pale face and darting brown eyes. She was barely five feet tall.

"You're wrong, Mister. I know you're wrong."

"If I am you made an easy ten dollars."

Spur lifted his Colt and checked it, then slid a sixth round into the empty chamber and let the hammer down gently on the live bullet.

He left the girl and walked up to the door of the small white house. Spur paused, then moved to the side of the door and opened it silently. He stood at the side of the door and peered around it. Inside a lamp gave off a soft glow. He could see no one.

He pounded on the door, then turned the latch and shouted.

"Phil! Hettie's been hurt! She says come quick!"

He paused behind the door jamb and out of sight.

"What the hell?" someone shouted. He heard feet hit the floor and some quiet cursing. Then a half dressed man rushed into the short hallway. He had no weapon.

"Phil Jamison?" Spur asked as he pushed into the open door, his six-gun cocked and pointing at the man.

In an instant Phil figured out the trick, dove back the way he had come as Spur's Colt roared. Spur raced into the hallway and edged up to the door that led off to where Jamison had vanished.

There was no doubt about who the man was now. The room would be a bedroom where Jamison would have his clothes and his iron.

"Give it up, Jamison. I've got three deputy marshals outside that window. The only other way is through me. You couldn't do it in the Territories yesterday and you won't do it here. Remember how Rorick went down?"

There was a roar of anger and three shots clipped the edge of the door frame. Spur edged back.

The next thing he heard was a window breaking. Spur darted into the room but the robber was already out the window. The black night closed around him. Spur edged up in the lighted room to look out the broken glass.

A slug tore into the window molding an inch over his head. He ducked back. Spur heard someone running and vaulted through the broken window, but he could see nothing. He ran to the dirt street and turned toward the middle of town. Spur saw no one in the blackness, heard no running footfalls.

He went back to the house. The girl in the alley had left. In the living room he found a pair of saddlebags. In one of them was a packet of five dollar bills. It still had a bank wrapper around it that had printed on it: "Willow Creek Fiduciary Bank $5's. . . $500."

Spur pushed the wad of bills and wrapper inside his shirt and walked out the door.

Solid evidence, the kind Judge Parker liked. Now he had enough to hang all three Jamisons that were left!

TEN

Phil Jamison had jumped through the low window in the small white house as soon as he recognized the gunman as the man who had killed Rorick in the Territories. He landed on his hands and knees, rolled to his back and leaped up.

Phil charged down the street into the darkness. He had taken time only to grab his gunbelt as he left the house.

Now he stopped half a block away, panting and strapped the leather around his waist and adjusted the big .44 in the holster.

"Come after me now, you bastard!" Phil whispered into the blackness. He saw a man come out of the house to the street, look both ways and then go back inside.

Phil figured he wouldn't stay long, and he was right. Five minutes later Phil watched the same figure come out of the house and stride the other way toward the business section of the little town.

Jamison had no idea what happened to the woman he had sent for more whiskey. Hell, Hettie might have been in on it with that sneaky bastard. It had to be the same guy who had gunned down Rorick in the Territories. How he had escaped the flames in that meadow Jamison would never figure out.

He slipped into the house by the unlocked back door, grabbed his hat and jacket then saw that the saddlebags had been searched. The bundle of five dollar bills was missing. Hell! So what, there was plenty more in his poke.

He went out the back door silently with all of his belongings and hurried to the livery stable. He had put his horse there when he got to town so it would have the best care. He took more pride in that roan than he did in his guns. Her dark red color was special, the best he had ever seen on a horse.

Phil paid the wrangler at the livery, saddled the roan and was on the road in five minutes. He crossed the Arkansas river on the ferry making sure the lawman who had gunned at him was not on board. As he mounted on the other side of the river, in Indian Territories, he began planning.

Phil had told the rest of the family what happened when they surprised the stranger near the hideout two days ago. Told them how the guy stuck to them, soon began hunting them! Now he was certain the man was a lawman. He must have recognized him in town and followed him to the house. Then when Hettie went out, he came to the door. The sneaky bastard!

Phil was so furious he almost made a wrong turn, and the longer he rode the madder he became. When he at last swung into the small ravine where they had built the little corral for the horses he was sputtering with rage.

Will Jamison gave his son a long shot of whiskey, sat him down at the table and tried to get him calmed down.

"When you think you can talk straight, boy, you go ahead and tell us what happened in town."

Phil gave them the story.

Will Jamison frowned and preened his drooping moustache.

"You sure it was the same varmint who shot down Rorick?"

"Can't be sure, Pa, nohow. But that's the only way I can figure it. How else would he know to call me by name?"

"Could have asked that girl you had there."

"Yeah, told her I was Phil Johnson. But that don't matter, I seen him up close two days ago. He saw me too. Important thing is what the fuck we gonna do about it! I want to get the bastard! I want to shoot him six times right in his damned face!"

Will held up his hand.

"You go charging off on half cock like that and you'll wind up buzzard food just like Rorick did. You want that, boy? Now calm down, Phil. Take it easy. Let's plan this out, way we always do. Got to be a way to even the score here. If it's the same man, we owe him for Rorick."

Dale finished cleaning his rifle and he assembled it slowly, lovingly. Then he lifted his brows.

"I say we go into town separately, find out where this joker is staying and we take him out. Three of us so that should be easy."

"He's gotta be one of Judge Parker's men," Phil said. "They the only ones who can come after us out here. Why the hell don't we ride in and dynamite the jail or Judge Parker's courthouse in there? Yeah! We could blow up the damn jail and let some of those folks go free and put a big stain on that new judge!"

"That's dumb, Phil. You ever used dynamite before? I sure ain't. Don't know nothing about it and I don't want to learn. We could just as well blow our hands off with that stuff. Any raid on the jail or Judge Parker is out. We try that, we might get it done, but if we did, Parker would have a hundred men out here searching every square foot of these Territories.''

Dale nodded. "Think Pa is right, Phil. We should stick to what we know. Forget about that gunner. He's just another lawman we got to go around. Hail, we been doing that for two years.''

"Catches in my craw! Makes me madder than hell. Besides, he ruined my night with Hettie. Been waiting six months to get her bare assed in bed with them big tits hanging out.''

Dale laughed. "Knew we'd get to it sooner or later. Hell, she'll still be there in a week. Take off a month and pump her six times a day until you get so tired you can't walk!''

They all laughed this time.

"Phil got a point, though," Will said. "Why not make some kind of a hit-back at them for what this lawman did? Got me to thinking too. If he was a Judge Parker man he'd have six or eight men with him. They always work in groups, remember all them wagons and six men riders we seen out here rounding up wanteds?''

"If'n he ain't with Parker, who the hell is he?'' Phil asked.

"Could be a U.S. marshal from Missouri or some other area where we been visiting," Dale said. "Don't matter." He turned to his father. "What do you mean hit-back at them?''

"Still figurin'. Tell you in the morning. Time we turn out the light and get some shut eye. Don't you two fret none, your Pa is working out something that will let them lawmen know the Jamisons are around, and warn them not to try to tangle with us.''

"Pa, we is down to three men," Dale said. "Really need five for our kind of work. You thinkin' of taking on some hired help?''

"Thinkin', Dale, thinkin'.''

A few minutes later they rolled onto their bunks and Phil blew out the last kerosene lamp.

Over a breakfast of venison steak and flapjacks, Will Jamison laid out the plan for his two sons.

"I figure we owe them for Rorick and for Gabe too. But I don't want us to charge into something we don't know nothing bout, like dynamite. 'Stead, we do what we do best. We rob a bank, not just any bank. We rob the Arkansas Riverman Bank, right there in Fort Smith! We take out the biggest bank in Arkansas with Judge Parker and his deputies just down the block! How does that sound?"

Dale had just stuffed half a pancake in his mouth and all he could do was grin and nod.

Phil jumped up and screeched in approval.

"Yeeeeeeeeeeeeha! I love it! Yeah! Great idea, Pa! When we going in?"

Dale got his food swallowed and he joined in.

"Best idea we ever had, Pa! Make them lawmen hunker back and think about us 'fore they say we can't touch really big banks. How much you think their safe would hold?"

"Don't know, twenty, forty, maybe eighty thousand in greenbacks. Nice sackful!"

"When we go in?" Phil asked.

"Right after breakfast," Will said. "We do it right. Phil, you'll have to stay out of sight or wear a disguise, maybe shave off your beard."

"No! I'll keep out of sight."

"We work it the way we always do. I'll get a room at the Railroader Hotel, that little one right in the middle of town. We'll work our plan from there."

They hurried finishing the meal, cleaning up, and then got on their horses and moved out.

Four hours later Will Jamison signed the register at the Railroader Hotel as Will Jefferson and took room 109 at the far end of the hall on the first floor next to the back door. That way they had three exits, front door, back door and the ground floor window.

Will looked out the window that opened on the street. Up the street a block he could see the Arkansas Riverman Bank. It sat on the corner lot. Will pulled binoculars from his carpet bag and focused. He could see the side of the front door and had a good view of the back door. Yes!

He met the boys who came on horseback and told them where the room was. Then he faded into the Bit and Spur saloon for a cool beer. He had no idea where they got the ice.

When the Riverman bank closed at three P.M., Will Jamison sat in a chair across the street reading the local weekly newspaper. He was sitting with the chair leaning back against the Fort Smith Hardware. Three other men sat there snoozing, talking or watching the women walk by.

Will watched over the paper as someone locked the front door of the bank from the inside, then let out two customers. When they were gone the same man drew a blind down over the door indicating they were through doing business for the day.

By four-thirty two men and one woman had left by the front door. Will had walked into the bank briefly about three o'clock, saw that there was no guard, there were three tellers, and two desks with bank officers behind them. A woman secretary or bookkeeper sat on the other side. Six employees.

Will closed the newspaper and seemed to snooze in the late afternoon sunshine. One more man came from the bank, then it was quiet.

At five o'clock Will stood, put down the paper and walked back to the hotel.

Dale was already there. Two men had come out the back door, a young man and an older one who made a big production of locking two locks on the outside of the rear door.

"The older guy had to be the president," Dale said. "He wore a good suit that must have cost him thirty dollars! He even had one of them English hats on, a derby! Looked like a Fancy Dan to me."

"Chances are he opens the bank in the morning by the back door. Probably the same young man will be with him and he is armed. Won't matter none. Phil and I will be at the back door if he opens it there from the outside. Dale, you cover the front door in case he opens it there. If he does, you get him and the gunman inside without attracting any attention."

"He'll come in the back," Phil said. "Bet it's a habit with him. He parks a rig out there in the alley, so he'll come in and out the back door."

"Knew we had you in this room for something," Will said. He looked at him. "Told you I got you a surprise, you ready?"

Phil nodded. "Since I can't go out of the room it better be a good one."

Will went to the door and opened it. Hettie walked in, nodded to Will and Dale, then ran and kissed Phil.

Will and his oldest son went to the desk for another room, then for dinner and some serious drinking.

Spur McCoy had spent the previous night catching up on his sleep alone in a good bed, then that morning he went to see Judge Parker, made a report about the sighting of Phil Jamison in town, and turned in the five dollar bills with the bank wrapper from the robbed bank in Missouri.

The judge had it recorded and entered in the record, then went into his courtroom.

Spur watched the proceedings for a few minutes. The jury had just been selected in a murder case. The accused had killed the man he was traveling with for his gold watch.

Spur edged out of the courtroom. He still felt washed out and hungry. Maybe he was losing his enthusiasm for fighting the bad guys and the rain and heat and mud on the trail.

Naw!

He had a steak for dinner that noon at the hotel dining room and figured he'd have another one for supper. He decided he needed one more day of rest before he went back after the Jamisons. They would not be moving anywhere for a while. They also needed two more men to make their bank robbing team as efficient as it was before.

He stopped for a cold beer at a bar and asked them about the ice. The barkeep showed it to him, a block two feet square and four feet long. He kept it in a big wooden trough that had been wrapped with thick wool comforters. Dozens of bottles of beer stood around the cake of ice.

"Insulation," the barkeep said. "Keep it all wrapped up and a piece that size will last for three or four days."

"River ice?" Spur asked.

"Right. Let it freeze in the winter in our ice pond, cut it up with saws and haul it out and put it in the ice house between thick layers of straw, then cover it up with straw. We usually have good ice here until the end of September. Fact is we're running low right now."

Spur thanked him, drank his bottle of cold beer and lost six dollars in a small stakes poker game. Then he went to bed alone and slept ten hours.

Phil Jamison had been right. The president of the bank pulled his rig into the spot behind the big brick bank building, met a man next to the corner and quickly unlocked the back door.

They were not quick enough. Will timed it just right, running from the alley as Phil came from the other way. Will slugged the gunbearer on the forehead with his .44 and pushed both men inside the bank as the door swung inward.

Phil shoved the unconscious man to the floor, stripped his weapon away from him and quickly tied him hand and foot with rawhide stripes and put a gag in his mouth.

The president was a small man, in a three-piece expensive blue suit complete with gold chain across his vest and a gold watch in each vest pocket.

Will backed the man up against the wall, pulled the watches from his vest pockets and shoved them in his own. The ugly snout of his .44 pushed hard upward into the soft spot between the bones under his jaw.

"Open the vault, right now!" Will snarled.

"Can't, I only have half the combination."

Will slapped him hard, rocking his head to one side.

"My name is Jamison, Will Jamison. You may have heard of me. I specialize in bank vaults."

Sweat popped out on the man's forehead and cheeks. His florid face became redder.

"Yes . . . yes, I've heard of you."

"So open the safe before you have a fatal accident. Reckon even Judge Parker can only hang a man once." Will chuckled as he watched the man. "Open it!" The .44 jammed upward until the man lifted to his toes to decrease the pressure.

"Yes! . . . Yes, I can do it."

Phil ran to the front door, saw three people standing there waiting. He let them in. And showed his pistol.

"No problems! Do exactly what I tell you."

The two men held up their hands. The woman

shivered.

"Any of you have guns?"

They all shook their heads.

"Good, lay down on the floor and spread your hands as far as you can reach. Now!"

They did. He expertly tied all three, hands behind their backs, feet tied tightly. Then he put gags in their mouths. Someone knocked on the door.

Phil looked up and saw another bank employee waiting. He opened the door, tied and gagged him as he had the others. No sounds were made. Nothing would seem unusual from the outside.

He opened the bank door again, then closed it quickly. It was the signal. A moment later Dale walked across the street, entered the bank and locked the door again.

The boys hurried back to the vault.

It was one of the large ones, with two locks, but now it stood open.

"Please!" the banker said, standing at one side as Will dumped drawers full of U.S. greenbacks into a sack.

"A lot of good people are going to be hurt, ruined if you do this."

"Should have thought of that when they trusted a bank," Phil said. "Now shut up!"

"But if you take just what you need . . ." Phil drove his doubled up fist into the banker's soft gut and he bent over. Tears gushed from his eyes, he groaned in pain. When he stood up he held a Derringer he had taken from his pocket.

The first shot from the Derringer slammed into the sack of currency and the sound made all four men think they had gone deaf.

Phil drew first and sent two rounds into the banker's heart before he could fire again. They watched him slump to the floor of the vault and saw him die within seconds.

"Beat both you guys!" Phil said grinning.

They knew the shots would be muffled by the vault and the brick building. Still they hurried now. They emptied the vault of every dollar of paper currency, looked at two drawers full of gold coins.

Phil shrugged and took six of them and put them in his pants pocket.

"For good luck," he said.

Dale checked the employees. They were all tied securely. The bank wasn't due to open for two hours yet.

The three went to the back door, looked out. They waited while two rigs went by, then made sure the door would lock behind them and stepped out into the alley. Each man carried a large brown sack about half the size of a gunnysack. They walked down the alley where they had left their horses, mounted up and walked their mounts out of town west toward the ferry.

No one paid any attention to them. They were a hundred yards from the ferry when a man stood up and stared.

"Goddamn, it's Will Jamison! The bank robbers!" The man drew a pistol and fired. The Jamisons returned fire, forcing the man behind a building. Then they rode hard for the ferry which had just docked.

They pounded on board the small ferry, ordered the captain to cast off at once and unlimbered their rifles as two men ran toward them with pistols.

Dale put a round just over the first man's head and he ducked behind a water trough. The second man turned and ran the other way.

The Jamisons laughed knowing there would be no pursuit. Not for a while at least. The ferry boat captain guessed there had been a robbery. The man alternately scowled and smiled from under a battered yellow oiled cloth cap. He battled the current of the rain swollen Arkansas for several minutes, then coasted into the calmer waters near the far side.

"Boys, I don't take sides in these matters. I just carry folks back and forth. None of my business. See, I don't want trouble. I ain't armed. I just don't want no trouble."

Will had put his pistol away and leaned against the little pilot house.

"I don't make it a habit to give folks any trouble," Will said. "Usually make it a point to mind my own business." He grinned. "Course I do give them bankers a mite of unhappiness. But everybody knows them bankers got too much money for their own good." Will laughed and the captain of the little boat joined in.

When they were across there was no one waiting to come back. The captain tied up the ferry at the rickety dock. The Jamisons led their horses off the ferry, then Will gave his reins to Dale and ambled down to the dock.

"You aiming to go back across soon?" Will asked.

"Depends anybody comes," the riverman said, looking around the trail's end.

"Be a good idea if you don't go back over there," Will said. "Could be a posse that wants to come looking for us." He drew his .44 and shot the riverboat man in the forehead. He was dead as he splashed into the water.

An errant current lapped against the boat, and when the captain surfaced, the waters twirled his body around and sent it toward the fringes of the faster water racing downstream.

Will untied the ferry, shoved it away from the dock and watched it catch the current, then spin sideways and shoot downstream with the current.

"Any little advantage," he said softly. "Man's got to take any little advantage that he can."

ELEVEN

Spur McCoy had been talking with Sheriff Kennedy of Sebastian County when a man burst in the door.

"The Jamison Gang just shot up the town, robbed the bank and took off across the river on the ferry!"

Ten minutes later Spur and a posse of ten men stood at the river and stared across. A witness said he had heard a shot on the other side, then seen the ferry drifting downstream with nobody on board.

"Far as I can go," the sheriff said.

"Not as far as we can go!" A heavy set man said walking up to the river. He had two pistols and a rifle. He pointed at the sheriff. "We got 'em this time, Sheriff Kennedy. I'm Maxwell. I'm heading up a team of six Judge Parker marshals. We got our rig already on a boat ready to push off. We'll be on the other side in twenty minutes and not thirty minutes behind them!"

"I want to go with you," Spur said.

"We don't take strangers. Find your own damn boat." Maxwell snorted, turned and strode off.

The sheriff shrugged.

"Them marshals play it just about any way they

want to. Lots of small boats up by the dock. Somebody'll be glad to run you across for fifty cents. Looks like we lost our ferry boat and our boatman."

Spur thanked the sheriff and headed back to the hotel for his gear and to finish putting his traveling kit together. He would be more than thirty minutes behind, but he had a hunch Maxwell had not come up against Will Jamison before. He would be in for some surprises.

It took Spur a half hour to find a boat to take him and his horse across the surging waters of the Arkansas river. Rains upstream had raised the level of the water to near flood stage. When they docked at the ferry landing on the far side, Spur gave the man a paper dollar for his trouble and moved north expecting that would be the route the Jamisons and the marshals had taken.

To his surprise he found no tracks to the nine horses or the marshal's wagon. He turned and rode south on the north-south route and quickly picked up the prints. With the marshals' mounts and a spare or two, plus the wagon tracks, Spur could tell little about which tracks were whose.

He followed the trail south for two miles, then heard rifle fire ahead.

Ambush, he figured. He rode hard for a half mile, then eased up as the sounds of firing continued and seemed closer. Just over a small rise in the train he looked down a long rolling valley that angled toward the river.

A marshal's wagon was a quarter of a mile from him, stopped dead, with three of the marshals on the ground under and around the sturdy rig in what looked to be a defensive firing situation.

He spotted two dead horses then two more which were still in the harness for the wagon. Quickest way to stop a chase is to kill the wagon. Good thinking by the Jamisons.

The ambush had worked that far. One or two of the spare mounts might be used in harness. It depended how far ahead the marshals had planned.

Spur heard firing now from the left, nearer to the river. Some of the Judge Parker men must have pushed the attack against the ambush and driven them off and pursued. Good cavalry tactics if you had enough trained and mounted men. Three against three would not be good attack odds.

Spur pulled down from the two of the rise on the reverse slope and rode toward the river. He found some light woods he could use as cover and moved closer to the rifle fire. It began tapering off, and by the time he wormed his way to the edge of a patch of heavy woods, all the firing had stopped.

In front of him he saw two mounted men helping a third man up to ride double. A horse lay without moving nearby.

The Jamison clan had no qualms about killing horses. Most cowboys and most western men considered horses like second cousins and almost never shot an animal on purpose. Kill the man not the horse, the cowboy said. The Indians and the Jamisons evidently took a more realistic attitude. Kill the man's horse and he can't follow you. Kill his horse and he becomes easier to kill.

Spur rode out slightly in front of the two marshals' horses so they could see him. He sat and waited for them to ride to him. The Secret Service Agent recognized Marshal Maxwell as they came closer. He had been the loudmouth at the river.

"What you staring at, civilian?" Maxwell bellowed as they rode up. He was the one who lost his horse and was sitting behind the saddle.

"Marshal Maxwell, my name is Spur McCoy. I'm a United States Government Secret Service Agent. I've already checked with your boss, Judge Parker. He's received orders from my boss in Washington.

D.C. General Halleck. I've been trailing the Jamison gang for two weeks. I could have helped you on your problem here if you'd let me. How many men did you lose?''

Maxwell looked confused. He swore softly. "Sir. We have one man dead, and one wounded. They ambushed us, killed our wagon horses, the bastards.''

"You have any replacements?''

"One and a saddle horse. We can just about get the rig back to the ferry and then go for replacement animals.''

"Sounds reasonable. When you get outfitted again, move north up this trail, not south. Their hideout is to the north about ten to fifteen miles, not too far from the border. I can always use some help with them.''

Spur hesitated. "But if you come up there you'll be working under my control and my command. Check with Judge Parker if you want to. Otherwise, don't come.''

"You some kind of a fast gun or something?''

"Something. I just don't like amateurs backing me. Maybe you should stick with the easy stuff out here. On second thought, tell Judge Parker that I'm requesting that he send no one to look for the Jamisons. If I'm not back at Fort Smith in three days, then he can send everyone he wants. I want your other two men to be sure that Judge Parker gets that message from me. Understood?''

The men nodded.

"Your names?''

"Flannery.''

"Gerunding.''

"Good. I'm moving back north. You men fell for the old broken wing trick by a mother bird when she leads you away from her nest. You better get your wounded man back to town.''

Spur turned and rode north, moving along at a trot as he began to eat up the trail. He came on the tracks of three riders moving up the trail a mile past the turnoff to Fort Smith. They had circled around the wounded chuck wagon and jail rig and headed for home.

The Secret Service Agent checked the trail where the horses had crossed a grassy section. Some of the blades of grass were just starting to lift out of the crushed position. He was behind them only an hour, maybe forty-five minutes. He was too close to them. They would split up, or stop and set up another ambush.

He pulled off the trail, concealed his horse in a patch of thicket and sat down against a tree. Spur nodded and dozed and stretched in the sunshine for an hour, smoked a long thin black cheroot, and only then got back in the saddle.

A mile up the trail he found where the first of the horses angled off into the brush.

It was far too early for them to be going separately into their cabin. Spur guessed they were still ten to twelve miles from the hideout. He kept tracking the other two and when one of them angled to the same side and vanished into the brush, Spur pulled off as well.

He followed the trail in the soft underfooting. It was not the trail of a man trying to get away from trackers. Surely they knew someone would follow.

Trap!

They were laying an elaborate trap. Not an ambush this time. They must know the territory well and were heading to a spot where they would have a sure kill on one or ten men following them. Any one of the three trails would lead through the trap. They all were well ahead and would double back, be waiting to close the noose when the victims were inside the kill zone.

Spur rode slowly for half a mile, then hid his horse, took his Spencer and two extra tubes of rounds and moved ahead on foot following the tracks. He moved only a hundred yards when he saw the trail entering a depression.

He had been moving like an Indian, not making a sound, not letting a leaf crunch or a twig snap. He paused behind a shortleaf pine and studied the area below.

It looked like a natural amphitheatre. What looked like terraced, grass-covered wide steps led down to a central area that was flat and bare of all vegetation. On three sides the step-like risers worked down to the center. In back there was a great slab of granite that formed a kind of sounding wall.

Standing beside the wall and picketed on a short rope was one of the Jamison's horses. A brown sack lay on the ground as if it had been dropped. Spur lifted his binoculars and saw bundles of banknotes spilling out of the sack.

Tempting bait.

He began to look around the edge of the brush for the executioners. At least one had to be here, perhaps all three. He found one man to his left, almost at the same level he was around the rim of the bowl. The man's rifle glinted where the bluing had worn off, flashing a stab of sunlight Spur's way. Then it was gone.

Spur studied the position with his field glasses for five minutes and found him. A man lay in the brush and small green plants totally concealed him except for the light shade of his face. He stared Spur's way but not at him. He was watching where the trail came to the bowl.

One.

Spur looked the other way around the bowl. It

took him ten minutes to find the second man, and that was by chance. The man moved at just the time Spur studied the spot where he lay. Only his head and shoulders showed beyond a pair of ancient basalt boulders that lifted four feet out of the ground.

Two.

Spur could not find the third man. He could be close at hand. He might be half a mile away keeping the horses quiet. How long would the Jamisons man this trap?

Spur laid out several plans of attack. He could zero in on the easiest target with the Spencer. The range to each man was less than fifty yards. He could kill one of them for sure. But the other two would get away clean. Or when he gave away his position the other two might return fire and blow him into that long, long sleep.

He could put down the horse below. Cut down the mobility of the trio.

He could wait for them to make the first move, which would be to collect the horse and money below and move out. At that time he could kill the man below and the horse. Or he could wait and watch and follow them.

Before Spur had selected the best combat move, he heard a wild trumpeting sound and looked below just as a large, magnificent black stallion pranced into the clearing and watched the red mare next to the rock. She lifted her head and nickered. He moved forward. Behind him ten mares of various shades and hues came into the flat area. With them were half a dozen colts of different ages.

The rifle shot came a moment later. It chipped a shower of rocks off the face of the granite. The wild horses shied, then panicked and the stallion led them across the flat section, up the slope and into the cover of the trees and brush.

When they were gone, Spur looked back at the granite wall.

Both the horse and the sack of money were gone. One of the Jamisons had used the horses as cover for getting the bait and making a getaway.

Somehow they knew he was there, or sensed he was there. They were the ones trapped, and used this lucky romantic approach by the stallion to escape with no one injured and no losses.

Next time, Spur told himself. When he checked the sniper positions on both sides, he saw that they were empty. The shooters had pulled back and were well on their way by now. Spur lay where he was. They could still be ready to ambush him if he moved too quickly.

He looked up at the blue sky with just a few high feathery clouds. It was a good day for tracking, and there was a lot of it left. He would wait a half hour before he moved a step. Such a wait could very well be the difference between living and dying.

When he figured the time was up, Spur rolled over and stared around him. He saw nothing. He sprinted to the first large tree away from the natural amphitheater.

Nothing happened.

He rushed to the next cover, then the next until he had moved a quarter of a mile back toward his horse.

All clear. He jogged on to where his horse waited.

Now all he had to do was track them again. The woods or the trail? They would move quicker now, that would mean the trail. He guessed they would ride hard to the trail and for five more miles north, then lay a confusing set of tracks that only a master tracker or a lucky man could follow.

Spur would let them do that. He already knew

where their hideout was, at least within a mile or so of it. He would go around their tracks, back to his known position and move toward that small mountain meadow where he had first surprised Phil Jamison and Rorick.

Spur expected no trouble on the trail for the ten or twelve miles north. The Jamisons probably figured they had stopped any pursuit, had blunted the attack of Judge Parker's deputies, so now they would vanish into the hills and relax until their next bank job.

A record of their attacks showed that they had followed a pattern during the last year. They would be quiet for a while, then surge into the border states around the Territories hitting one bank after another, usually three to five, before things got so hot for them they staged a "forced march" back to the Territories where they disappeared. The time period between raids was from three to six weeks.

Spur rode carefully, but making good time. He trotted his mare for a quarter of a mile at a time, then walked her, then trotted her. In this fashion he covered the ten miles in a little over two hours.

A pistol shot behind him made Spur spin around in the saddle as he drew his iron. Twenty feet away a horseman had come into the trail.

"Don't shoot, old pardner. You didn't show up at our meeting spot so I figured I better come looking for you."

Spur relaxed and holstered his weapon.

"Longjohn Ferrier, the bounty hunter deluxe. I thought I lost you for good."

"Not with sixteen thousand dollars on the hoof out here and us closing in on them."

Spur told him about Rorick and how he nearly got killed by the rawhider women, and the robbery at Fort Smith.

"You get all the luck. So where are the Jamisons?"

"About two or three miles from here."

"Let's get riding."

Spur held up his hand. "Ferrier, you ride with me, I'm the general and you're the damn private. You do what I say or I'll be shooting you, not the Jamisons. Do you understand? I am going to capture or kill the Jamisons. I don't give a damn about your reward money."

Ferrier spun his revolver and holstered it. "Hell, all I want to do it pick up the pieces and take them in for the reward. That's after we level their hideout and wing them a couple of times. You general, me private."

"Remember that when the shooting starts. You move or stay or shit when I tell you to. Got that?"

"Yes sir, general sir!" Ferrier gave what he must have thought was a salute.

Spur grinned in spite of himself. "I just hope to hell that you're going to be more help then hinderance."

They rode down the trail. Spur had no trouble finding the spot where he had followed the tracks entering the woods two or three days ago. A half hour later he had let his "nose" lead him until he found the meadow.

"Right over there is where I surprised Jamison and Rorick," Spur said. "All we have to do is backtrack them, but we do it slow and careful. Damn careful."

From there they both moved slowly forward.

Before he left Fort Smith, Spur had visited the hardware store and put together six sticks of dynamite. He fitted each stick with a thirty second burn fuse and a detonator cap. Then he bought big headed roofing nails and some sticky tape, and taped nails around each of the ten-inch long dynamite sticks.

When one went off it would be like a cannon filled with grape shot as those roofing nails exploded outward with the force of forty rifle shots.

They rode around the small meadow and found the double set of prints on the far side. It had been several days but hoofprints in the soft mulch under the hickory, oak and gum were still plain to see.

Spur and Ferrier worked ahead slowly, on foot, leading their mounts. Whenever there was a rise they tied the nags, worked up it silently and studied the landscape ahead. The third time they did this Spur saw a narrow gulley open to the left and what seemed to be a pole fence that had been built across it.

Spur worked closer until he was sure. Someone had made a corral out of the little gully. There were three horses in it, and all were still cooling out.

"Paydirt!" Ferrier whispered. "Their hideout's got to be close around here."

Spur and Ferrier left their horses tied to some brush. Spur stuffed four of the dynamite bombs inside his shirt and buttoned it again, then took his Spencer and three of the extra ammo tubes and moved to the far side of the corral looking for a path. He found several tracks, but no real path. The Jamisons must use different approaches each time.

He picked a trail and they followed it.

Spur and Ferrier moved like Indians again, never taking the next step until they were sure it would not make any noise. They checked a hundred and eighty degrees ahead as they walked.

A rabbit scampered away to the left. A blue jay and an owl ruffled their feathers to the right. Four times they stopped to listen, but heard nothing.

The next time Spur listened he heard a harmonica

giving out a baleful tune.

Spur grinned and Ferrier nodded. He patted his Winchester 1873 army rifle.

Hideout time!

They moved even more cautiously now.

The Secret Service Agent bellied down on a rise fifty feet from a small brook. Just across the stream lay a little clearing. There was no cabin, no building. But the area had a sense of being lived in. Then he saw a rack next to a tree. It was hung with strips of meat. Someone was making jerky!

Indians?

They would not hide their dwelling.

Spur looked more closely at the area. He took out his binoculars and studied it a section at a time.

Then an oblong section of the landscape moved inward, revealing nothing but a black hole.

A doorway?

Spur pointed at the spot then looked at the rectangle with the binoculars. Dimly he could see a door frame, then a glint of rusted hinges. He concentrated on the area until he could make out the shadowy form of a small cabin that had been built thirty or forty years ago flush against a tall, sheer rock wall. Trees and brush grew all around it.

Additional work had been done with cut brush to make it even more hidden.

A laugh drifted from the doorway.

"Fifty-seven thousand dollars!" a voice said clearly. "Almost twenty thousand dollars each!"

The voices faded then as someone closed the door.

Ferrier nodded. Both men realized they had found the hideout, and that the gang was inside. Now all they had to do was take them.

Spur stared at the objective. He motioned Ferrier back a little and they whispered.

"See that chimney on the far side? It must be for a fireplace. We'll blast them out. I'll drop the dynamite down the chimney. You be out here and knock them down without killing them. When they come wheezing and coughing out the front door. Remember, Judge Parker wants them alive."

"Easier to handle dead," Longjohn said. He shrugged. "Alive it is."

"If one of them breaks past you for the horss, you light out and follow him. Run him to ground and take him into Fort Smith. No sense trying to find me. Now pick your firing spot to cover that front door. You saw it?"

Ferrier nodded. Spur moved closer. They would have no guards outside. Why should they, they had been safe for two years.

He had spotted two windows, one on this end, one on the front. Both were small two pane affairs and high up. He could walk right up to the place.

Instead he moved up with cover as long as he could, then he crept to the side and came around the stone cliff to the side of the cabin.

He had spotted a stone chimney toward the back. It would be for a fireplace, and a straight drop into the hideout. He had a surprise they would get a bang out of.

Spur checked the sun. Five or six hours to sundown. Plenty of time.

The cabin had been built of chinked logs, sturdy hardwood logs that could last for a hundred years. The builders had not trimmed the ends leaving a convenient set of steps upward. Spur moved slowly, Indian quiet, making no noise at all on the log ends or the sod covered roof that sprouted brush and even a few small trees.

He worked forward slowly, laid down his rifle and two of the loaded ammo tubes at the edge of the roof over the door. Then Spur took one of the sticks of dynamite from his shirt and walked silently on the grass surface to the chimney.

The top of it was five feet above the roof. He found his packet of matches in his pocket, tore off one and lit the fuse. He let it burn for five seconds, then dropped the dynamite bomb down the chimney.

Twenty seconds later the blast shot soot and smoke out of the chimney. He heard the windows break and somebody scream as the rumble of the explosion died out in the heavy woods.

TWELVE

For a moment after the bomb went off inside the Jamison's cabin, nothing happened.

As the noise echoed through the woods, Spur heard a long chilling scream from inside the hideaway. The sound came out of the chimney, through both windows that had been blown out and through the door.

Spur was still moving toward his rifle when the scream took form and a man jolted out the door. His shirt was singed, his hair half frizzed and burned, and a long red tear on his cheek showed dripping blood.

He had six-guns in both hands and a saddle bag over his shoulder. The man was firing his revolvers as he charged out taking Spur by surprise. He sent round after round at the circle of brush around the cabin as he darted toward the nearest cover ten yards away.

Spur drew his six-gun and fired twice, but by then the man was in the woods. There had been no shots from the big bounty hunter.

"Ferrier, you asshole! Why didn't you shoot him?

He was yours! Now get moving and go chase him down. Wherever he goes you go until you bring him back! You hear me?"

Ferrier stepped from behind a tree thirty yards away and nodded. Then he drew his six-gun and charged into the woods after the fleeing man.

Spur was ready for the next one or two. He waited on the roof. Thirty seconds ticked past and no one came out. Had they both been killed in the blast? Not likely from one stick of dynamite.

Still . . .

Spur scanned the small clearing again, saw nothing. He could hear no movement from inside the cabin, but realized the foot of soil on the roof provided perfect soundproofing. He couldn't hear anyone if they were shouting.

He had to get to the ground and look inside.

Spur went down the log ends the way he went up. Window glass littered the dirt outside the small building. He carried the rifle in his left hand, and his six-gun in his right as he edged up to the door. It had been blown off its hinges and blocked half the entrance. Spur tried to look inside. He realized he was outlining himself in the outside light.

He looked both ways, then darted into the cabin. Smoke lingered in the air. A heavy layer of soot spread over everything. His eyes grew accustomed to the dimness quickly. Table, chairs, one tipped over. Bunks against the wall. An old kitchen cook stove with a stove pipe going into the fireplace stone chimney.

He squinted and checked it all again. No bodies. He had heard more than one man in the cabin. Probably three. Where were they?

Escape tunnel?

He looked for rugs on the floor. It was packed earth. At the far side under a bunk he saw boards that had been nailed together. They had been slid back in place but not far enough. Spur pulled them out.

A tunnel!

He dropped into it and crawled forward. For a second or two it was totally black, then six feet farther on he saw daylight. The short tunnel slanted upward at once and soon he came into the open behind a large patch of heavy brush.

Spur went to his knees and examined the ground. Bootprints, two sets. Two men had left. He also saw several drops of bright red blood that had not had a chance to dry yet.

Injured, wounded at least superficially. They both could still move. There was no foot dragging.

He moved ahead tracking them. Always tracking.

They ran at first. He could tell by the length of the stride, the way the heels and toes both dug into the leafmold. But gradually they had slowed, now they walked, moving steadily to the south. Why south?

Spur guessed they would run to the interior of the Territories.

Without warning the tracks turned east. Arkansas? Why would they turn that way?

Spur kept reading the sign. They were moving, making good time, there seemed to be no major injuries. He wondered what kind of weapons they had. Had they taken time to bring their money with them? He wasn't even sure if they had divided the last haul. The weapons worried him more than the money. Two Henry repeaters could throw out twenty-six rounds of .44 sized lead in one hell of a rush.

He came to a slight rise and scanned the country ahead. They were heading higher into the Brushy Mountains. Spur realized they had been climbing gradually for the last pair of miles. A small valley opened up below and a quarter of a mile down there he could see two figures moving slowly across the open area.

Five hundred yards. He could risk firing a half dozen rounds at them, but he was not sure how the Spencer was sighted in. He probably would only warn them he was trailing them. No. He would move in and nail one. Then they couldn't split up on him. He had to put down one, then go after the second Jamison.

Spur held the rifle at port arms and charged down the hill, running hard, making up ground on his quarry. He stayed under cover. They would be checking their back trail when possible. He was sure he could get within range before they made it to the woods on the other side.

He had seen a river coming down the valley, but he had no idea how big it was. Most of the creeks were small and easy to wade across. Anything else would change the Jamisons' plans in a rush.

He ran harder, then stopped to check the two fugitives. He had made up a hundred yards. He saw one turn and look back. Spur melted against a tree and remained motionless. The best way to be seen in the woods or in the open is to be moving. A still figure can be mistaken for a tree or stump.

Then he was moving again.

A hundred yards farther along he became aware of a sound. It was new. He listened again, and then he grinned. The small little stream ahead was not small and was not just a stream. What he heard was the sound of white water.

The river was going to pin the Jamisons on this side for some time. He would have a chance to catch them right here!

He ran hard again, then paused and looked down at the river. Here it was fifty feet wide and a boiling, churning melee of rapids and whirlpools and swiftly flowing currents. The rain earlier in the higher hills was now making its way toward the Arkansas river down this nameless stream.

Spur knew he had a chance to end it right here.

He leaned back on a rock and looked below. The two men were not in sight.

A rifle bullet chipped splinters off the rock he rested on and sang away into the brush. Spur rolled, grabbing his wrist where shards of the rock had gouged out a thumbnail of raw lacerated flesh.

He came up behind the rock and peered around it. Now they knew for sure that he was after them.

Spur crawled ten feet to the edge of a patch of woods and lifted up behind an oak tree. He checked the spot the rock was struck and where he had seen the Jamisons before. They were slightly upstream from him.

Good. He moved in short rushes, as if he were in the Civil War again, running from one cover to the next, taking every advantage of the terrain he could find. He wanted to get closer to the river, about thirty yards away, then move upstream after the pair.

They had at least one rifle, so they probably each took weapons before they left. How much of the money did they bring with them? It would only be natural to take as much as they could.

Spur got to the point he wanted to near the river. The white water and the power of the current made him think trying to cross the water would be a last choice. He scanned the area ahead and saw one of the men dart from a huge rock near the water into a thick patch of woods.

They might be moving upstream where they knew there was a spot they could cross on the rocks. Spur stayed to cover and run to within thirty yards of the woods that he had seen the man enter.

He crawled up to the edge of the cover and watched. At first he saw nothing, then he saw someone building a blind with small pieces of pine boughs. Pushing them into the dirt, then leaning them against each other.

Spur sighted in on the figure and fired.

The figure screamed and rolled out of sight. Spur put four more rifle shots into the area, but heard nothing else. He finished the last shot and rolled a dozen feet to the left. Just as he left another rifle from up the line of woods riddled his firing position with four shots. Spur returned fire at the second gunman, then moved again.

He reloaded, pushing a filling tube of rounds through the base plate of the Spencer. Then he ran. He slanted downstream sightly to a line of brush that would put him into the edge of the copse of trees where the Jamisons hid.

He let them know he was coming.

They had no shot at him and would not give away their new positions.

Spur dropped behind a big oak tree and looked around it. He took one of the dynamite sticks from his shirt, lit it and threw it near where he had seen the first shooter. The bomb with shrapnel-like roofing nails taped to it went off with a sullen roar.

Spur could hear the nails zinging through the trees. There was silence after the blast.

Then Spur heard a laugh.

"Somebody really wants the Jamisons bad, don't they?" The voice came calmly, in a full and powerful tone. It was a mature man's voice.

"Will Jamison I'd guess," Spur shouted back.

"Close enough. How much is it going to take to buy you off?"

"More than you have, Jamison. I don't do business with killers who slaughter people for the fun of it."

"Then you'll die. We have you in a crossfire right now."

"Not a chance. It must be Dale I just shot. He's

hurting bad. Tell him not to try the river. Too dangerous."

"Christ, you think it's safer on this side?" The new voice was softer, younger. It must be Dale.

"You'll both get a fair trial in Fort Smith," Spur said. "You come in now and it might go easier on you. A trial later is better than being dead in half an hour."

"Don't see no help you brought to do the job," Dale said.

Spur had pinpointed the voices now. They were closer to the rushing sound of the water. He eased forward a dozen yards toward the voices to a tall pine tree and stood behind it.

"Have all the help I need," Spur said. "Mr. Colt and Mr. Spencer here help out a lot."

Spur moved as soon as he said it, swinging toward the water. Soon he could see the white rushing flood.

He could hear the men talking, but he couldn't make out the words. Then one voice lifted.

"Damnit, try it then!"

Spur watched upstream as near the voices as he could see. There was a stretch of fairly calm water that showed a strong current. As he looked, he saw a form splash into the water. Saddle bags were tied around the man's chest and he had a pistol in one hand.

It was the younger man, Dale. He went under water, then came up pawing water, his gun gone as the current rifled him toward the white water ten yards below. It was a series of two foot drops as the water roared and raced around boulders, logs and broken end snags that had been ripped free somewhere upstream and floated down.

Dale went under again, hit the white water and bobbed a dozen times.

Spur watched him out of sight where the river

made a sudden turn into green timber. He looked up stream. For just a moment he saw Will Jamison on a rock, then he jumped back out of sight.

The Secret Service Agent put a Spencer round into the rock, then moved silently forward. He came out on a pile of boulders near the shore and commanding a hundred feet of the riverbank.

Always take the high ground!

Spur checked the area. There was no sign of the older Jamison.

"Give it up, Jamison. You've got no place to run, nowhere to hide. You'll get a fair trial."

"And then I'll hang!" The voice boomed out almost below Spur. The rocks shielded him from the outlaw who stood near the water below the ancient boulders.

"You got a name? Man likes to know the name of the man he's doing business with."

"Spur McCoy."

"Well, McCoy. I've got a business proposition for you. I've got my saddlebags that are stuffed full of packets of hundred dollar bills. Hundred of them in a stack. That's ten thousand dollars to the bundle. Then I have a batch of packets of fifties and twenties.

"I'd say I have nearly eighty thousand dollars in those bags. How much do you make a year, maybe four hundred dollars, five hundred at the most?"

"About that."

"Half of all I got is yours. Say forty thousand dollars. That's almost a hundred years wages for you. All you have to do it catch the half of the saddle bag and turn and walk back to your horse. No questions, no contact, no problems. You get rich, and I reduce the work load on Judge Parker's hangman. What do you say?"

"Always wanted to be a rich man. How do I know

you won't shoot me in the back as I walk away?"

"My guns will be on the rock."

As they talked Spur worked forward on the boulder. He could not see Jamison. He began to work his way around the side. Then he slipped and rolled down the sharp face to the ground ten feet below. He lost the rifle but held on to his Colt.

As he flew through the air he saw Jamison leaning against the big rock. He was holding his left arm which was bloody. By the time he got his hand to his six-gun, Spur had hit the ground and rolled out of sight next to the base of the rock Will stood on.

"Your time is running out, Jamison," Spur said. He was edging his Colt up and over the rock when he heard the man laugh. He had moved.

"Years yet, McCoy. I'm an expert swimmer. Sure as hell hope you are." The splash that followed brought Spur to his feet and leaping up on the rock.

Will Jamison had jumped into the river. Spur saw the saddle bags tied around his waist. Jamison stroked on top of the water, then came to the small rapids and he went out of sight for a minute.

Spur had to chase him. He searched the shoreline quickly, saw what he wanted and ran for it. It was a chunk of pine log about six feet long. Spur rammed his six-gun in his belt, picked up the log and dragged it to the water. It was dry and light, would float well, and Spur hoped keep him alive down the river.

He slammed into the water with both arms around the log and his legs around it too with his ankles locked.

The shock of the cold water stunned Spur but he held on. Then he was on a wild ride downstream. The first twenty feet went fine, then the rapids jolted and banged him against rocks until he thought he would loose his float entirely. His legs came loose and he struggled to hold on.

Twice he went under water but the log popped back to the surface quickly. He gulped in lungsful of glorious air just when he needed it most.

In a quiet stretch he looked ahead but could not see Jamison. White water sounded again ahead, but this time he steered himself around the worst of it going down one more abrupt drop but into a good pool at the bottom of the three foot fall.

Another quiet spot, but he saw no one.

Ahead he saw a blue shirt. He looked again. Dale Jamison was holding onto a snag that stuck out of the water. As he came closer, Spur realized Dale was not holding on to it. His head was under water and his body wedged in a "V" created by two logs that were wedged in rocks.

Two Jamisons to go.

The white water grabbed him again, jerked the log out of his grasp and drove him deep into a pool that had a whirlpool effect. Spur had to dig in with his crawl stroke and kick with every ounce of effort and strength he had left to get out of the whirling water.

Then he floated on the surface resting, not able to kick toward shore.

Again the white water tore at him, slammed him against one big boulder after another, and soon he learned to try to catch the rocks with his hands to buffer the blow.

He was almost out of them again when his head banged on a rock and he thought he was going to pass out. He fought it, splashed and clawed at the water to keep his head above the surface, then once more the water slowed and calmed as the river bed flattened out.

To his left was a narrow sandy beach. He kicked and tried to stroke that way. The current tugged at him, refusing to let him go without a battle, but when with one flurry of desperation kicks and fast strokes with his arms, Spur surged out of the current and drifted slowly up to the sandy shore.

Spur dragged himself up until he was half out of the water and lay on his stomach panting. His face rested on his arm on the warm sand, and for just a moment he knew that he had been near to drowning. He panted and sucked in all the air he could.

It was ten minutes before he felt strong enough to sit up. Twenty feet down the small beach he saw gray pants and a gray shirt.

Will Jamison!

Spur struggled to his knees, felt for his Colt in his belt. It was gone. He might still have the Derringer deep in his back pocket, but he was too tired to reach for it. He pushed himself to his feet and took slow steps down the sand.

With every movement his toes dug in the sand leaving long trails. The body had not moved since Spur spotted it.

He made the tremendously long walk, then fell to his knees beside the body. He had to identify it.

When he rolled Will over, his eyes came open and he coughed, spitting up water and wheezing.

He lay on his back, his eyes closed sucking in air.

"If this is hell, it don't look too bad!" Jamison said at last. He was too weak to lift his hand.

Spur sat beside him, legs out straight, his trail shirt still waterlogged and ripped by the force of the current. He took it off and wrung it out, then put it back on but could not manage the buttons.

"You almost made it," Spur said.

Jamison nodded.

"You saw Dale."

Tears seeped from the father's eyes, his head nodded once.

A half hour later, Will sat up.

"I'm taking you back to Fort Smith," Spur said.

Jamison laughed. "How you plan on doing that? Neither one of us can hardly walk."

"I'll manage." Spur stood. "Let's go, it's a long walk."

"Can't get up."

"Like hell you can't. Try."

Jamison moved his hands, tried to stand, dropped down. Then he turned and in his hand he held a derringer. Spur had reached with his left hand to help Jamison just as he fired. The .45 slug that should have hit Spur in the heart slammed through his left arm, broke the bone and glanced to the side into the water.

Spur automatically kicked out with his water logged boot, hitting Jamison's right wrist, slamming the derringer out of his hand and sailing it into the river.

"You broke my damned wrist!" Jamison shouted.

"Good, you broke my arm. Now get on your feet and let's walk."

"Hell no. You gonna kick me all the way to the gallows?"

Spur lifted his own Derringer which he had fished out of his pocket and shot Jamison in his left shoulder. Jamison roared with anger and pain holding his wounded wrist, then his shoulder.

"You bastard!"

"True, let's go. I have one more shot and I'll put it right through your right eye if you try anything. Dead or alive the posters say. I don't collect rewards anyway. You'll be out of circulation either way, that's my job. Take your choice."

Will Jamison stood slowly, glared at Spur and moved away from the river.

"We'll go back to the north-south trail and look for a ride from somebody. Hate to see you all worn out when we get back to Fort Smith and we have a parade in your honor down main street to Judge Parker's jail."

THIRTEEN

Spur stopped the march after half an hour. Will Jamison had three wounds in his left arm and wrist. He carried the arm tucked in his shirt. Spur did what he could with one hand to stop the flow of blood from Jamison's shoulder and arm.

Then he bound up his own left wrist. It still burned like fire. He had lost enough blood so he noticed it, and now the broken bone began to move. He had cut off one sleeve of his shirt and used it as a bandage and wrapper around the bloody hole where the bullet had ripped in and through his arm.

There was no chance to make a splint that would work. He closed his eyes for a moment to let the continuing pain filter away. The broken bones scraped against each other and every step brought a new jolt of pain.

Jamison was as tough as Spur figured he would be. Spur kept him walking ahead. They found the north-south trail after another half hour and took another break and rested. The battering fight and struggle down the river had drained more strength from them than they first suspected.

Spur hoped that a farm wagon would come along, but none did. Deeper into the Indian Territories were more than fifteen thousand whites, all living there illegally. Some of them just moved in and began farming and ranching. Others had married Indian women and taken over what land they wanted.

A few claim that they bought the land from friendly Indians who had no real right to sell it. Little was done to move the whites out of this Indian preserve. There were tougher, more demanding problems.

But as chance would have it, there was no farmer wagon going to Fort Smith this evening.

The sun worked closer to the horizon. Spur kept the Derringer deep in his front pocket. It was his one control over Jamison. Without it they would have a bare knuckle fight and probably neither of them could win it in their condition.

Spur heard a horseman coming, but when the rider saw the pair on foot he slanted through the woods and went round them. Just before dark a pair of riders came by.

Spur held the Derringer now aimed skyward.

"Evening. We shore could use some help. Would you ride us double down to the Fort Smith ferry?"

Both the mounted men were fresh into the Territories, they were too clean to be long time residents.

"Why the hell should we do that?" one of them asked.

"Get out of here," Jamison shouted. "He's a goddamn bounty hunter."

The men laughed and whipped their horses down the path.

"You just cost yourself a ten mile walk," Spur said. "I dont' know if you're going to make it or not."

"So what? Longer I can put off Fort Smith, I

figure is the longer I get to live. Also, I'm counting on Phil to come back and blow your head off so we can ride north."

"He the one ran out of the cabin?"

"Scorched the poor guy across the face. Damned vicious thing you did back there, McCoy, that dynamite."

"I fight fire with fire. I never do anything to an outlaw that he hasn't done, or wouldn't do if he thought of it."

Jamison snorted but kept walking.

"Never have trusted black powder. Now I sure as hell don't like this new fangled dynamite."

The sun had just rimmed the far landfall when a horse came up the trail heading north.

Spur moved Jamison into the brush and watched. The man on board moved slowly, and trailed a horse with a rider who had his hands tied to the saddle horn.

When the rider came nearer, Spur stepped into the trail.

"About time you're getting back, Ferrier. What took you so damn long?"

Ferrier grinned. Phil Jamison rode the horse behind him.

"You like a lift?" Ferrier asked.

"We both would," Spur said.

Will Jamison came out of the woods.

Ten minutes later Ferrier had rebandaged both men's wounds. He helped Spur into the saddle on Phil's horse and moved the outlaw behind Spur. Then Will lifted into the saddle behind Ferrier and they moved south. Ten minutes later it was dark.

They fired two shots from the dark ferry landing opposite Fort Smith and a light blinked at them, then they heard a boat coming across.

The boat chugged up to the dock a short time later and they all walked on board. Ferrier shouldered a pair of saddlebags he had taken from Phil Jamison. He also gave Spur his six-gun to help hold the prisoners.

"Suppose I got to turn in this saddle bag," Jamison said.

"Yeah, I suppose so," Spur said.

"I could have lost it out there, then went back and found it when all this robbery talk quieted down."

"True. I never did find Will's saddle bags, or Dale's. They must be in the river or on the shore or maybe in the Arkansas river by now."

Ferrier grinned. "Now that would be finders keepers if I stumbled on it one of these days."

"Technically the cash should be turned in."

"Ain't never been very technical. Besides, it's a damn treasure hunt. I love a good hunt." He took the saddle bags off his shoulder and draped them over Spur's right shoulder.

"I'm giving you almost twenty thousand dollars," Ferrier said. "Just a few seconds ago I was a rich man."

"You have eight thousand on the hoof right here," Spur said. "When I get patched up a bit we'll go back and get Rorick and Dale. That should be another eight thousand. You'll still be rich and you won't have to look over your shoulder the rest of your life."

"Yeah, right. You just struck yourself a bargain."

"Them guys the Jamison bank robbers?" the new ferryboat man asked.

Spur said they were.

"Damn! Gonna be a celebration tonight! You got back the money, didn't you?"

"Some of it."

"Yeeeeeeeha!"

As soon as the boat tied up, the ferryboat man ran into town spreading the word that two Jamisons had been caught. A half dozen sheriff deputies and a hundred men and women poured out of the saloons and gambling halls to watch the little march to the court house and the jail.

Judge Parker arrived to welcome his two famous guests. When it was all over Spur told the Judge that Ferrier deserved the rewards on the two.

"You give me about a day to get patched up and I'll lead a team of your deputies back to the cabin. Must be some of the money hidden around there somewhere. Rest of it is in the river."

"The other two in the gang?"

"Both dead, Judge. I shot one three or four days ago, and the other Jamison, Phil, drowned in the river yesterday."

"We'll need both bodies for the reward."

"Yes sir, we'll bring them in." Spur swung the saddle bags to the judge. "Here's about twenty thousand of somebody's money. The bank wrappers might still be on it. It's all yours."

"Fine, that's a start. Now, you better get yourself to a doctor." Judge Parker paused. He preened his goatee with his right hand and nodded. "Yes, McCoy, that was good work. I'll send your General Halleck a wire commending you."

"Will you need me as a witness in the trial, Your Honor?"

"Yes, it would help." He paused. "I'll schedule the trial for early next week, four days from now. That way you won't be held up here too long."

"Thank you, Your Honor."

The doctor waited for Spur in his front room offices at his house just off the main street.

The medical man was an old hand in the Fort Smith area. He unwrapped the shirt sleeve and looked at the mangled bones and the blue welts just under the skin.

He took a bottle of whiskey off the shelf and poured a glassful for Spur.

"Is it that bad, Doc?" Spur asked.

"Yes. Back in Boston I had all the sul-ether I wanted to use, but there just isn't any supply of it this far west. It will be used routinely someday. Did you know that ether was used on a towel during an operation in 1841? Here it is almost thirty-five years later and still a country doctor can't get it." He indicated to Spur he should drink up. When the glass was empty the doctor filled it again.

Two hours later Spur was so drunk he could hardly keep his eyes open. He hardly noticed when the doctor pulled the bones apart, forced them back into position and treated the gunshot wound. The medic wrapped the arm tightly against a stiff pine slat on both sides of the gunshot wound, but left the injured flesh available for treatment. Then he cast the arm around the wound with plaster-of-paris.

The next morning Spur woke up in the doctor's spare bedroom, which constituted the only "hospital" in Fort Smith.

The doctor fed him breakfast, laughed at his hangover and then told him that Judge Parker wanted to see him. He declined any pay, saying he would charge it to Judge Parker's deputy account as he always did. The cost was a dollar for setting the bone, fifty cents for the whiskey, and fifty cents for the overnight stay.

Spur walked with unsteady steps for a block before he got his head straightened out. Then he moved quickly to Judge Parker's office. His lower arm felt like an anchor with all of the plaster on it. He had to get used to it since the doctor told him he had to leave it in the cast for five weeks.

Judge Parker had changed his mind.

"I want you to lead a search party for the rest of the money in the hideout today," he said. "You can ride in the wagon or on horseback up to the site. But we should move quickly on this."

"I'll send eight deputies with you. Ferrier will go, too. Since these rewards are federal I'll authorize payment from here, but we won't have that kind of cash to give him."

Spur agreed, had a huge breakfast at the hotel with Ferrier, and left with the eight Parker deputies at ten o'clock.

Spur rode his horse and carried a flask of whiskey to help deaden the pain.

The trip went smoothly. They found Phil's cache of money in his metal box under the first bunk, and took the box back to the wagon. The hideout revealed three more hiding places for money, and Spur did not bother to count it. Much of it was still in original bank wrappers, and would be returned in due course to the right bank.

At the river they had less luck. The deputies fished Dale from the water. He had the saddlebags still tied around him, but one of them was empty and the other one held only six bundles of fifty dollar bills.

They did not find any trace of Will's saddle bags or his money.

A deputy was detailed to follow the small river and check every sandbag and bend in the water searching for packets of bills or the saddlebags. When they met him later in the day, he reported he found only two twenty dollars bills.

Spur and two deputies followed the trail Spur had ridden in his chase with Rorick and Phil Jamison. They found the body almost where it had fallen. Carion birds had eaten at the back of his neck and one hand was gone. They threw the body over a trail horse, tied the hands and feet together under the mount's belly and headed for the ferry.

Two days later Spur was nearly recovered. They had come back with eighty-two thousand dollars from the hideout, and Judge Parker was pleased.

Longjohn Ferrier had drawn two hundred dollars, and had Judge Parker send his letters of credit for the rest of the sixteen thousand dollars to a bank in St. Louis where he would pick it up or deposit it.

Then Longhorn bought new camping gear and went back to the river where Spur assured him there was something like eighty to a hundred thousand dollars in U.S. banknotes. He was treasure hunting. He wasn't going to pass up a chance to really be rich!

In a way, Spur wished he was going with him.

That noon in the dining room of his hotel, Spur had a window table when a woman walked up and cleared her throat.

"A real gentleman would help a lady sit down," she said.

Spur looked up and smiled at the pretty woman. She had long, curly blonde hair billowing around her shoulders, wide set eyes and a pleasing smile. Something about the smile caught his interest. He stood at once and helped her sit at his table. He had not ordered yet.

She sat down, waited for him to sit and then smiled at him. "I bet you don't recognize me, Mr. McCoy."

Spur slid into the chair, mesmerized by the beautiful woman across from him. She wore an expensive dress, her hair was combed and brushed until it shone like gold threads and her pretty face had just a touch of color added, but not enough to brand her as a painted dance hall girl.

She was dressed as a grownup woman, but Spur had a feeling she was younger than she seemed. Seldom had he been so attracted to a female. When her soft blue eyes looked at him, Spur wanted to start spouting Byron's love poems. That was ridiculous, he told himself, then he looked up at her beautiful face again.

"Mr. McCoy. I said I really didn't think that you know who I am or where we met."

"Uh . . . no, I'm afraid not. Usually I never forget a beautiful woman. Will you have dinner with me? I was about to order."

She smiled. "Yes, I will have dinner, thank you."

Spur signalled and a waitress brought a menu. She looked at it a moment, then ordered a steak dinner with three side dishes.

He watched her, but nothing hinted to him where he had met her or when. He had seen few of the town's women, certainly none to say hello to or be formally introduced. Absolutely not this beauty.

"How did you hurt your arm? Is it broken?"

"Yes, I'm afraid I was shot, but it's nothing serious." He sipped at his coffee. "Are you going to be in town long?"

"It depends. And you?"

"For most of the week. Legal matters."

Their food came and he was amazed at the way she made the thick steak disappear. He stared at her without apology. The dress she wore covered her to her chin and wrist, but it hinted at such loveliness underneath that it was more provocative and sexy than a gown that showed half of each breast.

At last he put down his napkin and reached for her hand.

"I'm sorry! I don't even know your name. Now that is unfair, you know who I am. What do I call you?"

She laughed and the sound touched his memory but nothing came clear.

"My name is Irma, Irma Woodhouse. Does that help your memory at all?"

Spur did not mind the teasing. He would have begged her to tease him so he could stay near her.

When the meal was over she stirred as if she were getting ready to leave.

"Please stay a moment," Spur said. "I'll go out of my mind if you don't tell me where we met. Was it here in Fort Smith?"

She shook her head and stood. Spur hastily paid the check and offered her his arm. They went to the lobby where she sat down in one of the upholstered arm chairs and indicated he should sit beside her.

"Before I tell you where we met, you must promise me something."

"Of course, just name it."

"I'm going to be in town for the next week, and I want someone to show me around, to take me to any plays or concerts that might be on, to go with me when I buy new things at the shops, to be my escort and guide. Could you do that?"

"For a month, a year!" Spur grinned. "Well, for as long as I can. I do have to be at one of Judge Parker's trials, but when I'm not there . . ."

"Good. Now, if you'll walk me up to my room, I'll tell you where we met. I just hope you don't change your mind."

Her room was on the second floor. She unlocked it and stood watching him.

"My real name is Irma Woodhouse, but I haven't used it for almost two years. I met you about a week ago in Indian Territories." She watched him closely. "My ma and my pa got killed and I lived with some other folks . . ." She reached out and touched his hand. "I was with the rawhiders, the old man and old woman who captured you . . ."

Spur's head snapped up in shock, surprise and wonder.

"You . . . the same person with those rawhiders?" He shook his head, walked away three steps, then came back. "It's totally unreal. How could you change so much? How did you get away from them . . . from him?"

She opened the door and walked into her room. He went after her but left the door open a foot. She sat on the bed and watched him.

"Yes, I'm the same Irma. My real ma and pa were killed by the old man, and they took me. I was only fourteen. We was going to Oregon but got lost from a train up in Kansas a ways. The old man shot my real pa, then raped my mother and killed her." Irma brushed her hand over her face.

"They took me and made me work, and the old man kept bothering me, and then one night he undressed me and started 'training' me about sex. At first the old woman screamed at him but gradually she didn't mind. I was just a kid then. But now I'm all grown up."

She wiped tears from her face. "I just sort of went along with them, it was easier. Then you came and it changed things. I told you I was trying to figure out which one of you to go with. But you tricked me and ran off."

"Next thing I tied up the old man while he slept. I took all the money he saved in his hiding spot, and I took ten of the horses and got all cleaned up, washed my hair and combed it and all, and came to Fort Smith. I sold the horses and got a room and took a bath every day and had my hair fixed, and then I bought some new clothes.

"Tonight I saw you sitting here, and that's it. Spur McCoy, I want you to help me learn how to be a lady!"

Spur kissed her cheek and then paced the room. He thought about the old woman and how she died. He thought about the wild, erotic way Irma Woodhouse had made love to him. He thought about the kidnapping of a girl and her introduction into crime and sudden death and rawhiding at its worst.

"Yes, Irma, I'll be happy to help you become a lady. The fact is, you're a lady right now. I don't know what I could do for you that would make you any more of a lady."

"Lots, you can help me lots. What my real Ma used to call the social graces. I ain't gone none. Teach me how to walk, and to talk to people, and what to say and how to act with strangers." She took a deep breath. "Teach me that I can't just jump in bed with every nice looking man I see." She was gritting her teeth. "Like I want to do right now with you!"

Spur stood and took her hand. "A lady does not allow strange men in her bedroom. So I'll step outside." He did. "Tomorrow morning my cast and I will call for you and we'll go shopping. I need some new clothes, and you can buy something. It will be a start."

Tears streamed down her cheeks. "Thank you," she said. "Maybe now . . . . maybe now I can turn out to be decent the way my mamma would have wanted me to be. At least now I have a chance."

She held out her hand to say good night. Spur shook it gently, then bent and kissed her lips with a feather touch and moved back quickly.

"While you're refining the techniques of being a lady, I'm going to have to use all my will power to try to be a gentleman. That's so I don't charge into your room right now and tear off your clothes!"

Irma smiled, then laughed softly. She closed the door and Spur heard the key turn in the lock.

He turned and walked down the hall toward his room on the third floor. It was going to be a frustrating afternoon and evening. Irma Woodhouse was the same female who had ravaged him in the Indian Territories! He was still in a state of shock.

He had business to keep himself occupied. First he

went to the telegraph office and wired General Halleck the results of his campaign and that Judge Parker requested him to stay and testify.

Then he went to the closest saloon and stared at one beer after another trying to make sense out of it. Irma Woodhouse was the same woman, the same sexy, erotic female he had mated with in the wilderness. He wasn't sure that he would be able to keep his hands off her for the next four or five days. He was not sure that he even wanted to try!

FOURTEEN

The next morning Spur slept in. His arm hurt. He had a headache. He did not want to play gentleman to a nymphet cum lady in the training stages.

He shaved and dressed, had breakfast at the ridiculously late hour of eight, then bought a new white shirt, a string tie and dark blue jacket. At least he could dress like a gentleman, even when he wanted to crawl between the sheets with the lady.

Christ what a lady!

Spur had himself under control by ten that morning when he called at Irma's door in the hotel. His arm cast would not fit into the coat sleeve so he had the casted arm in a sling and left the left sleeve hanging empty. It gave him that wounded soldier look.

Irma opened the door and he sucked in a quick breath.

His brows hadn't come down yet when she laughed. She was stunning. She had piled her long curly blond hair on top of her head showing off her slender neck and highlighting her coloring. The dress she wore was a simple print frock, but it made

179

Spur want to see exactly what it was hiding.

"Astounding!" he said at last. "I can't believe that you are the same woman I knew so well in the Territories."

"I could remind you about that mole you have three inches below your belly button." Irma grinned and he laughed.

"It's you, all right. I should get rewarded with at least a small peck on the cheek."

She caught his hand, pulled him into her room and closed the door. Then Irma put her arms around hs neck and pulled his head down and kissed his lips with fire enough to launch a cavalry attack. Her breast pressed hard against his chest and one knee lifted and gently rubbed his crotch.

When she let go and stepped back she giggled. "There, that's your reward for today. It's going to have to make do for the whole day, though."

Spur touched at a bead of sweat on his forehead.

"That will more than do. If you want to stay safely inside that dress, I'd advise you to get out of this room and stay in public until I get cooled off!"

She opened the door and went out, waited for him, then took his arm after he had closed and locked her door.

"First we are going to that little dress and hat shop just down the street. I bought this dress there, but I need something for the theatre tonight. I asked. There is a company of Shakespeare players in town and they are performing tonight at eight P.M."

Spur fumbled for something to say. "I tried out for *Hamlet* once in college. Those old Englishmen talked too fast for me. I couldn't even understand what they were saying, let alone memorize all of those lines."

"Who is *Hamlet?*"

He told her. "This will be your Shakespeare

education, so remember all of it. That will put you a dozen steps ahead of ninety-five percent of the other ladies in this town."

Spur sat in the outer sales room at the milinery and dress shop while Irma tried on three dresses. She bought all three. One cost four dollars, the second five and the third a silk dress that seemed to be the best in the shop, was fourteen dollars. The lady was making some alterations in it and Irma could pick it up later that afternoon in plenty of time for the theatre.

Outside Spur stopped Irma in front of a lawyer's office.

"Just how much cash did the old man have that you relieved him of?"

"I don't think I should tell you."

"Why?"

"You'd get mad at me."

"A lady would say that I would become angry with you. But I won't. Just curious. You're spending it like you have thousands. Do you know you just spent more than a month's pay for a working man?"

Tears edged into her eyes, and he turned around and screamed silently at himself for being such a clod. He looked back and the tears were gone.

"Sorry, none of my business. That old rawhider stole two years of your childhood. Nothing is too much to replace that."

"Almost six hundred dollars," she said softly.

"Six . . ." Spur laughed. "I'd like to have seen his face when he got untied and found his treasure missing."

"I did. I told him before I left. He almost had a seizure. Until you came along, I thought everything he did was right. I guess he had me hypnotized or something. I was under his spell."

Spur smiled and touched her hand. "Now I'm

under your spell. Where are we going next?"

"I thought an early lunch. I hear some ladies call it lunch instead of dinner when we eat at noon. You know, breakfast, lunch and dinner. The Eastern way of saying it."

"Yes, I've heard of that. The hotel or somewhere else?"

"The ladies said there is a nice little tea room down the block a ways that is run by an Englishman who came over here only a few months ago. He has a delightful accent."

They had tea and biscuits at the little shop. It had a British air about it. Two Union Jacks, pictures of London, a portrait of Queen Victoria held honored places at each end of the room.

The man who ran the tea room did have a delightful English accent. Spur talked to him a moment and soon discovered that his real name was Porloski and he was from Massachusetts. He had been a merchant seaman for a time and spent a year in England between ships. The tea shop sounded like a good idea.

Spur never did tell Irma.

A messenger tracked down Spur in the general store where Irma was buying a new set of combs and a hand mirror.

Spur read the note and caught Irma's hand.

"Judge Parker wants me in his courtroom right away. It will be a special hearing to charge the Jamisons. I'm one of the witnesses. This will broaden your knowledge of the court and justice system in the nation."

The hearing was underway when they arrived, but they were taken into the room and seated. The judge was informed Spur McCoy was there.

Two of the bank employees who had witnessed the robbery and seen the accused had testified. A third took the stand but broke down when asked to recall if he could the shooting death of the bank president. He testified that he had not actually seen the shots fired but said he had heard the younger Jamison say that he had beaten both his father and his brother in shooting the bank president.

The witness was excused and Spur called to the dock.

He was sworn in, then the judge stared at him for a moment.

"The court recognized Spur McCoy as a special law officer sworn to the United States Government. Did you capture these two accused?"

"I captured one. The second was apprehended by Longjohn Ferrier. We delivered them to your jailers."

"These men both had stolen bank notes on them when you captured them?"

"They did, Your Honor."

"The witness is excused. This court finds just cause to bind over the accused for trial. Said trial to commence Monday morning in this courtroom at 8:30 A.M."

Spur smiled as he led Irma out of the courtroom.

"That's what I like, quick movement of the law. In New York it would have taken three months for that case to come to trial. There would have been lawyers all over the place. This is a lot cleaner, faster and more satisfying."

"What if the judge makes a mistake in all the rush?" Irma asked.

"Then the wrong man is imprisoned or hung. But that doesn't happen often. I'll go along with Judge Parker, quick justice for murderers and rawhiders, and let the outlaws beware!"

"That was some speech."

"I might run for Congress. Now what are we going to do next?"

That evening after they came from the town hall

where the company of four put on several bits and pieces of Shakespeare, Spur was footsore and weary. His arm had been aching all afternoon and he wanted a shot of whiskey to help kill the pain. Now a new pain arose but he pushed it down.

She was so lovely his groin ached.

Irma held out her cheek. "You may kiss me good-night, if you don't think it's too improper."

He pecked her cheek, then reached round and pecked her on the lips but withdrew quickly.

"I think I better get out of here or your standing as a lady in town will be seriously jeopardized." Spur nodded to her and closed the door quickly. He noticed that she did not lock it behind him. He reached for the knob, but stopped just in time and turned and walked down the hall to his room.

Saturday and Sunday, Spur squired the prettiest lady in town to every social function, half the stores in town, and to church on Sunday. He never more than held her hand all that time, and he was starting to wonder if his arm or his crotch was hurting more.

Sunday night he stood just inside the door of her room, his foot wedged in the opening to stop the door.

She stood close to him. He noticed she had worn some perfume tonight and it had clouded his mind all evening.

Irma touched his cheeks and tenderly kissed his nose.

"Spur, I don't understand. You know what I want to do. I guess for the last two years I just thought everybody had sex whenever they wanted to. Now it's different." She put her arms around his neck and moved close to him so her breasts pressed against his shirt.

"Don't nice ladies ever make love? I mean they must if they have babies, right? I know what causes babies. So nice ladies must do it . . . sometime."

"With their husbands. Nice girls don't make love until after they are married. That's the key word. Get married and you can jump your husband twice a day and three times at night. It's perfectly respectable then."

"Oh, damn!" She scowled, then in a moment she brightened. "But what if nobody knew!"

"No. You said you want to settle down here in town, find yourself a husband and raise a family. Good. Then I'm not going to endanger any of that with a jump into your bed. It's just not worth it. So forget it."

He pulled her arms away from him, pushed her back a foot or so and edged out of the room. Before he closed the door her face came up close.

"How about a quick little kiss goodnight?" she asked.

She pushed her face into the opening. He leaned in and kissed her lips gently, then pulled away and closed the door. Again she did not lock it behind him.

The trial opened Monday morning on schedule. The charges were bank robbery, murder of the bank manager, and the murder of the ferryman in Indian Territories.

Spur sat with Irma watching the proceedings. The Judge said he would call Spur the first day so he could be on his way.

Judge Parker had a special situation in the Federal Court of the Western District of Arkansas. The former judge had been such an incompetent that he failed to cover up his own bribery and was forced to resign in the spring of 1875 or face impeachment and a possible prison term himself. Over ninety cases had stacked up that had not been tried by the former judge. Congress was thinking of combining the Western district with another one.

Then suddenly Congress had an ideal replacement in Judge Parker. He knew the situation and actually *wanted* the job! President U.S. Grant appointed him to the vacant judgeship and Congress quickly approved. He had arrived in Fort Smith on a riverboat on May 2, 1875.

By late September he had his legal machine functioning efficiently. The first eight weeks all cases pending had been tried and six men had been hung for murder. The springing of the trap in Fort Smith was music to the law abiding citizens' ears.

The judge's courtroom was so efficient mainly because there was no recourse to one of his verdicts. The normal channels of appeal were not open because most of the cases originated in the Indian Territories, which in effect was an independent nation, and outside the Constitutional guarantees. Only a direct pardon by the President of the United States could negate one of Judge Parker's sentences.

They were all jury trials. The jurors drawn from the working folks of the Western Arkansas area who were sick to death of the lawlessness in the Territories and in the western Arkansas counties as well. They went along with the judge's quick justice ideas.

Many times when the judge did not like testimony, or when he considered it prejudiced or that the witness was simply lying, he would refuse to allow it to be heard. Judge Parker ran roughshod over slick lawyers who tried to get clients off, bulldozed others into not practicing in his court, and soon showed the legal profession that he was boss in his court and he would have his way.

A flyer detailing the laws governing the U.S. Marshal and his deputies for the Western District of Arkansas, was different from others in the nation. In part it said: "U.S. Deputy Marshals for the

Western District of Arkansas may make arrests for murder, manslaughter, assault with intent to kill or maim, attempt to murder, arson, robbery, rape, burglary, larceny, incest, adultery, or willfully and maliciously placing obstructions on a railroad track.

"These arrests may be made with or without warrants first issued and in the hands of the Deputy or the Chief Marshal. It is always better for the Deputy to have a warrant before making an arrest, yet if he knows of any one of the above crimes having been committed and has good reason to believe a particular party guilty of the crime, his duty is to make the arrest."

Spur had heard that the deputy marshals drew two dollars for each arrest when the man was delivered to Fort Smith. The deputy got nothing for a corpse, unless there was a wanted poster on him with a reward. So the deputies shot to capture their suspects, not to kill them.

Spur settled down to watch the trial. As usual it got underway promptly at 8:30 A.M. and would be in session until nightfall. Now and then night sessions would be held. Judge Parker had plenty of customers for his justice.

No lawyer represented the Jamisons. Judge Parker appointed one who hardly knew his right hand from his left. The list of witnesses hastily drawn included bank employees, citizens who had seen the Jamisons leave the bank by the back door or on their ride to the river.

Again Spur testified about the capture of the two men, about the attack on their hideout, the subsequent drowning of Dale and the capture of the other two.

Spur was excused.

The outcome of the trial was a predictable one. Little evidence was given to show that the Jamisons had not robbed the bank or killed the president.

Spur and Irma left the courtroom and two new spectators eagerly rushed forward for their seats.

Late in the afternoon word came to the English Tea Room where Spur and Irma were eating. The Jamisons had been found guilty and would be hung the next day. Spur lifted his brows in surprise at the speed of the justice. It was fast even for Judge Parker. Then he heard that the two additional hangings would fill out a set of five that the judge would hang the next day.

Spur lifted his tea cup and sipped, then put it down.

"We were talking about Irma Woodhouse. She is a nearly grown woman. But she should have more education. You can read and write, and do sums, but these days a woman needs more than that. There are many women going into business, learning trades, becoming self sufficient. No longer is a woman tied to and must be dependent on her husband."

"But maybe I want to be dependent."

"Fine, but give yourself a choice. If you get married tomorrow and have five babies in the next five years, you will no longer have a choice."

"I have a choice right now. I could always be a fancy lady in a saloon. I know exactly what they do and how they do it and I'm trained to please a man and I must admit that I do enjoy making love."

"So you could have three options. Don't sell yourself short. You are a beautiful woman with a delightful young body. There are a lot of things you could do, if you want to try. But you'll have to make an effort."

"I've never seen a hanging. Can we go tomorrow?"

"Yes, a part of your education. It's not exactly a picnic but there will be wagon loads of people coming to town from all over the area. Sorry to say it will take on a carnival atmosphere. The trap drops at 9:30 A.M. Let's go down there now to the fort compound to look at the gallows. We won't be able to get anywhere near them tomorrow."

The gallows stood in the courtyard. They had been built especially to Parker's specifications. The posts and crossbeams were twelve inch square oak timbers. A narrow trap door ran the length of the platform. As many as twelve men could be hung at once with a single thrust of the lever dropping the trap door. Spur pointed all of this out to Irma.

Irma looked up at it and shivered.

"Judge Parker kills men here," she said. "Somehow it doesn't seem much different than what the old man did in the Territories. I mean, the men involved are just as dead no matter who killed them or how it happened, or why."

She walked the length of the trap. "Twelve men can die here at once? That's outrageous. The law. I guess I'll never understand the law."

"You don't have to understand it, just obey it and live a normal life, and the law won't hurt you. The best law is when you don't know it's there."

She touched his hand. "You haven't said a word about it these last three days. But I know you're still worried about the old woman. I could say I killed her in self defense. She came at me first with a knife. I had to defend myself." She stopped and watched him, then caught his hand and they walked back toward the hotel.

"Yes, I know I went a little crazy with the knife. She was dead and I knew she was dead and I went on stabbing her. Rage and fury were boiling out of me. They had kidnapped me, kept me. They had killed my parents. The old man had raped me and trained me to be a whore. The old woman had used me sexually when the old man was gone. They had robbed me of my youth. Suddenly a fourteen year old girl was a dance hall prostitute. I guess I'm not quite so angry at them any more."

Spur felt some of the tension draining from her. "Good, I'm glad you talked about it. Now it shouldn't bother you at all anymore."

They walked toward the hotel.

"You're not going to turn me in to Judge Parker?"

"What for?"

"The old woman who . . . died."

"What old woman?"

She smiled and they walked along in silence for a ways.

"Thank you. I'm not sure why you're being so nice to me. You'll probably attack me one of these times." She grinned. "Why don't you come up to my room and we can talk about books, and literature. You haven't told me yet when you're going to be heading out of Fort Smith."

"Tomorrow. After the hanging. The train will be through here at two in the afternoon. I telegraphed our office in St. Louis that I was testifying at the trial today."

"Oh."

"Nothing else to say?"

"I could plead with you to stay. I could ask you to marry me and take me with you. I could cry and plead and try to seduce you. But I'm not sure any of it would work."

"Tonight I'm going to start teaching you how to play bridge. A lot of the better people play the game. It's much more intellectual than whist or poker. I think you'll like it. Bridge is more socially acceptable than poker."

"Can we have some wine and cakes in my room while I learn?"

"Of course. Now, I better go see Judge Parker's clerk, and then send one more telegram. I'll be back to take you to supper, or dinner if you prefer, at

5:30. That will give you time to pick out a dress to wear tonight and then to lie down and have a short beauty nap."

"You think I need it?"

"No, but even perfection can be improved upon," Spur said. He kissed her forehead, then her cheek and slipped out the door. He tried not to notice if she locked it.

FIFTEEN

When Spur got up at dawn, he heard a bedlam outside his window. The street was filled with farm wagons, buggies, surries, cabriolets, and people on horseback. The flood moved slowly toward the courtyard . . . and the hanging.

He saw two three-seat full platform wagons that had more than a dozen people in them. There were road wagons, open buggies and rigs with tops and side curtains. He spotted one cut under extension top surrey with real leather seats and silver embossing on the sides of the seats that must have cost a small fortune. Two prancing blacks pulled it and a man and three women rode in it like they were royalty. For all he knew they might have been a prince or princesses from somewhere.

He washed, shaved and hurried downstairs. He found Irma standing on the hotel steps watching the show.

She grabbed his arm.

"All this for the hanging?"

"Right. It's been in the newspaper and word of mouth travels fast. Some of these people must have been driving for two days to get here. It will be a real celebration."

"To see five men die?"

"Not really. It's a celebration of law and order. They want to believe that this hanging will make them a little safer. That law and order and right will be more important and more possible now. It will pass, but for this time in this area, I think this kind of public hanging spectacle is a good thing."

They watched wagons filled with families drive by. There were blankets for sleeping, hampers and boxes full of food, and camping gear for outdoor cooking.

"Want breakfast first?" he asked.

Irma pretended to vomit, laughed and shook her head. "I couldn't eat a thing. I'm afraid I might throw it up when the trap drops."

They moved to the boardwalk, went down three blocks, then crossed the street with a dozen other people. They had to challenge the wagons and buggies to get across.

The courtyard was nearly packed already. No rigs had been allowed in to make more room for people. Some sat on blankets, but most stood waiting patiently. Spur and Irma squeezed into a free space.

"It's going to be over two hours yet before the hanging!" Irma said. "Look at all the people."

"There will be five thousand here before the trap springs," Spur said. They stood there watching the others. Talking from time to time. She caught his hand, then slipped her arm around his waist.

"This afternoon?" she asked looking up at him.

"Yes. I have to go. I have a job and duty calls."

"You could go deaf for a day or two."

"Could, but better not."

They watched young boys and a few girls climb

the walls around the old fort to get a better view.

In a roped off section right in front of the gallows stood fifty chairs. They were for the press. Reporters were there from St. Louis, Kansas City and Chicago.

The men on the fourth estate began drifting in, showing special papers to the deputy U.S. marshals at the gate and were escorted to the special chairs. The mayor of Fort Smith came with his entire family and sat just behind the reporters.

Soon the area inside the walls was filled and no more were let in. Wagons drove up along the walls and whole families stood on the wagon boxes to see.

By nine o'clock the sheriff and his deputies were on hand to control the crowd. It took some doing. The people were getting impatient. Babies began to cry. Mothers hurriedly nursed them to quiet the hunger pangs. Children became lost, screeching in fear and anger until a parent was found.

"Remember this," Spur told Irma. "You'll probably never see five men hanged at one time again."

"Lordy, I hope not!" Irma said and grinned at his expression of surprise.

At nine-twenty, Judge Parker's chief deputy and the U.S. marshal came out. They led a small line of men. Behind them came four ministers and a Catholic priest, then the five men who had been condemned. There were twenty rifle packing guards walking with the procession.

The U.S. marshal read the death sentences for each of the men. Then any of the five who wanted to was given a chance to speak.

All five were guilty of two or more killings, all unprovoked, and all done in the Territories for gain. One man who killed his friend for his purse and horse had nothing to say. The second man was being hanged for killing his wife and two children. He spoke for five minutes bewailing his mispent life and asking forgiveness. The marshal had to escort him back in line to stop him talking.

No one else spoke. The Jamisons snarled at everyone they saw, laughed at the ministers and priest and called them charlatans, hypocrites and worse than the devil himself.

The clergy offered prayers for the souls of the men, then led the throng in singing two religious hymns most of the crowd knew: *Rock of Ages* and *Nearer My God To Thee.*

When the last notes of the slightly off key hymn ended, a hush spread through the crowd. For a moment there was not a voice raised, not a baby's cry, not an animal whickering.

Two deputy U.S. marshals placed a black sack-like hood over each of the doomed men's heads and tied it around the chest. Then each man was led to his place on the trap.

George Maledon, the chief executioner, was a thin man with a full white beard and moustache, sad eyes and thinning black hair. He went to each man, placed a hand-woven, well-oiled Kentucky hemp rope around the man's neck and adjusted it exactly right so the heavy knot with thirteen loops around it would break the victim's neck the second he hit the bottom of the rope.

Maledon was a specialist, some said the best hangman in the country. The job had to be done right, otherwise the hanged man would twist and turn and die slowly of strangulation.

Maledon was often heard to say that he had never had to hang a man twice, and he never would have to.

When he had the fifth and last doomed man's noose properly placed he went back to the end of the gallows.

The hush that had affected the crowd intensified until the very silence could be felt.

Without any signal or announcement, Maledon sprang the trap.

The five killers dropped to quick broken neck deaths.

Spur let out his breath. He had no idea how long he had been holding it. He looked down and saw that Irma had dug her fingernails deep into the flesh of his arm. Three places showed traces of blood. She never knew she did it.

She gripped his arm tightly, staring at the swaying, black hooded figures on Judge Parker's famous oak gallows.

There were no cheers, no shouts. The crowd was stunned by the shock of the deaths. Families gathered and drifted away. The men of the press scribbled on pads of paper, looking around, then staring again at the slightly swinging figures before them. A few went to talk to the judge, others found Maledon the executioner and tried to get him to talk about his job. He turned them all away with a sad stare and a wave of his hand.

Spur guided Irma from the courtyard. She had not said a word since the hanging. Her hands both gribbed his arm. He felt her leg touching his as they walked. For a moment he sensed that she shuddered. Spur looked down at her. It had been a mistake to bring her here. She had seen her share of violence and death up close, ten times her share.

The crowd moved in near silence to the street and along it on various routes to get back to their rigs or homes. The bars and saloons were strangely quiet when Spur walked by them. No one was gambling.

From experience Spur knew that it would take two or three hours for things to get back to normal. By noon the gambling halls would be overflowing as everyone began to give his version of the hanging.

Spur found his way through the crowds to the boardwalk and then as quickly as he could to the hotel. He steered Irma straight to the second floor and into her room. Once inside she threw her arms around him holding him so tightly he thought she was going to crush him.

"Easy, easy, Irma. It's over now. It's all over. You never have to think about it again."

"No!" she screamed. "I want to remember it, always. It was the most thrilling, most exciting thing that has ever happened to me. I saw five men die at once!"

She reached up and pulled his face down and kissed him. Her mouth was open and she drove her tongue into his mouth. As she held him she stumbled backwards, then fell on the bed dragging him with her.

"Oh, yes! Yes! Right now while I still feel that jolting, that sound as the men all dropped at once!"

She tore at her dress, ripping buttons, pulling her bodice open, tearing the chemise off until her breasts were bared.

"Right now, Spur! Right now! I have to have somebody make love to me! Right now! Don't waste time!"

She pulled at his fly, ripping it open, digging inside for his genitals.

Spur lifted up, saw the wild, frantic look in her eyes, and knew that he had to humor her. He pulled his pants off and lay on top of her. Her hips beat a tune against his. She pulled his face down to her breasts and he ate his fill. Then she turned him over so she lay on top, pulled her tattered dress off over her head and quickly kicked out of the soft silk underwear she had bought only the day before. She lay on him, naked, her legs spread wide, her hand urging his turgid member toward her crotch.

Spur felt her need, sensed that this was somehow tied in with the rawhiding. She might never be rid of the violence, the death and how it was all tied up with the sexual act.

Then she had thrust him into her and she rocked and bounced on top of him. She climaxed almost at once, and he saw how it reduced her tension. She kept moving and two minutes later she shivered and the tremors rocked through her. This time she shrieked until Spur got his hand over her mouth. She writhed and jolted longer than Spur could remember her doing before, then she sagged on top of him. But when he tried to move her away, she shook her head.

She pumped him again and again, then slid down and took his penis in her mouth and played with his balls until he could not stop and jolted his load into her mouth.

She nodded, and then lay beside him, her arm around his shoulders as they rested.

A few minutes later she lifted up, pushed her breast into his mouth.

"Again, damnit, fuck me again! I need it again!" She turned over and held out her arms. Her knees came up and she screeched at him. "Spur McCoy you make love to me right now!"

He saw the frantic glint in her eyes. Why had he taken her to the damn hanging?

He soothed her, kissed her, moved over her slowly. He wasn't ready yet, but she solved that quickly with her hands. She pulled on him as he began entering her, then she sighed and relaxed and let him move at his own pace.

She climaxed again, and then again. Spur thought she would never stop, but at last she did and just as quickly she closed her eyes and her breathing became spaced, deep, even.

She was asleep!

Gently he came out of her and lay beside her. She slept on. Spur got up and dressed silently, then pulled a sheet over her and tucked it in around her shoulders.

Spur thought back to the rawhiding. Remembered how the women had argued over who "got this one first." So it had happened before. They captured a man, robbed him, the women fought over him, made love to him, and then what happened? Spur felt a shiver roll through him.

He remembered what the old man rawhider had said when Irma had been making love to him in the Territories. He asked Irma if she was ready yet. Ready for what? She had said no, she "wanted to keep this one for a while."

This one.

Keep this one for a while.

Then Spur remembered that the old man had held a six-gun in his hand. When Spur looked up the .44 muzzle had been pointing directly at his head.

Had they worked out a routine where the old man shot Irma's lover while he was still coupled with her?

Spur shivered. What had the old man done to this beautiful young girl? The hangings must have brought it all back. She had a strong tie between sex and death.

Would the compulsion fade, would a loving, strong man wean her away from any memories of those terrible two years in the Territories?

He stroked her golden hair and she reached out in her sleep and caught his hand. She brought it to her lips and kissed it, then put it over her breast. Spur left it there.

She woke up an hour later. Spur had not moved. She smiled.

"You've dressed already? Don't you have time for one more?"

"No. I have to get packed."

"That was wonderful, our making love. I don't care if anyone here knows. I just don't care!"

She sat up, careful to keep the sheet over her breasts. She looked down and laughed. "That is silly, being modest now." She deliberately lowered the sheets showing her breasts.

"Please stay longer."

"I can't. But I'll stop by to say good bye after I'm all packed and checked out. The train comes at two this afternoon and it won't wait. We have a couple of hours. Do you want to have lunch or dinner?"

"Yes," she said.

"I'll be back in half an hour."

He slipped out, sold his horse and saddle at the livery, paid his hotel bill and checked out with the judge's assistant. Then he took the most beautiful girl in the world to dinner at the hotel.

They talked of everything and nothing. He could see her becoming more and more tense.

Spur touched her arm.

"Irma, you're a lovely woman, a fine person. I know you're going to be very happy here. Go to church, join the choir and get to know the people. Men will be smashing into each other in three months to marry you. Wait and see. Forget all about me, about the Territories and everything that happened there. Start over, start fresh, and enjoy life."

He reached over and kissed her cheek.

"Now I have to hurry to the train."

He stood and watched her.

"Spur McCoy, I'll always remember you," she said. Then she smiled one of her perfect, beautiful smiles. "I hope you will remember me too. Somehow

I think you will."

He touched her hand, paid the bill and went to check out. His one small carpetbag was packed and ready.

Spur looked off the railroad coach at the small town of Fort Smith. Soon it would be only a memory, of a broken arm, a wild ride down a river filled with death and white water, and the capture of all that was left of the Jamison bank robbery gang.

And Irma Woodhouse.

He would never forget Irma. Such a beautiful girl. But such a tremendous problem. He wondered how she would do in Fort Smith. As the train lurched and pulled away from the station, he hoped that she would find a kind man, settle down and never be anywhere near to death or violence again. He had a feeling she would no longer want to go to the hangings in Fort Smith.

Spur settled down to the "jake" train ride that would eventually put him in St. Louis. It had been a year since he had been back there, since he had visited "his" office and talked to Fleurette Leon, the half French green-eyed blonde sweetheart who also was related to his boss in Washington D.C. He would worry about that when he got there.

Two days, the ticket man said. By the time they jigged and jagged across the state and then moved up toward St. Louis and the main line, they would have eaten up most of forty-eight hours.

Spur tried to relax. The cast was bothering him again. Yeah, it was itching under there! Why hadn't modern medicine developed some way to stop a cast from causing the skin to itch?

He went toward the dining car, found a "club car" where he could get a drink. It would help him stand the low grade but continual pain of the broken arm. He deserved it. Just one little drink.

He got a pair of beers and went to a seat next to a

window. The country slid by, and after a half hour it stopped being interesting, and picturesque, or even educational.

Face it, the country was dull.

He looked up from his beer and at a blue sheer silk skirt that must be on a woman who was standing next to his small table.

"Mind buying a girl a drink?" she said.

Spur looked up, then jumped to his feet.

"Irma! What are you doing on the . . . I thought you were going to stay back in . . ."

She sat down. "Sorry about surprising you, but even as a little girl, I always liked surprises, for me or on me." She looked at the two bottles of beer beside him.

"You drinking both of those, or could a lonely girl talk you out of one of them?"

He pushed the beer to her and set up his unused glass beside the bottle.

"Hi, Spur McCoy. How is the arm?"

"Fine, yeah, just fine."

They stared at each other. She took a drink of the beer from her glass. He tipped his bottle. They went through the ritual again.

"Sorry about the hanging. I shouldn't have taken you."

"No, no I wanted to go. I knew that something was rattling round in my skull. I wanted to see what would happen." She covered her face with both hands.

"Lordy, did I find out what happened!"

After a moment she looked up and smiled. "It's all right. I think I know what's going on. I have tied the two up for so long, and I was so young when it all . . ." She looked out the window. "I can handle it. I know what to stay away from. I can avoid those experiences, and then I won't . . . won't go all to pieces that way . . . I mean I can handle it now."

"We don't know that for sure, Irma, do we?"

"No, not for sure. I may never find out for sure, because I will avoid problems like that, situations, places where . . . like that. It won't be hard."

"You decided not to stay in Fort Smith?"

"Yes. It's too close to the . . . to the Territories." She looked up at him. "I thought St. Louis would be a good place to start over again, or just to start."

"Hope it works for you."

"Won't you be there?"

"This is the first time I've been back to St. Louis in almost a year."

"Oh." She finished the beer. "Well, would you walk me back to my seat?"

"Of course."

They went into the first car, then to the second. She stopped in the car that had been divided into compartments, small rooms, with the walk way at one side of the car instead of down the middle.

She used a key and opened the door. "This is my seat. Come on in."

Spur laughed. "Going in style, I see."

"For as long as the money holds out." She sat on the bed made up for two. "There is one bit of my education I am lacking. I hoped that you would help me one last time."

"Anything I can do."

"I have never really been seduced. I don't know what a man is going to do. I promise not to help, not to protest too strongly. I just want you to show me what happens, what a man does when he tries to get me to . . . you know, go to bed with him."

Spur chuckled and walked to the door.

"The first thing they do is lock the door, so no one will bother them. Probably the next thing would be a kiss." He sat beside her on the surprisingly soft bed and kissed her lips. She kissed him back.

"No, hold it, no helping. You would not kiss back

204

when you were not interested in the man. Let's try it again, and this time try to get it right."

Spur kissed her and she sat without reacting.

"Yes, better, much better. He'd try to kiss you four or five times, then he would try to touch your breasts."

Spur kissed her again. After all, he had said he would do anything to help her. It was tough duty, but he had to keep his word. Spur slid back on the soft bed a little farther, kissed her and against her gentle protests slowly leaned her back on the bed. Then he kissed her again.

It was forty-five hours to St. Louis. They would find some way to while away the time.

SALOON GIRL

1

There was a starkly beautiful place where the trail topped the last hill and fell away from the blue sky with its fleeting white clouds and raced downward toward the green of the valley floor along the river, then stretched farther east and north into town. This was a place a man could look down on the world spread out before him, watch the hawks circling far below in their graceful, constant search. Along this trail a man came riding.

John Ringo pulled up his bay mare where the trail slanted down and sat a moment staring out at the quiet valley of the Grande Ronde river. He never thought he would get to Oregon, and never this far off the well traveled routes.

He had been visiting his three sisters in San Jose, halfway up the long state of California, when a letter from Texas told him an old partner of his had holed up in La Grande, Oregon, a small town out on the high and dry eastern half of the state where they raised cattle and cut timber.

It was 1867 and John Ringo never liked to let a
debt go unpaid, especially one of five hundred
dollars that was three years overdue. He cut
short his visit to his sisters, who knew him as
John Ringgold. He had changed his name so they
never would learn of his lawlessness and
reputation as an outlaw in Texas, Arizona and
half the western states. Now all he wanted was to
ride down into La Grande, find Curley Johnson
and extract the five hundred dollars.

Ringo was a tall man, almost six feet, two
inches, and Texas-lean with a somber face and
light blue eyes. He gambled, usually drank to
excess and had most of his killing fights when he
was drunk. In Tombstone, Arizona, where he
spent most of his time, he was known as the
fastest, deadliest shot around. Nobody came to
town to try to make a name for himself by
shooting it out with John Ringo.

He had taken the train up the coast and then
the stage two hundred and sixty-four miles from
Portland to La Grande. It was a rough two and a
half days in a Concord stagecoach, and Ringo felt
all tied up from the close quarters. They arrived
just after noon and he promptly rented a horse
and took a ride around the town, then up the
stage road west. Now he felt better. He would
find Curley Johnson tonight.

Ringo tipped a pint bottle of whiskey, took a
long pull and capped it.

He turned and rode down the hill into La
Grande.

By the time he tied his rented horse up in front
of the Sagebrush bar, it was dark. He went to a
small cafe nearby that offered a "one pound
steak" dinner. The steak was fair, but not Texas

quality. He told the owner so as he paid, then he turned toward the Sagebrush bar where Curley Johnson was supposed to be tonight.

His partnership with Curley was not the legal kind—quite the opposite. They had teamed up to relieve some stage coach passengers of their valuables and found a drummer traveling with over a thousand dollars in cash on him. They took it from him and left the area quickly. Much later that night after John Ringo drank himself into a stupor, Curley had relieved John of his half of the cash.

Now Ringo was going to get it back.

There was a swagger to the way John Ringo walked, and even he was not sure if he did it on purpose or if it had grown into his normal movement as a kind of warning and defensive mechanism. At any rate, it worked. His two pearl handled revolvers hung low, lean and mean and ready, and while few knew his name in Oregon, they recognized the low tied six-guns and the no-nonsense expression on his face.

Gunfighter!

Any sane man took two steps back around such a man.

He pushed his way into the Sagebrush saloon and looked around. At least it had a plank floor. There was a long bar against one side, a dozen small tables for drinking and poker, and two larger poker tables at the back. The far side held a small stage and an upright piano much the worse for wear. The music box had taken a bath in two rivers on its way across the plains twenty years ago in a covered wagon. It had been reworked and refitted but it played almost as good as new.

Ringo did not see his ex-partner at any of the

tables or at the bar. He let his right hand relax a little and strode to the bar.

"Whiskey, the good stuff, a bottle!" Ringo spat out. He took the offered bottle and glass, dropped a quarter eagle, a two and a half dollar gold piece, on the counter, and walked away. He kicked a chair back from a small table near the wall and sat down. He could see anyone who came in the door and everyone inside the gin mill.

For an hour he worked on the bottle of whiskey. It was fair, as rotgut whiskey went this far from home. Texas would always be home. But he could never go back. He had been only fifteen when a cattleman-sheep herder feud flared into violence. John's only brother was killed and he swore vengeance. He hunted down the three men responsible for his brother's murder and killed each one. Then he had to flee the state and dodge an occasional bounty hunter who came looking for him.

Now he peered over the glass and watched every man who came in the front door. There were three tainted, painted and shopworn saloon girls in the Sagebrush. Each had tried to interest him in her charms, but he had roughly pushed them all away.

By nine o'clock the fifth of whiskey was half gone. Ringo's eye was clear and he could still walk a straight line across the floor. He looked up and saw Curley Johnson walk in. He was immediately hugged by one of the bar girls who put her arm around him and headed for the back cribs. Curley pushed her away and went to the bar.

Ringo roared in anger and stood, tipping over

his small table, and smashing the whiskey bottle as it hit the floor.

"Sonofabitch!" Ringo screeched. "Curley, you thieving bastard, I'm calling you out, right now!"

Johnson turned slowly, his hands on his shoulders. He had one six-gun on his right side, tied low.

"Ringo! Wondered what happened to you when we got separated. This gang jumped me, robbed us both and . . ."

"Liar!" Ringo thundered. "You robbed *me*. I want the money back now, or a chunk of your hide!"

"Now, Ringo, take it easy. I'll make up what they stole, damned if I won't. What was it, about five hundred? I can make that up . . . sooner or later."

"*Now*, you thieving sonofabitch!"

Curley began to sweat. "Ringo, can I reach for my wallet?"

"Long as it's got money in it."

Curley brought it out. He opened it so Ringo could see the bills inside; greenbacks, several. When Ringo squinted his eyes to see the denominations, Curley dropped the wallet and his right hand darted for his hip.

It didn't look like Ringo moved quickly, but before the eye caught the jolting movement of his right hand, it came up with iron and three shots blasted by the time Curley's fingers closed around the walnut handle of his .44. He never got it out of leather.

The three rounds came fast from the double action revolver, and all three .44 caliber slugs slammed into Curley, nailing him to the bar for a moment. Two slashed through his heart, killing him instantly. The next hit his throat as his lifeless body began to fall.

The Sagebrush Saloon had gone deathly quiet as the two men argued. Prudent men edged away from the combatants, leaving an empty alley behind and between both men. The barkeep had slid well out of range and reached for a sawed-off shotgun he kept below the counter loaded with double-ought buck. He didn't need it.

By the time the apron lifted up from behind the bar, Curley was dead and John Ringo had straightened up his table, sat down and signalled one of the saloon girls to bring him more whiskey.

Five minutes later, Sheriff Quincy Younger, who was fifty-two years old and had been elected to his four year term the last four elections, walked in the door. He had the look of a lawman who would rather argue the law than try to enforce it.

Sheriff Younger was half a head shorter than Ringo and had developed a fondness for his second wife's cooking. She had twice had to let his pants out. He checked the dead man.

"Get him out the back way and over to Zed's undertaking parlor," the sheriff told two men standing nearby. They picked the body up by hands and feet and carried him through the back door.

Sheriff Younger grunted as he got off his knees after examining the corpse. He walked over to John Ringo's table and sat down.

"Evening, Sheriff. Buy you a drink?" Ringo waved to one of the girls who brought another glass. He poured two fingers of whiskey for the lawman.

Sheriff Younger took the whiskey in two gulps. He needed it. It had been six months since he'd had a killing in town. He had recognized the man in front of him at once. John Ringo was wanted in half a dozen western states and territories. Right now Sheriff Younger had no thoughts of arresting the gunsharp. Younger cleared his throat.

"Mr. Ringo, can you tell me what happened here?"

"He shot down Curley, that's what he did!" a saloon girl named Belle screeched and ran at Ringo. He held out one arm, fending her off as she swore at him and flailed her thin arms. Two men pulled her away and she calmed down.

"Sheriff, it was self defense. That man drew first. Ask anybody. He went for his six-gun, so I had to defend myself."

"Three shots?"

Ringo laughed without humor. "Five years ago, Sheriff, I might have trusted one shot. These days I'm not taking so many chances. I've seen more than one man shot down and killed after he thought he'd killed his opponent."

The sheriff looked around the saloon. He pointed at two men and motioned. They walked over.

"You both saw the killing?"

They nodded.

"Tell me what happened." He indicated one of the men.

"This man, Mr. Ringo, was in the place drinking. He had a bottle. Been here long as I have, an hour. Next thing I know, I hear him yell at the other guy, Curley. They were talking about some money, then the dead man went for his gun. He made his move first. He was just too slow."

The second man told the same story.

Sheriff Younger sighed and stood up. "Mr. Ringo. I'll go along with self defense, but I want you to come around the office tomorrow and sign a statement to that effect. All right?"

"Whatever you say, Sheriff. I was just having a few drinks."

"Will you be in town long, Mr. Ringo?"

"Not sure, I have some more business here."

"I hope nobody else owes you money."

Ringo laughed. He had frowned slightly at first, then he laughed. He had won, he was free. John Ringo felt good. One debt had been paid, with blood.

Sheriff Younger motioned to the glass. "Thanks for the drink. Now I better get back to the office."

A few minutes later, Sheriff Younger leafed through a stack of wanted posters that he had accumulated from the mail. He had heard about John Ringo for years. His usual haunts lately had been around Tombstone, Arizona where he played cat and mouse with the Earp brothers. Had Ringo come all this way just to shoot down a man who owed him money?

He found a poster. The picture was not a good likeness. The poster was from Texas where a much younger John Ringo, also known as John Ringgold, was wanted for three murders. There was a three thousand dollar reward.

The sheriff kept looking. Deeper down in the pile he found another wanted poster from New Mexico Territory. Ringo was wanted there for murder as well. Five hundred dollars reward.

Sheriff Younger pushed the posters back in the stack and stuffed them in his bottom drawer.

There was no chance that he was going to try to arrest Ringo on the strength of the posters. Texas was too far away. He couldn't spare a deputy to take Ringo back. If any of them lived through trying to arrest Ringo. No, there was not the ghost of a hope that he would arrest John Ringo.

When someone opened the front door, he looked up to see his wife coming in with a late night snack in a small basket. She brought it every night he worked.

Charlotte Younger was twenty-six, half his age. She had been a widow for a year when he married her. He couldn't ask for a better wife. She was so young and fresh and beautiful that he said a prayer of thanks every day. She had flowing black hair she kept long at his insistence. It framed her face and swept half way down her back.

"Pumpkin pie with whipped cream!" Charlotte said, uncovering the dish containing the quarter of a pie wedge.

She sobered. "I hear there was some trouble."

"All taken care of. Self defense. No problem."

Charlotte smiled and pushed a strand of greying hair back behind his ear. "Good, because even I have heard of John Ringo. He's a bad one. I hope he leaves town soon." She took a big breath and hugged him.

"Quincy, I had one husband killed while he worked out of this office. I am certainly not going to allow that to happen a second time!"

Sheriff Younger chuckled and kissed her soft cheek. "Sweet Charlotte, I am on your side. I don't want that kind of a problem to pester you either."

She hugged him again, then kissed his cheek.

"You see to that, Sheriff. I just won't allow you to turn up dead." She grinned and ran out the door and half a block down to their house.

Back in the Sagebrush Saloon, Ringo had bought another bottle of whiskey and was doing some serious drinking. He watched the featured attraction of the saloon, a lady singer! She came on the small stage and accompanied herself on an old piano as she sang. Ringo blinked.

He wasn't sure if she were pretty or not. He could see that she had a small waist and good breasts. He shook his head, picked up his bottle and walked with elaborate care out of the saloon toward the best hotel in town where he had already registered. He would finish the bottle in his room. Yes, good idea. Kill the bottle and think about what he was going to do tomorrow.

2

Spur McCoy stepped down from the stage coach at noon the next day, his back sore from the two and a half days of pounding by the coach. Half way he had given up his seat with a backrest to an older woman, changing to her place on the bench in the middle of the stage where there was no back. Sometimes he thought it was easier to ride his own horse than the stage.

He looked around the eastern Oregon town of La Grande. He knew little about it. Cattle mostly, a little bit of timber. Nothing large scale would happen there until the railroad came through.

McCoy stood six-two and weighed a solid two hundred pounds. His reddish brown hair fought with his collar and half hid his ears—when he remembered to get it cut. Green eyes showed over a full reddish brown moustache and long side-burns just a inch this side of mutton chops.

Hidden in his wallet between two other cards pasted together was his identification as a United States Secret Service Agent. Spur called St.

Louis his headquarters, and had as his responsibility the whole western half of the nation. It was too much, and he was not given any help. Budgets were tight for manpower they told him.

Spur was not your usual lawman. He had a Bachelor of Arts degree from Harvard University in Boston. He had been an Army Captain during the big war and an aide in Washington to a U.S. Senator.

When the Secret Service was established in 1865 he had applied and was accepted as one of the first agents. Since his was the only federal law agency that could chase criminals across state boundaries, that made for more work than they could possibly manage.

Originally the agency was created to handle one crime only, counterfeiting. He still worked many funny money cases, but now everything from murder to kidnapping to bank robbery was on his assignment sheet.

He was in La Grande to investigate the death of a U.S. General Land Office Agent and the destruction of all of his records, files and house. His wife had been seriously burned in the fire.

William Wood, the director of the agency, had sent Spur his assignment via telegraph to Portland. It came from General Wilton D. Halleck, the Number Two man in the agency. It said simply:

PROCEED TO LA GRANDE ORE AND INVESTIGATE DEATH OF LAND OFFICE AGENT JONAS KING. MURDER, ARSON SUSPECTED. FIND KILLER, PROSECUTE, RE-ESTABLISH LAND OFFICE IF

POSSIBLE. WIRE UPON COMPLETION YOUR LOCATION.

It was signed by Gen. Halleck, who listed himself as president of Capitol Investigations, Washington D.C.

Spur walked over to the Grande Ronde Hotel with his one big carpet bag and registered. He was in room 202 front looking right down Main Street.

Spur used water from the big china pitcher in his room and gave himself a quick sponge bath. He shaved closely and then dressed in clothes that were not trail dusty and went to see the sheriff. His name was Quincy Younger, and he had been around long enough to know this county inside out.

Sheriff Younger looked at Spur's identification letter with surprise.

"Never even heard of your group," Younger said. "But then that's not unusual. Half the things the Federal Government does never filter down to us way out here anyway. So, what can I do for you?"

"Sheriff, I'm a lawman, the same way you are. I'm here to investigate the death of Jonas King, the man who ran the U.S. Land Office here."

"Yes, Jonas. Terrible tragedy. Fire evidently started about three o'clock in the morning. It was gone before us volunteers got there with our buckets. Someday we'll have a real pumper here to use on fires!"

"Sheriff, we think Jonas was murdered. He wrote his boss in Washington a letter a week before he died. I have a copy of it. He said there had been threats against him. I understand he was also doing the work of the county clerk on a temporary basis.''

"Jonas murdered? That's a real surprise. Who would want to do a thing like that to a nice young man like Jonas?''

"I want you to give me some answers to that question. Who in the county could benefit if all the county ownership land records, and the land office records of homesteads and other federal land transactions were wiped out, gone forever?''

"I don't know. We've had considerable homesteading in this valley, some in the mountains. You can homestead a stand of timber just as easy as a river bottom, you know.'' Younger shook his head. "Benefit? Hell, I don't know. You better talk to the banker. Best one in town is Hirum Follette.'' He scowled at Spur.

"Can't say I'm too happy knowing that we even *might* have a killer running around town. Course, now that I think more on it, the big ranchers around caused the most uproar about the homesteads. Most of them were grazing public lands they figured they owned, but they didn't. Then a homesteader drops in and fences off his eighty acres and plays all hell with grazing and trail driving.''

"Like the RimRock Ranch?''

"The same. But Wade Smith wouldn't do nothing like this. Not murder!''

"Let's hope not.'' Spur stood to leave. "Oh, and Sheriff, I don't want a word of this to leave this room.''

"Yes, yes, I understand. Hirum over at Cattleman's Bank would be a reliable source for you.''

Spur said goodbye and headed for the bank. It was closed. He tapped on the window until someone came. A brief conference through a barely opened front door, and Spur was let in.

Hirum Follette was a short, round man, with fat cheeks, clean shaven and nearly bald. He was not yet forty years old.

After Spur told him the story he paled.

"Oh, God! Not another killing. We have just finished a minor struggle between the big ranchers and the homesteaders. The ranchers got their noses bloody in that one. Served them right; they were dead wrong. They never had title to the land they claimed but wanted to go right on using it."

"Could this tie in? With the records of the county clerk and the land office gone, who can prove they own anything?"

"Copies. All those recordings had to be done in triplicate, with the land owner keeping one copy. Course, more than likely over fifty percent of the owners have lost their copy. They could always get a new one from the County Clerk—up to now."

"Couldn't those owner copies be changed or rewritten to include more land than they did originally? Who could disprove it, especially the federal lands through the General Land Bank?"

"Yes, it's a problem, all right."

"Mr. Follette, my job here is to find out who killed Jonas King. Do you have anyone I might begin to talk to? Who would benefit most from this fire?"

"Wade Smith, at the RimRock Ranch, and Travis Odell at the Twin O Ranch. Opposite sides of the county, so they never fight much, but they would like to roust every small rancher and homesteader out of the county."

"Fine, that's a start. What about town people? Any retailer trying to buy up all the property?"

"Not a chance. Nobody is that ambitious."

"Mr. Follette, I would appreciate your not mentioning this to anyone. If it is murder, I want to nail the killer before he knows I'm after him."

The banker agreed and let Spur out the side door. He went down the street two blocks to the edge of the business district to the blackened remains of the U.S. Land Office, and the temporary office of the Wallowa County Clerk. Only a few two by fours stood in one back wall. Nothing had been done to rebuild or clean up the ruins after a month. Some kind of official search had been made, Spur guessed, by the looks of the blackened remains.

But there were no soggy burned masses of paper. When files burn they often singe the edges, burn around the outside, but closely packed paper is not as prone to burning as people think. To burn completely files need to be opened, books must be torn apart, their pages ripped out and the burning remains stirred. He found bindings of the large plat and land ownership books, but none of the pages.

There had been a systematic destruction of the records inside the office before any fire was evident on the outside. No wonder it had taken all night and until three A.M. to finish the job. Jonas could have surprised them, or simply been captured and killed or tied up and left to die when the place caught on fire.

At the far side of the place, away from the street, he found two metal cans. He sniffed them. Coal oil. Each would contain a gallon. Kerosene would be ideal to help burn a building right to the ground. He kicked the cans and wondered what else he should do.

The widow should be next.

He asked at the closest doctor's office. It seemed to be the only one in town, belonging to Dr. William George. The doctor had his office in one wing of his home, and from appearances he had a clinic or small hospital facility in the other section. Spur walked into the office. It was a little after five P.M. and there were three people in the waiting room.

Spur talked to a woman on duty and she said Mrs. King was in the clinic, and yes, he could visit with her for a short time. She was still severely burned, but recovering. The nurse led him through a hall to a hospital-like room.

Mrs. King lay on a bed. She was bandaged over both arms and half of her face. Spur guessed she had many more bandages under the sheet. She smiled with one good eye.

"I am the luckiest person in the world!" she said with an optimistic lilt to her voice. She meant it. "Or maybe the Lord has something else for me to do in this world. Now, how can I help you, young man?"

"Mrs. King, my name is Spur McCoy. I'm interested in the fire at your house. Can you remember anything about what happened that night?"

She blinked back sudden tears, then lifted her brows. "*Remember*. That's about all I can do for another couple of months. It was just a regular day. Jonas often worked late trying to get all the work done. I told him he had two jobs, but he wanted to help out the county until they could get someone reliable. Then too, there was an election coming up in two months to fill the empty post of county clerk."

"Did he say anything about anyone threatening him, Mrs. King?"

"Threats? In La Grande? My goodness no."

"Mrs. King. I don't want you to tell anyone, but he sent us a letter to Washington D.C. advising his superiors about threats. We think the fire was deliberately set to destroy all the land records in the county, and that your husband was murdered."

"Oh, my goodness!"

"Please try and remember anything your husband said that last week before the fire. Anything you can remember will help."

Her one green eye looked at him with fear, but that quickly changed to anger.

"Yes, Mr. McCoy, I'll certainly remember something!"

"You're a brave woman, Mrs. King. I'll see you later. I hope this hasn't upset you."

She shook her head but he saw tears growing in her eyes.

Back at the doctor's office, Spur asked to see Dr. George. He said it was official business. The woman showed him into a room and shortly the doctor came in. He was thin, short, with a moustache and thinning hair. He looked to be about fifty, energetic, tired, but friendly.

Briefly Spur introduced himself.

"We think Jonas King was murdered, Doctor. Did you find any marks on the body that might support that theory? I'm scratching for some kind of a lead."

Dr. George shook his head. He sat down in a chair and took a deep breath. "No, I'm afraid not.

There wasn't enough left to examine. The flesh was almost all burned away, some of the smaller bones had burned. The skull had no bullet holes in it. But that's not much help. There wasn't enough soft tissue left to tell me anything."

"Not a lot. Oh, Doctor, did you smell anything unusual or foreign to the body when you examined it?"

"Yes, there was something that baffled me. There was a strange odor I always associate with my home at night, or perhaps just as I go to bed."

"Could it have been kerosene smoke?"

"Oh, my God!, that's it!"

"Kerosene that was poured on the body to make it burn faster?"

"Yes! I should have caught that. Damn them! Then it was murder and arson. Who in this little town could be capable of doing such a thing? We don't have more than four or five hundred people here."

"I was hoping that you might have some suggestions for me along those lines, Doctor George."

The doctor shook his head. "I specialize in healing people, making them well again, not in destroying them. But if I get any ideas, I'll be sure to contact you. Where are you staying?"

Spur told him, thanked him and then stepped out into the pre-dusk of the high plains land of eastern Oregon. It had a different feel than the great plains, not as arid as the deserts of the southwest. Somehow a more gentle, softer feel to it. Gentle for everyone but the killer.

3

The tall, slender man who sat in the rocking chair
on the far end of the porch at the Grande Ronde
Hotel, let the monocle drop from his right eye. It
fell on a thin silver chain attached to the watch
pocket of his vest. The vest matched the dark
blue pin stripe suit. He signalled with his first
finger and a man wearing a simple white shirt and
blue trousers hurried up to the man in the rocker.

"Yes, Sir Jeffrey?"

"It will soon be time for dinner. Do you know
what is on the menu tonight?"

"No, sir. I'll go at once and find out."

"That's a good lad, Edward. Good lad."

The young man of no more than thirty years
hurried away toward the hotel's dining room.

Sir Jeffrey Mountbatten watched his man,
Edward Long, vanish through the front door of
the biggest and best hotel in La Grande. So far, so
good, he thought as he watched the people
coming and going along the boardwalk of the
small western town. It wasn't at all what he

thought it would be, but he was ready to accept it as it was—especially when he owned it, even for a short time.

He bowed slightly with a nod to a matron who came up the steps. More and more of the "better" ladies of the town were "just happening" to stop by the Grande Ronde hotel to smile at him, and some were so bold as to come and ask after his good health.

The Americans did go crazy, he thought, when it came to British royalty. They had such outlandish ideas about Lords and Ladies. Sir Jeffrey stood and walked into the lobby, then up to the second floor where he had the three room Presidential suite.

In the hall two matrons smiled at him and they paused.

"Sir Jeffrey," the younger one said. "I wonder if you could tell us about what English ladies wear. I mean do they wear grand gowns all the time?"

She was about twenty, he guessed. She was probably with her mother, a much older woman but still attractive. As she spoke the younger woman turned so he could see the top of her dress which showed a generous portion of cleavage.

He smiled. "Ladies, you both are beautiful and charming. I'm afraid I'm no expert on English women's apparel. However, they do dress almost as nicely as you are now." He paused. "But I must say they are not as cordial and friendly as I find American women. It is most refreshing. It's been delightful talking to you."

"Sir Jeffrey, might I have a word in private with you?" the older woman asked. She was in her forties, a bit stout but with a large bosom.

"Certainly." He moved down the hall a few steps and she followed.

"It's about my daughter. She is a bit shy, but I was hoping that you might be my guest for tea tomorrow, in our rooms here. My daughter, Daisy, is a most engaging girl, and she's interested in getting to know you better." The woman smiled, then went on quickly. "After tea, I would have to leave for an hour or so, and I'm certain that anything you wished to do with Daisy would be all right with her, and me."

"Yes, that's most flattering. However, I do have an inspection ride tomorrow scheduled."

"Oh, well, if you prefer older women, Sir Jeffrey, I should tell you that I'm a widow and truly missing the attentions of a handsome man. Tomorrow would be fine with me as well."

"Thank you, but I'm really afraid I do have this engagement tomorrow. Business, you know. I simply can't avoid it. Perhaps at another time."

"I hope so. I'll be in touch again."

He smiled, bowed slightly and hurried on to the Presidential suite.

When he left Sir Jeffrey on the porch of the hotel, Edward Long slipped out the side door of the hotel and walked down the street to the first saloon. Inside he paid for a nickel beer and mixed, watching poker games and moving closely to several other drinkers.

His nimble fingers worked quickly and when he had two wallets and a soft pull string purse, he faded out the front door and hurried back to the hotel before the men missed their pokes. Once inside the Presidential suite, he closed the door and only then felt safe enough to laugh softly. He had heard about swift Western justice at the end of a rope. Long wasn't sure if that included the small misdemeanor of picking pockets or not.

"Once more I bail you out, *Sir Jeffrey!*" Long said the title and name with elaborate care. He dropped on the bed and took out the billfolds. One had only six dollars in it, and some silver. The other had almost thirty dollars. He untied the soft leather pull string purse with expectation.

"It could be gold!" he said.

Sir Jeffrey came from the other room and stared at the money on the bed. He stepped forward as Long poured out the coins from the soft purse. Long counted the coins with obvious glee.

"Three double eagles, three eagles and some small ones—almost a hundred dollars! Who would be carrying money like that in his pocket?"

"I don't have the foggiest notion, Edward, but he's going to be doubly careful the next time he goes into that saloon. You better not work that one again for a few days." Sir Jeffrey reached for the money, but Long slapped his hand away. "Me dip did the do, so I keep the loot," Long said, dropping into a cockney tinged accent.

"Quite so, old boy. You are excellent at your trade. I have nothing but the utmost respect for you."

Long grinned. "Besides that I'm feeding your arse, as I have for the past two months, ever since Boston. When is this bloody big score going to be coming through that you keep promising me day and night?"

"We start the wheels in motion tomorrow. Within three days half the land owners in Wallowa county will be ready to do business with us."

"Then it's bloody well fifty-fifty, the way we promised?"

"Of course, of course. What could I do without you?"

"Damn little, gov'ner. You're getting me pecker hot again."

Sir Jeffrey smiled and patted the shorter man on the head. "Not until after dinner at least. We should go eat while it's still fashionable."

"Besides, now we have the scratch to pay the bill," Long said.

Dinner was always a time to show off. Long hovered around the great man, making sure he was served properly. When he was settled down to eat, Long slipped away to a back table and ate a steak and all the side dishes.

Lord Mountbatten was bothered by a dozen or more ladies of the town who stopped by to say good evening. Mountbatten loved it. He shyly flirted with each one but offered none the chance to sit down.

By the time dessert was over, Edward Long was hovering around Sir Jeffrey Mountbatten again, acting as his manservant, holding the chair, settling the bill, leaving the tip, doing it all for his master.

An hour later up in their suite, Edward dropped on the bed and laughed.

"It's a bit of fun, laddie, but I'm getting tired of this servant routine. Ain't it about time I get to be the lord again and you the servant?"

"Perish the thought. Not now. We have this whole county just about where we want it. Another two days at the most. Come here and look at this map."

He spread out a large scale map of Wallowa

county which was the north-eastern most in the state, bordering Idaho on one side and Washington on the other.

"We are talking about all those lands that are drained by the Grande Ronde river, the Joseph and the Innaha rivers. That means all of the Wallowa mountains, the big valley of the Grande Ronde and this whole bloody corner of the state. We'll be billionaires!"

"If it works. I think we might have to hit and run fast."

"Not a chance. We've got this one set up so well, planned so completely, that it will roll for at least two months. Think what we can do in two months!"

"And then we take the stage to Portland and vanish in the big city." Edward nodded. "Yeah, it sounds good. I just hope it all works!"

"It can't fail, if you keep up your good work making me look like the bloody duke himself."

Edward snorted. "Bloody, fucking queer duke *you* would make! Where would the bloody next generation come from?"

A knock sounded on the door. Sir Jeffrey vanished in the far room, Edward went to the panel and opened it a foot.

"Eight o'clock, right?" a woman's voice said.

Edward grinned. "Damned if I 'adn't forgotten all about you, love. Come in, come in. Sir Jeffrey has retired for the night in the master bedroom. We won't bother him a bit."

The girl stepped into the room. She was from one of the saloons and had come as promised. She held out her hand. "You're telling me Sir Jeffrey isn't for fucking tonight. I'd really counted on getting my first British nobleman in the old kip."

"Afraid not, love, just me and my little pecker to play with. He's tired out, wouldn't be any sort of fun anyway."

"Too bad. Leastways I'll get me a real Englishman. Be a good change from these farmers and loggers and cowboys." She held out her hand. "That's three dollars, ducks. Three for house calls when there's no duke or earl or prince involved." She laughed. "And I damn well will give you your money's worth."

"You better, ducks," Edward said. "Or I'll bite off one of your nipples!"

Lil giggled. "Oh, you do sound wild and British and all. Do you foreigners do it the way Americans do?"

"Do what?"

"Fuck?"

"We'll have to see. First you show me all the ways you've ever been fucked. Then we'll figure out some new ones for you that are strictly British. Have you ever done the Queen Elizabeth?"

"No, love. Can't say as I have." Lil giggled again and began pulling off her clothes.

"No, sweet one," Edward said. "Slow and easy. I get the fun of unwrapping the package. Now lay down on the bed and look fetching."

In the other room, Sir Jeffrey looked through the two-inch space where he had edged open the connecting door. His face showed a flushed excitement, one hand worked at his crotch and soon his fly came open and he held his stiff penis in his hand. Slowly he began stroking, but he did not watch the girl on the bed, he watched Edward as he slid out of his trousers and dropped bare-assed on the bed.

4

When Spur McCoy left Doctor George's office late that afternoon, he saw a few people looking at him curiously. This was a small town, extremely small, and a stranger stood out here like a peacock in a flock of white leghorns. He shrugged. Strange and curious looks he could live with. He angled across the street and headed along the livery stable on his way to Main Street.

Halfway along the block, a pistol barked from the shadows near the back of the livery. A bullet whizzed over his head and Spur dove toward a thick oak tree that grew near the fence. He peered around the trunk. He saw no one. The shot sounded as if it had come from along the back fence of the livery.

Spur pulled his long barreled Colt and raced along the fence. He saw nothing. He froze against the unpainted boards and listened. Someone was humming *Clementine*. He listened again, then moved slowly toward the sound.

Twenty feet ahead in the weeds beside the fence

sat a man with a six-gun in his lap, and a pint of whiskey in his fist. He didn't hear Spur approach. Spur grabbed the revolver and sniffed it. It had just been fired. He checked it and saw there had only been one round in the cylinder.

The man shook his head and squinted up at Spur.

"I did it! I did it!"

Spur squatted down beside him.

"Yeah, but you missed."

"So what? You said just shoot at him, not hit him." The man tilted the glass bottle again. "Hail, you know I can't hit nothing no more."

Spur took the bottle, threw it against a rock, smashing it, then grabbed the man by the vest and dragged him to his feet.

"We're going for a walk, can you make it?"

"How far to the nearest bar?"

"Not far."

Spur found that the sheriff was not in his office, but a deputy waved at Spur's bushwhacker.

"Know him?" Spur asked the Deputy.

"Sure. That's Park. He's so far down the trail he doesn't even know his name half the time."

"He just took a shot at me."

The deputy took Park's chin in his hand and turned it up to him. "Park, you've been bad again, you know that?"

"Just a little job. Got me a jug and a silver dollar."

"You could have killed this man. Do you realize that?"

"Just one round, never could hit nothing."

The deputy scowled. "Where is your silver dollar?"

"Left it with Lefty at the bar, the Sagebrush

Saloon. He always keeps my money."

The Deputy let him go and turned back to Spur.

"Not much I can do. Park can be hired by any-body in town to try almost anything. The man who hired him could be anybody. Why would somebody try to shoot at you? You're new in town, right?"

"Right, almost six hours, by now. Looking for a somebody I need to find."

"He have a name?"

"Yep, I just don't know it yet. You can have Park. Why don't you dry him out overnight?"

Spur went back to the street. A bar bum, a drunk had taken a shot at him. He hadn't been in town six hours. Did somebody know why he was here, or was it just mistaken identity? This was the first time he'd been in Oregon. Nobody here could know him—unless they recognized him from somewhere else. Entirely possible.

Spur headed for the Sagebrush Saloon. It turned out to be the biggest, noisiest bar along Main Street. The Sagebrush had windows across the front, the foot square kind that were cheaper to replace. Dozens of kerosene lamps burned inside.

Most cardsharks liked to gamble at night. The low lighting in gambling halls made it ideal for their bottom dealing and card exchanges. Spur slid through the swinging bat doors and went to the bar.

A man with a white apron around his stomach moved up and eyed Spur. "What's the stranger in town need tonight?"

"A beer and some information."

The apron slid a bottled beer toward him and Spur stopped it.

"Now the question?" the barkeep asked. He was about thirty-five, a little heavy, open and friendly.

"Are you Lefty?"

"Yep."

"Park been in today?"

"Sure, he's always here. Sleeps in back sometimes when I don't catch him."

"Hear he earned a dollar today."

" 'Pears. Leastwise he had one. I kept it for him. A dollar all at once could buy enough rotgut to kill Park."

"You're his banker, or his nursemaid?"

"A little bit of both, but he never has a very big account."

"How did he earn it?"

"Told me he was gonna take a shot at somebody. I warned him not to. As usual he was too drunk to listen."

"He missed me, Lefty." Spur paused to let the message sink in.

"Whoa, none of my doing. I didn't hire him. I'm just his banker. I don't want him to drink himself to death before he's twenty-nine years old."

"And I'd rather he not shoot me even if it is through no fault of his marksmanship. Who hired him?"

The apron waved his hand around the establishment where there were only thirty men and three saloon girls.

"Take your pick. Could have been anyone of these, or anybody in here since we opened when the stage got in at noon." He paused. "Why would somebody want to shoot you? No, that's not right. If they wanted you dead it would have been a real bushwhacker. Somebody is just trying to scare you."

"About the size of it. I don't scare easy. I've only been in town for six hours. I was on that noon stage."

"Damn peculiar. Anybody know you wēre coming?"

"Nobody in town. What else is happening?"

"You've heard of John Ringo?"

"The Texas Terror? He's been in Arizona the last few years, mostly at Tombstone. Sure, most people know about Ringo."

"He's in town. Killed a man last night. Sheriff agreed it was self defense."

"Was it?"

"Yeah. Shot him down right there at the bar. The dead man went for his gun first. Man! That Ringo is *fast*!"

"I've heard." Spur thought about it as he took a pull on the beer.

"Ringo have anything to do with your problem?"

"How long has he been in town?"

"Came yesterday."

"He's not my worry, then." Spur looked around and saw the bar filling up.

"Why the sudden trade?"

"In ten minutes our new songbird sings. She's a looker and she can sing. Full house last night. She calls herself Colette Paris, whatever that is. But she can sing."

"When does all this happen?"

"In about five minutes. She sings for a half hour. Maybe again later if we have enough customers in the place."

Spur worked on his beer. Who could have been worried about him so quickly? Before he had it figured out a whisper shot around the saloon.

"Ringo!"

The man stood just inside the door, his pair of pearl handled six-guns tied low. He wore range pants, a blue shirt and a brown leather vest.

Ringo scowled at the group around the tables and walked directly to the bar.

"A bottle of that same whiskey," he said. He put three one dollar gold pieces on the bar and took the bottle and glass when the apron set them out. Without another word he walked to a poker game where there was an empty seat, and without asking, sat down.

"Name's John Ringo," he said. "Deal me in."

When the buzzing stopped, the rest of the poker games continued. Somebody plunked on the piano, not a professional, just some cowboy who had taken a few lessons in Milwaukee or Boston or Atlanta, and wished he were home.

A barrage of hoots and yells soon silenced the beginning piano student.

Then the big room was filled with a crashing fanfare on the piano. Spur turned as did everyone else. A small, pale girl in a bright red dress sat at the piano wearing an off the shoulder dress revealing slender arms. She was a brunette with lustrous hair falling halfway down her back and cut straight over her eyes in bangs.

When the fanfare was done she turned to an absolutely quiet house and smiled.

"Good evening, gentlemen, I'm Colette Paris and I'm here tonight to entertain you with some songs, and some piano playing and maybe a memory or two. How many of you remember *The*

Bloody Monogahela?'' She hit a few chords and launched into a tearful ballad about the Civil War.

It was over quickly and she stilled any shouts of one side or the other by charging quickly into *Rosie, You Are My Posy*, and then *My Love is Buried on the Wabash*.

When the three songs were over she stood and bowed and the whole place broke up into a hooting, shouting and clapping uproar of approval. When the applause died down, she smiled and half the men in the place knew she had smiled directly at and for them.

She was a gamine, small and pretty, with a slender body and generous breasts, but it was the sparkle in her eyes and her happy, friendly style that won over her audience.

She did another set of three songs, then asked for requests from the crowd. Quickly came *Old Dan Tucker*, and then *Jimmy Cracker* followed by *Simon Kenton's Revenge*, another song about the Civil War.

Spur sat enthralled by the showmanship of the small girl. He had seen many performers in New York and Washington, but few of them could match this girl who called herself Colette Paris.

Halfway through the next song, John Ringo jumped on the stage and leaned over the piano as she sang. She motioned him away twice, and when he wouldn't leave, she picked up a glass of water from the piano and threw it full in his face.

For a moment there was a shocked, deadly silence, then Ringo roared with laughter, and the shocked and fearful audience joined him. He bowed from the waist and in the sudden silence, doffed an imaginary hat.

"My apologies, Miss Paris. I thought I might have known you in Houston, but I was mistaken." Still chuckling to himself, John Ringo returned to his poker game.

He looked at his whiskey bottle. It was scarcely one quarter gone. Disdaining the glass, he tipped the bottle, lowering the level by an inch and reached for the cards.

"My deal," he said knowing that it wasn't, and challenging anyone at the table to contradict him.

The next few hands went wrong for Ringo. He was a crafty poker player, but luck was not with him, and quickly he lost fifty dollars. The pots were averaging about twenty each until a new player joined the game and the betting picked up.

The next pot was over a hundred. Ringo lost it. He set his mouth firmly and picked up a new hand. Ringo had four nines! On a hand of draw poker he knew that was an extremely good showing. Only a few hands could beat him. Ringo bet his last dollar calling the new player. There was over five hundred dollars in the pot.

The new player now showed that he was a professional gambler. He calmly laid down his hand, four tens.

John Ringo was on his feet in a second, one of his big revolvers drawn before the others could grab a second breath. The muzzle pointed straight at the gambler with the winning hand.

"Cheated!" Ringo thundered. He didn't look to the other men for confirmation. There were no chips at this table, only greenbacks and gold and silver coins.

Ringo looked at the four men around the table. They made no move. The gambler stared at the muzzle and shook his head slowly.

"Mr. Ringo. I did not cheat. However, if you want the pot so badly, why don't you take the money? If you'll excuse me I'll be going back to my hotel." The gambler stared at Ringo for five seconds, then calmly turned his back and began to walk away from the table.

There was hardly a sound in the saloon except the man's footfalls.

Ringo watched him a moment, then looked down at the pot on the table that held more than five hundred dollars. It was two years wages for the average working man. Ringo reached for the money with his left hand. The gambler spun suddenly, his right hand pulling a .32 caliber hideout gun with a two inch barrel from his pocket. He had it drawn but not aimed when Ringo fired his .44. The round went through the gambler's heart, slamming him backwards on the top of a poker table, smearing the cards and the money with blood as he skidded off, hit the plank floor and died.

Ringo held his gun on the man for a moment, heard the rush of air from his lungs in a death rattle, then holstered his .44, picked up the money on the table and walked out the door.

The barkeep quietly sent a flunky out the back way to get the sheriff.

Colette came to the bar to talk to the barkeep, who it turned out also owned the place. They talked for a few minutes, and she nodded. Then she turned to Spur who still stood there.

"Miss Paris, you sing extremely well," Spur said.

"Thank you." She smiled. "You're from the east, Boston?"

"I went to school there and picked up a trace of

that accent."

"I thought so. I come from Portland, Maine."

"Could I buy you a drink?"

"No, no thanks. I'm to do another show later on. I must keep a clear head. Now I need to rest." She paused. "You know my name, but I don't know yours." She was frank, open, friendly.

"Spur McCoy, Miss. I'm staying at the Grande Ronde Hotel."

"Nice to meet you, Mr. McCoy. Perhaps I'll see you again. I'm at the same hotel." She turned then and went behind the bar to what was probably an office or private quarters.

Spur lifted his brows.

The barkeep/owner smiled. "A nice lady. She is not to be confused with our saloon girls."

"That would hardly be possible," Spur said. He paid for his second beer, finished it and headed for his hotel. He took a roundabout route, staying in the shadows, backtracking, and watching his back trail.

No one was following him. Five minutes later he eased into his hotel room and lit the lamp. A long white envelope lay on the floor just inside the door where someone had slipped it under the door while he had been gone.

Spur locked the door, then picked up the envelope.

5

Spur tore open the envelope. A piece of purple, scented stationery came out. On it in a dainty feminine hand he saw the message.

"Mr. Spur McCoy. You could help me. I need your aid. Please come to Room 215 as soon as possible."

There was no signature.

Spur read the note again. It certainly didn't look like a set-up. Still, someone had hired a drunk to take a shot at him, to scare him. How could a purple, scented stationery using woman hurt him? It would be the man in the closet or in the hall or waiting in a room with a connecting door who could do the damage.

And it could be a lead to a killer.

He checked his appearance, combed his hair and brushed back his moustache, then put his clip on holster in his boottop with the hideaway derringer and went down the hall. Room 215 was on the same floor as his. He found it, surveyed both ends of the hall, but saw no one move. He heard nothing. Gently he knocked on the door.

It opened at once.

The girl standing there was tall, maybe five-seven, her hair was light blonde and had been cut short. Huge brown eyes gazed at him and a smile lit up her pretty face. She wore a dress buttoned to her chin and wrists.

"Oh, Mr. McCoy! I'm so glad you got my note. I missed you at supper. Please come in."

Spur had left his hat in his room. He took one more look up and down the hall, then stepped inside.

"Yes, I am Spur McCoy. And who might you be?"

"You can call me Maggie. I live here. I fix my room any way that I want to." She spun around like a school girl. "Isn't this a nice room?"

"Indeed it is, Maggie. You said you needed some help."

"Oh, yes. I'm just so bored and unhappy and sad, that I think I might just take my own life. You wouldn't want that to happen, would you? So what I decided when I saw you get off the stage, was that you could help me. It isn't hard, and if you're short of money, I can even—you know—help pay your hotel bill or whatever."

She saw him look up quickly.

Maggie shook her hand in front of him when he saw how forcefully he reacted to that idea. "No, forget about that, but I do need your help desperately. I get so depressed and I really don't want to shoot myself, although I do have a gun, a .32 caliber I think it is, and that would be plenty enough to kill me."

Spur frowned. "This sounds more like you need a doctor, maybe Dr. George. He would know what to do more than I would."

"Oh, no, no! I can't go to him. I've known him all my life and it wouldn't be the same. Don't you see, I need someone I've just met to talk to, so I can tell you all my problems and worries and you won't laugh at me."

"I would never laugh at such a pretty lady," Spur said.

"There! See what I mean? I feel better already. You just said I was pretty. Now Dr. George would never tell me that, right? So you have to stay and help me. I want you to tell me all about yourself, just as if . . . as if you were here courting me. Then I can tell you about myself, and I'll feel just ever so much better."

"I'm afraid this isn't my usual line of work, Maggie. Now if you'll excuse me, I really should get back to my room."

"No! you can't go or I'll kill myself! I will!" She darted to the dresser and brought out a business-like .32 caliber revolver. She pointed it at him without putting her finger on the trigger. Spur could see that there were lead slugs showing through the end of each cylinder.

He changed his attitude, held up both hands, and sat in the room's one straight backed chair. There also were two other upholstered chairs, and a table at one side. The bed was on the far side. He realized the room was at least twice as large as his own. It must face the alley.

"Good." I'll put this horrid thing away. I really don't want to use it, you know."

She sat on the bed facing him. "Now, what shall we talk about? You first."

"What about your family, Maggie? Can't you talk to them?"

Her face turned sad. "Yes, I wish I could. They died, my mother and father and a brother. Indians. It was terrible. A year ago now. But I'll never forget it." She shook her head and her face brightened. "Now, Mr. McCoy. Tell me about yourself." As she said it she unbuttoned her dress at her wrists.

"Oh, you don't mind, do you? It is a little warm in here." She undid her wrists and rolled the sleeves back, then undid the buttons at her throat but only three or four. "Now, what about you, Mr. McCoy?"

"I come from New York City, where I went to school. My father owns a store there."

"How exciting! Are there really all those people living in one place, in one town?"

"Yes, I should say. Almost two million people in the city. It's really like a lot of little cities all pushed together."

"So many people." As she said it, she undid more of the buttons at her throat, they extended all the way to her waist.

She undid two more buttons.

"Tell me how it was to grow up with all those neighbors." she laughed. "Goodness, around here we have three hundred people and sometimes it seems tremendously crowded."

Again she undid more of the buttons.

"So what kind of a business does your father have?"

"He has several, really," Spur said. At first Spur thought she was just opening a few of the buttons down the front, now she kept moving her fingers, and the buttons opened lower and lower. He could see white fabric showing through the opening.

"Maggie . . ."

She smiled. "Spur McCoy, am I embarrassing you? They're just buttons. I'm still entirely covered. See." She spread apart the front of her dress and the white chemise was indeed covering her breasts.

"Really, Maggie, I don't think . . ."

"Hush, Spur McCoy. I told you I need you. I do. I'm going to show you just how much I need you." She shrugged out of the top of her dress, then in one quick move lifted the chemise over her head. She sat there calmly, bare now to the waist, her breasts still bouncing slightly from her motion.

The twin peaks were still pointed with youth, creamy white and tipped with soft pink areolas and small darker nipples. Before he could move, she scrambled forward and sat on his lap. She put her arms around his neck and kissed his cheek, then nibbled at his lips.

"Spur, darling Spur McCoy! I need you desperately. Don't you understand? Do I have to say it? Please, darling Spur!"

Spur groaned softly.

Maggie giggled. Her hand moved down by her hips and she touched his erection which was growing by the second.

"I can feel part of you who is glad to see me all bare. Do you like my titties?"

Spur could stand it no longer. He bent and kissed her breasts, then licked her nipples, slowly at first, than faster and faster as he saw them grow and enlarge. He held off as long as he could, then he sucked one of her luscious mounds into his mouth, and chewed and licked and ate her as Maggie moaned low in her throat and her hand rubbed at his crotch.

"Christ, we better at least lock the door," Spur said.

"I'll do it," Maggie said. She jumped off his lap, pushed him out of the straight chair and forced the back of it under the door knob and tilted, angled out resting only on the rear two legs. Then she took a key and locked the door and turned the key half a turn to leave it in the keyhole so no master key could be used.

Her breasts bounced and swayed and jiggled as Spur watched, his pressure building.

She came to him, and he lifted her off her feet, kissing her open mouth, his own mouth exploring hers as deeply as he could. She wiggled to be put down. Quickly she slid out of the dress, then four petticoats slipped away until she wore only billowy pink underpants that came to her knees. She jumped on the bed and patted the spot beside her.

"Now it's my turn to undress you," She said.

"Be gentle with me," Spur said and she laughed at him, then took off his vest and town shirt and marveled at the black hair on his chest. She toyed with it, tried to braid it, then kissed it and played with his man breasts.

His boots came next and then his pants. She stared in anticipation at the bulge in his short underpants, and when she pulled them down, she sat back and stared in frank admiration.

"I still don't understand how it can get so hard and stiff that way, and then just moments later he can be so tiny and short and soft."

"It's known as rising to the occasion," Spur said, enjoying himself. It was nice to be the one being seduced for a change. She pulled his underwear off his feet and sat on his stomach. Then slowly she bent over him until her breasts hung enticingly inches away from his mouth.

"Want a bite of a sweet cookie? I have chocolate on the right, and vanilla on the left."

He compromised by licking and chewing both.

She wiggled with delight, her still covered crotch dropping and grinding against his erection. She rolled over and pulled down the pink silk undergarment, then kicked it across the room.

She came to her knees beside him, her legs spread, the pink wetness of her slit showing past a brush of blonde curls. Slowly she pumped her hips forward, her crotch coming almost to his face as the opening puckered and opened.

She kissed his mouth hard and pulled away quickly.

"Darling Spur, I have three holes, which one do you want first? We're going to do all three tonight, I promise you!"

"You pick," he said, sitting up. She kissed his mouth again, then his chin and his neck, worked down a string of hot kisses cross his chest and his little belly and through the black hair around his crotch.

"First," she said, and slid her mouth around his pulsating penis.

Spur groaned with delight, his hips pumped upward and she sucked him in her mouth, gurgling as she pumped up and down. He came out of her mouth, rolled her over and knelt stradling her shoulders as she lay flat on her back. He slowly bent forward, inserting himself into her mouth. Her eyes went wide, then she nodded and took him as he provided the motion, gentle at first, pumping in and out of her mouth.

Sweat beaded her forehead. She moaned in joy as he worked faster and faster. Spur had always had a special feeling for making love this way. It meant a special commitment by the woman and he never forced one. But when she offered . . .

He felt the urgency building. Deep down the seeds of new life were stirring. Then he felt them surging forward, the undeniable journey had started. He groaned and bellowed in expectation as the pulsating came closer and closer. Then with one final surge he shouted six times, one for each spurt as he emptied himself and at the same time sensed she was swallowing and sucking at him.

He heaved once more and lifted away from her, rolling over on his back, panting like a steam engine gushing out hot breath and dragging in new air to feed his starved cells.

She snuggled against him, taking one of his hands and cupping it around her breast. He massaged her mound gently and she purred.

"Was that good?" she asked.

"Great, the best ever. You are marvelous. How did you learn to be so good?"

"Nobody has to learn, it's natural. Everyone can fuck good. How else would we have so many people? Nobody teaches the animals. I've seen them on the ranches."

They both laughed. Then she took his hand and brought it down to her crotch. "Do me," she said softly.

"What?"

"Rub me, play my little guitar, strum me! Make me go out of my mind!"

She put his finger on her clit and he explored a moment, found the right spot and began twanging her. After only a dozen strokes she was wailing and pumping her hips against him. Then she screeched softly, and he saw that she had her face in the pillow. Her whole body rattled and vibrated like an earthquake, shaking like she was going to come apart. She gasped and shivered.

Slowly her wails into the pillow slacked off, and her hips slowed in their tattoo against him. At last she reached down and pulled his hand away from her and gave a long, slow sigh before she reached up and kissed his cheek.

"It's so much better when a man does me that way," she said, then she heaved a sigh and went to sleep. Her face still had a soft smile on it.

Spur lay there holding her in his arms as she slept. He grinned, afraid to move, not wanting to awaken her. At last he moved slightly and she awoke and sat up. She watched him a minute, then grinned.

"Don't mind me," she said. I always nod off for a minute after I have a good one. You did me just great!" She laughed at the surprise on his face. Slowly she reached over and kissed him, then her hands were busy at his crotch. Her hands had a marvelous effect on him.

"Come on, Big Boy, you've had enough rest. It's playtime again, playpen time. The choices are now down to two."

Spur leaned back, put his hands under his head and relaxed. It was going to be a great night, and this was only the start. If somebody was planning on blowing him into pieces tonight in his bed, they would have a surprise. This was the best defensive move he had made since coming to town, and certainly the one that he had enjoyed the most.

Unless, of course, Maggie was the one who wanted to blow his brains out.

6

Spur had always thought of himself as a light sleeper. In the wilderness he would wake up if an Indian came within a hundred yards of his camp.

He had to rethink his ability the next morning when he woke up about six A.M. and the tall blonde with the short cut hair was gone from the room. She was not only gone, she had moved out. Nothing that was hers seemed to still be there, but his clothes, his guns and his purse were untouched.

Spur got back to his own room, shaved and dressed in his town clothes, a clean shirt and lightweight doeskin brown vest and dark brown pants. He gave up on the string tie and went down for breakfast when the dining room opened at seven.

Maggie was not there. Strange. Interesting girl, but a little on the weird side. She had been delightful when it came to making love.

Right after a stack of buckwheat cakes and syrup covered with three sunnyside-up eggs,

Spur went to see a man represented as the best lawyer in town. His name was Irvin Dunlap, and he had been practicing law in La Grande since the area became a territory back in 1848.

A wooden ramp led up the two steps into the lawyer's office. Spur went in and talked with a young law clerk who said Mr. Dunlap was busy, but he would be free to consult with Spur in ten minutes. Spur took a walk up and down the three block long business district, noticing nothing unusual or different from most frontier towns. The people were a bit more friendly, he decided, but that was about it.

Back in the law office, Spur walked into the private room and found Irvin Dunlap sitting in a wheel chair. He introduced himself, shook hands and grinned.

"Been several people wondering about you, Mr. McCoy. If I had to guess, I'd say you were a Federal man interested in what happened to the General Land Office and all those records."

Spur laughed. "Remind me to get you to defend me in Oregon if I ever have the need," Spur said. "You're partly right, Mr. Dunlap. I am interested in those records. For example, I have a long time deed to property up the valley a ways, but I've lost my piece of paper. How do I prove it's mine?"

"Be damn hard. I'm trying to put together some stopgap procedures such as filing of affidavits by at least six unrelated individuals who will swear as to ownership and approximate boundaries."

"Stopgap sounds right. Who settles disputes?"

"We haven't got that far yet. I'm trying to work with the state legislature and the state's attorney general. It's all up in the air."

"Heard anything from the Land Grant people in Washington?" Spur asked.

"I notified them of the fire, nothing else. If you're from there you're the first one."

"They at least should have records in Washington D.C. of all land grant activity, homesteads, leases, land sales. Or do they?" Spur was puzzled.

"We think so. But frankly, Mr. McCoy, by the time any such proof gets here, we could have a land fight that will rank right next to the Civil War."

"Who in the county stands to benefit most by the destruction of the records, Mr. Dunlap?"

"Ah ha! The true colors start to show. Figured you were Federal but I just didn't have any idea in what capacity. Now I've got it pegged. You're enforcement. You're here to find out who set the place on fire, and how Jonas was killed. At least I have that worked out."

"Right, Mr. Dunlap, but I'd appreciate your not spreading it around. I suppose you know that the records were not just burned, they were *systematically destroyed* by burning. You may have tried to burn paper, packed together paper. It's hard to burn it up completely unless it is stirred around and separated."

"Agreed. I took a look at the remains over there, too."

"So who will be the big winner?"

"The ones who always win, the entrenched, well established land owners. Cattle ranchers, the timbermen who are just waiting for a railroad to cut through here so they can get their lumber shipped out. Those are the big winners. They can bloat their ownership by hundreds of thousands of acres and no one can say that they are over-stating the truth. This could be a headache, a morass of conflict and lawsuits for generations."

"RimRock Ranch?"

"Of course, the largest in the county and the other huge one, the Twin O Ranch run by Travis Odell. Both outfits have ownership of about five thousand acres. But, like others, they have been grazing public lands so long they sometimes think it's theirs. Now I don't know where the homesteaders will settle down. How can they tell what's left to homestead?"

Dunlap rolled in his chair to the window and looked out on Main Street.

"Damn, I wish this hadn't happened. Without those records a lot of people are going to lose what little they own. We're going to see the biggest case of land grab greed that's ever taken place. And I don't have a prayer of an idea how to stop it." He shook his head, then rolled back.

"Frankly, I've been expecting you. I've got a letter for you here to Judge Farley Inglesia. He's the circuit court judge making his rounds, and he's here for two more days. Take this over to the county office where we have our one court room, and see if you can talk to him. In this letter are my suggestions for putting the stopgap plan into action.

"Talk to Judge Inglesia. He's a smart man, and a fair one. He might have some ideas."

Spur tried. A law clerk took the letter to the judge along with Spur's invitation to dinner. He had to eat after the morning session. Ten minutes later the clerk came back with a handwritten note.

"Dear Mr. McCoy. I must work through my

noon meal. I can tell you nothing more about the local land record problem. Mr. Dunlap is the local expert. Go with his suggestions. Good luck in your work."

Spur changed plans, had a quick bowl of soup at a cafe and went to the La Grande Stables. He rented a horse and saddle, and a 7-shot Spencer repeating rifle. Then he got directions to the RimRock Ranch, and turned the big roan upstream along the Grande Ronde river.

The stable man told him it was about eight miles to the ranch. It took Spur two hours to ride there, including the time he got lost. He could see the big overhead archway type gate at the ranch just off the main trail. He turned that way and saw a rider swing away from a cluster of cattle and ride to meet him.

"Howdy," the ranch hand said.

"Afternoon," Spur said. "This the RimRock Ranch spread?"

"Peers as how."

"Good. I need to talk with Wade Smith."

"He's up at the main ranchhouse. I'll be glad to show you the way."

Spur wasn't sure if it was an escort or a guard who rode with him, but both purposes were served. The man led him to a wide veranda that looked out on the Grande Ronde river less than a quarter of a mile away.

A small, heavyset man with arms as thick as cedar fenceposts worked over a battered oak desk. He looked up as they came on the veranda.

"Mr. Smith, you have a visitor," the hand said.

"Thanks, Bert," Smith said. He stood and held out a rope and rein in a gnarled right hand. "Smith is my name," he said.

"Mr. Smith. I'm Spur McCoy." They shook.

"Yep, heard you were in town. Got to be something to do with the Land Office, right?"

"That's one of the things I like about a small community, Mr. Smith. Actually I'm not from the Land Office."

"Oh. Well, fine. What can I do for you?"

"Do you know who killed Jonas King?"

"Killed? I thought it was an accident?"

"That's what the killer wanted everyone to think. The fires got so hot so quickly he didn't have a chance to take away two gallon cans that had been filled with coal oil. Also, Dr. George told me that the burned body had the odor of kerosene on it, and the residual matter from burned kerosene as well. Someone deliberately poured the fluid on the body to burn it beyond recognition."

"Who the hell would do that?" Wade Smith asked. "Certainly not me, or any of my hands."

"Mr. Smith, who would benefit most if all of the county and federal land records for the county were destroyed?"

"The biggest land owners in the county. Me and Travis Odell."

"Exactly. Without those records, proof of ownership could be in the courts for twenty years in this county. We need to do something about it."

"And the rich get richer. As well as homesteading would come to a halt," Wade Smith said. "Nobody would know what land was available."

"Which would never make a big rancher angry. Mr. Wade, I want to enlist your help."

"Hell no! I ain't gonna help tie the noose to

hang myself with. Not a chance in hell! You come out here and practically tell me I'm suspect in a killing, and then tell me you want me to find out who did it. Hell no! Now you get yourself off my spread before I sic one of my boys on your tail. You rode on here nice and peaceful. Now you go get on your horse and you ride off the same way."

"I'm not accusing you of anything, Mr. Smith."

"Daddy?" a woman's voice came from the door into the house. A woman stood there, looking into the veranda. "Daddy, I thought I heard another voice. I just don't understand this at all. You should have told me we had company."

Spur turned, the voice vaguely familiar. When the woman came in the light of the porch he saw the tall, slender form, then the short blonde hair. Maggie! She was the same girl who had invited him to her room and into her bed last night! She smiled formally at him and looked at her father with more than a little touch of impatience.

"You could introduce us, Father."

"No sense, Mr. McCoy was just leaving."

"Oh, Mr. McCoy." She held out her hand. "It's nice to meet you, Mr. McCoy. I'm Margaret Smith."

Spur was jolted by the surprise. From naked in bed with her ten hours ago to this formal introduction was such a surprise that it was almost more than he could believe. But she was the same woman. The short blonde hair, direct, piercing brown eyes, and the quick smile. He even knew how she looked under her cool blue dress.

"Mr. McCoy, we get visitors so seldom, I do hope that you can stay to supper."

"No, Margaret. I told you, Mr. McCoy is just

leaving. There's no cause for you to be here."

Spur at last found his voice.

"Yes, Miss Smith, I'm sorry, but I do have business back in town. Perhaps I could invite you to supper sometime at the hotel. I hear they have some excellent dishes."

"Oh, I'm sorry. I don't get into town much."

"Good bye, Mr. McCoy," Wade Smith said sharply. "A shame you had the long ride for nothing."

"Quite to the contrary, Mr. Smith. I have learned a lot. I'll be talking with you later." he turned to Margaret. "Miss Smith, that supper invitation is open any time. I'm staying at the Grande Ronde Hotel."

He turned and walked out of the house. Margaret started to follow, but a curt command by her father stopped her. By then Spur was off the veranda.

Spur's horse was where he had left it. The rider who brought him in was waiting to escort him out to the gate. Spur noticed that the man had a six-gun on his left hip and a Winchester in his boot. The man was a guard after all. They said little as they rode to the gate.

They had just passed the gate, when the cowboy held up his hand and they both stopped. The man eyed Spur with more than a little anger.

"Mr. Smith has a message for you, big man. He says don't come back on RimRock Ranch land again, unless you're asked. And don't under any circumstances try to see or talk to his daughter. He wants you to understand them two points real good. You do understand them?"

"Yes, understood. Now, I have a message for Mr. Smith. You tell him I'll go on anybody's land where I think I need to go, and my two buddies, Mr. Spencer and Mr. Colt, will be with me. As far as his daughter goes, that will be strictly up to the lady. Whatever she wants to do is fine with me."

Spur turned and rode away.

He was two miles from the ranch gate, just riding down into a low spot where the trail wound near to a bend in the Grande Ronde River, when a rifle shot jolted into the quiet countryside. Spur heard the flutter of the air as the round passed within two feet of him. He dove off the horse to the left and rolled toward some rocks left exposed by the river at flood stage. It was two feet high.

Two more rifle shots sent hot lead toward him. One round went over the rocks, the second hit the granite and shattered. Spur looked around the rock and saw the faint trails of blue gunpowder smoke two hundred yards to the left, slightly above him in a heavy stand of pine. Two more shots sounded and the bullets sang overhead.

He was pinned down. There was no place to move to that would give him any protection. All the bushwhackers had to do was work around behind him and shoot him full of lead!

7

Spur ducked as a rifle round sang off the rock and careened away into the high plateau of Eastern Oregon. He had just been shot at from ambush. He dove off his horse and now evaluated his situation. One gun or two out there? He figured two. They had the high ground and cover. He had a six-gun and not much to go on.

His rifle! He had to have the Spencer or they could circle around and cut him to pieces. His roan mare stood munching on spring grass ten yards toward the trees. The Spencer rested in the boot on Spur's side of the mount. With three strides he could put the horse between himself and the rifles on the slope.

There was nothing else to think about. Spur leaped to his feet, boots churning the ground as he darted to his horse, grabbed the reins and ran with the big roan mare. She half dragged him but he kept up with her by jerking back on the reins. With one hand, he pulled the Spencer from the boot and kept running.

Three shots sounded and he felt one tick his boot as he ran. Then a fourth shot came and the mare bellowed in rage and stumbled. She crashed into Spur, spinning him away as she fell, rolling once, scrambling to her feet and galloping straight downstream as fast as she could go.

Spur shook his head, rolled and came into a crouch, the Spencer still in his left hand, his right checking the six gun to be sure it was still holstered.

Dirt spurted in front of him from a rifle slug. He darted the other way, got his bearings and rushed twenty feet to the side of the river where the stream had cut a six-foot gorge in the land that was now a dry former water course.

He dove the last six feet as four more rifle shots sprayed around him. He rolled over the lip and fell to a ledge and scrambled to his feet. He was out of sight, and unhurt.

Spur knew the mare had moved downstream. He could get her later. He was more interested in identifying at least one of the men bushwhacking him. He ran upstream where the gully swung close to the pine grove.

Five minutes later he was out of the dry stream bed and into the timber. He moved swiftly now, taking care not to make any noise as he ran through the typical eastern Oregon pine woods. There was little brush, almost no hardwoods, just the pines growing straight and tall.

After moving fifty yards forward, he stopped and peered around a two-foot thick Ponderosa. Ahead he could hear someone talking. He made sure the rifle had a round in the chamber and was ready to fire, then he ran with the weapon at high port, gliding from one tree to the next, moving toward the voices.

Another twenty yards ahead he paused. He could see through a slight clearing to the fringe of trees along the edge of the grove. Two men lay along the downslope watching the river.

"Hell, he's long gone by now," one said.

"Not a hindtail chance. He's the kind who comes after guys who hurt him, and we hurt him. He's on foot. Ain't nothing makes a cowboy madder than a wet hen than to have to walk. He'll be coming."

"You watching our arse-end backside?"

"Now and then."

Spur slid to the ground and lifted the Spencer. He sighted in on the closest man and his finger began to tighten on the trigger. He wanted to blast both of them straight into hell, but he relaxed. He was a lawman.

McCoy kept the man in his sights and yelled out his warning.

"Don't move either one of you, I've got you covered. You're both under arrest."

At the first words, one man rolled out of sight behind a log. The second one tried the other direction but there was no cover. Spur slammed two shots at him as he moved, the second one plunged into his stomach, slanted upward through his lung and cut his heart in half.

Spur was up and running. The second man had vanished. A moment later Spur heard the sound of hooves on the soft pine woods floor and the second bushwhacker rode off through the trees. There was no chance for even one shot.

The Secret Agent went back to the first man and checked him. He was dead. Spur found the man's horse where it had been left and brought it back. He tied the dead man over the horse just behind the saddle, mounted and rode for town.

He found his roan mare a mile down the river munching on new grass. She had a bullet crease across her rear quarters, but was not hurt seriously. She let him ride up and tie her reins to his saddle.

There was no chance to identify the man who got away, but someone in town should know this one.

An hour later, Spur tied up both horses at the sheriff's office. Half a dozen men gathered round the deadman. The sheriff came out, glanced at Spur, then went to the corpse and lifted the head so he could see his face.

"Tex Abbot. Been around town for a year or so. Works now and again as a ranch hand. Never been steady with any spread. Heard he was good with his six-gun. Guess he wasn't good enough." The sheriff told one of the gawkers to take the body over to the undertaker, and motioned Spur inside.

Spur told the story to a grim sheriff.

"Far as I know, Wade Smith could have sent him after me, told him to wait until I got off the RRR land and fill me with lead."

"Not likely. Smith don't go for Texans, likes to keep his crew all northerners. Besides, he never uses part timers. He hires on a hand, he stays on year round."

Spur sighed and stood up. "You do the paper and I'll sign it, Sheriff. This don't help me much on my problem. Oh, the horse and saddle were his. That should pay for his burying. I got to get my nag back to the livery."

The dead man helped little. If Spur had

wounded him he could have made him tell who hired the pair. Damnit!

He couldn't help but think about Maggie Margaret Smith. She must sneak into town for a fling now and then. It was obvious that her father kept a tight rein on her. When she got the chance to come to town she let out all of her frustrations. He wondered why she wasn't married and settled down. But he knew. No one in the area was "good enough" for Wade Smith's darling.

Spur went to the doctor office where he talked with the widow King again. She was sitting up now and some of the bandages were gone from her face. Her right hand had not been burned but the rest of that arm was still covered.

"Mr. McCoy, I've been remembering things. Jonas told me he was worried about something and was going to write a letter to Washington D.C. He never said what it was about."

"We got the letter, it has helped. That's why I'm here."

"Good. That night of the fire, I remember that Jonas was working late. He said he had some more county work to do. He was looking forward to the special election to name a new county clerk. The former one got so sick he had to quit."

Spur handed her a glass of water. She went on.

"That night I kept hearing people talking. It wasn't all that late, but people did come to do business at night when they saw Jonas working. But when I woke up much later, I could smell something. It was kerosene! The whole upstairs seemed to smell of kerosene. Then the flames came and I had to run down the stairs. That's when I got burned. Could it have been kerosene?"

"Yes, Mrs. Jonas. We're convinced that someone deliberately set the fire, and they also killed your husband. It wasn't just an accident."

"Oh no!" tears seeped from her eyes onto the bandages.

"I'm sorry, Mrs. King. I'm going to bring them to justice. Is there anything else you remember about that night?"

"No, but that was the same day that the Englishman came in. He wanted a map of the county and thought it would be free. Jonas said he was rude, not at all like he imagined a titled Englishman should behave."

"An Englishman. How long has he been in town?"

"Maybe a month or so. Jonas said the talk is that he's looking for a cattle ranch to buy. But mostly he sits in the hotel or on the veranda watching the people walk by."

"Interesting. Mrs. King, do you remember your husband saying anything about disputes over land ownership lately? Did anyone come in for copies of his deed to prove ownership?"

She shook her head. "Not recently."

Spur thanked her, said goodbye and went to the hotel for a change of shirt, and then supper in the dining room. He had completely missed his noon feeding time somehow.

After supper, Spur smoked a long, thin, black cigar as he sat on the veranda and watched the sun go own. He had thought through the case but had little more to go on. The big ranchers were still the ones who would profit most by the land records problem.

He gave up on it and went to the Sagebrush Saloon for a drink. The singer, Colette Paris came by and sat at his table.

She smiled at him. "I hope you don't mind. I just had to get out of that little dressing room, they gave me. I'm not due to go on for another half hour. I could use a sarsaparilla. Anything else is hard on my voice."

Spur went to the bar and brought her back one of the carbonated, non-alcoholic drinks. "It's a beautiful voice. How come you're doing the Wild West circuit?"

"Reasons. Partly because I got tired of the eastern cities and the crazy people who live there."

"Except New York," Spur said.

She laughed. "Yes, except New York."

"How long will you be here?"

"A week, maybe two weeks. Depends how long Lefty can keep on making money with me. When he starts losing money, I move on to the next town."

"Pendleton," Spur said remembering the next little town toward Portland.

"Wherever, it really doesn't matter."

"You don't have a husband or a fiance somewhere, then?"

"No."

Before she could elaborate, John Ringo came into the saloon. Everyone knew at once that John had arrived.

"Where the hell's the big money action in this town? I want to play me some goddamned poker!"

He looked around, saw Colette and barged up to the table. He ignored Spur, looked at Colette and sat down quickly.

Spur could see the man was drunk, but this one

was more dangerous and a better shot drunk than sober.

"Well, if it ain't the little pussy who threw her drink in my face. Now that ain't nice. Didn't your mamma ever tell you that? But, what the hell, we'll forget all about that. Why don't we dance?"

"There isn't any music."

"Then get the piano player to play something. Have him play *Harvest Moon's Courting Time*. I like that one."

"We don't have a piano player here."

"Damnit! why not? Hell, we'll just go upstairs and I'll unwrap your pretty little package and we'll have a wild time in bed."

"You must be out of your mind. Get away from me!"

John Ringo laughed, stood, swept the small girl up in his arms as she hit him with her small, ineffectual fists.

"Now, calm down little hellcat. Enough time to do all that when I'm laying on top of you."

Spur stood and faced Ringo. "Put her down, John. The lady isn't going anywhere."

Ringo focused on Spur, seeing him for the first time. "Shut up, asshole! This is none of your business. Go fuck yourself!"

Spur swung his right fist with all his two hundred pounds behind it. Ringo had no way to defend himself. The big fist collided with his jaw, powering him backwards. His hands sagged, dropping Colette. Spur jumped forward and caught her just before she hit the floor. He was back on his feet in seconds.

But there was no fight left in John Ringo. He sat on the floor holding his jaw, then he began to weave and fell on his face on the planks.

Spur stood up Colette and knelt beside Ringo. He pulled his hands behind him and tied Ringo's wrists together with a length of rawhide he took from his pocket.

"Go get the sheriff," Spur said, snapping the order to a man standing nearby. The man stood up straighter as if he had been in the Army.

"Yes sir!" he said and ran out the front door.

Spur rolled John Ringo over. He was still unconscious. Spur picked up a half filled mug of beer from the table and poured it in the outlaw's face.

Ringo came to sputtering and swearing. When he saw he was on the floor and his hands tied he screamed in fury.

When he quieted, Spur knelt beside him. "Ringo, you're drunk and you're going to jail."

"What for?"

"Drunk and disorderly, and assault and battery on a female."

"Didn't hit her. What the hell you mean? She's a fucking saloon girl!"

Sheriff Younger came in and scowled down at Ringo. The county lawman motioned Spur to one side. "What the hell you doing? I'm hoping Ringo will ride out of here in a day or two. What did he do?"

Spur told Sheriff Younger. "You jail him now, or I'm swearing out a warrant for him myself. Take your pick."

Younger shrugged. "Help me get him to a cell. And you better be there tomorrow when I let him out. I'll hold him overnight, but after that he's gonna be gunning for your hide, not mine. I'll make that damn plain."

"I bet you will, Sheriff. You're all guts. Let's

get him into a cell and then worry about it."

Just before they led Ringo out of the place, Colette touched Spur's arm. "Thank you, Spur McCoy," she said softly. "I owe you, and I am a person who always pays my debts."

Spur touched his hat and led John Ringo to jail.

8

Sir Jeffrey Mountbatten sat at the small table in the suite of rooms at the Grande Ronde hotel. Half of it was covered with books, and papers and directly under the lamp lay a document with fancy borders and scrolled work that looked as if it had all been done by hand with a quill pen.

Sir Jeffrey picked it up and a look of awe covered his face.

"It's beautiful! Magnificent. The man who did this was really a great artist. He probably painted nights and holidays on his 'better quality work' which never sold. These certificates he made for a living. Extraordinary!"

Edward Long lounged on the couch in the middle room of the suite, the sitting room. He was buried in a dime novel featuring "Wild Zack and His Daring Rescue." He cocked an eye at sir Jeffrey.

"Done with the bloomin' thing yet, mate?"

"Done? Gads, man. This is a lifetime of work here. It has to be right or we might as well give

up. Another half hour and I should be done with
it."

"About time. You file it with the judge
tomorrow?"

"Maybe, maybe. I want it to be perfect."

Painstakingly he traced in the last of the border
work. He leaned back and inspected it. Yes, good.
The printing had been done somewhere in
Missouri with old English block letters and
looked absolutely genuine. It only had to go back
to the year 1845, not even thirty years ago.

He compared his work with an engraving in a
book, and smiled. Yes. It might not fool the
experts in the Tower of London, but out here in
the backside of America, it would take months,
perhaps years to disprove this certificate.

"Edward, see you're lifting the level of your
reading. Up to the trashy dime novels, I see.
Good lad. When we come into our fortune, you
can buy some real books."

"Where would we keep them, guv'nor, in your
carpetbag? We're not the type to carry too much
luggage, especially when we're running to catch a
stage or a train."

"Once you have money, dingo, nobody cares
where it came from. Just having it is what's
important. You'll see. We'll go back to New York
and set up a flat and be the rage of the town's
social season. We can do that with money.
Especially here in the colonies."

Sir Jeffrey filled in the missing date by hand,
since that was how the rest of the certificates had
been drawn. There was little left to do. He would
keep the finished document in the sun in the
morning to help yellow it just a bit and to heat in
the new ink and give it a touch of age. Not too

much, it was supposed to be only thirty years old. The parchment paper he had used would be almost impossible to assign a date to, no matter how hard they tried.

His ink was of the oldest variety he could find in London. This was an operation that had been planned well in advance. And within a week at the most, the juicy plums would start falling into their grasp!

He pushed the parchment aside, carefully put away the two books and the letters and samples, and then stared down at the parchment with satisfaction. It was going to work! They had a shot at becoming millionaires! A million dollars, American. Two hundred thousand pounds sterling! The sum was staggering.

He put everything away, locked the cases and made sure the parchment lay between clean pillowcases to prevent any damage. Tomorrow he would give it the sun treatment, then perhaps present it. The Circuit Court judge would not be in La Grande much longer.

Edward checked his pocket watch, put away his novel and straightened up the room. Sir Jeffrey hardly noticed. When the knock came on the door, Sir Jeffrey scowled.

"Not again, you didn't invite that whore here again tonight!" Sir Jeffrey whined.

"No," Edward said, grinning. He swung open the door. "I invited two fresh ones, one for you, one for me. No, no, old friend, don't thank me. Just take your pick, and hurry into your room with her. These two are both hot and we don't want them to cool down."

The two saloon girls rushed into the room, spun around, and then began undressing. Sir Jeffrey cowered against a chair.

"Edward! You know perfectly well that I don't care for this sort of thing."

"He's shy, ladies. Takes a bit of warming up." Edward pulled Sir Jeffrey to the side of the room. "The taller one is yours. She's not a big titted whore. Brought her for you. She's got such small tits you'll think she's a boy. Roll her over on her belly and have at her hard little ass. You'll think she's a sixteen year old lad, you will. Now have a go at her. If that don't work she's got a well trained mouth, I can vouch for that. You can do a little putting instead of taking, old man!"

By this time both girls were naked, prancing around the middle of the room. Edward grabbed the one with breasts and vanished into one of the bedrooms.

The tall, thin girl came up to Sir Jeffrey and rubbed his crotch. Then she knelt in front of him and had his fly open before he knew what was happening. Sir Jeffrey closed his eyes as she stripped him and led him into the other bedroom.

Edward had been right. With his eyes closed she did feel like a ripe young sixteen year old male ruffian from London. It might not be such a wasted night after all.

It was nearly eight-thirty that evening when someone knocked hard on the Presidential suite door. Neither Sir Jeffrey nor Edward wanted to answer it. After eight knockings, with each one becoming more insistent, Edward pulled on his britches and went to the door.

A tall, thin man with a three day stubble of beard pushed into the room. His hands hung at the end of long arms like afterthoughts. His eyes roamed the room, then stopped at Edward.

"Where's the rest of my money?" the man said, his voice a rasping, unhealthy sound.

"Digger, you fucking idiot! You got your money. Why are you bothering us?"

The hands shot upward, caught around Edward's throat and squeezed suddenly and hard. At once Edward's eyes bulged, he couldn't breathe and began wheezing and gasping. His arms flailed at the man. One fist hit the tall man's eye and he let go of Edward and turned away to the side.

They stared at each other. Edward at last got his breath back and the tall man held one hand over his wounded eye.

"My money," the man Edward called Digger snarled. "You still owe me fifty dollars."

"Maybe so. Let me talk to my partner." Edward pulled open Sir Jeffrey's door. He was just coming away from the woman who lay on the bed on her stomach.

"Thought you'd like that," Edward said with a knowing grin. Then he frowned. "There's a bloke out here who claims we still owe him fifty dollars. Didn't you pay Digger the whole thing three weeks ago?"

Sir Jeffrey shook his head. "We were short, remember? He's here? Pay him and get him on his way to Portland. Do it right now!"

"I thought he was out of the state by now," Edward said. "Damn! Got to do every bloody thing myself." He went out banging the door. Sir Jeffrey shrugged and crawled back on the bed.

"Now show me that trick you have of getting me ready to go again fast!"

In the next room, Edward dug into his poke and

came up with two double eagles and a gold eagle and gave them to the tall, thin man.

"I want you on the first stage out of here in the morning, do you understand?" Edward said.

Digger stared at the money and ignored him.

Edward grabbed a knife from his pocket, snapped open the blade and pressed it against the tall man's throat.

"Mate, I'll tell you once more, then I'll save me fifty dollars. You be on that stage coach for Portland in the morning the way we agreed, right?"

Slowly the man's anger faded enough so he could nod. He grunted an assent.

"Now get your bloody arse out of here, and use the back stairs. If I see you anywhere near this hotel or us again, I'll slice your throat from ear to ear, mate. You understand what I'm telling you?"

"Yes. I waited for the money. Your fault, not mine." The man glared at Edward, turned and went out the door. He continued down the back stairs, anxious not to be seen by the hotel people. They had thrown him out several times. He did not like any of them.

Nobody ever liked him. Wasn't his fault. They were afraid of him. Not very many, he hadn't hurt very many of them. When he did they stayed hurt. He laughed, remembering the fire. Now that had been fun! He liked to watch things burn.

Just because people called him Digger wasn't his fault, either. So he dug the graves out at the cemetery. Somebody had to do it. They paid him a dollar for every one, digging and filling in. He even had a little house out in back of the grave-yard. Just one room and he made it himself. He didn't have to pay rent.

Damn, that fire had been fun! He wasn't sure
what the other two guys were doing, but he had
sure as shit burned down that fucking house in
good order! Yeah! He thought about it and
remembered how it was, and soon he was
breathing faster and faster. He realized he was
getting all heated up. Damn prick stood straight
up inside his pants! A fire, yeah, he *needed*
another goddamned fucking it to hell fire!

Digger ran now, straight back to his shack
behind the graves. He took out the two one-gallon
cans of kerosene, the kind everybody had for their
lamps. He shook them. Both were full. Yeah, he
had filled them just yesterday down at the hardware store. They had a big barrel out on the back
dock.

Digger grinned as he lifted the cans. One might
do it, this time. No, he wouldn't be inside, he
better take two. He felt along the inside of the
shack up high where he kept the matches. He
didn't want no mouse to bite into a match and
burn down his shack!

The tall, gaunt man with dirt from today's
grave still on his pants, carried the two gallons of
coal oil as he walked down one alley after another
trying to pick a good house to burn down. He
wanted just a house, not the whole town. Lordy,
he couldn't stand it if more than one place burned
at a time! Both his hand and his prick would just
wear out!

Digger laughed. It had been two or three weeks
since he'd laughed.

The big house on the corner looked like a good
one. All wood and white paint, two stories tall,
and already the lights were out in the big house.
He had no idea who lived there. It would make a

beautiful fire, and everyone could see from all around. He walked past it, then went into the alley behind it and melted into a shadow.

Digger was good at waiting. He had to do a lot of waiting in his business. He had learned to be patient. An hour after he got there he saw someone come home to the big house. Lights flared, and burned for two more hours. Then, about midnight the last lamp was blown out on the second floor.

He gave them another half hour to get to sleep, then moved cautiously through shadows to the side of the house. One window had not been locked. He lifted it silently, cautiously and looked inside. A sitting room. Curtains. He reached inside and splashed half the gallon of coal oil and let it soak into the rug and furniture.

Then he went to the other side of the house. The window he wanted was locked. He took off his shirt and held it against the glass, then broke it with one sharp, powerful blow from the side of his fist. The glass broke, but the sound had been deadened by the cloth. Quickly he dumped the rest of the first gallon of kerosene inside, then put his shirt back on. He went to the back porch. Porches were always good. He tried the screen door. It was held by a hook and eye. With his knife he slit the screen wire and lifted the hook free. The door swung open.

Inside the back porch, he poured out two quarts of the kerosene, then left the can half filled beside the wall. Now he lit the fuel, and tore up some newspapers to help it burn.

Digger ran to each side of the house, firing the evaporating coal oil with burning newspapers. Then he walked away rapidly. He was a block away when he saw flames behind him. They shot out a window on the side of the house.

Someone screamed. He sat down on a small lawn a block away and watched. It was past midnight.

Digger heard more screams coming from down the block. Then men appeared from houses. They were wearing trousers, pajamas and slippers. Each man carried two or more buckets and ran quickly toward the fire.

The tall, thin man with the sunken eyes and nervous, claw like hands walked that way. Five minutes later he was in a line running buckets of water to the house. There was no chance to save it.

After half an hour the whole upper floor was burning. One man had jumped from the second floor. He had a broken leg.

"My wife's still up there!" he screamed again and again. Two men held him down so he wouldn't try to hobble back into the fire to find his wife.

Digger sat on the lawn across the street with a dozen or so other men from the bucket brigade. All were soaked and sweating; smoke clouded their eyes and black smudges showed on their clothes.

"Hell, we tried," one man said.

Digger nodded. "Damn right, we tried."

9

From the county jail, Spur went back to the
Sagebrush Saloon to check on the girl, be sure she
was all right, and he wanted to hear her sing
again. He enjoyed it. There wasn't a lot of enter-
tainment on the range out here. Half the men
evidently in town felt the same way.

The Sagebrush was packed when he walked in
the front door. Men sat on the stairs, stood
shoulder to shoulder in front of the stage and
those at the tables in back had to stand up to see
when Colette came out and played her fanfare on
the old piano.

Everyone in the bar went as silent as a silver
moon on a clear lake.

"Good evening, gentlemen. I'm glad that you
came to hear me sing. Don't be bashful about
buying your favorite refreshment while you're
here. I also invite you to feed the kitty on the bar
if you like my singing. Just between you and me,
I don't share that kitty with Lefty who owns this
place." The audience laughed and the kitty began

making the rounds.

Colette romped into a dozen songs, mostly old favorites the men knew, as well as a few Civil War songs and a new tune or two that none of them had heard before.

The half hour of singing and piano playing was over too quickly and the men coaxed another five minutes of song from her. Twice she had caught Spur's eye while she sang. He had been standing at the back beside the bar.

Lefty came down the bar, wiped the spot in front of Spur and set out a cold bottle of beer.

"Courtesy of Colette," he said softly. "She says if you have a minute she would like to talk to you in her dressing room after the show. Usually I don't let anybody in there, but with you I guess it will be all right."

Spur took the cold beer with him and went through a small door at the side of the bar. It opened on a short hall with two doors. One was open and he saw Colette sitting in front of a mirror inside. When she saw him she stood and smiled.

"I want to thank you for saving my skin tonight. Nobody has had the nerve to handle John Ringo the way you did. He was going to rape me, you know."

"Yes, it occurred to me."

"My last show is a ten-thirty. I hope you can be here. I want you to walk me back to my hotel. I don't like being out late at night and alone. It's only two blocks, but . . ."

"I'll be here. Looks like you'll have a job here at the Sagebrush for quite a while. The men love hearing you sing and play."

"Good. Only then I'll have to get some new

dresses. I can't show up on stage every night in the same old clothes."

"Tough problem," Spur said grinning.

"Nice kind of problem to have." She walked near him and put one hand behind Spur's neck and pulled his face down to meet hers. She stood on tiptoe and kissed his lips softy, then let him go.

"That's a first thank you. Now I usually try to have a small nap between shows. Idea! here's twenty dollars. Play poker with it for me and see if I win anything. That will give you something to do between shows."

"Fair enough. Maybe we'll get lucky tonight." She smiled. I hope so."

Back in the saloon and gaming house, the crowd had thinned out to a normal number, and Spur found an empty chair at a small stakes poker game. No bet over a dollar. He sat down, got change and concentrated on his poker.

He used only her double eagle as his stake, and before the last show was announced at ten-thirty, he had almost fifty dollars on the table in front of him. The game broke up and he took Colette's winnings and moved closer to the stage.

It was a great performance, with half the songs new. Colette seemed to know almost every popular song that the men requested during that part of her show.

Again the bar was filled shoulder to shoulder, and the extra barkeep was kept busy selling drinks along with Lefty. When the show was over most of the patrons finished their drinks and left. It was eleven o'clock, late for a farming, ranch oriented kind of people who lived in La Grande.

Spur sat at the end of the bar near the small

door and waited. Ten minutes after the show ended, Colette came out wearing the same dress. She now sported a small hat over her long black hair.

"Ready for your guard duty?" she asked smiling.

"Anytime you are."

She said good night to Lefty, told him she would be back at eight-thirty the next evening and they went out the door. She put her hand out holding his bent arm, and looked up at him.

"I really appreciate this. I still get the shivers remembering how easily John Ringo picked me up. I was paralyzed."

"Think about something else, like the twenty dollars that grew into fifty for you tonight. You won thirty dollars!"

"That's a whole month's wages! I should stake you every night." She shook her head. "No, I can't do that. I'm still upset about John Ringo."

"Think about something else."

"Home. I usually think about home. I guess I miss the storms most, those fierce storms that sweep in from the Atlantic in winter, smashing things, battering the cliffs, changing the coastline. It generates an excitement in the whole town. You never know if you're going to be washed away or blown away."

"Sounds like a place I'll stay away from."

"You would love it. Don't you like a noisy thunder and lightning storm? All that power, that force, and puny little man is down here looking up and hoping a lightning bolt doesn't hit his house or barn."

"I admit I enjoy a good lightning display."

"I'm here at the Grande Ronde Hotel, she said.

Second floor."

"That's a popular floor. What room?"

"Two oh one."

"The first one by the stairs. In case of fire—a quick escape."

Colette nodded. "Most people never think of that." She fished in her small reticule for her room key, unlocked the door and stepped inside. "Come in for a minute. I have a new bottle of what is supposed to be really good wine. You must sample it with me."

The room was a copy of his, looking out on Main Street. She took off the small hat and found the bottle of wine in a suitcase under the bed. She magically produced two glasses.

"I stole the glasses from the saloon."

The wine was corked and she found a corkscrew and let Spur do the honors opening the bottle. He screwed the metal into the cork as far as he thought he dared, then holding the bottle pulled slowly on the cork. It came out with a resounding pop, and for a moment he wondered if it were champagne.

"No, just a good red wine," she told him.

She poured.

The wine was surprisingly good.

"It's from California," she said. "I think they have at last learned how to make wine down there."

She put the glass down and sat on the bed and motioned for him to sit beside her.

"Spur, I have a favor to ask. I don't do this very often, but tonight is special, and I think you are a special man. I want you to softly, and gently, make love to me." She watched him for a moment, then bent forward and kissed his lips, easily at first, then with more and more desire.

When the kiss was done she smiled. "You don't seem surprised."

"Very little a beautiful woman ever does surprises me. I'm pleased, flattered, interested, anxious. But not surprised."

He bent forward this time and kissed her lips, then both her eyes and then the side of her throat.

Her voice was very soft and low. "Spur, you will have to seduce me. I may even protest a little."

"But you are sure?"

"Oh, yes! I want to be with you, right here, right now."

He kissed her again, then put his arms around her.

"Now, tell me about Portland, your home. Tell me all about your family and how you learned to sing, and where you memorized all of the songs."

She began talking, and as she did Spur kissed her and held her and now and then stroked her breasts throug the fabric. She looked at him quickly at first, then smiled. It took him ten minutes of talking and stroking before she let him keep his hand over her breast. The soft massaging led to her gasping with pleasure and a smile now and then.

It took him a half hour to get the front of her dress unbuttoned, and another half hour before he could slip his hand under her chemise and hold her bare breast.

Slowly he pushed the dress off her shoulders and let it fall around her waist. Then little by little he lifted her chemise away so her breasts were uncovered.

He kissed them and she whimpered with excitement. At last he found the combination to the dress and lifted it over her head. The three petticoats went down off her feet and she lay on the bed, topless, her face a combination of surprise and wonder.

Twice he had moved her hands to his crotch, but she would not open his fly. At last he did so himself and pushed her hands inside. Cautiously, slowly they explored until they found his erection.

She moaned with delight.

He stripped his clothes off, locked the door and pushed a chair under the handle, then sat on the bed beside her. She reached out and touched his erection, then grasped it and watched him.

His hands touched the drawers she wore, cotton underpants that extended down each leg to the knee.

"Sweet Colette, I think it's time we take these off, don't you?" She nodded, but her hands held his hands.

"Maybe we should just get dressed again," she said.

Spur sat up. "Fine. You want to get dressed, fine with me. Then I can get to my room and get some sleep."

"No! I want to do it, I really do. Help me, please."

"Give me your hands."

She did. He put both of them around his erection.

"Now, don't move your hands, all right?"

Colette shivered, but nodded.

Spur unbuttoned the drawers, and slowly took them off, pulling them down her legs.

Colette whimpered softly. He kissed her. He

caught her hands and put them round his neck, then he kissed her and slowly, gently he rolled over on top her.

Colette trembled and her whole body went stiff. For a moment she didn't breathe.

"It's all right, Colette. Everything is fine. This is normal and natural." He kissed her then and she relaxed and opened her eyes.

"Am I being terrible?"

"No, just frightened. I can't figure out why. Have you ever made love before?"

"Not soft and gentle, not this way."

"Oh, It should always be this way." He bent and kissed her breasts, licking her nipples until he saw them lift and enlarge.

"Does that feel good, warm and nice?"

"Yes."

"That's how making love feels."

When his hand at last moved down to her crotch, she was soft and wet. Slowly, gently, he edged against her and then inside. She moaned and smiled and then grabbed his buttocks and pushed him in harder until his long shaft was all the way home.

Colette sighed.

"I think I like this," she said softly.

Spur found her hard clit and twanged it four times. She gasped and yelped and then surged into a shattering, stunning climax that kept her vibrating and throbbing for over sixty seconds. When the tremors passed sweat streaked her forehead and her face.

"That, that . . . that was so *wonderful*! That has never happened before. Never! So fine, so marvelous." She was beaming. Colette looked up and kissed his lips. "Now nice man, Spur McCoy, who has been so patient with me. It's your turn."

Spur had been holding back for the past forty-five minutes. Now he stroked a dozen times and exploded with a punching series of thrusts, then he settled beside her on the bed.

"You are fantastic in bed," Spur said.

Colette laughed softly and stroked his chest. "You are the one who helped me to find that out. The next time will be a little easier. But I think I always will remember too much about before."

Spur frowned. "What about before? Can you tell me about it?"

She shook her head. "No, that is for forgetting. I never will be able to talk about it. Just thinking is bad enough." She picked up his hand and moved it to her crotch.

"Make me feel so wonderful again, wonderful Spur McCoy."

His finger found the spot and this time she sailed for twice as long over the moon and the stars and saw the wonder of the universe. When at last she settled beside him again, she thanked him and slowly drifted off to sleep.

Spur lifted away from her, slid into his clothes, and closed the door so the chair would slide under the door knob. Back in his room he found that nothing had been disturbed, no one had been there. He locked the door and window, then dropped into bed.

When the fire burned down the mayor's big house that night, just after midnight, all of the commotion and shouting and screams two blocks away did not even wake up Spur McCoy.

10

Spur heard about the fire the next morning at breakfast. As soon as he was through, he went to the burned house and looked at it. The sheriff had been there and left. Near where the back porch had been, Spur found a tin can, the kind kerosene usually came in.

Another similar can that had burned almost to the point of melting, still sat beside the back wall of the house inside the old porch. The rest of the house had burned completely. Only part of the heavy staircase had not gone up in smoke.

Spur took the can that had only been scorched by the fire. There was still some printing on the side of the rectangular can. Who would sell kerosene? He checked at two stores before he found one, the hardware dealer.

The man was in his sixties, loved the hardware business and said he was a problem solver.

"What's your problem, young man?"

Spur held up the can. "This come from your store?"

The hardware man took it and turned it around, read the printing left on the metal and nodded.

"Right you are, but I can't say when. Sell a few of these fresh, but most folks bring them back for a refill from my big barrel out in back. Less expensive that way."

"You fill any yesterday?"

"Half a dozen. Seems like we do about that many a day winter or summer. Course, now, in the winter lots of folks have those little coal oil heaters, the round kind that don't need a chimney. Makes the house smell a little, but it's a quick way to get some more heat in a place. We sell lots more kerosene then, usually in five gallon cans."

"Remember who got refills last couple of days?"

"Not off hand. I could think on it."

"Good, I'm working with the sheriff. We just might have a fire starter in town. The mayor's house was torched using coal oil from that can. You might help us find out who it was."

"Well now, don't that beat all! A fire starter! I'll work up a list for you right off."

Spur thanked him and walked over to the county sheriff's office and jail. He heard John Ringo swearing as soon as he came in the front door.

Sheriff Younger shook his head. "You got to get that guy out of here, McCoy. You said you'd talk to him, you'd take responsibility. So do it!"

Spur went back to the cell. John Ringo shook the bars and glared at Spur.

"Calm down Ringo, or you'll never see daylight again. You could be in big trouble. No self defense involved in this."

"In what, damnit? You hit me."

"You were committing assault and battery on a female. You were threatening to rape her. Oregon courts could give you five years in prison for that. They protect their womenfolk out here."

Ringo calmed down. "But I was drunk. I don't rape women. All women are special. I must have got some bad whiskey."

"You were roaring drunk, I brought you in. Now, you want to get out of here without a trial?"

"Yeah."

"First you agree to be on the one o'clock stage for Portland. Give me your word."

"Hell . . . okay. My job here is done. I'll be on the damn stagecoach."

"Good. Next I want you to promise not to hurt the sheriff or any of his deputies. They were just doing their job. Give me your word on that."

Ringo looked at the sheriff who came to the side of the cell.

"Right, all right. I won't gun down any of the sheriff's people here. Now you have my word."

Sheriff Younger still looked scared. He frowned at Spur and motioned him to one side.

"You going to take the word of a killer like Ringo? That won't mean a damn thing to him."

"With Ringo, it does. I've heard that he is scrupulously honest about standing behind his word. I'm betting on it. If not, I'll be around. Get the keys."

Sheriff Younger shook his head, hesitated, then at last gave the key to the cell to Spur. McCoy unlocked the cell door.

"Pick up whatever you had in your pockets at the desk," Spur said.

Ringo snorted and went through the door to the

front of the office where Sheriff Younger was taking items from a drawer.

"A hundred and ten dollar and twenty seven cents, a knife, two small rocks and a harmonica."

Ringo nodded. "Sounds about right. Now my two six-guns."

"You a man of your word, Ringo?"

"Damn right. Give me my guns."

Sheriff Younger handed the gun belt and the two Colts to Younger who strapped them on. He turned and looked at Spur who leaned against the wall.

John Ringo stared at Spur with a deadly gleam in his eyes.

"Yeah, now I remember. Spur McCoy, big time Federal lawman. Heard about you in Arizona. I made my promises not to hurt the sheriff, but that didn't include you, McCoy. I want your hide!"

"Could be trouble for you, Ringo."

"And could be dead for you, McCoy."

"Let's have a real Texas walk-down. One shot each. Whoever shoots first has to stand pat after he fires. If he hits the other man, fine. If he misses or just wounds him, the one who hasn't fired yet can walk down the line and blast the other one from two feet if he wants to. A Texas Walk-down shootout."

"Not a chance, Ringo. I'll take you on the regular way. Five rounds in one gun and fifty yards apart. Then we walk forward."

"Fifty yards? No damn six-gun is good at that range. Fifty feet maybe if you're lucky."

Spur drew the special Colt from his holster. It had a ten inch barrel on it.

"It's not fast draw, Ringo, but it's damn

accurate at forty yards. You still want to call me out?''

"Damn right! You probably can't even hold that thing steady. Since I have to be on the one o'clock stage, let's make our showdown at high noon on Main Street. Right outside of the doctor's office so he can pronounce you dead.''

Spur grinned. "Suits me. The sheriff will have a couple of men there with shotguns to insure a fair fight.'' Spur turned and walked away. He had never liked call-outs, and avoided these duel-like shootouts whenever he could. But this one was not to be denied. Ringo's pride had been injured, and he would not stop until he had a chance to repair the damage. Killing Spur would suit him just fine.

Until noon, Spur had work to do. He headed back toward the hardware store hoping the owner would have that list. Whoever torched the house was hired by someone, or was the brains behind this whole land grab. It could be a good lead. There was no reason the person who used kerosene had bought it during the last two days, but it was a chance. Right now Spur would take any kind of help he could find.

He passed the courtroom where the circuit judge was in his last day of hearings before he moved to the next town. Someone came running out of the building, his face ashen, fear crowding in on his stern features.

"My god! it can't be! It just can't be true! Twenty years of hard work for nothing?''

Spur stopped the man. "What's going on?''

"Courthouse. Some Englishman claims he has a British Crown Land Grant that covers almost all of Wallowa county. He says he owns the whole damn county, the town the hills, everything. He claims everyone here is a trespasser on his land!"

Land again. Land! It could tie in with the land records burning! Spur ran for the court and squeezed into the packed room. Sir Jeffrey Mountbatten was standing near the judge talking.

"Your Honor, I don't know how to make it any plainer. This document has recently come into my hand. The Royal land grant was made in 1845 to my father the late Earl of Mountbatten to reward him for long service to the queen. I am his only heir and now own the land grant. Queen Victoria made hundreds of land grants.

"As I'm sure you know the Oregon territory was jointly occupied by the United States and the British Empire by agreement in 1818 and renewed in 1827. The boundaries were finalized in 1846 when the 49th parallel was established as the international boundary between the British Canada and the U.S. The boundary extended from the Pacific Ocean to the Rocky Mountains.

"There seems little to dispute. Her Royal Majesty, Queen Victoria, had the absolute right to award a Royal Land Grant in this territory. Simply because the document was lost or not claimed for the past thirty years, has no bearing on its authenticity.

"I'm sure you have numerous ways to check the form and content of such a document. And when you do I am certain that you will find it authentic in every way. Even though I own this vast area of land, I realize that I now am under the authority and legal jurisdiction of the United States Government, and your court.

"That is why I have brought the document to

your attention just as soon as I received it by post and messenger from London. I have been in town for almost a month waiting for it to arrive. I'm sure you understand the delays that occur on ocean as well as land transport."

Judge Farley Inglesia stared at the paper in his hands. It was a fine parchment, and the royal crest and printing all looked accurate. He read the description of the area again and was thunderstruck.

"... that the grant shall include all of those areas drained by rivers said to be named the Grande Ronde, the Joseph and the Innaha from their sources to their joining the Snake river."

"Mr. Mountbatten. The court would have appreciated some kind of advance notice of a land claim of this magnitude. Nothing of this sort has ever taken place in Oregon before. In fact I can think of no British Royal Land grant ever having the support of law anywhere in the Western part of the nation.

"Numerous Spanish Land Grants have been ruled valid in California, but those were entirely different circumstances. There the owners had been long time residents and toilers on the land they claimed."

"Your Honor, I understand the shock of this revelation. I, too, was surprised by the extent of the claim. I have been touring my land lately and it indeed is extensive. However, I am more than willing to wait for the decision of this court in the matter. I am a law abiding, peaceful man, and I urge everyone in the county to have patience."

"Mr. Mountbatten," the Judge said. "There is no possibility that the court can rule on this document today. Indeed it would be my first opinion that it would have to be taken up with the Federal District court in Portland. However this court will retain the document which has been properly marked and recorded by the clerk.

"Knowing the gravity of this claim, the court will seek all possible haste and forward the document to Portland on the stage which I understand leaves this noon. It will be sent by an armed and bonded messenger to insure its safety. A copy of the wording and descriptions will be made by the clerk and made available here through the county offices."

"Your Honor, do you have any estimate about the length of time the Federal court might take . . ."

"None whatsoever, Mr. Mountbatten. However, I urge the people of the county not to jump to conclusions. Since this type of land grant has never been presented before, we can not know how the court will rule. It could rule it invalid under international law. Or it could rule it valid. We'll just have to wait for the decision of the court."

"Thank you your honor." Sir Jeffrey Mountbatten closed a small leather case he carried, nodded to his man, Edward Long, and they made their way out of the small, packed court room. Spur moved out behind them.

Once on the street a man who had followed them out charged Sir Jeffrey and knocked him down.

"If I had a gun I'd kill you!" he screamed. "My whole life's savings are tied up in my land and my house. I'll never let you have them." He kicked at Sir Jeffrey and Edward Long jumped to his aid.

Spur's long pistol came out and he fired one

shot in the air.

"Stop it! That's enough! The matter is up to the court."

A dozen more men stormed from the court chambers and headed for Sir Jeffrey. Spur saw that it was quickly developing into a riot he could not control. He grabbed the Englishman and raced him down the alley, then along another block until they came to the livery.

"You would have been ripped to pieces back there in another five minutes," Spur said. "You should have expected some violent sort of reaction to a bombshell like this."

"Really I had no thought that there would be any violence. It's a matter for the law."

They panted for a moment.

"You don't threaten two or three thousand people with the total loss of their land and houses and businesses and their whole future without expecting some reaction. Now we better get you out of town before you two go to a necktie party with a real hemp rope."

11

Spur quickly rented three horses with saddles
and they rode down the alley, across three back
yards and around a small farm. Then they were in
the open range and Spur angled toward the river
and a grove of trees which was about three miles
from the main part of town.

"I don't believe it," Sir Jeffrey said. "We are
actually running for our lives. How droll."

"If you don't want to be shot down, or get your
neck stretched by a rope, you better concentrate
on riding, and forget the try at being funny,"
Spur said.

Spur watched behind but could see no
immediate pursuit. That didn't mean someone
would not raise a gang, a small mob and come
charging after them later.

"We can't just stay out here in the wilderness,"
Sir Jeffrey said.

"Oh, for bloody hell . . .!" Edward Long burst
out suddenly, glaring at Sir Jeffrey. Then he
stopped quickly.

Spur eased the pace down to a walk. They were almost to the woods.

"All you have to do is wait out here and hide if anybody comes looking for you. As soon as it gets dark, ride back into town and I'll meet you in back of the hotel. I'll have rented a room for you. Don't go back to your regular rooms wherever they are. You can bet somebody with a loaded shotgun has already visited them."

"These people mean business, don't they?" Sir Jeffrey said, more serious than he had been before.

"You threaten their whole way of life in this county and reduce everyone living here to a pauper. That is bound to come as a shock. I don't see how any court can accept the authenticity of your Royal Land Grant. It would mean chaos in the county, and upset things in this half of the state."

"I can't argue that point with you. But the land really belongs to me, to my family . . "

"We'll let the court decide. But none of that will matter to you a bit if you're dead and buried. So keep a sharp lookout. You have a watch?"

"Yes, of course."

"I'll meet you in back of the Grande Ronde Hotel at eight o'clock. It will be dark then. Don't let anyone recognize you as you ride into La Grande.

Spur turned his horse and rode away. He circled the little town and came in from the opposite direction.

Back in the three block long business section, the whole of La Grande was in an uproar. Everywhere on the street groups of men were talking. Some were urging that they raise a posse and go hunt down the Englisher. Others said such a claim would never hold up in court. No Royal Land Grant like this had ever been sanctioned by the courts in Oregon before.

A few wondered if the claim was real or not. They wondered how a judge in Oregon would be able to rule on a document that might or might not have been signed by Queen Victoria in London.

Spur worked his way through the people to the little hospital wing. On the way he had stopped at the La Grande General Mercantile and bought a box of chocolates.

He gave them to Rebecca Jonas. She now had both eyes uncovered. Neither was damaged, but her right cheek was still bandaged.

"Nobody done brought me chocolates in ten years," she said. "Jonas was a good man, but not a romantic." She offered Spur one of the delicacies but he declined.

"Have you remembered anything else about the night of the fire?"

"Yes, I have, Mr. McCoy, and I think it could be important. The key word is duplicate. I remember Jonas saying part of the extra work he had was because the former clerk kept all of his records in duplicate. He made two entries on two sets of permanent record books. The old man was terrified of fire.

"So when Jonas took over, the old man made him promise to keep up all of the duplicate records."

"Duplicate. If the former clerk was so worried about fire, he must have kept one set of the records in another place. Did Jonas ever say anything about having to take things to another building, or did he work at the city owned building?"

"He never said anything like that. I just know he was doing two or three men's jobs. He worked twelve to thirteen hours every day, except the Lord's day, of course."

"Did the land office ever have a safe?"

"No, we didn't handle money. Oh, for the records? Land sakes no. Those big books are almost three feet square. Take a whole vault to hold them."

"Vault, the bank. Let me go give Mr. Follette a call. That might solve a lot of our problems." Spur smiled down at the woman. "Now, Rebecca, you just eat those chocolates and hurry up and get well. I'll see you again."

Five minutes later Hirum Follette shook his head. They had just probed and moved things and looked in every square inch of the bank's new vault. It was made of six inches of steel and concrete, and was absolutely fireproof. But there were no county land records inside.

"Sorry, McCoy. I really hoped that those ledgers had been brought over here. Guess not."

Spur thanked him and left. There were fewer people on the streets now, but everywhere the topic of conversation was the Queen Victoria Land Grant. As the shock of it wore off, more and more people were downplaying it. Something like this could take years to resolve going through the courts.

More and more people wondered if the Land Grant was really from Queen Victoria. Spur had thought of the chance that the paper was a complete fake. His half hour with the two Englishmen did nothing to dispel that possibility. If it was a phony, the courts would discover it quickly, but that wouldn't help Spur find out who had killed Jonas King, or where the duplicate land records were.

He went to the burned out land office. It was just the way it had been. He found a solid two-by-four and began probing the ground. The building had been pier-block and joyce built, and all the flooring and most of the supporting joyce had burned away. He walked through the blackened jungle, probing with the two by four, stabbing the ground, looking for a cave, a hole, even the hard surface of a big floor vault where the records might have been kept.

Jonas and Rebecca had moved into the old home which had been taken over by the count to house the county clerk's office. So the former clerk could have had a little cellar dug. But after two hours of probing and falling down and ruining a good shirt with the charcoal and ashes, Spur decided there was no hidden area under the house.

What next?

He sat on the small swatch of grass in the front yard. The only other chance was the small stable house where one horse could be kept. Spur was about to move in that direction when he checked his watch. It was five minutes until noon. He had a date with John Ringo.

Spur had no desire to shoot it out with Ringo close-up. But with his long barreled pistol he had an even chance. That was better odds than he usually enjoyed.

Three or four years ago, Spur had gone to the longer weapon. He found it shot much straighter and more accurately, and that he could hit what he aimed for at ranges well over a hundred feet.

Most six-guns with their seven and a half inch barrels were notoriously inaccurate. His only hope now was to aim straight and shoot first.

Word of the gunfight had spread almost as fast as that about the Land Grant. Fifty people had come out of stores and stood on the boardwalks watching.

At the far end of the long block in front of the Sagebrush Saloon, stood John Ringo. He held a fifth of whiskey in his left hand and from time to time took a drink.

Spur McCoy came out of the side street and stood at the other end of the block. He adjusted the long weapon in his holster and waited.

"You wanted a long walk, you got it," Ringo called.

"You have one last chance to get on the stage without a bullet in you, Ringo." Spur answered.

"Not a chance," Ringo said and turned, showing that he only had one gun. He corked the whiskey bottle and tossed it to a man on the boardwalk. "Save that for me, I'll want it again in about two minutes."

"Let's do it, Ringo," Spur called. They stared at each other and then began walking forward. They were about fifty yards apart. No one was behind either man, but the boardwalks were filled. More people ran in to watch.

Spur drew his long weapon after five full strides. He stopped, spread his feet apart and lifted the weapon.

"Look at the barrel on that Colt!" somebody called.

Spur brought the gun up to shoulder height and reached out with his left hand, using both arms and hands to steady the weapon. He sighted in on Ringo's right shoulder, blinked as Ringo took another step. He would fire just before the next step by Ringo's right foot. The gunfighter's weapon was still in leather. They were thirty-eight yards apart.

Spur held his breath, refined the sight again on the shoulder and squeezed off the shot.

The blast of the .44 round came like a thunderclap, only to be topped by the shouts of surprise and amazement as John Ringo took the round in his left shoulder and sprawled backwards in the dust of the unpaved street.

He glared at Spur, but his right arm hung useless. His own six-gun had spilled from leather and lay three feet away. Ringo grabbed at it with his left hand, but already Spur had sighted in and fired. The chunk of .44 caliber lead it the cylinder of the Colt .44 and slammed it a dozen feet backwards out of the reach of John Ringo.

Spur walked up and looked down at the famous gunfighter.

"Told you I had no cause to kill you, Ringo. You go see Doc George, and then you still have forty-five minutes to be on the stage. I'll keep that ruined .44 of yours."

Spur turned and walked away. John Ringo stared at Spur for a moment, then laughed.

"Damned if that long gun of his didn't beat me. Damned if it didn't! Learned something today." He looked around. "Who in hell has my bottle of whiskey? And where is that doctor's office? Somebody show me the way. I got a stagecoach to catch for Portland."

Spur kept walking to the building where the county held its court. Circuit Court Judge

Inglesia had canceled the rest of his afternoon calendar. His clerk said the judge would see Spur.

Spur had out his Federal identification when he walked into the judge's private, if temporary, chambers.

Judge Inglesia looked at the letter and nodded. "That's why you wanted to see me before. Now things are different. You know about the land grant claim?"

"Yes, Your Honor. I think it ties in with the land record fire. Nobody can prove who owns anything. Then the Royal Land Grant drops on the court and before you can blink, the Englishman owns everything."

"You're telling me you think the Englishman had something to do with burning up the land records?" The judge paused. "Yes, it would seem to follow. I have sent the document off to Portland. I really can't do anything else."

"I understand. I have a question. If that document turns out to be spurious, a forgery say, would it be a state or a federal crime? Who would have jurisdiction?"

"The Federal courts, no question. The Circuit Court is merely acting as a messenger service in this case."

Spur knew what he wanted. He thanked the judge, went back to his hotel and had his noontime meal, even if it was late. The rest of the afternoon he poked around the blackened ruins of the land office house, then checked with the hardware owner. He had four names of people who had bought more than one gallon of kerosene the previous three days in one gallon cans.

Two of them were women who lived alone. The third was the owner of the livery stable and the fourth the town's grave digger, a truly strange man known only as "Digger."

"Where does this Digger live," Spur asked.

"Where he works. He has a shack down in back of the graveyard. Spends most of his time down there when he isn't digging or filling in graves. A stranger man you'll never find, at least in this county."

Spur decided to pay the man a visit. The graveyard was at the end of town, closer to the big bend in the river. Spur walked, found the small shack at the far end of the unused section of the cemetery. No one was home. The Secret Service Agent leaned against a tree and waited for half an hour. Nobody came, so he went back to the hotel.

Digger had seen Spur coming through the cemetery. He was a stranger to Digger, and strangers usually meant trouble. Digger slipped into the brush along the edge of the Grande Ronde river and hunkered down, watching. The man called, knocked on the side of the wall, and then waited.

Digger had no idea why the man waited. When the stranger at last moved off through the cemetery, Digger remained hidden for a full hour before he left the trees and went back to the shack. He didn't want anything to do with strangers. Not a thing.

12

Well before eight o'clock that night, Spur had a ground floor room rented only two doors down from the side entrance of the Grande Ronde Hotel. He explained that someone was trying to find him he didn't want to see, so he wanted to register the room under the name Mark Smith. The clerk grinned thinking it was a love tryst.

Just after eight, the two men rode up on the horses.

"McCoy? Is that you?" Sir Jeffrey whispered.

"Yes, leave the horses here. I'll take them back. Now be quiet and we'll get into the room fast before anyone can recognize you."

Spur took them into the room, told them to lock the door and let him in when he got back from the livery.

When Spur came back he brought a fifth of whiskey and two kinds of wine.

"You men had anything to eat?" Spur asked.

"Hell no, and I'm hungry," Long said.

"We could do with some food," Sir Jeffrey said.

"I'll bring some plates from the dining room for my sick friends. Take a few minutes."

As Spur waited for the food to be fixed he realized how quickly the temper of the town had cooled off. Now less than ten hours after the first announcement of the Land Grant, La Grande had settled down and most people were willing to let the courts handle it. Many said no United States court was going to let some weird foreigner take their land away from them.

Spur brought the men dinners from the dining room, and then broke out the whiskey and soon both were feeling happy and talkative.

It was nearly two hours of drinking later before Spur got around to what he wanted to talk about with the two men.

"If you don't mind my asking, Sir Jeffrey, just why didn't your father come claim the land thirty years ago?"

"Oh, that's simple. He took sick and went to bed. He never told anyone about the grant, wanted to keep it as a surprise. Then a year later he died and only his solicitor knew of it. Father made him promise to wait to tell me about it until I was responsible. I was only a lad of six at the time, you see."

"Interesting," Spur said. "Here, let me freshen up that drink for you, we've got plenty for tonight. I'd guess that by tomorrow you'll be able to go back to your regular rooms. Tempers have cooled off a lot around town."

"Good. I'm tired of this small room already. Only one bed."

"Sir Jeffrey, how did your solicitor find you?"

"I wrote for money. I get a yearly stipend and it was due. He said now that I was thirty-five I

was eligible for the Grant. Well, it was a shock
and a surprise for me, I should tell you."

An hour later they were still drinking. Sir
Jeffrey was showing signs of going to sleep. Spur
had been sipping at his glass while pouring as
much as he could for the Englishman.

When Sir Jeffrey passed out on the bed, Spur
concentrated on Edward Long.

Spur laughed. "Now that old stuffed shirt there
is blotto, we can talk, Edward. Is he really an
Earl? I heard somewhere that he's a phony,
making up all this Earl and Lord stuff to impress
the ladies."

Long laughed. "Him impress the ladies? Not a
chance. He'd rather pop you right now tonight,
than the prettiest cunt you can find. He's bloody
queer he is." Long took a good pull on the
whiskey. "Things I could tell you about him.
Gawd, you'd turn in your seat, you would."

"Is he a real Earl?"

"Nah . . . he lost his title cause he didn't go into
the Queen's Service. Not really a Lord at all, but
the Americans like to think he is. So we go along.
Things I could bloody tell you about His Lord-
ship, there. In Boston and then in New York. But
loyalty is what I've got." He shook his head. "I
must be drinking a little!" He laughed. Then had
a long drink and blinked at Spur.

"Bloody stories I could tell. Good old Land
Grant. Gonna be millionaires soon. Me I get fifty-
fifty. Not that I did so much, but I'm part of the
bloody team. Stories I could tell!"

"Edward, is the Land Grant Certificate really a
forgery?" Spur asked.

Edward looked at him but never heard. He
slumped sideways, then fell face down on the bed,

passed out and began snoring in a moment.

Spur decided he had asked the most important question about a minute too late. He closed the door, locked it from the outside and slid the key under the door, then went up to his room. Long would be the better of the two for a little bit of Yankee informal questioning, but only after he recovered from tomorrow's hangover. The questioning would take place in what might be considered strange and wild circumstances. Spur smiled just thinking about it.

He unlocked his door and slipped inside. At once he smelled a perfume he remembered.

"Maggie Smith, you have returned," he said. He heard her giggle before he lit the lamp. He lit the wick, lowered the chimney and turned.

She sat on the bed wearing a soft cotton night-gown. Her brown eyes were alert and dancing. A smile creased her pretty face and she stretched.

"I've been waiting for you, hoping that you wouldn't be too late."

"Your daddy know you're in town?"

"Of course, I'm staying with my school chum. She always lies for me. I tell her when I'm in town. We are best friends, but she's already married."

"Did you come to stay the night?"

"Of course."

"You ran out early last time."

"I was worried that Daddy might come to town and stop by to see me. So I left here and rode back to the ranch."

As she said it she pulled the nightgown over her head. It barely fluttered her short cut blonde hair, but made her breasts jiggle from the motion.

"You make a pretty picture."

"I believe in going after what I want."

"What is that right now?"

"To have you come to bed with me and see how many times we can make love, a different way each time."

"You've had a lot of experience then, I would guess and know all about getting pregnant."

"No. I'm a ranch girl. I know all about breeding. I know when my fertile period is. Just after it's over, that's when I play married folks with you."

"Now."

"Yes."

"Do you mind if I lock the door and get undressed first?"

She giggled.

He locked the door, turning the key half way around so no one could get in with a pass key, then sat on the bed and pulled off his boots.

"I wish we had a bathtub here," she said. "I want to take a bath with you, but there's no chance." She moved up behind him and nibbled at his ear. Then she pushed her tongue into his ear, tickling him.

"Hurry!" she said.

She put her arms around him and unbuttoned his vest, then his shirt.

A moment later he was as bare as she was and slid under the one sheet she had left on the bed.

His arms went around her and she pressed hard against him.

"You have such a marvelous body! So strong and hard." She rolled over on top of him.

"Darling Spur, the first time this way! Oh, Please! Then you get to choose the next position.

I've never been done on top this way. It would be exciting!"

He pulled her head down and kissed her open mouth, then chewed and nibbled and sucked on her breasts hanging down at him like pointed, ripe mellons ready for picking.

"Do you know how it makes me feel when you're chewing on my titties? I get this warm, wonderful glow, like everything is wonderful and I'm pleased and happy. And then it grows and I get hotter and hotter, and if you lick my nipples I think they are going to burn right off! Did you know that? Lick my nipples again, darling Spur, oh please!"

She had found his pole and held it with one hand, stroking it back and forth gently. He licked her nipples and she groaned as a climax ripped into her slender form, rattling her like a tin cup in a bucket. She bounced and jolted and shivered. She let out a long, low wail and stopped pumping his penis.

Maggie gave one last shudder and relaxed on top of him, her breasts crushed against his chest, her chin just past his shoulder. She rested for two minutes, then pushed up and kissed him.

"Push it inside me quick before I scream!"

Maggie helped. Spur laughed as she rode him. She was panting and puffing and then she climaxed again just as he did and they roared and rumbled and came at the same time nearly knocking the springs out of the bedstead. At last they slowed and calmed and lay in each other's arms panting and gasping for breath.

A few minutes later she raised up from where she lay beside him. She had a strange smile on her face.

"Why is it always so good with you, and so bad every time I try it with someone I know? I get all tense and tight and I can't relax and nothing happens."

"It will, give yourself time. Some things take practice."

"I'll practice with you every night for ten years!"

"And never get pregnant?"

"There are ways."

"And none of them work, all the time."

"They will for me."

"How old are you?"

"Twenty."

"And your father doesn't think there's a man in the whole county who is good enough for you?"

"How did you know? I've had two suitors this year, and Daddy threw both of them off the ranch. I saw one of them in town, but he was so scared of Daddy that he wouldn't even talk to me."

Spur kissed her. "Give it another year, until you're twenty-one. Then move to town, or in to Portland and tell your old man to go to hell."

She grinned. "I'd love to do that. One of my brothers did. Then he came back."

She sat up, threw off the sheet and began kissing his chest.

"Again! Again! I don't want to waste another minute!"

"You want to see a soft little worm?"

She looked at his crotch. "Oh, the poor little darling!"

"Make him well again."

Maggie knew exactly what to do. Two minutes

later her head bobbed up from his crotch and she laughed softly.

"He's standing up and raring to go." She rolled over and got up on her hands and knees.

"The first animals I ever saw fucking were dogs. Do me this way, darling Spur! I've never fucked dog fashion before!"

Spur knelt behind her. "You're sure?"

"Just hit the right hole!"

Spur lifted and probed a moment, then slid into her and leaned over her grabbing a hanging breast with each hand. He stroked and felt his staff rubbing against her clit. After a dozen probes she climaxed and wobbled and vibrated and moaned. Halfway through she lost her balance and fell on her stomach on the bed. Spur rode her down and the climax left her gasping for air. Then she laughed.

"Guess we fell down."

"I like it this way. Okay?"

"Sure, it's different."

He started moving again and felt her respond and soon he was shooting the moon and riding the cloud trails until he shot his last load and sagged down on top of her, catching his weight with his elbows and knees.

"You are wild!" she said. Then she cried.

He moved and turned her so he could hold her. The sobs came and she blubbered for five minutes. Spur knew there was nothing he could do but wait. When she tapered off and the sobs turned into an occasional gasp, he kissed her forehead.

"Now, tell me about it, Margaret Smith."

She sighed and looked up at him. "You're a man, you wouldn't understand."

"Let me try."

She scowled, took a deep breath. "Well, it's just that I want to get married so damn bad! Daddy doesn't understand. He thinks things should be done a certain way, at a certain time. He says I should wait until I'm twenty-two to get married, so I'll be settled down.

"Bullshit! I want a man now! I want somebody I can take to bed every night for two years if he'll have me. I want to get fucked until I'm so sore that I can hardly pee. I'm a woman. I'm the only woman in the ranch house and Daddy just doesn't understand."

She gasped a pair of times as the crying jag was playing itself out. He kissed her cheek.

"And so?"

"And so, I want to tell Daddy that I'm going to move into town and stay with my aunt here, so I can meet men and find one to marry. I don't care if he doesn't own half of Oregon. I don't care if he's a clerk in a store or runs a railroad somewhere. I just want to find my man, the man I'm supposed to love and have babies with. My father simply can't understand that."

"Have you talked with your aunt about it? Maybe the two of you could persuade him. Invite him in to your aunt's house and you come and tell him what you want. Does he have a cook at the ranch?"

"Yes. And one of the ranch hand's wife is housekeeper. He doesn't need me out there."

"So do it. Talk to your aunt tomorrow before you go back, get it set up for this week. The Land Grant thing is going to be over in a week or so. Don't worry about it."

She sat up, wiped the tears from her eyes and

off her cheeks, and urged him up. Then she hugged him so tight he thought she was going to crack a rib.

"Love you, love you, love you! You have helped me tonight more than you'll ever know! Now, while you rest up, I'll fix the snack. I can't expect you to do all this tough physical exercise without providing you with some nourishment. I know you ate up my titties, but this is better for you."

He sat there as she jumped out of bed as bare as the day she was born, found a sack at the side of the dresser and laid out on top a picnic of cut apples, wedges of cheese, chunks of fresh baked bread and a bottle of wine.

"Now, this is what I call service," Spur said. They stood at the dresser and nibbled on the cheese and bread, ate the apple sections and sipped at the wine.

"Don't eat everything!" She said sharply. "We have to save some for our three A.M. snack."

"How are you going to wake up at three o'clock," he asked.

Maggie laughed and nibbled at his ear. "You foolish man. You didn't think I was going to waste any time tonight sleeping, did you? Now hurry up, I'm getting curious about how we're going to do our fuck-fuck the next time."

Spur downed the last of the wine in his glass and slapped her on the bottom.

"Yes!" she said squealing softly. "Spank me! Not too hard but just hard enough. That really gets me all hot and ready! Come on, right now, I have been a bad girl and you need to spank me until my little bottom turns all red!"

He did.

Then he lifted her legs on his shoulders and

drove into her so hard and fast that she yelped in surprise, then she wailed.

"You touched something deep inside me!" she said. "It felt so unusual, so weird and wild. Do it again!"

They had their snack at two-thirty instead of three, and made love twice after that and Spur McCoy watched her dress and get ready to leave at four.

"Darling, I'll go back to Paula's house and sleep until noon, just in case Daddy stops by. But soon I'll be living full time in town, or in Portland."

She knelt on the bed and kissed him, then hugged him tightly.

"Spur McCoy, I'll never know how to thank you. She flashed him a perky smile from those big brown eyes, then slipped out of his room.

Spur checked his pocket watch. It was four-thirty. He turned over and slept until eight.

13

That same night, Colette Paris closed her third round of singing at the Sagebrush Saloon with a haunting, touching love song, *My True, True Love*. A young cowboy waited for her in her dressing room. When she opened the door, Colette stopped suddenly, her hand to her mouth in fright.

"Oh, no, Colette, don't be frightened. I just wanted to tell you how wonderful you sang tonight. You were better than anybody I've ever heard in Chicago! Really you sing just beautiful."

She began to edge back toward the bar.

"Come in, Colette. I'm Hank, from the triple R. Mean you no harm. Lordy no! Just want to be here with you a minute or two, is that too much to ask?"

"You surprised me, Hank. I'm usually not so touchy. It was nice talking to you. Now I need to rest. I always rest a few minutes after each performance."

"I could wait just outside. I thought maybe we

could talk a while. Be more than glad to walk you back to your hotel. Heard you stay at the Grande Ronde. That's a nice hotel. I never stayed there."

"Hank, it was sweet of you to come back and see me, but now I really do have to sit down for a few minutes, alone. Would you go back to the bar, please?"

Hank, a cowboy about five feet eight, grinned, turned his brown low crowned hat in his hands and bobbed his head.

"Yes, Miss Colette, I most certainly will. Anything you ask, that's what I'm gonna do just quicker than a spring calf finding his mama." He moved toward the door. He stopped beside her.

Colette shivered.

"Oh, Miss Colette, would you mind my giving you just a little kiss on the cheek?"

"Yes, I would mind!" She said it sharply.

Hank shrugged. "Figures. Don't hurt none to ask. I'll wait out in the bar if you want me to walk you to your hotel. Sure hope you do. Some rough, mean no-a-counts roam around this time of night out there on the street." He touched one finger to his forehead in a kind of salute and went out the door. Colette closed the door and leaned against it.

For a minute she thought she was going to cry. Then she fought back the emotion and sat in the chair and carefully wiped off most of the traces of makeup she used around her eyes and on her lips and cheeks. It was not blatant color like the saloon girls used. She was not a saloon girl. She was a singer!

It took her ten minutes to stop her shaking. She took a quick drink from a small flask of brandy.

Someone knocked on her door.

"Yes?"

"Lefty, you okay? Saw some guy trying to sneak back here."

She opened the door.

"Somebody was in here when I came back. Hank. I got rid of him. He scared me, Lefty."

"I'll watch your dressing room better," he said. "You want Billy to walk you to the hotel?"

"No, that's silly. I'll be fine. I'm almost ready to go."

Lefty nodded and left.

She checked her small windup clock on the dressing table. It was eleven fifteen. Colette put on a small hat, took her reticule with her hotel key, and went out to the bar. She did not see Hank among the dozen or so patrons. She waved at Lefty and walked out the door.

Hank waited for her half a block down. It was too far to run back to the bar.

"Evening, Miss Colette. I was going this way, mind if I walk along?"

"Boardwalks are made for everyone."

"I figured as how."

"Did I tell you I'm from Chicago? Grew up in the city and now I'm a cowboy. Isn't that strange? Always wanted to come out west. This is about as far as you can get."

Colette decided she would go straight to the clerk when she got to the hotel. If Hank was still there the clerk would take care of him. He had done it once before for her.

Hank talked about Chicago as they walked. He continued up the steps and right into the hotel.

Nobody stood behind the clerk's desk.

No one was in the lobby.

"Thank you, Hank, for seeing me safely home.

I'll be fine now. Goodnight."

"Goodnight, Miss Colette."

She turned and walked away. She was at the top of the flight of steps to the second floor before she realized he was right behind her.

"No, Hank, go away or I'm going to scream."

"Now, pretty, great singing little Colette, you wouldn't want to do that."

He stepped up beside her, caught her arm in a firm grip and walked with her down the hall. He knew which room was hers and stopped at the door.

"Open it, Colette. I could kick it open but you don't want that, do you?"

She couldn't talk. Slowly Colette took the key from her purse and put it in the keyhole. Hank turned it, opened the door and took the key out. He walked her inside the room, and closed the door.

He snapped a match into flame and held her as he moved to the lamp on the dresser. A moment later the lamp burned brightly as he adjusted the wick.

She had stood where he left her.

"Now, isn't this cozy?" He said. He went to the door and locked it, pocketing the key.

"Miss Colette, you and me are going to get to know each other one hell of a lot better. He grabbed her chin in his hand and his fingers pinched her cheeks painfully. "And don't think that I'm afraid to hurt that sweet little body of yours to get what I want. You know what that is."

He turned her to him and kissed her lips, a hard, demanding kiss. She didn't respond.

"Little Colette, I'm gonna fuck you, you know

that now. I'm gonna fuck you half a dozen times until I can't get my prick up stiff anymore, and you're going to love every stroke of it. Now, let's get busy and get you out of all of those clothes."

He grabbed the top of her dress. "You want me to rip this thing off you?"

"No! No. I'll take it off."

"Don't look so scared, pretty pussy. You've been in bed with lots of men. You like to fuck as well as you like to sing. Just think that you invited me up instead of the other way, and then you'll enjoy getting banged and sucking me off as much as I will."

Slowly she undid the snaps and buttons on the dress and pulled it over her head. Her mind was whirling. What could she do? She was frantic. She wasn't a virgin, having sex with the man did not bother her, but the idea that he was forcing her to do it made her furious.

She had to think of something. What? After he had climaxed! Yes, when he was exhausted and his guard was down. She would do it then. He would not be expecting anything. She would smile and pretend that she was *enjoying* having sex with him. Oh, God! Was she that good at acting? she had to be. He could kill her right there if he suspected.

Colette watched him unbuttoning his shirt. For a moment a picture flashed in front of her eyes of another man taking off his shirt. It was in her family house in Portland, Maine. The buttons came off and she saw the manly chest and she heard someone scream. She had screamed that day and ran from the house but he caught her in the woods in back of the house.

"Hey, you gonna undress, or I got to help?"

She shook her head to come back to the present and lifted the chemise over her head. She did not wear a binder, that long strip of cloth to keep her breasts from bouncing. She hated them. Now her big breasts bounced and jiggled as she dropped the chemise.

"Oh, yeah, big tits. I bet the guys you had big boobies. They look like they need chewing on."

He lunged across the room, fondled her a minute, then bent and sucked one of her big breasts into his mouth. He was vunerable right now. If she had a heavy knife she could plunge it in his back.

He came away, grinned at her and went down on her other breast.

"Damnit, get the rest of your clothes off!" he said between bites on her boobs. "Hurry up!"

She opened the buttons on her drawers, and pulled down her last protection, the knee length underpants. He pushed her on the bed and stripped the cotton garment off her legs, then grinned the way her legs had spread. She pulled them together and he laughed.

Quickly he pulled off his boots and his pants. His penis was hard and slanting out at her, the head large and now purple with the engorging, hot blood.

"Oh, yeah!" he said softly. "There is nothing so good as nookie, good old pussy, cunt all naked and waiting on a bed. Yeah, in bed with your shoes off!

She spread her skirt to the side and folded it.

"What you doing?"

"You're so slow that I'm just being neat."

"I can get faster!" He pushed her flat on the

bed away from her skirt and spread her legs with his feet.

"Now, sweet little pussy, just how good are you?" He drove between her legs probing, searching. When he found the right spot she was dry. He swore, spit into his hand and wiped the saliva over his penis, then probed again.

He drove in hard and she screeched in pain.

"Easy!" she yelped.

"You wanted it fast, this is fast!" He made no attempt to satisfy her, simply powered into her, thrusting hard and long, his breath starting to come in furious pants as he rocked back and forth on his elbows and his knees.

She felt the soft glow begin to spread through her body and fought against it. This was not like last night. No! This was rape and she was furious! With her hand she grabbed the edge of her skirt and worked it slowly toward her. He noticed.

"I like to touch my clothes, makes me feel better."

He pulled the skirt against her side and then grunted and wailed in pure joy as he climaxed. He was panting and spent as he dropped on top of her. She used her right hand, worked through her skirt until she found the pocket.

Carefully she pulled the object from her skirt's hidden pocket and lifted it over Hank's back. With her left hand she reached up and quietly unfolded the four-inch knife blade and heard the brace lock in place.

"Whatcha doing?" Hank mumbled. "Damn that was fine!"

Colette lifted the knife, holding it firmly in her right hand and drove it down toward his left side.

She aimed it just under his ribs and pushed the blade into the hilt, then turned it and tried to rip it out.

Hank did the work for her, springing away from her only to collapse on his back on the bed.

Colette's eyes flared, her lips came open and she swung the bloody knife downward, ramming it between ribs into his chest. Hank looked at her once in disbelief, then his eyes rolled upward.

She drove the knife into his chest a dozen more times aiming for his heart. At last he stopped twitching.

She sat there on the bed, his bloody body in front of her. For a moment she wanted to vomit, then she pushed back the feeling and sprang to her feet. She put the pillow from the bed on the floor, then rolled him off the bed onto the pillow. She pulled the pillow and tugged at him, scooting him across the six feet to the alley window.

Quietly she lifted the window and peered out. No one was in the alley. She pushed his feet upward the twenty-four inches to the open window and forced them out. By struggling and shoving with all her strength she got him halfway out the window. Then she squatted over his head, grabbed his shoulders and straining every muscle in her legs and back, she heaved his torso up and forward.

Hank slid out the window, turned halfway over and hit the ground of the alley below.

Colette panted for a moment, sat on the floor looking at the room. The pillow had absorbed most of the blood from his body. There were few spots on the hardwood floor to clean up.

The sheets! They were covered with blood. Quickly she wrapped them up, washed off a spot of blood on the cheap mattress, and then checked out the window. She threw the sheets out as far down the alley as she could, then dressed and checked the linen closet down the hall. She found two fresh sheets, a pillow and a pillow case.

As quickly as she could she made the bed, cleaned off the knife and put it away in her skirt pocket. Then she slipped into her nightgown and lay in the bed.

He had deserved to die. He was as bad as all the rest of them! She blew out the lamp and lay in the darkness, her breath coming more naturally now and her furiously beating heart settling down.

It was over.

She could sleep now.

An hour later she had the same dream. She was being chased by a man. She ran out of the small house into the trees, but still the man came after her. Colette tried every way she could to get away but he countered her until at last he caught her.

Slowly, he took off her clothes and forced her to do all kinds of sexual acts with him. Again and again it happened, then one day she had a large folding knife in her skirt pocket. Just after he had raped her, she surprised him and slashed his throat, then cut him again and again and again.

She woke up with a start just as she slashed his neck. Colette was sweating and crying. She washed her face, and dried it. The man had been her brother, and she had been thirteen at the time. She would never forget it. But also, she would never be without that same four-inch folding knife.

It was well into the morning when a banging on her door wakened her. Colette got up, put on a robe and went to the door.

"Yes, who is it?"

"Sheriff Younger, Miss. Could I talk to you a minute?"

She said of course and opened the door.

He barely looked at her, instead looked at her bed.

"Interested to see which bed doesn't have any sheets. Nothing to be worried about. Little thing like you just couldn't have done it. Sorry I bothered you."

The sheriff turned and went down the hall to the next room.

She closed the door, not really understanding. She had the dream again last night. By now reality and the dream had merged and flowed together, until she could not tell which was fact and which was memory. She remembered the man who came to her room, but after that the man began to look like her brother and soon all she could see was her older brother who had been nineteen.

Colette, took a deep breath. She was hungry, she wanted to have a bath, and then have a good breakfast and take a long ride somewhere. At least she had learned to ride a horse on this Western trip. She loved to ride.

Colette looked at a red stain on the window sill. She got some water and a cloth and wiped it up. She wondered how that red mark got there.

14

Victor White had been working the south forty of his homestead when the three riders came over the ridge. The south forty had been laboriously plowed with a single bottom hand held plow and a mule, and he was ready to float it down with a tough oak log he had cut especially for the job. He wiped sweat off his forehead and looked up from where he had hitched the mule to the single tree that hooked the mule's harness to the log.

"Hold it right there, sodbuster!" The angry shout came from one of the riders who had out his six-gun and aimed it at Victor.

"No cause for firearms," Victor said. "Ain't got one on me. What can I do for you gents?"

"For starters, unhitch that mule and drive him back to your cabin. Got plans for you."

Victor spat a stream of tobacco juice into the plowed ground.

"Figure not. I got to get me this forty floated down by sundown so I can plant tomorrow. Getting late as it is."

The gunshot boomed in the morning air and the slug slammed into the sod an inch from Victor's boot.

"No time for arguments, sodbuster. You want the next one in your head or your heart?"

"He mean it?" Victor asked the man on the horse ten feet away.

"Damn right, move the mule or die where you stand."

"You boys usually ride for the RimRock outfit, as I recall. Wade sent you?"

"Never heard of any RimRock Ranch, said the first man who held the gun. "Now move it before I get unhappy."

Ten minutes later Victor slapped the reins on the back of the mule and prodded the sterile creature back to the tiny farm yard of his homestead just off the banks of the Grande Ronde river.

He saw three other men at the cabin. His wife, Etta, was loading up the wagon with things from the house.

"What is this?" Victor asked.

The big man from the roan horse had swung down, but stll held his weapon on Victor. He took three steps toward the homesteader and slammed his gloved fist into Victor's jaw. The farmer-rancher spun around and lost his balance and fell in the dirt.

"Victor, no more dumb-assed questions. You have half an hour to load anything you want to keep on that wagon over there. Then hitch your mule to it, climb on board and hightail it out of the county. We're running you off your place, case you are too stupid to figure it out."

"My homestead!"

"No way to prove that. Land office records all burned up, didn't they? You've got twenty-eight minutes left. You better hurry. And don't try to get to a hidden gun. We've got six men and twelve guns, including six rifles. You want to go up against that much hot lead?"

"No." He hesitated. "You promise you won't hurt Emma or the boys?"

"Nobody gets hurt long as you do as you're told. Now get!"

The men on horseback walked their mounts around the small "proved up" cabin watching the tight-lipped Etta White push boxes of goods into the wagon. She soon ran out of boxes and used pillow cases to hold clothes. At last she rushed back and forth and threw loose items into the wagon box.

Victor helped for a while, then he hitched the mule to the wagon and went back to the small cabin. He had built it from logs hauled in from his own land. Now strangers were running him off his homestead. Five years he'd been here.

"Five minutes left," the big man on the roan said.

"What about my cattle?" Victor asked.

"I don't see no cattle," another of the armed men said.

"We find any strays with your brand, we'll send them along to you," another guard said.

All the mounted men laughed.

Victor ran to the small lean-to that served as a barn, and saddled his one cow pony. He tied a lead line to a halter of a colt not yet six months old and led him out of the small fenced pen.

"You call this a ranch with only one horse?" one of the rousters said. "Damn, I wouldn't be caught dead having a place like this."

Etta looked at him with fire in her eyes.

"If I had got to my rifle in time, you would be dead!" she spat at him.

The cowboy laughed, pointed his six-gun at her and said, "Bang, bang." Then they all laughed again.

"Time to move out," the leader said.

"Ain't got the bedstead yet," Victor said.

"Tough. Do it, boys."

Two men ran inside the house.

"Get on the wagon, Smith, we're leaving. Get those two little brats too, wherever you've been hiding them."

Etta called and two boys about five and six, ran from a patch of woods and jumped on the wagon.

"We going to town, mamma? Are we?"

"Yes, now hush."

Victor looked at the cabin he has worked so hard to build and saw smoke coming from the front door.

"No!" He roared. He jumped off the wagon and ran for the house. A lariat snaked out, circled his shoulders and jolted him to such a quick stop that he fell to the ground.

"Noooooooooo!" he screamed.

A pistol round dug up dirt beside him and the sharp report seemed to bring him out of his frenzy. Victor stood, brushed off the dust from his work clothes, then walked around the semi-circle of mounted men and looked searchingly at each face. Only then did he climb on the wagon and pick up the reins to the mule. The horse and colt followed on a lead line tied to the wagon.

"I got me a good memory for faces. Just want to tell you I'll never forget a one of your looks.

You'll be hearing from me one of these days. You owe me one homestead, a cabin and my livelihood. You'll be hearing from me!"

Etta sat on a cushion in the front of the wagon, her long skirt hiked up to show her ankles. She didn't care. She let the tears come then. She would not watch the cabin burn. Smoke came from both broken out windows now and the front and back doors. It would be nothing but a pile of ashes the next time she saw it. It had been a good five years.

"What are we going to do, Victor? What in the world are we going to do?"

"First off we go to La Grande and see the sheriff. If he can't do anything, I get myself a rifle and come back to my land. Any man who sets foot on it gets his head blown off!"

The warm spring sun had just passed its zenith, when Victor White and his family drew their wagon up in front of the Wallowa County courthouse and the sheriff's office. Another wagon sat nearby with a woman and four children in it. Victor tied the reins and jumped down.

"Take care what you say, Victor," Etta cautioned.

He hurried off toward the sign over the door to the sheriff's office. Inside he found Sheriff Quincy Younger talking with a man obviously right off the farm in his bib overalls and narrow brimmed hat.

"Just won't stand for it, Sheriff! You got to do something about that damned triple R bunch of thieves!"

"Mr. Nelson, I understand the problem. I'll get out there and see what I can do. Can you identify the men that run you off your property?"

"Hell, yes! Man never forgets faces of men who do that."

"Sheriff," Victor said. "Six RimRock Ranch hands drove me and my family off our place, too. Then they burned down my house. I want to charge them with arson and anything else we can come up with. Better get a posse, there's thirty men on that spread and they all got six-guns and rifles."

Sheriff Younger looked up. "Victor White isn't it? You said some of Wade Smith's hands forced you off your place, too? That makes three this morning. What the hell is he trying to do?"

"Easy what he's up to, Sheriff. He claims he worked that valley of mine for twenty years before I come. Says he owns it by rights of development. Them hands as much as told me he was taking back what was rightly his. With all the land office records burned up, how can I prove that the land is mine? I proved up on that eighty acres!"

Spur McCoy eased in the sheriff's office. He motioned the sheriff to one side of the room to talk.

"That makes three, Younger. We better move."

"Go see Wade Smith?"

"Right now. I'd suggest two more men and you and I. We leave the men run off their land here in town. We don't want any hotheads on this side. Can you go?"

"Half an hour. Have a rifle and six-gun and we'll take a ride."

They made the ride in under two hours, met a guard at the gate who led them down the long lane to the big ranch house. Wade Smith was on the porch waiting for them when they rode up. He did not invite them to get off their horses.

"What the hell you want, Younger?"

"Three families have been burned out and run off their homesteads near your ranch. What do you know about it?"

"Not a damned thing."

"Watch your tongue, Smith!" the sheriff barked. "I have evidence enough right now to charge you and a dozen or more of your men with arson, rustling and a half dozen other crimes. Just watch how you talk."

"I don't know a thing about anyone being chased off their homesteads. But I do know that I own land where some of these families have been squatting. Over twenty years ago I bought this land from the Yakima nation. Paid them with beef and salt and provisions for two years. I have witnesses."

"Then you admit you run off these three families?"

"Don't know what you're talking about."

"Your riders did it, Smith. And they don't do anything without orders from you. We can identify every man on the three raiding parties. You can't afford to let them all run. You'll pay for everything you destroyed, Smith, and you'll rebuild those houses, better than before."

"You made a fatal mistake, Mr. Smith," Spur McCoy said. "Just because the local land office burned down, don't think all of the records were destroyed. All such records are made out in triplicate. One copy goes to Washington, D.C. and two are kept by the local office. Those records are still safe and can be used at any time."

"McCoy, I told you to get off my land once."

"And I told you I'd come back anytime I wanted to. I told the sheriff we should arrest you right now. He said to give you one more chance."

"He's got to get elected again here, you don't, McCoy."

"One more incident, Smith, just one more homesteader gets run off land near your ranch, and I'll come out here and take you back to town for trial, and fifty guards around your house won't stop me. Remember, the attacker always has the advantage."

"I'm scared, fast gun, just damn scared," Smith said. "You better worry about that con man of an Englishman. I heard about his plan to take over the county. I saw his kind before, in Boston thirty years ago."

"The courts will settle that," Sheriff Younger said. "The three families you burned out will be settled by me, and damn soon. Now, will you agree to stop this taking the law into your own hands until the courts settle the Englishman's Royal Claim?"

"That could take months!"

"Two weeks at the most," Spur said. "If I can prove that Sir Jeffrey Mountbatten is a fraud and perhaps a murderer, it could be settled in a day or two."

"Good, I'll let you make your play. But just remember this whole end of the valley is mine! I've developed it, I've grazed it for twenty years!"

"Grazing public land doesn't make it yours, Smith. You know nothing about the law. Get a good lawyer and ask him for some advice. You're going to need it." Spur turned his mount and the other three moved with him.

They rode slowly away from the buildings and down the long lane. The guard did not come with them.

"Don't look back," Spur said so the other three could hear. "We've stopped him. He won't run off any more homesteaders. Now we have to talk to the survivors and get statements and any identification they can make. Descriptions at least of the riders. Eighteen of them. There must be a way to identify those men with certainty."

The sheriff scratched his chin. "Sure as hell gonna try. This kind of range warfare I don't want in the county. The big ranchers have too much power now. Let Smith get away with this and there will be no way to hold him. We have to stop him dead in his saddle right now!"

15

Wade Smith watched the sheriff and the three men ride off his ranch. He called his foreman over and gave him curt instructions, then Wade went back in the house.

When the owner of the RRR came out five minutes later, he was ready for the range. He left with twelve men, four of them heading in three different directions. They carried the equipment they would need.

Wade went with the group nearest his ranch headquarters, a long arm of land that he had neglected to buy from the government when he had a chance before the homesteader moved in five years ago. The eighty acres bordered the river and controlled access to a half mile long stretch that he needed.

He sat on his big gelding at the small rise and looked down on the piece of land he wanted and he would have it! First he had a small job to do.

The four cowboys spread out on a sweep down the quarter mile wide stretch of land pushing all the cattle they could find in front of them. The land was open, part of the glacial formed four mile wide depression that had attracted a river.

The cattle were not the best, a few longhorn mix and the general range cattle of Eastern Oregon.

Wade was not so interested in improving his herd as eliminating that of a competitor. When the homesteader returned to his land, if he won in the courts, he would find no house, no barn, no buildings of any kind and no cattle.

The owner of the RimRock Ranch estimated there might be two hundred animals in the small strip of land. It was lush grazing land and could support that many. He would drive them north, past the edge of the man's property, toward a box canyon well beyond his own ranch boundary and into federal land.

The cowboys knew their jobs. The smart cutting horses could anticipate every move of a steer or a cow and calf and turn at just the precise moment to move the animal the way the rider indicated.

In an hour the cowboys had rounded up every critter and bunched them. Then they began the slow process of driving them north. The animals did not want to leave the good grass, nor the handy drinking water.

Wade looked in wonder at the quality of some of the stock. He was surprised. They all carried a brand, the FP ranch. Wade laughed when he figured how easy a running iron could change that brand into his own RRR. And that was exactly what he had in mind.

They got the critters into the box canyon early and immediately bunched them. Two men started a fire and threw in the long running irons. One iron was simply a right angle bend in a straight piece of steel so it could be used to form straight lines. Another iron from the RRR would make the rounded section of the "R." A third iron was the "R" from the regular branding tools.

At the site of the fire, Wade stepped down from his horse. He had spent years in the saddle, and could do any job on his ranch better than his men. That bred respect for the boss. He checked the fire and the irons, then when they were glowing red hot, he signalled the ropers.

They picked out a steer and began the ballet of roping. Wade insisted his men use the head and heel catch. The first roper used an overhand throw of his lariat to catch the head of the steer. He tightened the line and led the critter away.

The second roper came up behind the steer and made a heel catch on the back two legs using a sidearm cast. This slipped the rope under the steer's back feet. The rider pulled up the noose and held the steer. They slowly stretched out the steer by pulling on both ends. Since both rear legs were noosed together, the animal soon lost its balance and fell on its side.

Now it was ready for branding or castration or any other attention needed.

Wade walked up to the first thrown steer and looked at it. The owner's hip brand the FP showed plainly. He checked for other marks and found only a small ear notch. There was no jaw brand or wattle mark or road brand. Wade smiled.

"Brand them," he said. And make a fresh ear cut over that small one. There won't be a fair day in hell anybody'll be able to say these cattle aren't regular triple R stock."

The branding began. Soon the thrashing cattle turned the area around the fire into a barren, dusty arena. Red hot irons seared the flesh, burned hair off and left a triple R brand on the animal's hip, the owner brand.

Deftly the running iron put a curved line around the end of the "F" and created the top half of the "R." The running iron lanced a line down from the loop to complete the "R." Sometimes the "R" branding iron was set directly over the old letters to create new ones. When the expert branders were done the ear was clipped removing the old ear mark with that of the RRR.

Then the bawling calf, steer, bull or cow was untied and two cowboys herded it into a new holding area.

They worked until it was too dark to see the brands. Half the cattle had been marked. They rolled out blankets and slept. They would go to work again as soon as it was dawn and be finished before noon. Then they would return to their normal duties.

Wade left the branding at dusk and rode to the other branding site where the smaller herds from the other two homesteaders he had burned out had been gathered. There were only about fifty head, and they had all been branded and would be driven to the major holding box canyon at day-light.

Wade thought of the sheriff and he snorted. Anyway it turned out, he won. Nobody would be able to identify any cattle. He might have to rebuild the buildings he burned down, but the cattle he took were worth much more than three shacks.

He rode back to his ranch with his foreman and three cowboys from the last branding. It had been a good day's work.

Later, Wade leaned back in his big rocking chair on the porch and watched the moon glinting off the Grande Ronde river. Why in hell hadn't he sired any sons? What does a man build up a big ranch for? He had no intentions of giving the place to some snot nosed kid who Margaret just happened to marry. She had about as much sense in judging men as a heifer in heat.

If his wife hadn't died so young . . .

He could always marry again, find some young, wide-hipped woman with big tits who could produce two or three sons for him in three years. An idea. A good brood bitch was what he needed, but where did a man find one in La Grande?

Virginia came out on the porch and sat in the other rocker.

"Daddy, I've been thinking about moving into town. I am away from everything out here."

"No."

"Daddy, you can't run my life for me. I want to go places and do things. I've never been out of the county! Do you realize that? I want to go visit my aunt in Portland. I'm going to write her a letter and ask her if I can come. I'll stay a month and then come back."

"Absolutely not!"

"Why?"

"Don't have to give you a reason, you're my daughter."

"I'm a grown woman. Lots of the girls I used to know from church are married. One has four children already! Do you want me to be an old maid!"

"Virginia. You stand to inherit this whole spread some day. And the man you marry will get it as a gift. I want to be sure you marry a good man."

"I don't want your old ranch! Sell it. Move to San Francisco and you can go to the whorehouse every night instead of just on Saturday nights the way you do now!"

Virginia jumped up and flounced away.

Wade watched her go and only with a great effort did he hold his angry words. Slowly he began to smile. So she did know where he went on Saturday afternoons. Good. But that also meant that she was a grown up woman. He would have to think about what to do with her. It might be a good idea to let her stay in town for a while. Then she would forget about Portland.

Portland was out of the question. She'd get married and bring home some city feller who would ruin the ranch in five years. Maybe he should sell it. What was he killing himself for to make the triple R bigger and bigger?

Wade slapped his hand down on his dusty denim pants leg. "Hell, just to do it!" he said outloud. Just to prove to everyone else in the valley that he was smarter and meaner and a better rancher than they would ever be. That was enough.

Hell, it didn't make that much difference what happened to the triple R. When he was in a pine box six feet under the ground it wouldn't matter a whit!

Wade stood slowly and walked through the

night toward the small house to the left of the
ranchhouse where his cook for the past ten years
had lived. Her name was Mildred and she had
been his foreman's wife before the man got gored
by a range bull. Wade promised him to keep
Mildred as cook before he died.

He watched and saw no one in sight. He slipped
in the back door of the four room place and called.

"Milly?"

"Yes, Wade. I'm in the bedroom."

He went in and saw her at the mirror combing
her long black hair. She turned and smiled. Milly
was forty, and enjoyed eating her own cooking.
She was short and heavy with huge breasts that
sagged from their weight. Her small, round face
had bright blue eyes, pink cheeks and a smile that
charmed every hand on the place. She had almost
married one three years ago, but he drifted off
when he found out Milly was barren.

Milly turned. She wore a soft cotton nightgown.

"Problems, Wade?"

"A few. I just got to thinking about the ranch,
and Virginia, and what the hell I'm doing all of
this work for."

"Tell me all about it." She put down her comb,
stood and walked to him. Her breasts bulged the
nightgown. She unbuttoned his shirt and slipped
it off.

"Want me to heat up some water? Only take a
half hour or so. That would give us plenty of time.
Later you can have a fine bath."

He nodded, then reached out and caught one
big breast with each hand.

"Christ! but you feel good."

"It's been almost a month, Wade."

"I know." He massaged her breasts, then kissed her. He came away. "I'll get the fire going."

He used kindling and then bigger wood to get the fire started in the wood stove, then moved the copper boiler on top of the stove and Milly poured in two buckets of well water.

Wade stoked the fire again, then Milly pushed against him, and began unbuttoning his pants.

"Right here in the kitchen, woman?"

"Any place as long as you got it hard!" she said and smiled.

They hurried to the bedroom and she undressed him, then slid out of the nightgown. She was fat, her large breasts sagged and Ward laughed and rolled her on the bed.

"I'll take comfort over speed any day," he said and began licking her breasts.

Milly purred softly. "I've got some surprises for you tonight, Wade," she said. "Something that we've never done. I think you'll like it."

"Woman, that's got to be during our fourth or fifth fuck. I've got plans myself before that. You'll have to wait your turn to choose."

"I'll wait," she said and reached for his crotch.

Upstairs in the big house, Virginia watched the lights come on in the kitchen of the cook's house. Then the light went off as the lamp must have been carried into the bedroom.

She knew her father was there. Good. She liked Milly, who had been like a mother to her the last ten years. Milly had told her about her bleeding time, and sat up with her for hours one night when it finally happened, talking to her, soothing her when she cried.

Virginia wondered about the new hand they

had taken on. He was not much over twenty, had sandy hair and was tall and sturdy. He spoke with a funny accent. He said was from New York. She had liked him the first time she saw him.

But she knew better than to let on. If her father had even the smallest inkling what she was thinking, he would run the man off the ranch. No, she would take her time, see how he fit in with the crew, and then, one day, maybe, when there was no one around she could get a note to him.

They could meet down by the river. For just a moment she wondered how it would be. Then she was off in a fantasy. She lay on the bed and when she thought of his hands touching her, she touched herself. He was so bold as to rub her breasts, but she said it was all right.

Virginia rubbed her own breasts. His hands wandered then, and so did hers and then he was over her and she was on her back, her knees spread and raised, and he was entering her!

She found the candle in her nightstand and put saliva on it and lowered it between her legs and then surged upward against it as it slid into her hot, wet slit.

"Oh, yes! yes!" she murmured as her finger found her hard little clit and she stroked it.

"Yes, darling, so good!"

Then the ranch boy was lost in her thoughts and it was Spur McCoy over her and stroking into her and she was overcome with emotion as he reached her climax.

Five minutes later she smiled into the darkness.

"Lovely, Spur McCoy, just fantastic. I won't let you get away so easily the next time."

16

When Spur McCoy, the sheriff and his two deputies were on the way back to La Grande after talking to Wade Smith, they found a strange group just outside of town. It was a smartly out-fitted democratic buggy with four horsemen riding shotgun. When they came up to the group, the guards saw the sheriff and relaxed.

Inside the buggy sat Lord Jeffrey Mountbatten and his manservant Edward Long.

"Sheriff, just the man I wish to see," Lord Mountbatten said. "The tenor of the population has quieted and now seems to be fairly stable. The people have accepted the idea that the courts will decide in their favor, so the animosity toward me has reduced.

"However, as you can see, I am taking no chances. I don't want to get shot dead and then win the judgment for all of this beautiful land and not be able to enjoy it."

"Seems the folks have quieted down after the first panic, Mr. Mountbatten," the sheriff said.

"You might be a lord and knighted in your country, but that don't mean a damn thing here, Mountbatten. You obey our laws or you get your neck stretched. That good and plain enough?"

"Truly my good man. We have sheriff's in England as well. I understand your position. But I also wish you to understand mine. Just because I own the whole county, it is still a political entity of Oregon and the United States, and must be governed as such. I'll only be the freeholder of the land and buildings. Laws will still apply, the city and county governments still exist.

"I totally understand all of this, my good fellow. I've been looking over some of my land. It is vast, much larger in reality than it looked on the map. Yes, it will take me days, perhaps weeks to visit all of it."

"No need to do that until the court makes up its mind about that document of yours," Spur said.

Mountbatten smiled at Spur. "And I understand Mr. McCoy is a lawman of some repute engaged by the United States Government. That all is quite impressive. I expect to cooperate completely with the government entities and to participate in the governing function wherever needed.

"I really see no practical purpose to disposses anyone from any land or building. Quite simply only the ownership will change hands. I am working out some applicable share cropper tenant basis for the farms, ranches and businesses. An equitable plan I assure you, Sheriff, that should keep everyone happy.

"Perhaps later the living units will be assessed some type of rent, I'm not sure yet. You see, gentlemen, as the Duke of Wallowa, I will rule in a way. I was born to rule, to lead, and by God I will do my best!''

He nodded to the sheriff and motioned for his driver to move the rig on upstream along the Grande Ronde river.

The sheriff watched the entourage move away.

"Something I don't like about that man," Younger said.

"Join a growing group," Spur said. "Somehow he's too slick, too sure of himself. It's not the British accent, there's something else there that bothers me."

Back in town, Spur let the sheriff talk to the dispossessed, and went back to the wreckage of the burned out office. Basement and cellar were still the key words. He probed the entire floor area of the house with a steel rod, ramming it hard into the ground to find any hidden basement or hiding area.

After two hours he found nothing.

Spur saw the Englishman ride back into town and go into the hotel. Spur went back there as well, cleaned up and changed his shirt, and walked up to the third floor to see the Duke of Wallowa. Two guards stood in the hall.

"Tell Mr. Mountbatten that Spur McCoy is here to see him."

One of the guards knocked on the door and when it opened a crack he relayed the message. The door came open fully.

Edward Long smiled at the Secret Service agent.

"Mr. McCoy, of course, our Irish cousin. Won't you come in? The Duke is in his room, he'll be out shortly."

Lord Jeffrey came out at once. "Ah, Mr.

McCoy. Just cleaning up a little. What can we do for you?"

"Your ancestoral home in England. I was wondering where it is?"

"Actually it lay in Sheffield. My father became the Duke of Sheffield, the title I inherited."

"Interesting. Is there a castle and everything?"

"No, no. Just a manor house. It is quite extensive by local standards. It's on two square miles of wooded hills with a trout stream and a herd of deer. The house itself is thirty-six rooms with servants' quarters in another building. It's quite adequate."

"I would guess you have farm lands?"

"Oh, quite. All done on a sharecropper basis as you blokes would say. Perhaps I could ask you for some advice. You seem to be well traveled."

"Fire away."

"I understand there are great stands of virgin timber in my mountains in the Wallowas. Pine and fir. The pine is the prime lumber tree in this area. Would it be practical for me to start a logging or lumbering operation in the mountains?"

"Impossible. Whoever harvests that timber will need a railroad to get the logs or the lumber out to the markets. You can't haul logs out for sixty miles, and then get it from here to the railroad. It's just too far."

"Pity. I had the same conclusions. The nice thing about steers is that they have their own transportation devices, four feet."

"True, driving steers is much easier. That's why the big ranchers have developed here, not big lumberyards or sawmills."

"As you can see, sir. I am learning as I go along."

"All of us do, Mountbatten. Might I ask how you hope to establish the authenticity of your Royal Land Grant?"

"You may ask, but my barrister will have to answer. I engaged legal representation this afternoon."

"Sorry, I don't want to talk to a lawyer. Thank you, but I have an appointment and I must rush away. Maybe we can talk again sometime."

"Yes, I would enjoy that. I want to learn more about Washington, D.C., your capital."

Spur said goodbye and stepped into the hall. He was halfway down when a man arrived staring at each door number. Soon he found the right one with the two guards.

"I'm Bill Amos. I need to see Sir Jeffrey."

A moment later the man who was dressed in a Sunday suit entered the room. Spur frowned but continued on to his own room.

In the Englishman's room he had moved behind a small desk and now looked up at the new visitor.

"Ah, Mr. Amos. Have you considered my offer?"

"Yes, and I've about decided to go ahead." Amos was thin and nervous. He kept running his fingers back through his hair.

"Decided that I can get a deed from you now, I'll be free and clear if you win the court case. If the States won't honor your claim, then I still have my property."

"That's the La Grande Mercantile, isn't it Mr. Amos?"

"Yes, right. I have drawn up a bill of sale granting to me and my heirs or assignees all rights to the building and the land under it to me for the sum of two hundred dollars."

"We mentioned a figure of three hundred."

"That's a year's wages, Sir Jeffrey. All I can raise is two hundred, take it or leave it. That's all I can afford for this kind of insurance."

Mountbatten stalled. He walked to the window and was counting up the firms he could squeeze for two hundred each. If he could get twenty or thirty of them, they would ride out on horses in the dead of the night, take their money with them and catch the stage well out of town.

He came back to the desk.

"All right, Mr. Amos. I'll do it for you, if you will spread the word to those you can trust about this service. We can't let the general public hear about this. I'm dealing only with reputable businessmen of integrity such as you. Also we don't want the sheriff or the court involved. There is nothing at all illegal here, it's a matter of double insurance if you will."

"I understand. Just sign at these two places, and I sign under them."

"You did bring cash, Mr. Amos?"

"Just the way we talked about."

"Mostly ten dollar bills, is that all right?"

"Perfectly acceptable." He signed the papers. "Now, if you have one or two friends you can trust not to let this get out . . ."

"Yes, I think I should tell some friends. Should they contact you here?"

The Englishman counted the money, let it lay on the table and held out his hand.

"Mr. Amos, a pleasure helping you this way."

When the merchant had gone, Edward Long ran out of the connecting room and counted the bills.

"Glory be! What a good thing we got going here, guv'nor. I've got three more men waiting in the hall. They wouldn't say why they wanted to see you. Think I'll bring them in and put them in the spare bedroom so not anyone else will see them."

"Capital idea, old man. Now let's rush it. We could have ten visitors tonight! I told them anytime up to midnight."

By midnight the Duke of Wallowa was so excited and nervous he could hardly keep a straight face.

"The idiots!" he exclaimed softly when the last of the merchants had left. They had sold back property the men owned or had been paying mortgages on to fourteen men. All were properly glad to take the small risk. The amounts were from two hundred to three hundred, and Long had kept the tab and the cash.

Long came out of the bedroom with a flushed face, his eyes dancing.

"Gawd! I can't believe it. We've got three thousand five hundred American dollars in our kip!"

"Now this is a good night's work."

"Let's leave tonight! Let's get out of here while we still have our skulls in one piece, mate. These blokes are going to get on to us damn quick I've a hunch. We can rent horses and be ten miles out on the way to Portland when the stage comes along the road. We pay and get on board."

"Just the start, Edward, just the start. We can

do as well for three days and have ten thousand dollars!''

His eyes glinted at the idea. They locked the door and went into the bedroom and looked at the bills stacked on the bed.

Sir Jeffrey ripped off his shirt and began unbuttoning his pants.

"Money makes you horny, doesn't it you old cock!"

"Damn right. I want to lay in all that money naked! I want you to put it to me right on top of three thousand five hundred dollars!''

Jeffrey was naked, he fell on the bed on his back, then rolled over and lifted his bare ass into the air.

"Come on, Edward, ram it into me right now. This is one that I'll never forget. The day we made three thousand five hundred dollars and you buggered me right on top of all that cash.''

"Fifty-fifty, you promised me.''

"Damn right, now get your fly open and that delicious prick out and throw it into me. Now!''

Colette had sung beautifully that night. One of the clerks from the hardware store had stayed for both performances, and fell into step with her as she left the saloon.

"Miss Colette? I hope you don't mind if I walk with you to your hotel? I'm Gerry Todd.''

"I'd rather you didn't, Mr. Todd.''

"Call me Gery. That's okay. No problem. I'm going that way. Really appreciated your singing and playing. We come from Baltimore and there's performers there lots of times. But you were better than any of them I ever heard.''

"Please don't walk with me, Mr. Todd."

"Come on, now Colette. I'd really appreciate it."

"I do have to make a short detour."

"No problem, I have time. Nobody waiting up for me."

"Oh."

They walked a block and she turned down a dark side street.

"I must see a woman down here."

"Fine, I'll go along."

When they came to the middle of the block she stopped.

"I didn't want anyone to see. Gerry, I like you. Would you like to kiss me?"

"What? Like to? Damn, I'd half kill to kiss you. Right here?"

"Nobody can see us. No houses or businesses open."

"Now?"

"Yes, now."

He kissed her and she held him tightly. When he started to move away, she opened her mouth and his tongue darted in. She felt his erection building. When they came apart she took his hand and placed it over one of her breasts.

"Oh, damn! I never expected anything like this!"

"Are you excited Mr. Todd?" She reached down and felt of his fly, found his long hard lump and smiled at him in the half light. "Yes, you are excited." She opened her blouse and pushed his hand inside. "Play with my titties, Todd. I like it!"

"Jesus!" He kissed her again with his hand on

her breast as she rubbed his crotch. Then she pulled him back into the short alley away from the street and sat down on the ground behind a carriage.

She quickly opened her blouse and lifted the chemise. "Play with them!" she commanded him. Gerry did.

"Show me your big cock, Gerry Todd," she said softly.

"Oh, damn!" he said. He fumbled at his waist and then his penis sprang out, hard and ready.

While he did this she reached quickly into her pocket and took out the knife. She opened the blade, heard the lock snic into place so the blade could not fold back.

When he looked down at his hard penis, she swung the knife. The razor-like blade slit Gerry Todd's throat from side to side, opening both carotid arteries. Then she grabbed his penis and using the knife, sliced it in half.

She had moved away from the spurting blood from his arteries. None of it splashed on her. His hard pumping heart sprayed blood from his throat as Gerry Todd died in less than a minute.

Colette wiped the bloody knife on the man's shirt, unlocked the blade and folded it, then slid it back into her skirt pocket. She stood, brushed the dust and dirt from her dark skirt, walked back to Main Street, turned right and was soon in her hotel room undressing.

Only for a moment did she think of Gerry Todd. Then his face became that of her older brother who had raped her so many times. She smiled thinly, remembering the blood gushing from her brother's neck. Then she frowned. Or was it Gerry Todd? She wasn't sure.

Colette put on her nightgown, made sure the door was locked and lay down on her pillow. She was smiling as she went to sleep less than two minutes after blowing out the lamp.

17

After Spur left the hotel room and his fruitless talk with the two Englishmen, he went down one floor to his own room in the same hostelry. He was twenty feet away when an explosion shattered the door to his room, blasting half of it into the hall and filling the area with thick smoke.

Spur bent low under the smoke and worked his way to the splintered door. The window had blasted out as well and now the wind blowing in quickly cleared the room of smoke. The place was a mess. The bed had been blown apart. Bedding, springs and mattress parts were all over the room. The dresser had tipped over, the porcelain pitcher shattered against the wash basin.

His carpetbag under the bed had been ripped open and slammed to one side wall. Chunks of plaster from half the ceiling had fallen over everything.

Before Spur started his examination, the hotel clerk came charging into the room.

"What the hell?" he asked.

"Bomb," Spur said. "Most likely dynamite. Not sure how they set it off yet. It wasn't thrown through the window because the glass all blew outside. I locked the door when I left. Of course anyone with a pass key could get in here."

"This has never happened before, Mr. . . ."

"McCoy, Spur McCoy. If it hasn't, then you're lucky." He found what he had been looking for a few minutes later. A white candle, the cheap kind you could buy for three cents in a hardware store, had been blasted against the front wall. He picked it up. It had burned about half way down, leaving a three-inch stub. He showed it to the room clerk.

"Here's how they set off the dynamite. Wedge the candle into a solid place and wrap the dynamite fuse around the candle. When the flame burns down to the fuse, it lights it and sets off the bomb. Simple, effective and can let the bomber be up to an hour away from the scene before the bomb goes off.

"I'm sure you'll pay for the damages, Mr. McCoy."

"I'm sure I won't. I may charge the hotel for damage to my equipment and my clothing. Find the bomber, he's the one who should be paying."

Spur gathered up his clothing and everything else he could find that he owned. "I rented a room on the first floor yesterday, I think it was. I'll move down there. As far as you know Spur McCoy has checked out of his room."

"Yes sir, Mr. McCoy."

In the room that Spur had rented for the Englishmen, he settled in, saw that the bomber had also stolen his backup .45 Colt and two boxes of shells. Swell person. Spur decided he better

buy a new weapon and headed for the hardware
store which had a selection of handguns.

He walked outside into the late afternoon. It
was nearly four o'clock. This far north it would
not be dark until nearly nine that evening. He
turned toward the store and stumbled on a loose
plank in the boardwalk. Just as he pitched
forward a rifle snarled from across the street and
a slug zapped through the air where his chest had
been a split second before.

Spur dove to the ground, rolled on the boardwalk and fell off it behind a water trough at the
near edge of the dirt street. Two more rifle slugs
jolted into the heavy boards of the trough, then
Spur heard a horse pounding down the alley at a
gallop. He came up with his long barreled Colt
but the man was too far away. The black horse
was ridden by a tall man in a dark shirt and dark
pants.

He headed toward the route south out of town.
Spur watched him a moment, saw a cowboy just
getting off his horse in front of a saloon.

"Can I borrow your horse, cowboy?" Spur
shouted as he ran up to him. "That snake just
tried to bushwhack me!"

The cowboy nodded. Spur jumped on the
mare's back, slid into the saddle and raced after
the gunman. He checked but the cowboy did not
have a rifle in his saddle boot. Spur tried to
remember how many .45 rounds he had for the
Colt. Twenty in his gunbelt, but none in his
pockets. He hadn't planned on a shootout.

He rode through the alley, charged to the left
where he had seen the rider turn. Now there was
only a few houses between him and the prairie. He
could see the rider ahead, galloping hard, heading

straight at the ridge to the west of town.

Spur slowed his horse. There would be no trouble following the bushwhacker. The river flowed in the other direction. There was little timber this close to town. It was mostly rolling land with a few gentle hills, in an open and wide valley. The gunman was at a disadvantage.

At the first tree, Spur looked ahead and found some small groves of trees. They were mostly ponderosa pine and white pine, with little brush or undergrowth. Not a good spot for another ambush.

Spur rode to the left of the area the man in black would have entered the woods if he continued on his same route. He guessed that the man he chased would find a spot and stand and fight. He was not supplied for a long run. His first move would come from a good position. It was Spur's job not to get caught in an ambush where the gunman could be successful.

At the very edge of the pine grove, Spur stopped and listened. He held the muzzle of his mount but heard no sounds of movement, no call from the other animal. He moved ahead cautiously.

A rifle shot blasted in the virgin wilderness, and at once Spur knew his horse was dead. She took the slug in the head and collapsed at once. Spur jumped to one side and came up running.

The one shot told Spur a lot about his opponent. The man was a hired killer who would stop at nothing to get his man. No cowboy would shoot a horse, that was a sacrilege. This killer had no such moral cautions.

Spur slid behind a big pine and looked to the left where he figured the shot had been fired.

There were fifty yards of open space with only scattered trees, then a spate of heavy brush that could conceal the killer and his horse.

Spur began moving toward it from tree to tree. He changed directions so the gunman could not get a bead on him for the next charge.

When he had covered half the distance he stopped and listened again. This time he heard a horse blowing somewhere ahead. It was quickly cut off as if hands had grabbed the muzzle.

Good, the man was still with his horse. Easier that way.

Spur charged to the next tree, a slender foot thick pine that afforded inadequate protection from a rifle, and at once he changed angles and jolted to a two-foot tree at right angles to his main line of attack.

A rifle shot barked into the quietness and the sharp sound was swallowed up by the green foliage. It missed. Spur stopped behind the big tree and worked on his attack plan. Right now he had little to go on. The man might have a whole box of shells, or he could have brought only three or four in his pocket, planning on a quick kill in the street and then fade into the townlife.

His best bet: no six-gun, one rifle, a knife probably and not more than a dozen rifle rounds. He had used three in town, and three more so far. He was down to six rounds. Maybe.

One was enough to kill.

Spur checked his next tree. It was fifteen yards away. Plenty of time for a good marksman to sight in and fire. If Spur ran a yard a second it would give the rifleman fifteen seconds. Too long.

Spur checked other trees. None good enough. He found a good sized rock directly behind his tree. It was hand sized. He threw it the opposite way he was going to run, aiming it at some small brush so it would make some noise.

As soon as the rock hit, Spur darted for his tree. The noise should pull the gunman's attention away from the point where Spur had been last seen.

When Spur was four strides from the tree, the rifle spat out blue smoke and hot lead. But the aim had been hurried. The lead only sliced through Spur's pantleg by his ankle, missing flesh and bone. Then he was safely behind the tree.

Now he was within ten yards of the hiding spot. Spur saw the blue smoke where the shot had been fired. He edged his long barreled Colt around the tree and sent a .45 slug into the brush three feet to the left of the smoke.

"Fire and move, fire and move." His old infantry training was still practical, lifesaving. He counted on most men being right handed and most would roll to the right after firing.

Spur heard no sound of pain from the brush.

He had twenty-four rounds left.

From this point the trees grew closer together. In one strong surge he could top the small rise and see behind the shield of brush. As Spur was getting ready for the move, he heard the sound of saddle leather creaking. The man was riding out!

He surged around the tree and charged the ten yards to the break.

The tall, gaunt man had just settled in the saddle on a big roan. Spur lifted his iron and fired all in one shot. The lead blasted into the left shoulder of the bushwhacker as the mount charged forward. Before Spur could aim another shot the pair plunged into the light brush and were gone.

Spur ran into the spot he last saw the horse only to find it vanishing into another clout of brush thirty yards downslope.

McCoy dropped to the ground on his knees, and pushed two more rounds into his pistol. He would carry six rounds now and take the chance. He had wounded the man, a tall, dark, lean individual Spur couldn't remember seeing before.

The man was hurt. That would slow him down.

The bushwhacker might be a local. If so he wouldn't run, he would try to finish his job or go back to town and get his shoulder treated.

Now Spur had the advantage. He ran toward the brush and as he suspected the killer was not waiting for him, Spur eased through the small growth and looked out into an open area of two hundred yards.

Near the far side he saw the roan standing behind two big ponderosa pines. He could not see the man. Much too far out of range for even Spur's long barreled Colt. But fish-in-a-barrel range for the rifle which Spur figured was a Sharps by the sound.

Spur edged back out of sight so he could watch the area where he figured the gunman had to be. The stranger had taken the first advantage. Kill the victim's horse and put him on foot. He had another advantage with his long gun, but so far that had not been the controlling factor.

Spur ran to the left. He was a natural warrior. He did not sit down and logically figure out his moves. If he had to do that he would be as good as dead in a combat situation. He had learned that in his days in the Civil War as an infantry officer.

Instinctively he knew what to do and how to do it.

The Secret Service Agent slanted around the clearing and past the big ponderosas toward the still visible horse. Almost too late he realized it could be a trap. The horse was visible but not the man.

Trap!

He slowed, bellied down beside a white pine and edged up so he could look around it at ground level. Few men will watch for a an attacker on the ground. He scanned all the area around the twin ponderosas but could find no evidence of a man. He sectionalized the area, concentrating on each square yard of the trees and brush at one time.

In one spot a foot-high pine tree leaned at an unnatural angle as if an elbow or a shoulder nudged it to one side. If it had been trampled with a boot it would be righting itself gradually. He watched, it did not move. Then it did! depressing a little more.

Spur was forty yards away. He leveled out the long-barreled Colt and sighted in. With both hands he held the weapon and refined his sight again just to the right of the small pine.

McCoy fired six rounds into the area as fast as he could pull the trigger. He had practiced holding the weapon solid against the recoil for fast shooting. His sturdy hands and wrists were like steel.

He saw the first bullet slam through the light brush exactly where he wanted it and the other five made a pattern around the spot.

A scream of rage slanted through the silent pine trees.

Quickly Spur kicked out the spent brass and

shoved in six more loads from his gunbelt.

He saw no movement among the brush.

Spur ran again.

This time he took more chances. A rifle round whispered over his head but he was behind a tree again, then he jolted forward, circling the spot where the enemy lay.

The attacker was still alive.

He was still deadly.

The Secret Service Agent came up from behind where he had seen the brush move. The horse was still in place, tied he could see now, some ten yards from the former target.

Spur lifted his six-gun, concentrating on the same spot where he had seen the small pine tree move.

The suddeness of the rifle shot caught him off guard. The bullet from the Sharps smashed into his Colt on the side of the cylinder, jolted it from his hand nearly breaking his trigger finger. His Colt spun twenty feet to his left. He knew that it would never work again, at least not until it had been retooled by a gunsmith.

Spur shook his numb right hand and hunkered down to where he had rolled behind a pine tree.

What the hell could he do now? His ambusher had killed his only weapon.

Except the four-inch sheath knife on his belt. A knife against a rifle?

A fine way to die.

Spur watched ahead. Nothing. The man was a master at waiting, a cautious, patient man who had everything to lose. McCoy threw a rock to his left.

No reaction.

A cautious, smart man.

Spur checked the terrain again. He was on a slight uphill from his target. A gentle breeze blew down the slope. He reached in his pocket, found a wad of "stinkers" the frontier matches pasted together on a waxy base with sulphur tips. He cautiously gathered long strands of dry grass from around him, wrapped them around a rock until he had a heavy ball that would burn and he could still pitch.

He made three of them, watching the spot where he had seen the haze of blue smoke where the rifle had last spoken.

When the third fire ball was ready, he struck a stinker, lighted one ball, let it burn a moment, then lit the second from the first. He threw the first fire ball toward the dry grass near the bushwhacker's hiding spot. Then lit the third ball and threw the last two in the same direction.

As the second fire ball hit, the rifle snarled twice more, but Spur was already behind his protective pine tree.

The bushwhacker could have only three rifle rounds left. Maybe.

Spur watched the fire balls catch the grass on fire. It would not produce a forest fire, but could smoke out the gunman. The grass blazed up and the fire pushed it forward. It was ten feet from the place he figured the gunman was when a figure lifted up.

Spur stood and threw four hand-sized rocks he had gathered. He thought one of them hit the man. He ran after him, feeling safe for a moment since the smoke concealed him. He jogged around the small patch of flames and ashes and saw the man twenty feet ahead. He was down.

The bushwhacker had lost his rifle. He held his

right, bloody shoulder. His left leg had twisted under him and Spur saw a spot of blood on his pants leg.

Spur took out his sheath knife and walked forward slowly.

"I won't kill you unless I have to," Spur said evenly.

The man made no agressive move.

"Do you have a pistol?"

"No."

"Your rifle out of rounds?"

"Yes."

"That leg broken?"

"Damnit, yes!"

Spur walked up to him. "Stay very still or this blade goes six inches into your spine!" Spur checked his pockets and ran his hands down each leg. He had no hideout gun. Spur looked at the shoulder. It was broken and bleeding. The bushwhacker gritted his teeth.

Spur attempted to move the broken leg, but the man screamed.

McCoy sat down opposite the man and lit a thin, crooked cheroot. As he smoked the man watched him.

"What's your name?"

"Digger."

"Came to see you the other day."

"Didn't want to talk."

"Who hired you to kill the Land Office man?"

"Didn't do that."

"I'm betting you did. Do you want to get back to town?"

"Yeah, sure!"

"Who is going to help you?"

Digger stared at Spur for a long moment, then

snorted. "And you won't unless I tell you. Is that it?"

"About the size of it. You could hop all the way back to La Grande, I guess. On one foot it could take you a week. You'll be dead before then."

"Yeah. No sense fooling you. It was the Englishmen, they hired me. Wanted him dead and the records all burned."

"Swear that in front of a judge?"

"Sure, if I don't hang. I'll point the finger at them if I only get ten years in prison. I been there before."

"Deal." Spur moved away, came back with a slab of bark two feet long and three stout green sticks the same length.

"I have to splint that leg or you'll lose it. Compound fracture?"

"I guess."

"You'll probably pass out when I do it. But you have my word, you'll get to the doctor before dark."

That's the way it happened. Doctor George promised to keep Digger out of sight for three or four days, and swore his wife and one nurse not to let on he was there.

Spur smiled. He knew who, now all he had to do was smoke them out . . . and find those duplicate land records.

18

The next morning at breakfast, Spur was laying out his day's work. The records were primary. As soon as he found them he could go after the Englishmen. He was sure now the pair of imports from Britain were phonies. An English aristocrat was unlikely to pay someone to murder. Spur, however, knew that he still needed more proof.

He was almost through a big breakfast when a small boy brought him a note and scampered away. Spur opened the lavender scented paper and read.

"Mr. McCoy. My name is Charlotte Younger. I am the sheriff's wife and I must see you this morning. It is an urgent matter. Could I ask you to meet me two blocks in back of the hotel on the corner? I will be in a closed carriage and will stop beside you. This is terribly important to me. Hope to see you there soon. I will be waiting for an hour."

Spur fininished his coffee, folded the note and put it in his pocket. He had worn working clothes for the city, good trousers, boots, a plain white shirt, string tie and his doeskin brown vest.

Outside he read the note again. It must have something to do with the case. Perhaps the sheriff wanted to tell him something but had no other way to get a message to him. Although the logic of the last reason was thin, Spur smiled. He was always ready to see a lady who went to so much trouble to meet him. The closed carriage especially interested him. He had no fears of being ambushed now, since the man who had tried, and who had bombed his room, was safely tucked away with a broken leg, and his good arm was handcuffed to the bedstead.

Spur walked out of the hotel and down the street. He had decided to meet the lady, and walked briskly. He had a lot to get done today and hoped this small detour would not take too long.

He saw the buggy ahead with a prancing black mare in the traces. McCoy walked up to the near side and saw the leather side door with a small glass window in it swing open.

Inside sat a prim lady whom he guessed was short with long, flowing black hair that fell to her waist. She had dark eyes a small smile on her pretty face and a slender, boyish form. She could be about thirty years old.

"Mr. McCoy?"

"Yes, ma'am."

"Come closer, please."

He moved up to the edge of the door and held it. "How can I help you, ma'am? Is it some message from the sheriff?"

"In an indirect way. Would you please get in this door and drive, I need to talk to you."

"Yes, of course."

He stepped into the rig as she pushed over on the seat. Once inside he took the reins, looked out the open front of the rig and clucked at the beautiful black. She stopped prancing and eagerly stepped out as if anxious to get moving again.

"Yes, ma'am?"

"Mr. McCoy, my name is Charlotte, and I just wanted to thank you for the efficient and masterful way that you handled John Ringo. Everyone in town was scared spitless of him. We knew he was a famous gunshark from Arizona and Texas. You see, I had one husband shot down in a gunfight when he was a deputy sheriff. I don't want to lose another one, and John Ringo would have killed Quincy sooner or later if you hadn't been here."

"No way to know that, ma'am."

"Call me, Charlotte, please."

"Yes, all right."

"Would you drive north along the river? There's something I want to show you."

"Ma . . . Charlotte, I really have a lot of work to get done today."

"This won't take long, and I think you'll appreciate seeing this. It isn't far."

They talked about the big land grab and the land office, and he found her intelligent and understanding. Also pretty in a soft casual way.

They came to a heavy growth of trees along the river and she asked him to turn off into the grove through a narrow lane to a point where a house had once stood before it burned down.

When the horse stopped, she got out and asked him to follow her. They walked five minutes to a spot by the river that was shielded on both sides.

"This is my hideaway when I want to come for a swim," she said. "Would you like a swim?"

"No Charlotte, not just right now."

"Maybe I can persuade you." She caught his neck and pulled his face down to hers and when their mouths met hers was open and she licked his lips until his opened and they kissed long and passionately.

When it ended she had one hand inside his shirt rubbing his chest.

"Spur McCoy, I want to thank you properly the best way a woman can for saving my husband's life. I want to make love to you. And don't deny me the pleasure." She kissed him again before he could move, and then stepped back and unbuttoned her blouse. She wore nothing under it. Before he could react the blouse was off and her small breasts pointed proudly toward him.

"You better hurry and get undressed or I'll be in the water before you will. Don't you see, out here, we don't need any bathing suits!"

She sobered as she unbuttoned the side of her skirt.

"Spur, I don't do this with just anyone. I am determined to thank you for saving my husband's life. After the swim it's your party. Anything, any way you want to."

She dropped her skirt, then one petticoat and was naked. She giggled and ran for the water.

Spur undressed slowly. She was slender with solid hips and small breasts. All that long hair was a delight. He plunged into the water beside her and found the Grande Ronde river only three feet deep. They sat in the cool water, splashed each other and then kissed. He found her breasts under the water and she caught his flaccid penis.

They both laughed and kissed again. Her hair was not wet yet except on the ends.

"Time," he said and they walked out of the cold water to the grass. She was so small he picked her up and put her legs around his waist. Then he adjusted her and bent his knees and gently drove his erection into her wet and throbbing pussy.

"Oh, oh, oh!!!! I've never been had this way. It's wild! Absolutely wild."

Spur pounded into her a minute, then slowly dropped to his knees and forward on his hands, putting her on her back on the grass.

"My ass in the grass!" she said softly and laughed like a teenager.

She kissed him then and pulled away. "Please! Hard and fast, do me hard and fast! I want all of you deep inside me right now!"

He felt his long thick tool strumming her high clit on every stroke and soon she was wailing and screeching like a cat in heat as she climaxed again and again and again.

Her excitement rushed Spur and he exploded before he wanted to, nailing her soft bottom into the grass and shoving it forward with six, eight, then ten powerful strokes.

"Oh, Lord!" she said as the last of the tremors faded from her body. "I'll never be the same. You fuck so hard, so good. I could feel you spurting inside of me! I've never felt that before!"

"Making love outdoors in the grass might just excite you more. You'll have to try it often."

She kissed him and held her arms locked around his neck so he could not come out of her.

"Sweet cock, I'll try it four more times with you right here if you can hold out."

"Why not five or six?"

"It's your party, we'll try for a dozen!"

She unlocked her hands, pushed him away and jumped up.

"Let's play tag in the water!"

They did, for ten minutes. By then her hair was thoroughly wet and she swirled it around her as she swam under water in the clear but cold stream. They both shivered and ran to the grass and lay in the warm sun.

Soon they were kissing and petting and anxious to make love again. This time she was serious and soft and gentle. He played with her small breasts and almost had to seduce her before she let him spread her legs. Then it was so gentle and serious and meaningful that Spur was moved. Just as she climaxed she whispered in his ear.

"Spur McCoy, I.... I thank you for saving my husband's life."

Afterwards they lay in the sun, feeling its warmth. She told him how her first husband was killed by a wild drunk gunman in a bar in town. She was left with one small son and no income and no means of making a living. She lived with friends for two months, then Quincy Younger a dedicated bachelor of forty-two had married her after a two week courtship. They had two children together.

"Your debt is paid, your thanks given," Spur said.

She rolled over on top of him and pushed one of her small hanging breasts into his mouth.

"Good the debt is paid, now I get one for myself, just for the fucking fun of it!"

She devised the positions, she called the shots, and she wound up chewing on him almost to ejaculation, then moving up and with him on his back riding him like a stallion until he blasted his juices halfway through her slender form and she climaxed at the same time, screeching and wailing like a wild animal.

A half hour later they dressed each other. Back at the buggy she took out a towel she had brought and dried her hair. Then they sat in the sun until it was totally dry. Soon he drove slowly back to town.

"Mr. McCoy, if we pass in town, I will not know you. You see, we've never met. This was a one time . . . one time fuck." She giggled, embarrassed saying the word now with her clothes on.

"I understand. It was a remarkable gesture by you, a certain sacrifice, and I am impressed and I appreciate it. I wouldn't think to impose on you."

She smiled, touched his cheek with her fingertips. "I must say I am bowled over by you, Mr. McCoy. If I wasn't married I'd set my cap and flip my skirt if I had to in order to try to marry you. You're nice!"

She reached over and kissed his lips gently, then pushed over to the far side of the buggy seat.

"You better drive me back to town quickly before I forget my married status and start crawling all over you . . . again."

They both laughed. Then they talked about the case he was working on during the twenty minute drive back. He left the carriage at the edge of town and walked quickly away. She drove in a round about way back to her house.

It was almost noon. Spur knew what he had to do now. Last evening he had found his long barreled Colt and brought it back to town. He took it to the best gunsmith in La Grande. All it needed was a new cylinder and a little bit of alignment. The man would have it ready in two hours. Spur bought a backup Colt .45 to replace the one stolen and two boxes of .45 rounds. First he refilled his gunbelt loops, then went back on the street and walked to his hotel.

He had to find out if the Duke of Wallowa's man servant was in his room. He asked the room clerk. The man on duty did not know. Spur went up to the third floor door and knocked.

For a moment no one answered. Spur knocked again. He hoped they had not felt the fakery slipping and run away. After the third knocking, he heard movement inside.

When Edward Long came to the door it was plain to see that he was hung over. He could barely open his eyes. Spur grabbed him by the shirt front and jerked him into the hall.

"Edward, my man. Just the Englishman I was looking for. You and I are going for a ride."

19

Spur took Edward Long down the stairs and out the back door of the hotel. In the alley he backed the man against the wooden siding and slapped him twice sharply across the face.

"Mr. Long. You are under arrest. I'm a Federal officer and you and I are going for a walk, and then a ride. If you make any move to disagree or to run, I'll shoot you down without a quiver. Do we understand each other perfectly?"

"Y . . . Yes sir."

"Good. This won't take long. You can ride a horse?"

"Every Englishman can ride, sir."

"Not true. We'll see just how good you are forking a quarter horse."

A half hour later Spur and Long had ridden north then west into the sagebrush covered plateau of Eastern Oregon. They could see twenty miles in one direction to the Wallowa mountains. There was little forage on the land for grazing. A lot of sand and scattered sage, clumps of struggling brush in water courses was all. The timber was all in the mountains and foothills.

"Do you know where you are?" Spur asked Long.

"Hell no. Somewhere outside of La Grande."

"Which direction is it?"

"Damned if I know. What do you want from me?"

"The whole thing, the whole swindle with the phony Royal Land Grant."

"Don't know what yer talking about, mate."

"You sure?"

"Damn sure."

"Fine. Dismount."

"You aim to strand me out here?"

"Get off the horse or get shot in the shoulder. Which would you prefer?"

Edward dismounted.

"Take off your shoes and socks and pants."

"What kind of games you playing?"

"We call it barefooted rattlesnake keep-away."

Spur got off his horse, tied the other mount on a lead to his saddle, and walked over to Edward. "Boots, and pants, now."

"I don't understand."

"Tell me about you and Jeffrey or start stripping."

"Nothing to tell."

During the next five minutes Spur got the man's boots, socks and pants, tied them up and put them on his horse. All the time he was telling Edward about the rattlesnakes in the area.

"Not so big, but damn deadly. They have all sorts of names, but most people just call them diamond back rattlers because of the marks on their backs."

Spur found a branch and began turning over rocks. Under the third one he found a rattler. The forked stick nailed the rattler's head to the ground. Spur picked it up holding the deadly snake directly in back of the head so it could not strike at him.

When he carried it to Edward, the smaller man shivered and backed away.

"Get that damned thing away from me! I hate snakes."

"These guys don't like you either. He's real mad by now. I'll just drop him here near you. Don't worry about him. One strike and you're as dead as a bloated steer."

Spur dropped the snake in front of Edward. It coiled for a moment, rattled the ten buttons on its tail, then uncoiled and slithered away.

Spur mounted and rode a dozen yards off. "You think over my proposition, Edward. You tell me everything I want to know, and just maybe you won't have to dodge rattlesnakes trying to find your way back to La Grande."

"Nooooooooooooooooo! You can't do this to me!"

"Why not? I don't hear any citizen complaining. You're just an alien without funds, and my guess without proper papers. Why should I listen to you?"

Spur rode a half mile off, found a small pine tree on the edge of the foothills and relaxed under its shade.

He could see Edward standing on one foot, then the other. He tried to sit down, then jumped up.

Two hours later, Spur rode back to the man. Edward stared at him with angry eyes.

"Bastard! Bloody, fucking bastard!"

"That's the spirit. Now it looks like you can talk. The deal is this. First you tell me what you know and I let you live. That's the big one. You tell me all I want from you and you get your clothes back one piece at a time. Eventually you'll be dressed and on your horse."

"Bastard!"

"You think everyone in this country is stupid?"

"So far. Up to you. If I talk will you see that I get a light sentence. No more than five years, maybe deportation?"

"We'll see. I will try. Questions, Long. Sir Jeffrey is a phony. Tell me about you two. Who are you and how did you get here?"

Long looked at the arid land, the rocks where snakes could be hiding. Slowly he began to talk.

He told Spur about jumping ship from a British freighter in New York, and how they worked the East coast for a while with con games and some pickpocketing.

"The Land Grant is a fraud, right?"

"Bloody right. Got the idea in Chicago. Had some printing done, found some paper, had a bottle of old British ink. Then did some research in the Chicago library."

"Who is the artist?"

"Jeff. He's good. Could have made a living that way if he'd had a mind to. Too lazy."

"And you're a dip and a seaman?"

"About the size of it. We had to get to Oregon or Washington to make the Land Grant scheme work."

"First your names. I want your real names, and the address of one of the places in New York City where you stayed. I was born in that town and grew up there so don't try to fool me."

Edward gave it all to Spur who wrote it down with a pencil on a pad from his rear pocket.

"The Land Office. Who burned it down?"

"I never had nothing to do with that! I didn't even know. It was Jeff. His idea. He figured if the land ownership was up in the air anyway, we would have an easier time of it. He talked to somebody here in town and arranged it. A damned bloody surprise to me."

"Who did he talk to?"

"Gent named Digger. But he's long gone from La Grande by now."

Spur tossed him his boots. Edward slipped into them.

"Get on your horse. We're going back to town. Don't tell anybody where you've been or what we talked about. Especially don't tell Jeffrey. I have a man watching the stables, and another watching the stage. If either of you tries to get out of town you'll be hauled off to jail. Is that clear?"

"Damned clear, g'uvnor. I've got your word that I can't get more than five years in the jail house?"

"I'll send that recommendation to the court. Just don't tell Jeffrey a thing about this."

"Righto, mate. I'm bloody tired of running anyway."

They got into town before dusk and Spur let Edward off at the edge of town so he could walk back to the hotel.

After a big dinner, Spur went back to the burned out building where the Land Office had been. This time he concentrated on the small stable building which was intact. It was little more than a lean-to with a front and side walls.

The rear of it was open and down wind. There were two stalls for horses and pegs on the wall to hang harnesses and tack. A feed box to one side held oats and some mixed ground grain. Two bales of hay sat unopened near the front.

The left side seemed more open than the right. He probed with his iron bar again across the stalls, around the bales of hay, and then on the far right hand side. There he hit something hard. Under an inch of dirt he found a trap door four feet wide and about that long.

When he lifted it by the ring, he found it was mainly a root cellar with potatoes, and sacks of apples and some root crops all stored there. But near the back were two large wooden boxes. He dragged one out and saw that it was closed with a hasp and held with a nail.

Inside the box he found sets of record books, smaller than the normal, but all wrapped in oiled cloth to protect them from the dampness.

When he opened the first one he found the set of duplicate land records for the county and the Land Office. He stared at the books, then wrapped them up and put them back. He closed the trap door and covered it with dirt, then straw.

Spur found Sheriff Younger still in his office. He knew they should be moving on the Englishmen as soon as possible. He told him about his run-in with Digger.

"Digger is the man who probably killed Jonas King. He tried to bushwhack me. He's in custody over at Doc George's right now."

"Digger? He's harmless," the sheriff said. "Leastwise we always thought so."

"Digger also likes to set fires. He torched the Land Office and the mayor's house. He did the first one for money."

"Who paid him?"

"The Englishmen. It's all a part of their con game to swindle property owners in town."

"Can we prove it?" the sheriff asked.

"Not yet. I need to make up some official looking arrest warrants, can you help me?"

The sheriff said he could. Then he motioned to Spur. "A man down here I think you need to talk to. From what he tells me, our British friends were hard at work on that land swindle you're talking about."

The man at the desk in a separate office was writing on a yellow pad of paper. He looked up and stopped.

"Hirum, I think you've met Spur McCoy."

The banker stood and held out his hand. "Indeed I have. Do you know what's going on here?"

"Some of it, Mr. Follette," Spur said. "What else is happening that I don't know about?"

"Friend of mine said this English Lord offered to sell him back his own property. Said it was an 'insurance' kind of deed. Then if the federal court ruled in Lord Mountbatten's favor, the man would own his land free and clear. If the court ruled that land grant was invalid it was just a few dollars of insurance money the property owner was out. Simple insurance."

"That ties together," Spur said. "I knew it was a fraud somehow, but I couldn't figure out how they were going to make any immediate payoff."

"Twenty or thirty business men in town must have fallen for the scheme by now," Follette said. "At even two hundred dollars each, that could be over six or seven thousand dollars."

"Sheriff, I'd suggest you put a deputy on the livery stable and make sure our Englishmen don't decide to take a quick night ride anywhere."

The sheriff agreed and left to send a man.

The banker nodded. "So this all ties in with the Land Office fire. If folks were a little worried anyway about the accuracy of their land records, they would be more prone to go along with a scheme like this. What the hell can we do now?"

"We keep them in town, and then we get them to start accusing each other of murder, that's what we do, Mr. Follette."

It was well after dark when Spur got back to the hotel. Spur opened the door to his room and struck a match. When the lamp flamed up into a good light and he put the chimney in place he saw a man sitting on the bed with a six-gun aimed directly at Spur's chest.

"Okay, McCoy, you can quit pretending. Where the hell have you hidden my daughter, Margaret Smith?"

"Is this a joke, Smith? Just because you own the triple R, the biggest ranch in the county, is no sign you can run around with a gun accusing people of crimes."

The man jumped off the bed, but was careful to keep the six-gun trained at Spur.

"No damn joke! If you've got her in another room under some fake name, you better tell me."

"Put the gun away, Smith before you get in trouble."

"When you show me where Margaret is hiding, I will."

"That could be quite a while," Spur said, "because I don't know. The last time I saw your daughter was at your house that first day I was out there when she was trying to be polite and you were your usual, nasty, stupid, offensive self. Now get out of my room. I want to get some sleep."

"Not until you tell me where Margaret is."

"Then I hope you don't mind my taking my gunbelt off and putting it on the dresser."

"Easy, keep your hands away from the iron."

Spur unbuckled the belt, turned and put it on the dresser. At the same time he wheeled and lashed out with his left foot in a round kick. He aimed the blow at Smith's gun hand and the move caught Smith entirely by surprise, smashed into his gun hand and jolted the weapon from his fingers. It fell on the bed. Spur brought his foot down, spun and slammed his right fist into Smith's jaw before he could dive for the gun.

The rancher fell on the bed on his stomach and Spur dropped on him with one knee in his back. McCoy grabbed Smith's hands and tied them together behind his back with a rawhide strip.

"Let me up, damn you! You touch that girl and I'll kill you!"

Spur stood and let Smith roll over and fight the rawhide a moment.

"Now, Mr. Smith, do you want to start over? Are you reporting to a peace officer that you have a missing child?"

"What the hell you talking about? I just told you. Margaret came into town this morning, said she was going to stay with a friend of hers. I came in for some supplies and got the mail. She got some important mail at the post office pickup window and I wanted to give it to her. But the woman school friend admitted she hadn't seen Margaret."

"So you assumed that I had captured her and that I've been raping her all day and evening."

"Well, no. But she did take a shine to you that day. I saw it, and she started making wild plans."

"Smith I can charge you with assault with a deadly weapon for pointing that six-gun at me, you know that? I can arrest you and throw you in jail right now. Is that what you want?"

"Hell no. I got a ranch to run."

"You also have three small ranches to rebuild."

"Not until somebody shows up with legitimate land records."

"If I let you go, will you act half way civilized? Your daughter is what, twenty-two or twenty-three? She has a right to live her own life. You can't live it for her."

"You sound just like she did. You put those ideas into her head. She's only twenty."

"Twenty? Lots of women have three kids in tow by that age. You should be horsewhipped. You probably chase off every young fellow who comes courting. Behave, or I'll leave you tied up all night."

"Okay, okay. I'll stop bothering you. Maybe she isn't here."

"You make trouble for anyone else in town and I'll bring my charges tomorrow and you'll serve at least six months in the county jail. You remember that!"

"Yeah. Maybe I have been too strict. Maybe."

Spur cut the rawhide from Smith's wrists, took the rounds out of his six-gun and handed it back to him.

"My advice to you, Smith, is to get a room here, have a good night's sleep and in the morning ride back to your ranch and go to work. Let the girl live her own life.''

Wade Smith muttered profanities under his breath as Spur opened the door and pointed him into the hallway.

20

Spur ushered Wade Smith out of his room and closed the door. The man would have to change his mind about his daughter sooner or later or he would lose her completely.

The Secret Service Agent was in the middle of checking and cleaning his newly acquired six-gun when a knock sounded on his door.

Spur opened the panel and began talking before he saw who was there. "Smith I told you that I . . ."

Colette, the saloon singer, stood there with a big smile watching him.

"I'm not Smith, but may I come in anyway? We need to talk."

"It's late."

"I know, I just finished singing at the Sagebrush." She walked in and he closed the door.

"Colette, if it's about the other night."

"It is about that. I don't think . . . no I'm certain that I have never been more thrilled, more delighted, or more happy. I want to marry you!

Will you be my husband?" She laughed. "I guess I should at least show you what you will be getting." She unbuttoned the top of her form fitting dress.

"Colette, I'm not sure this is a good idea. You seemed so hesitant the other time."

"I was a virgin, you had to seduce me. Now I'm more experienced." She opened the top of her dress, then walked up to him. "Kiss me a few times, before you decide," she said. She reached up and kissed him. For the second kiss she opened her mouth. Then she sat down on the bed, pulling him with her, stretching out and urging him on top of her.

She looked up at him and smiled. "Yes, I think I like this. It feels good with you on top of me. Play with me. Undress me. Spur McCoy do anything you want to with me!"

Spur moved to one side and sat up.

She sat up beside him.

"Colette, you are a talented lady, a marvelous performer, you are a beautiful woman. Why are you throwing yourself at me?" ———

"For love. I want love. I want you to make love to me and marry me and keep me safe. I don't want to hurt anyone else!"

"I don't understand. How can you hurt people? You make them happy by singing for them."

"Yes, but I hurt some, too." She lifted up and raised her skirts and quickly took the dress off over her head. She took off her chemise and sat beside him bare breasted. "Play with them, pet my titties!"

Her breasts were large, with sturdy nipples that already had swollen with her excitement. When he touched them she moaned and her nipples stood out taller. Spur bent and kissed her mounds, licked her nipples and she leaned down and kissed his neck.

"That is so wonderful, so good!" Her hands fumbled at his crotch. "Please show your big one to me, Spur. Please get him out right now!"

Spur sucked half of one breast into his mouth and chewed on it, then came away and opened his fly. A moment later his erection popped out, hard, pulsating and ready.

"Oh, yes!" Colette whispered. Her right hand slid into the pocket of the skirt of the dress she had dropped beside her. Spur saw her hand move and wondered about it.

"Kiss my titties again! That feels so wonderful!"

Spur did but watched her right hand. He saw it come away from her skirt with a folding knife. She moved it over his back and her other arm brushed his back as it came up.

The Agent listened and he heard a small snic when a metal sound came from behind him. He quickly rolled away to the left and lifted his hand to grab her right wrist which held the open four-inch blade that was locked in place.

She tried to stab him. He powered her arm down so the knife drove into the bedding.

"Noooooooooo," Colette wailed. "I didn't want to do it. You're the only one who has ever been kind and gentle with me. The only one. I didn't want to hurt you!"

She cowered back, dropped the knife and pulled the dress over her bare breasts. "Don't look at me!" she commanded.

"Colette, I won't look if you tell me all about it. Tell me about the first time a man molested you."

Her eyes were open wide and she looked right through him for a moment. Then she nodded. "Yes, I can do that. But first you turn around so I can get dressed." She hesitated. "Unless you are too . . . worked up. My brother used to say that. He would say he was too excited, too worked up to stop."

Spur turned around. "Go on, Colette. Tell me about your brother."

She pulled on the chemise and then let the dress down over her head. When Colette had the buttons up the front all fastened, she told Spur he could turn around. She sat primly in the straight backed chair. Spur sat on the bed.

"My brother Zach was older than me. I must have been about thirteen at the time and we lived on a little farm with a few pigs and two cows and some dogs. My brother was always feeling horny and he tried to touch my breasts whenever he could. We used to watch the dogs mating and laugh and he'd say he wanted to do that. I'd laugh and say all he had to do was catch the old bitch dog and try.

"Then one day the folks were gone to town in the wagon and he came in my room in the house. He said this was the day he was going to fuck my cunt just the way the male dog did the bitch. I knew what he meant but I'd never heard those words before.

"I was well developed at thirteen. My breasts were as big as they are now and he always wanted to play with them. Now he came over to me and stripped me to the waist. He was rubbing his crotch as he just looked at me and then he pushed me down on the bed and began playing with my boobies and kissing them.

"Then he began to moan and sweat. He pulled out his thing and pushed it against my stomach and began pumping his hips and he spurted his juice all over my tummy.

"That didn't _stop_ him, he pulled off my skirt and my drawers and played with me. I told him not to, and I cried and tried to beat on him with my fists. He slapped me and told me to shut up, and then he was hard again and pushed his thing into me.

"It hurt awful and I cried and screamed the whole time. He just laughed and said I was a tease. He fucked me three more times before the folks were due to come home. Then he put his pants on and ran out and began shocking the cut hay the way he was supposed to be doing."

"I never told Ma. I knew she'd tell Pa and he would beat up on my brother Zachary. Pa might have killed him. But then every time after that we were alone Zach wanted to do it. He called it fuck-fuck and he was always ready. When Ma wasn't looking he'd grab my breasts or try to stick his finger in my crotch.

"The next time I let him, thinking it might feel better, but it hurt again and I screamed and we almost got caught."

"He planned to get me alone then, down in the field, by the river, even in the haymow.

"I was afraid I'd get pregnant the way the old bitch dog did, and I told him to stop. I got a stick I carried and I hit him a few times. Then he grabbed the stick and slapped me hard and fucked me four times. I was so sore I didn't want to go to the bathroom.

"That went on for more than a year, maybe a year and a half. He knew when he had time and the right place. He'd catch me every two or three days and pump away. I was too scared to tell anyone.

"I decided that was enough. By then I had put up with it for way too long. I was almost fifteen and had a nice boy I wanted to marry when I turned sixteen. He wanted me too, course I never told him about Zach and what he did.

"I bought this knife in town and made a pocket in every skirt I had and I always carried the blade. The first time I opened it and waved it at Zach and scared him off.

"The last time I forgot it until he had my breasts bare. We were in the cornfield and the tall corn really hid us. When I remembered the knife I grabbed it and opened the blade. He slid down on my legs and spread them ready to enter me.

"I slashed the sharp knife out wildly. It cut across his throat and he looked at me in surprise and then horror. I slashed his stiff cock too, cutting it almost in half, then he fell to the side and I got up and dressed and ran through the corn.

"I never looked at him. But I knew he was cut bad. I'd seen Pa bleed a butchered calf by slitting his throat. I cleaned off my knife and hid it in the barn, then ran in the house and was sick all over the kitchen floor.

"Ma put me to bed. They found Zach two days later and the sheriff said must have been attacked by some runaway slaves, or maybe just a drunken no-good."

She went to the pitcher and had a drink of water.

"Ever since then, Spur, when a man molests me, I try to use my knife on him."

"Have you used it here in La Grande?"

"Yes. Twice I think. I get so confused. Every man becomes Zach and he's leering at me, bending over me, hurting me and I slash out at him and it's somebody else I hurt. I'm really only trying to hurt Zach."

"I understand, Colette. It's a sickness. There are doctors who can help make you well."

"I'd like that. I hate it when I use the knife."

"We could throw it away."

"I'd only buy a new one. I've tried that a dozen times."

"Colette do you know how many men you have hurt thinking they were Zach?"

"One every couple of weeks. I don't know. I'm twenty-four now. It's been a long time since I was fifteen."

Spur's brows raised. Twenty-five a year for nine years!"

"Colette, would you like to rest here for the night? You can have the bed, I'll sit up in the chair."

"No, I'll go back to my room."

"It might be better if you stayed here. I'll keep anyone else from bothering you. Some of the men in town know which room you live in here."

"All right. Let me go get my nightgown and some things."

Spur went with her. When she came back she acted as if she were alone, undressing, putting on her nightgown, then turning out the light without another word to Spur. He stretched out on the floor on a spare blanket and snoozed lightly. Every time the springs squeaked as Colette moved, Spur became wide awake. He had no desire to join the nearly two hundred men Colette must have cut or killed with her folding knife.

In the morning Colette was embarrassed to find herself in his room in her nightgown. She made him go outside while she dressed. She remembered nothing of the time she had spent in his room.

"Did we . . . I mean were we . . . intimate?"

"We just talked. You told me about Zachary, your brother."

She frowned. "Yes, I remember him. He hurt me."

"He also made you ill, Colette. There are doctors who can help you. This morning we'll go over and see Doctor George. He'll know where you can go for treatment."

"Then I won't get to sing anymore?"

"I'm sure you'll be able to sing every evening, just like now, only for a different audience."

They had breakfast in the dining room at the hotel, then walked slowly to Dr. George's. Spur explained the situation privately to the doctor.

"Mentally over the edge," Dr. George said. "There's a state hospital in Salem where they are starting to take in people like Colette. She'll be safe there at least. I don't know how much treatment she will get. But it's the first step."

"She's a talented performer, Doctor George. I don't know if you've heard her sing or not, but she's good. Be sure to tell them that so she can perform for the other patients."

"Yes, that would be good for her. I'll keep her here for a day or two, then have someone go with her to Salem. The county can help with the cost."

"Good. How is Rebecca King?"

"Much better. There will be little scarring on her face and arms. She was a lucky lady."

Spur thanked the doctor and hurried on to the

sheriff's office. He had to get the right papers made out as quickly as he could. There were horses the Englishmen could steal if they were desperate enough to leave. He just hoped that Edward Long had not caved in and confessed his blabbermouthing to Spur.

At the sheriff's office the clerk wrote out the warrants of arrest. They made out one for Phineas J. Bull, alias Jeffrey Mountbatten. The charge was grand larceny, conspiracy, and murder of Jonas King.

A second warrant was written for Edward Long, charging him with conspiracy, grand larceny, fraud and pickpocketing.

A third warrant, all carefully written by hand by the clerk, charged Phineas J. Bull with armed robbery in New York City, and listed his New York address.

The last warrant was for Digger, also known as Alan Underwood, for the murder of Jonas King, and arson of the Land Office house and the Mayor's residence.

Spur told the sheriff about Colette.

"We have two recent murders, both with a knife. The first one could have come out of Colette's window. We'll mark them solved. Too damn bad."

Spur told the sheriff that the missing land records had been found.

"Great!" Sheriff Younger said. "That takes one hell of a lot of worry out of this. With the land records back in place, we'll have no more problems with the big ranchers. Wade Smith will be forced to rebuild and restock those three ranches. And the whole problem of the Royal Land Grant will be labeled a hoax."

"Let's go get those records and store them in the bank vault until the county can build a new county clerk's office," Spur said.

The sheriff went with Spur and two deputies, and the men carried the two wooden boxes into the back door of the bank where the boxes were opened. Hirum Follette agreed to store the records and to keep them safe.

"Those books are worth more than their weight in gold," Hirum said. "We'll take good care of them."

21

Spur and Sheriff Younger talked with Hirum Follette, the banker for a few more minutes, then Hirum went over to the hotel to find the Englishmen. There were two ranchers waiting in the hall in front of Hirum just outside Sir Jeffrey's door. He knew both of them.

"Will, this guy is a fraud," Hirum told one of the men. "There is no way legally that he can sell you what you already own. It's a confidence game, a fraud. I can guarantee that the land records are safe and that they will be found. Don't tell anyone."

Will watched the banker. He had known Hirum for ten years. Slowly he nodded. "If you say so, Hirum. But if that is so, why are you here?"

"Working with the sheriff, Will. We're about ready to trap these Englishers and arrest them."

Will smiled. "You dang double sure about the land records?"

"Positive, Will."

The man leaning against the wall shook

Hirum's hand. "If you say our land is safe, I'll go along with you, Hirum." He whispered to the man next to him and they both walked along the hall and went down the stairs.

A minute later the door opened and a man Hirum knew only casually came out. Edward Long peered out after the man left.

"I guess you're next, sir," he said. "Right this way."

Hirum walked into the room and saw Sir Jeffrey busy at a small desk.

"Good morning, my good man. And what can we do for you today?"

"A friend of mine said you had a kind of insurance policy I could buy on my bank and three stores I own, is that right?"

"It certainly is. My name is Jeffrey Mountbatten," he said holding out his hand.

Hirum took it and shook. "Hirum Follette. Be interested in what kind of a deal you have."

"Straightforward and simple, Mr. Follette. I give you a legal and binding bill of sale and grant deed for your property. As you must have heard from your friend, if the disputed Royal Land Grant I have is valid, I own this land. But with this insurance I have already sold your former property back to you at a low, low, bargain price. In the event the Land Grant is declared not valid, you still own your land, and you are out only the 'insurance' fee we charge."

"Sounds reasonable. How much is the fee?"

"For your four parcels, we could give you a bargain price, Mr. Follette. Usually we charge four hundred dollars a property, regardless of size or location. But since you have four of them, we could accommodate you for two hundred and fifty dollars each, or a total of a thousand dollars. That's a six hundred-dollar discount!''

"Sounds reasonable. I understand you deal only in cash?''

"Yes, that's right.''

"All right, draw up the papers and I'll sign. Then I'll get the cash for you from my assistant who is outside. As you see, Sir Jeffrey, I am a banker, a cautious man.''

Jeffrey Mountbatten smiled. "I can see that, Mr. Follette, and the people of Wallowa county are lucky to have a man of your intelligence and caution safeguarding their life savings." He worked for a moment on some papers on the desk.

"Now if you would give me the names of these properties.''

Hirum did and Jeffrey worked again on the papers.

"All right, we're ready. You inspect them, and sign them. Then as soon as I get the money, I'll sign and the deal will be complete.

Five minutes later the details were finished. A clerk from the bank waiting in the hall gave Hirum a valise with two thousand dollars in it. He counted out the thousand and Jeffrey signed the documents. The clerk took the valise and went out the door.

That was the signal. Spur McCoy, the sheriff and two deputies burst into the room and arrested Jeffrey.

"I don't understand," the Englishman said.

"You, Phineas J. Bull, alias Jeffrey Mountbatten, formerly of 1476 Fourteenth Street in New York City, are under arrest for fraud, conspiracy, and the murder of Jonas King.''

"No! there must be some mistake!

"Are you Phineas J. Bull?"

"Never heard of him."

"We have a witness who will swear that is your real name. Also that you are not a real Lord, that you are a merchant seaman who jumped ship in New York."

One of the deputies took the thousand dollars in greenbacks off the desk.

"This money is evidence for your trial, Bull," the sheriff said.

Spur looked in the far room. No one was there. He checked the third room in the suite and found it too was empty. Then Spur found the second outside door that led into the hall. He looked out the window and saw a man rush out of the hotel on the street below, grab a horse that had been tied to the rail and jump aboard.

The man was Edward Long.

Spur raced down the three flights of steps to the street, borrowed a horse from a stranger and gave chase. That reminded him he had to pay for the horse Digger had shot. He caught up with Long half a mile out of town and put two pistol rounds over his head. Long brought the horse to a stop and lifted his hands.

"Going somewhere, Long?" Spur asked as he rode up.

"Thought it might be a bloody good idea. You had us cold and hard with no place to fudge."

"About the size of it. Our deal is still good if you can prove you didn't help in planning the killing."

"Bloody right bout that, mate. Surprised the hell out of me, it did."

Spur took the valise off the Long's saddle horn.

Inside were packets of greenbacks. Spur guessed the total at eight or nine thousand dollars.

"You took your spending money with you, I see," Spur said. "A lot of merchants in town are going to be unhappy with you two."

"His doing, I'm just his lowly man servant."

"That's your role in this stop. I'd wager at the next town you are Sir Edward Long, Duke of Kent or some such, and Jeffrey is your man servant. You probably take turns."

"How in the bloody hell did you know that?"

Back in town, Jeffrey Mountbatten, or more correctly Phineas J. Bull, was in jail. Edward joined him in a separate cell. Spur had explained to the sheriff the deal he had made with Long. It should hold up.

Two deputies brought Digger over to join the jail bird crew.

The sheriff had set up a table inside the office and was checking records that Bull had kept, and paid back the money the merchants had spent so unwisely for insurance.

The sheriff kept the thousand dollars from the banker for evidence.

Sheriff Younger knew that paying back this fake insurance money should cement his re-election for three or four more terms.

The sheriff sent a letter to the Federal court in Portland explaining the arrests and certified that he had a witness who swore that the Royal Land Grant was a hoax, a forgery, and that the court should disregard it.

The county attorney had formally charged the three men with a variety of crimes, and set a hearing for two days hence.

Spur searched out the cowboy in the saloon he

had been headed for, and paid for the man's horse and saddle.

Then Spur relaxed in the sun outside of the sheriff's office for a minute. Already the word was all over town about the swindle, the fakery of the English "Lord" and his part in the death of Jonas King. The word had spread as well that the land records were intact and safe in the bank vault.

Spur felt that the whole community seem to let out a held in breath. To threaten to disenfranchise three thousand people of their property and life's savings had been a terrible strain. The danger was over, they were safe again.

Spur walked down to Doctor George's office and talked to Rebecca King.

"So it's all clear now, Mrs. King. The Englishman hired Digger to burn down the Land Office. Somehow in the process your husband surprised him or the Englishman, we're not sure which, yet, and they killed him so he couldn't talk. He was a fine man, and defended the county property with his life. He will get a medal and a plaque to his honor mounted in the court house. I've arranged it with the sheriff."

Rebecca sat up now and smiled. Her face had healed more and the doctor had been right, there would be almost no scarring.

"I'm glad you were here, Mr. McCoy. Without you it might have remained a mystery, and my husband's killers gone unpunished. I thank you again."

"Oh, by the way. The county is going to need a temporary clerk, until the election at least. The county officials have named you to that post as soon as you are able. I hope that you will run for the office when the election comes."

Rebecca King blinked back tears. Spur patted her hand and left the room.

His next call was on Colette. She would be leaving on the noon stage for Portland.

She wore a different dress now, a simple calico print that swept the floor and buttoned high on her throat and each wrist.

"I'm going on a trip today!" she said excitedly. Her eyes sparkled. "Doctor George says his wife needs to go to Portland, and she's going with me. Isn't that wonderful?"

"I'm glad for you, Colette. I'm sure you'll find some extremely good people in Portland."

She came toward him. "Mr. McCoy, Spur. I know that you helped me. I'm not exactly sure how, I can't remember much of that time, but I thank you." She reached up and kissed his cheek. "Thank you for everything."

Spur patted her shoulder and walked out of the room. He heard the door lock solidly behind him. He hoped that wherever she went they would have a piano she could use.

Back on the street, Spur paused for a moment. He had nothing to do! What a marvelous feeling. All the loose ends had been tied up. He could lay over until the next day and take the stage back to Portland where he could telegraph his office and headquarters.

He decided to change clothes, then have a leisurely lunch and sit in a tilted back chair on the boardwalk in front of the general store for an hour or two to soak up the atmosphere of La Grande. He might not be back this way for some time.

As soon as he walked into his hotel room he knew he was not alone. He closed the door and found Margaret Smith smiling at him.

"Hi cowboy," she said.

"Did your father find you?"

"Not yet. He went back to the ranch this morning, just the way you suggested."

"He'll try to kill me if he finds you here."

"Probably."

She moved forward and put her arms around his neck, then kissed him hungrily. The kiss grew into half a dozen and they soon were sitting on the bed.

"This time my father will think he knows where I am. My woman friend and I are on a horseback ride along the river hunting cattails." She put his hand over her breast.

He hesitated.

"Oh, no! You're rejecting me?"

Spur kissed her to put a lie to the words. "Just thinking about protection. Your father knows about this room. I'm going to go down and rent another one, on the top floor. You wait here."

Ten minutes later Spur and Maggie Smith sat on the bed in the third floor room.

"Why don't you stay over a couple of more days," Maggie said as Spur unbuttoned her dress. "I'm sure we could figure out a few new ways to make love."

"A couple of days? Sounds reasonable. My work here is done, I do need some rest and relaxation."

She unbuttoned his fly and pushed her hand inside the cloth.

"My, my! I certainly know part of you that is not what I'd call relaxed! And I like him that way!"

Spur growled at her and bent her back on the

soft bed. "Maggie, I'm going to show you about a dozen ways that you will like. I hope you have that many new and exciting ideas for me."

"Shut up, McCoy. Get my dress off and show me number one before I explode!"